Shadows from the Past

Judith Erwin

Published by
Emerald Cat Press

Printed in USA

First Printing: September 2015
Second Edition 2018

First Edition ISBN 978-0-9863367-2-0
Second Edition ISBN 978-0-9863367-8-2
E-Book ISBN: 978-0-9863367-3-7
Library of Congress Control Number: [To be provided]

Published by:
Emerald Cat Press
Jacksonville, Florida 32217

Editor: John C. Boles
Cover Painting: Nancy H. Duty

ALSO BY JUDITH ERWIN
Shadow of Silence
Shadow of Doubt
The Ballroom
The Ballet

*To my son, William Erwin, Jr., and my
daughter, Allison Erwin Norton,
You have filled my life with joy, love,
and pride.*

ACKNOWLEDGEMENTS

While fiction is a creation of the writer's imagination, there is often a thread of truth that kick-starts the process. Therefore, I must acknowledge my paternal grandmother's brother, James Sheridan, who spent over thirty years of his life in the mental institution at Milledgeville, Georgia. My curiosity as to why he was there, even though I never met him, spawned the idea for Shadows from the Past. However, that is where the truth ends and the fiction begins.

In unwrapping Fury O'Quinn's story, I had the love and support of my precious family, close friends, and a brilliant writing group. To all, I say thank-you for being there, believing in me, reading my work, providing insight, wisdom, and knowledge. You are: my family by blood—Bill, Allison, Judson, Trevor, Brooks, Sarah, Mary Caroline, and Amelia; my family by affinity—Perry, Lynda, Marshall, John, and Keri; my dearest friend—Nancy Duty, who gave form to the MacGregor mansion; medical consultant, Carlos Sotolongo, MD; my literary family—John Boles, Julie Delegal, Keith Gockenbach, Marcella Beeching, and Michael Heubeck; my publishing family—Cheyenne Knopf, Darius, Carrie and all those at Online Binding; and last but not least—Heidi, who inspired the creation of Apache, and Juliette, after whom Gypsy was modeled.

DOLAN-O'QUINN FAMILY

Thomas Dolan
(M)
Ellen McGuire

Children: Julia — Michael — James — Mary — **Bridget** (M) Conor O'Quinn — Thomas — Rebecca (M) Walter Clark

Bridget (M) Conor O'Quinn
- Ronan
- Mary (M) Sean Doyle
- Saoirse
- Maura
- **Michael** Patrick (M) Kathleen Murphy

Rebecca (M) Walter Clark
- Colleen Clark (M) Charles Lester

Mary (M) Sean Doyle
- Casey (M) Margaret O'Casey
  - Evanne

Michael Patrick (M) Kathleen Murphy
- Megan
- Michael
- Cory (M) Donald Reynolds MD
  - Alexandra (Sandi)
  - Susan Leigh (Suzi)
- **Fury**

MACGREGOR FAMILY

John Graeme MacGregor (J.G.)
(M)
Emma Langley

Arabella (Sissy)

Louise
(M)
Phillip Grant

John Graeme II (Graeme)
(M)
Dorothy Vanderlin

Martin

John Graeme III (Jack)
(M)
Zaira Ross

Valerie
(M)
John Butler

John Graeme IV (Gray)

CHAPTER ONE

The summer sun cast long shadows across a blanket of wild grass, still wet with dew. Fury O'Quinn, accompanied by her sister and two young nieces, weaved through the trees and overgrowth of vines and weeds, searching for the graves of their ancestors.

"When you invited us to come here with you, I pictured a manicured cemetery with plots neatly lined up on a grid—not a stroll through a spooky jungle," Cory said.

"This is an old cemetery, Cory. Look. Some of the graves predate the Civil War." Fury pointed to a crumbling rock marker with 1827 – 1872 carved below the name of Isaac Bartholomew Carson.

The cemetery, located behind St. Mary's Catholic Church in Arabella, Georgia, dated back to 1843. Abandoned as a burial site in the 1980s, it suffered from years of neglect. A variety of headstones, monuments, and plaques, some crumbling from age, marked the sites of those buried in the randomly scattered graves. A haze of slowly dissipating fog added to the eerie feeling of the surroundings.

"It's daylight, and I have a creepy feeling. I wouldn't want to walk through here at night," Cory said.

A rustling sound came from behind one of the old gravestones.

"What was that?" Cory jumped. Her eyes grew large as she looked around. "Was it a snake?"

"It was a squirrel, Mommy," Cory's seven-year-old, Sandi, said, tugging on her mother's blouse and pointing toward a tree where the small creature warily eyed the trespassers.

"Don't be such a sissy, Cory. There's not a single species of wildlife in here bigger than you are."

"Have you forgotten that I was born and raised in the asphalt jungle of Brooklyn where the wildlife wore jeans and tee shirts?"

Fury rolled her eyes. "I appreciate you mustering the courage to come with me."

"I'll survive. I hope."

"Think you're brave enough to search by yourself? We could find the Dolan graves faster if we split up."

Cory hesitated.

"Come on, Cory. Nothing is going to bother you."

"Okay, but if I scream, you'd better come fast." Cory took five-year-old Suzi's hand and headed slowly toward the west side of the property. Sandi trailed behind. Fury navigated her way eastwardly.

As she searched, Fury pulled away overgrowth on some of markers and periodically paused to read epitaphs. Six or seven minutes after the sisters separated, Sandi called out.

"Aunt Fury. I found a Dolan."

Following the direction of the voice, Fury hurried through the trees to the area where her sister and nieces stood next to a cluster of graves.

"Sandi found what looks like some of our family," Cory said as Fury approached. "Look, there's a double grave with a Thomas Dolan, who died in 1935, and his wife, Ellen, who died in 1924. Weren't those Dad's grandparents?"

Fury hardly heard Cory's question, because an impressive headstone of marble had caught her attention. The inscription read:

James Patrick Dolan

Beloved Son
of
Thomas and Ellen

1904-1970
Here lies a good and innocent man.
Robbed of life forty-five years before death.
May eternity bestow on Jim the peace and
comfort denied by evil on earth.

"Fury! Did you hear me?"

Fury nodded, not taking her eyes off the monument. "I heard you. Come here and look at this."

"Don't you want to see the ones Sandi found?"

"Yes . . . I do, but I want you to read this first."

Cory walked to where Fury stood and looked down at the monument. Reading the epitaph, she said, "That's strange."

"I know. How did he rate such a large monument? It must have cost a fortune. What a cryptic statement." Fury turned to face Cory. "In my dream, the red-haired ghost in the gossamer gown was saying, "Help Jim. Help Jim.""

"I don't believe in your ghosts, but you're giving me the creeps. Remind me again about how you got started with this genealogy project."

"A fellow author at the conference last month recommended looking at ancestors for potential stories. I borrowed the family Bible from Dad and started checking out some of the names that Mum had recorded from his American relatives."

"Right. And then your overactive imagination gave you a nightmare."

"Call it anything you like, but I believe it was a vision." Fury took out her small camera and snapped photos of the grave. When finished, she turned to her niece and said, "Now, show me what you found, sweetie."

"It's over here," Sandi said, tugging at her aunt's shirttail. "There are a lot of them."

Smiling at the child's exuberance, Fury followed Sandi to the site of four graves—three identified with flat marble headstones. In addition to the double grave Cory mentioned, there were three singles, one of which had a small marble marker with a cross engraved on one corner and an angel on the other. The inscription read:

JULIA MARY DOLAN

1899-1908

Cory had followed. "How sad. She was barely older than you, Sandi."

"She died?" the child said.

"They didn't have good medicine, or smart doctors like your daddy, in 1908, sweetheart," Fury said, putting an arm around the little girl's shoulders.

The other two graves were those of Michael Francis Dolan and Thomas Ardyn Dolan, who died in 1957 and 1965, respectively.

After taking a photo of each grave, Fury returned to the site of James Dolan and sat down at the foot, staring at the inscription.

"What are you doing?" Cory asked.

"Thinking."

"About what?"

"You're not intrigued by this?"

"I give you that it's peculiar, but I'm not hypnotized like you appear to be."

"Cory, something was amiss there. Read that inscription—'evil on earth.'"

"That could be some standard graveyard language."

Shaking her head, Fury said, "No. I don't believe that. Look at the size of that monument, compared to the rest. Some secret is buried in this grave, and something led me to find it."

"You and your imagination."

"Don't knock it. It makes a pretty good living for me. But, this isn't my imagination. Do you remember that we met some cousins of Dad's from here when we first moved to Atlanta?"

"Vaguely, but that was ten years ago. How could you find them?"

"In a community this small, I bet we could ask around—especially here at the church office. This is an old church and the only Catholic one in the area. They must have records of the family."

The inquiry was successful. The church secretary provided a wealth of information from sacramental records in the registry and even copied some of the pages for Fury. From the records, they traced a current parishioner, Colleen Lester, a first cousin of Mike O'Quinn.

"Ms. Colleen is a widow and both of her sons moved away years ago. I'm sure she would welcome a visit from relatives," the woman had said.

"Thank you," Fury said. "I'll call her."

As they left the building, Cory said, "The secretary was certainly nice to take so much time with us."

"Yeah, and I'm lucky that she was willing to give us the information. I bet it would have been a lot more complicated in a city church."

"Are you going to call Colleen now?"

"No. I'll do it when I get back to Atlanta. I have a lot of questions, and I'm sure the girls are bored. They've been so patient. I can wait."

CHAPTER TWO

Two weeks after their visit to the cemetery, Fury drove the thirty miles from her Atlanta condominium to Cory's home in Redbridge, Georgia. When she reached the Reynolds house, she parked her blue, Mini Cooper on the circular driveway and walked up the porch steps. Cory opened the front door before Fury could knock.

"I see you have the top down."

Fury nodded. "I needed to blow the cobwebs out of my head." She took off her floppy brimmed hat and shook her short, red hair free.

"Judging from the look on your face, it didn't work." Cory said, stepping aside to give her sister space as she passed by.

"Not really. Do you have any iced tea?"

"Sure. Have a seat."

Returning from the kitchen with a tray, Cory asked, "Here or on the porch?"

"Let's go outside. I need the peace and tranquility of birds, flowers, and fresh air to calm down."

"What's wrong? I'm assuming that your new designer purse means trouble in paradise."

"Among other things, starting with the speeding ticket I got on the way here."

"Not another one. Fury! You are going to lose your license. Do I dare ask what's going on with you and Carl?"

Fury shook her head and then said, "It's a done deal."

"I suspected as much when I saw the purse."

"What can I say? When love goes wrong, guys go to a bar; girls go to a mall—heartbreak therapy."

"Heartbreak? You? I doubt that, but what happened?"

"Night before last. I told him that I'm going to Ireland to do more research on our family history. He went ballistic. He said, 'You're doing no such thing—travel to Ireland alone—no way. All those sexy Irish accents—no way.'"

Cory shook her head, frowning. "And you said?"

"Nothing at first. I was fighting the desire to throw my ice water in his face. But, I didn't. I just stood up, grabbed my purse, and said, 'Excuse me. I have packing to do. Go arrest yourself.' I walked out and called a cab."

"Typical of Fury O'Quinn—leave no man standing. Think there's any chance of patching it up?"

"No." Fury took a drink of her tea.

"Fury, you're never going to find a perfect man. They aren't made the way you make them up for your novels."

"Then I'll have to do without. I won't compromise."

"So you're really going to Ireland?"

"I am. I'm committed to the idea of a book about Granny and her brother. Something definitely happened at that big house in Arabella—Forglen."

"You really think so? What did you find out from our cousin?"

"She knew a lot about the family, and there was a trunk in her basement with old postcards, letters, and newspaper clippings about Dolan family births, deaths, and weddings. Colleen said that our uncle, James Dolan, the one with the large monument, spent his adult life in Milledgeville—the insane asylum."

"Let me guess. Forty-five years?"

"You got it."

"What was wrong with him?"

"Colleen said that all she ever heard was that he threatened to kill his boss, a man by the name of J.G. MacGregor. Cory, according to Colleen, that marble monument on Jim's grave appeared there mysteriously. No one knew where it came from or who bought it. The other Dolan graves had those modest markers that were complimentary for all MacGregor Marble employees and their families. Granny's father and three brothers were all stonecutters at the quarry. Jim was the last to die, but he had not worked there since 1925. MacGregor is still the largest business in Arabella, and Forglen is still the MacGregor home."

"That is strange. Is Forglen that huge house that looks like someone shipped it over from Europe?"

Fury nodded.

"James Dolan was committed to the asylum the same week that our grandmother, Bridget, left Arabella for good. She was only sixteen years old. I found Bridget listed on the passenger manifest for a ship to Ireland in June of 1925 and matched the dates."

"And you're thinking there's a connection."

Fury nodded. "There has to be."

"Was there any information in the letters?"

"Oh, yes. Bridget must have worked at Forglen. There were letters from her to Colleen's mother, Rebecca, in which Bridget talked about being homesick but missed taking care of the wee MacGregor children at Forglen. She also said that thinking about Jim made her cry because he should never have been taken to the asylum. He was confined there from 1925 until he died in 1970."

As Fury talked, Cory listened with interest. "What are you thinking that means?"

"There's a secret buried in that house that cost our uncle his freedom and changed the course of our grandmother's life."

"I have to admit that I'm impressed with the work you've done," Cory said.

"You probably aren't going to believe this, but several days after I went to Colleen's, I had what you are going to call a dream, but I think it was another vision."

"Another one?" Cory gave her sister a dubious look.

"Don't pass judgement until you hear me out. I saw Uncle Jim's face." Fury cringed. "He was like a zombie from Michael Jackson's 'Thriller' video. His voice had an eerie echo and tears were coming from the holes where his eyes should have been." She moved her fingers down her check. "He kept repeating: 'MacGregor. It was MacGregor.' I could see a rotting sign over broken doors in the background behind him that read: 'Georgia Asylum.' It's haunting me. I haven't been able to get that image out of my mind."

"You and your dreams. That was just a nightmare."

Fury shook her head. "That's what Carl said—the jerk. I know that it was more. There was the vague figure of a woman in a white, gossamer gown on the other side of the doors—like the ghost in my first dream. It was hazy, but I think her hair was red. I just know that it was Granny and Uncle Jim calling out to me from the past. I'm going to find out what happened and write about it, even if you, Carl, and my agent think I'm crazy." She reached down in the handbag and drew out a book. "You should read this. Jim Dolan spent his entire adult life in this place." She handed the book to Cory.

"*Damnation Hospital?*" Cory fanned through the dog-eared pages.

"The author of the first part, *There but for the Grace of God*, was the chief psychologist there about fifty years ago, during the time Jim was a patient. The place was a virtual torture chamber where thousands of people were confined. I can't believe that even if Uncle Jim made such a threat that it was right for him to spend the rest of his life in that place. There's no newspaper article, police report, or court record showing a crime was ever committed. Pretty harsh punishment for just making a verbal statement, wouldn't you agree?"

"Maybe, but why would digging into our family history matter to your agent?"

"First, because I have postponed my upcoming tour until next year, so that I can make this trip; and second, because she doubts that she can sell the book. Sarah said that if I publish such a book, and it bombs, sales of my next romance could be adversely affected."

"Then, why are you doing it? What can it matter now?"

"I can't explain it, but I just know that I have to expose the truth. Dad has a sister still living in the O'Quinn family home in Ireland. I'm hoping that there may be clues stored away there—letters, journals, newspaper clippings—evidence of what really happened."

The energy in Fury's voice accelerated and her eyes sparkled. "I 10 think I'm on to a *really* good story. Either Uncle Jim or Granny

may

have known something about Mr. MacGregor, and he wanted them out of the way. Maybe he had committed a crime, and they found out. Or, maybe Uncle Jim was messing around with Mrs. MacGregor. Who knows? In those days, a person could be committed to the asylum on the word of one doctor for anything from 'novel reading' to 'nervousness.' A rich and powerful man could make it happen to anyone."

"If you find the information you hope to find in Ireland, are you going to write a novel or a true story?"

"I don't know. It depends."

"You'd better make it fiction. The MacGregor family is still around. I've seen pictures of the current MacGregor scion on the social pages of the *Atlanta Constitution*. I don't believe that you want to take them on. And, how do you think Dad is going to like you using his family secrets, maybe skeletons?"

"Dad was a cop. If there's something wrong, I think he would want it exposed."

"Have you told him?"

"No, not yet."

Cory brushed her bangs back. "I remember Dad talking about how much you remind him of Granny."

"It's the red hair." Fury tossed her pert haircut. "Hearing him tell stories about her has always made me curious. I wondered why she left the United States even before I knew how young she was at the time. Her parents came here for a better life. Why would she go at sixteen?"

"Good question. But maybe you should stick to writing what you've established that you're good at. You're living the dream—travel, a posh condo, beautiful clothes—expensive purses." Cory gestured with a sweeping movement of her right arm.

"Don't get me wrong, I'm grateful for my success in writing romance, but I want to write a story where I don't know the ending before I start."

"The history is interesting, but you'll have to forgive me if I can't buy into the paranormal idea. What if you find out that Jim was just crazy and tried to kill the man?"

"Whatever. But, Cory, what if he was innocent? It was forty-five years. His entire adult life spent in that place! Read that book and see what they did to patients. I know he was reaching out to me."

"You've always been filled with wild ideas." Cory gave her sister an admonishing gaze.

Fury frowned. "I'm *destined* to write this story." She stood, picked up the tray with the empty glasses, and started toward the front door. "Right now, I have to decide how to approach Dad about digging into the family dirt. I might need his help with his sister. What do you think he will say?"

"Your guess is as good as mine. You know Mike O'Quinn—larger than life and reckless as a teenager on speed. But, he cares about his family. I would say that it could go either way. Why don't you include him—take him with you to Ireland?"

Balancing the tray, Fury turned the screen door handle and then put her foot in the crack to hold it open. She paused as if mulling over the idea. "You think he would go? He's never been back since Mickey died."

"He's getting older. I think he might like to go. And you need someone to travel with you."

"They do speak English over there, Cory. I would be fine alone."

"I'd feel better if Dad went along."

Fury returned to the porch as an SUV pulled onto the Reynolds' driveway, stopped, and two young girls popped out of the backdoor. "Aunt Fury," they both shouted and ran up the porch steps with arms open wide.

"How are the two most beautiful girls south of the Mason-Dixon Line?" Fury said, doing her best to respond to the hugs from both at the same time.

"How's my favorite sister-in-law?" Don Reynolds said as he flicked his door closed.

"I'm your only sister-in-law but fine, thank you."

"She's got a new purse," Cory said.

Shaking his head, Don smiled. "Shot another one down?" He said as he hugged her.

Fury nodded. "I'm looking for a sweet, handsome doctor like my sister married," Fury said, grinning and pointing toward his chest.

"If you'll come by the hospital, I'll make introductions if you promise not to break too many hearts."

Fury smiled. "Might take you up on that. But, for now, I'm massaging the bruise on my heart left by almost falling for the cop who gave me my last speeding ticket."

Don looked at her with a puzzled expression.

"I'll fill you in on that later, honey," Cory said. "Right now, you need to get ready. Our dinner reservations at the club are for six-thirty."

"We want to go to the Varsity, Mommy," the youngest Reynolds daughter, Suzi said, her eyes peering up like two king-sized, blue marbles.

Fury grasped the child in a bear hug. "If that's where you want to go, princess, then I'm all for it."

"Suzi-Lee, we're not taking your aunt to a hamburger place to celebrate the success of her new book. This is her big night—maybe her last one. We're going to the club."

Don turned around and looked at Fury as if expecting an explanation.

"No, Don. I'm not quitting. I'm just taking a chance on writing something different."

Don emitted a spontaneous belly laugh.

"What's so funny, Dr. Reynolds?" his wife asked.

"The two of you. If I were Mike, I might be wondering if I fathered you both. Fury, I'd say was a definite, but you, sweetheart? If I didn't know better, I would think you came from an entirely different gene pool."

"She's a Murphy, Don. You didn't know Mom. She was the conservative one—slow, cautious—had to have a plan, a list, and a schedule."

"That must have been an interesting household. Mike drives his life like he's Jeff Gordon behind the wheel of a Bugatti Veyron," Don responded while Cory rolled her eyes.

"We can't go to the Varsity?" Suzi asked, tugging at her mother's shirttail with tears about to roll down her pink cheeks.

Don motioned to his five-year-old. "Come here, kitten. We'll go to the Varsity this Saturday, I promise, but tonight we're going to have a celebration. Mommy has made reservations."

CHAPTER THREE

He had not said a word since boarding—totally out of character for Michael O'Quinn.

Fury watched his face as the flight attendant went through the drill, wondering whether her dad was nervous about flying or about returning home. When the recitation was over, Fury tapped him on the arm. "Are you okay?"

"Of course," he said, louder than necessary and patting her hand. "Nothing a spot of the Jameson wouldn't cure."

Fury smiled. "A spot? It's going to be a long flight."

"I think I can keep this bird in the air with just a wee bit of the drink."

Fury laughed. "Please do. That's a big ocean underneath us, and I'm not a good swimmer, but try to go light on your liquids."

Mike gave her a don't-go-there look and reached for the book of crossword puzzles he bought at the terminal newsstand. "I sure hope these aren't as difficult as those in *The Times*."

He was working hard to appear casual, but Fury knew him too well to buy his bluff. He had not seen Ireland since he and her mother left their homeland after the death of their only son, which was six months before Cory was born. She suspected that Mike was haunted by past memories. Any childhood questions the sisters had posed to Kathleen about why the couple exited Ireland, leaving family behind, were always met with a brusque, "We don't talk about that."

Likewise, Kathleen refused to discuss her firstborn child, whose picture was in the silver locket she wore. All Fury knew was that Mickey died before his fourth birthday. She had learned that from Mike, late one night when he had consumed a fair share of Guinness and was shedding drunken tears. She was only nine at the time but wise enough to know that it was not a subject to be probed.

The plane started to taxi down the runway. As it lifted off, Fury saw Mike grip the armrest—his knuckles white. Very little frightened the big Irishman, but the takeoff appeared to be getting to him. Mike had spent a lifetime pursuing degenerates: first, as a police officer in the Irish Garda, then in Manhattan where he rose to detective, and finally with the Atlanta Police Department. Although retired, he still worked as a private investigator or bounty hunter when his pension ran short. The move to Georgia had come after the death of Kathleen when Fury was fifteen and Cory was twenty-one.

Watching her father fill in the squares of his puzzle, Fury wondered if this was a mission of duty or pleasure. "Cory made you come with me, didn't she, Dad?"

"No. No, she didn't. I wanted to come. I just didn't want you paying."

"That's no problem. But, I want you to enjoy it. You don't have to babysit. When we get there, you go wherever you like. Don't feel obligated to hang out with me." She looked into his blue eyes, the mirror image of her own, and wondered what he was truly thinking. His initial reaction to her quest had been reserved.

"You're going to the town of my birth. Why would I want to go anywhere else? Nearly everyone left of the family is there. Besides, you'll be needing me to translate."

"Yeah, right. As if living with you and Mom my whole life didn't educate me well on English, Irish style."

"At the very least, you'll need me to introduce you and maybe vouch for your intentions. You *are* aiming to pry into the family history."

"I admit that I am nervous about that. Do you think any of them have read my books?"

"I've not a clue. But I'm warning you, now. Don't let a young whippersnapper sweet talk you into staying over there. I'll not have my girls on opposite sides of the Atlantic."

Fury laughed. "Why in the world would you worry about me falling for a guy over there when I've managed to avoid doing that at home? I'm not exactly the type to be swept off my feet."

"Just be on your guard."

The plane reached its cruising level, and the seatbelt sign went off. Mike seemed to relax and unbuckled for a trip to the restroom. Fury took her leather portfolio from the seat pocket and started making notes.

As the evening progressed, fortified by several shots of whiskey, Mike settled in for the overnight flight. To Fury's surprise, he was the one who actually fell asleep while watching the inflight movie. She tried but, even with a sleep mask, it was hopeless. Book tours, conferences, and New York meetings with her agent and her publisher had accustomed Fury to air travel. However, the prospect of seeing Ireland for the first time, meeting her relatives, and researching the family archives kept her awake. It was one a.m. before she drifted off, leaving less than two hours to sleep.

The landing at Dublin Airport was smooth and on time. Before exiting the aircraft, Fury and Mike adjusted their watches to reflect that it was eight a.m. After clearing immigration, they did an exchange of currency and rented a car.

"I'll do the driving," Mike said.

"I'm not helpless, Dad. I can drive."

"I'll not hear of it. At least not until we get out in the country a bit. You've never driven on the left of the road, nor a car that steers from the right. You let me handle it while we're in Dublin." There was no use protesting.

It was raining as they emerged from the terminal. "If I weren't so tired, I would be annoyed with this weather," she said, brushing her wet hair back as she settled into the small car.

"Get used to it, pet. It rains all the time, but it will clear."

Although he would never admit it, Fury could tell that Mike's Irish driving was rusty. He eased onto a main road, far more cautiously than she had ever seen him do in the States. The hotel was a short distance away, which had been by design in Fury's plan. She knew that jet lag would interfere with activity on their first day. The plan was to stay in Dublin for three days before traveling to Cork to meet the relatives.

The hotel exceeded Fury's expectations. It was an old, red brick, four-story building with dormer windows across the top floor. The walls were partially covered with ivy. The grounds were beautifully landscaped with patches of colorful flowerbeds and stone paths. Mike said nothing as he drove to the front entrance. A valet came out for the car, along with a bellhop who took charge of the luggage. Fury's travel agent had made all the arrangements, including payment for their stay. As they entered the reception area, Mike's eyes grew large and his mouth silent.

"What do you think, Dad?"

"It is far too grand for a bloke like meself."

"Nonsense. You are going to enjoy it. And yes, it has a pub, see." She pointed to a hallway with an easel displaying directions to the bar and restaurants. "Don't stay too late, Dad—okay?"

"I never stay out late." He frowned.

"Right."

Their adjoining rooms were on the top floor. Fury had an executive suite, complete with lounging furniture, a small work area, a table, and four chairs. Mike walked to a window, pulled back the sheer curtain, and gazed out over the area—a wistful look on his face.

What is he thinking?

"Want a soda from the minibar, Dad?"

He didn't answer.

Fury popped the top of a Coke and walked to the window. The rain had cleared, and the midmorning sun showcased the park-like setting below. The grass and foliage were rich in varying shades of green, highlighted by beds of flowering plants and stone pathways. Graceful trees provided shade for randomly placed wooden benches.

"It's a lovely view," she said, holding back the sheer window covering. Mike still didn't respond. "What are you thinking, Dad?"

Dropping his side of the curtain, he shook his head as though to clear confusion. "Just an old man reflecting on the might-have-beens instead of relishing the joys of today." He reached around and affectionately squeezed her shoulders. "Think I *will* have me a cold drink."

Fury smiled and put an arm around his waist. "I'm glad you came with me. It's going to be a good trip. But, right now, I've have to take a nap. If you go out, leave me a note." She walked toward her bedroom. "Don't count on me for anything before dinner. If I'm not up by five, wake me."

The next morning, Fury was awake and dressed early. After checking her email, she went down to the hotel restaurant to have breakfast. Mike had stayed in the hotel pub after dinner the night before, telling stories of his youth to anyone who would listen. She had left him there close to midnight and had no idea how late he stayed. Giving him an extra hour to sleep seemed a wise decision. Her plan was to sightsee in Dublin for two days before moving on to the village where Mike was born and starting her research into the past. She had a list of places she wanted to visit in the city, beginning with Trinity College and the Book of Kells.

After a hearty Irish breakfast of sausage, bacon, eggs, and potatoes, Fury sipped a cup of tea and read the local paper for an hour before returning to their floor.

"Dad," she called out as she eased open the door to his adjoining room. "Are you decent?"

There was no answer for a moment. "A sight more decent than the hour. What's the rush?"

"It's ten-thirty, Dad. If we're going to work in all the places I have on my list, we have to get going. That is unless you want to do your own thing, and then I'll go without you." She put a tall beaker of steaming coffee down on the dresser.

"Not a chance. I'll have that coffee and be ready to go faster than a Leprechaun can steal a coin."

By the time they drove up to Trinity, Mike was in full command of the car and the day. In his typical fashion, he took in everything with gusto. The line to view the Book of Kells was out the door. Knowing Mike's lack of patience, Fury said, "Maybe we should come back early tomorrow morning. I know you don't want to stand in that line."

"No, no. It's doable. And, I've been meaning to mention to you that I think we should be on our way tomorrow. No sense in spending another expensive night at the posh inn."

"Dad." She tipped her chin and cut her eyes at him. "Stop worrying about the cost. I have it more than covered."

"I don't want you spending all your money. We can move on to the country where lodging will be more reasonable. We might stay with some of the kin."

"No." Her expression indicated that she meant business. "We're sticking to the plan." If a look could kill, Michael O'Quinn would have been a candidate for last rites.

"I was right to call you Fury," he muttered under his breath. "The name suits you fine." Raising his voice, he said, "I concede. We'll stay until the Goddess gives a go."

Fury smiled. "Nice to have you agree."

"So, what did ye think?" Mike asked as they left the college.

"Words fail me, Dad." She shook her head. "I can't believe that the incredible artwork was done by hand over a thousand years ago." Fury was talking about the ancient *Book of Kells*. "The colors are so brilliant. It makes me wish I remembered more of the Latin I took in high school so that I could actually read the words of the Gospels."

"Aye. I would admit that when me mum and da brought us to Dublin to see the book, I paid it little mind, but seeing it again just now, I'm in awe as well."

"I need to sit and let my mind thoroughly absorb what I saw. Let's grab some lunch."

"Dandy idea. Why not the Temple Pub? It's on that list of yours, is it not?"

"At the pub, both ordered shepherd's pie. Mike asked for a glass of Guinness. Fury requested a Coke. "It's good to sit for a while. My feet were killing me at the college." Under the table, she eased off her shoes for a minute or two.

With his usual, larger-than-life personality, Mike engaged an American family sitting nearby in conversation when the husband expressed difficulty reading a tourist map of the town.

"I know the place inside out," Mike said. "Spent the first of me adult years as a Garda, right here in Dublin City."

"A Garda?" the wife asked.

"Garda, Irish cop—the unarmed kind. Police are a lot different over here than in the States."

"Really?" the middle aged, Iowa woman said, focusing intently on Mike. "Like the London bobbies?"

"Aye. Not that we'd want to be compared." Mike took a sip of his Guinness. "When I got on the force in New York, they assigned me a gun and holster as soon as I graduated from the academy. I was pretty impressed with meself."

"You're a New York policeman like on *Law and Order*?" the young boy of the family asked, his eyes wide with awe.

"No, lad. Not anymore. I lost me dear wife when Fury, here, was still a girl. I thought it best to leave the city—get a fresh start. Moved me girls south. Sort of retired now, but work sometimes as a bounty hunter."

The boy's eyes grew even larger. "Like *Dog*?"

"No. He's not like *Dog* on TV," Fury interjected. "He's primarily retired but works as a private investigator and sometimes as a bail recovery agent." Instantly she wanted to bite her tongue. *Why did I say that? Can it hurt that he wants to be known as a bounty hunter?*

Mike did not register that he had been contradicted, carrying on with his usual flair and reciting anecdotes from his work until the family finished eating and left the pub.

Watching him, Fury reflected on the tragedies of life he had sustained and wondered whether it was good or bad to have brought him back to the site of his first sorrow. *We are all shaped by the scars of life. He drinks a little too much, talks a little too much, but he's genuine and his heart is pure gold.*

"We'd better get a move on, Dad, if we're going to see anything else before we go back to the hotel. We'll need time to dress for the play at the Abbey Theatre."

"Ready I am, colleen. The mug has gone dry." He reached for the check, but Fury snatched it away.

"How many times do I have to tell you that this trip is my treat?" She laid her credit card on the table. "I sell a *lot* of books."

Mike served as an excellent tour guide for the remainder of their stay in Dublin. The gap in time had not hindered his ability to navigate the city. The next afternoon, they rode through a neighborhood of terraced housing, and Mike pointed to one of the doors. "That's where your mum and I lived." He made no reference to the little boy he lost there. Although there was no sign of emotion in his voice, Fury sensed that he could neither slow down nor elaborate further.

Their last morning in Dublin, Mike was up first. By the time Fury was dressed, he had his luggage packed and standing at the door, ready to transfer it to the car.

"How far is it to Kilkerran" Fury asked.

"Forty miles—no more."

"Then we have plenty of time to enjoy a leisurely breakfast. It's only eight-thirty."

He nodded.

Breakfast was quiet with Mike saying very little.

By eleven, they were on the road. Mike stared straight ahead from the driver's seat. If Fury asked a question, she got a reply; but left to his own social devices, he was silent. As sunlight fell gracefully on the lush countryside, the beautiful scenery that bordered the two-lane road entertained Fury.

"It's really lovely here," she said, looking over at Mike.

He nodded.

"Has it changed much?"

"Some."

So much for conversation.

They approached a hotel. "Is this where we're staying?" Fury asked.

"No. We've a little farther to go. You said the reservation is for the Purple Duck B&B, didn't you?"

"Yeah."

"There. It's right ahead."

Just off the road was a two-story, country house of gray stone. Situated on a large tract of land with a reed-filled pond on one side, it looked to be several hundred years old and was covered with vines. A pair of ducks were sunning on a small island in the middle of the water. "Here we are," Mike said, pulling into the drive. "You'll now get a taste of the land on which your da cut his teeth."

Fury's heart raced. As she climbed out of the car, she took a deep breath of country air. "It's beautiful, Dad. I love it."

He smiled and opened the trunk to retrieve their luggage. "It is a good land."

The bed and breakfast was furnished with eighteenth century, dark wood pieces. Winged-back chairs and an overstuffed sofa with ample throw pillows created an inviting and homey ambiance in the entry salon. The period motif was carried through in the bedrooms where a pot of yellow chrysanthemums added an additional layer of warmth. Every room had a fireplace, framed with white woodwork and topped with a matching mantle. Plump comforters and pillows were on the beds. Fury's room was done in shades of green, while Mike's was in shades of blue. Each had a tea station.

"Perfect," Fury said as Mike put her luggage down. "I couldn't ask for more." She walked over to a window overlooking the water. "Let's unpack, go into town for lunch, and then try to contact the family."

"Did you tell them when we would be arriving?"

"Not exactly. I told you that I spoke with Evanne, Aunt Mary's granddaughter. I said we would be here sometime this week, and I would call."

"I'm surprised that my sister, Mary, is still alive. She's got to be nearly eighty."

"Evanne said that, even though she's got health problems and has trouble hearing, she's still full of spirit and excited about seeing you again. I can't wait to meet the family. You realize that you and Mom are the only relatives Cory and I have ever known."

"I hope they'll be happy to meet you after they hear what it is that you want to do."

CHAPTER FOUR

"It's four-thirty, Dad. We need to leave for Aunt Mary's."

"I'm ready," Mike responded as he closed the door to his hotel room.

As they headed to the farmhouse where Mike was born, he asked, "How is it that you plan to bring up the purpose of this trip?"

"I've not a clue." Fury took a sip from a bottle of water. "Any suggestions would be welcomed."

Shaking his head, while staring straight ahead, he said, "Can't say that I have any."

"But, you know her. I don't," Fury said.

"Might be better said that I *knew* her. As I remember, she was a bossy old hen. We young ones called her the O'Quinn Gestapo Queen." Mike slowed the car to accommodate a gaggle of geese crossing the road. "Queenie patrolled us wee ones like it was her sacred duty— forever barking her orders: 'Wash up, Mick. Clean the mess, Maura. Do your chores, Ronan.' And Ronan was older than she." Taking one hand from the wheel, he reached for a tissue to wipe his damp brow. "And if she turns you down? What then?"

"I guess I go home like I came. Right now, I'm not even sure *when* to bring it up. What do you think?"

"I dunno. How much did you say to the granddaughter?"

"Only that we were coming for a visit and that I hoped to learn more about my family's history."

"Best play it by ear. No way of guessing how it is that Mary will react."

"Are you okay about staying for dinner?"

"Since you've already accepted, I will have to be. But, I don't have a problem with it. You're sure to have an authentic Irish meal," Mike said, smiling.

"Isn't that what I had all my life? Evanne said they are having a traditional chicken supper—the bird, chips, gravy, peas, and onions. Her father and mother, Casey and Margaret, are coming."

"You don't say. Casey was just the lad when your mum and me left."

The O'Quinn homestead was set back from the road outside of Kilkerran. Behind it were acres of green pastureland, giving home to a substantial herd of sheep and a large garden. Mary's son, Casey Doyle, ran the farm and lived with his wife in the guesthouse at the back corner of the property. Evanne had moved into the main house to help care for her grandmother.

When they reached the property, the double gate was open in anticipation of their arrival. As Mike turned the car onto the gravel drive, Fury looked around the site.

"It's larger than I had pictured, Dad. It's a *big* house. I thought your family was poor."

When he did not respond, Fury turned her head to look at her father. He appeared stiff. Leaning forward to see his face better, she saw that his eyes were glazed over, a tear creeping down the side of his nose.

"Are you okay, Dad?"

"It's a bit to take in, luv. I grew up in that house—me mam, me da. Sheared those sheep but couldn't wait to get off the farm—had to get me to the city. I never said we were poor, but we weren't rich. Seeing this just now, I'm wondering why I was in such a hurry to leave."

The car came to a stop, but Mike did not kill the motor. Fury's eyes were glued to her father, who continued to stare at the house.

"Take your time, Dad. We can sit here for a few minutes."

Instantly, he snapped out of his reverie. "No way. We've come the distance. Let's introduce my darlin' daughter to my kin."

As they left the car and started up the stone walk, bordered by flowering plants, Fury gazed at the two-story, gray stone house, dating back two-hundred years. Originally a watermill for grinding stone, the wheel had been removed and the building converted to a home by Mike's grandfather. It had been a working farm for seventy-five years. The narrow river, which once fueled the water wheel, now nourished the livestock. The sight of the blue water with graceful trees lining its banks, emerald-green grass covering gently sloping fields, and the herd of black-faced, white sheep created an artist's delight. Out of sight, behind the house, an arched, wooden bridge crossed the stream adding a romantic touch to the pastoral scene.

As Mike rang the bell, he said, "All's we had was the brass knocker." The door opened, and a young woman with dark hair and blue eyes stood smiling.

"Cousin Mike, Fury, come in," Evanne said. "Granny is dying to see the two of you." She immediately hugged each as they entered.

Mike's eyes sucked in the surroundings.

"Has it changed much?" Evanne asked.

"I would say not so much," Mike answered. "A bit quieter."

"It's beautiful," Fury said, "just as I imagined."

As they entered the living room, white-haired Mary O'Quinn Doyle attempted to rise from the Victorian sofa, holding on to her walker.

"Mick, you scallywag, come here and give your old sister a hug."

Fury looked at him, quizzically. "Mick?"

Smiling, he shook his head. "Haven't been called that since I left Kilkerran."

"And this is your wee colleen. Jesus, Mary, and Joseph, she's the spitting image of our dear, sainted mam."

Wrapping his arms around the teetering old woman, he kissed her on the top of her gray chignon. "Favor Mam she does and every bit as spirited."

They sat in the living room for more than an hour, drinking tea and exchanging stories. Mike and Mary did most of the talking with Fury and Evanne listening with interest. At five-thirty, Casey and his wife, Mary-Margaret, arrived as Nuala, the housekeeper, announced that dinner was ready.

Passing a bowl of fried potatoes, Evanne said, "I want to read your books, Fury. Can I order them from Amazon?"

"You can, but let me send you a set."

"That would be lovely," the dark-haired, young woman said. "You might want to read them as well, Granny."

"That I would. That I would."

Watching her hosts, Fury wanted to broach the purpose of her trip but each time she felt there was a potential segue into the subject, guilt stifled her. *I feel like a fraud, coming here for an ulterior purpose. They are so happy to see us and think we came for familial reasons.*

The visit passed without a mention of the true mission.

"I kept awaiting for you to bring up your purpose, but you didn't," Mike said as they walked down the hotel corridor.

"How could I, Dad? I felt like a hypocrite. Maybe tomorrow when we go to the home to see Uncle Ronan."

"Would it help if I talked to Mary?"

Fury thought for a minute. "No. It's my project and my responsibility to deal with. I'll find a way tomorrow."

"Maybe you should wait until someone in the family reads a book of yours."

Fury's eyes lit up. "You know what? I'm going to Dublin tomorrow morning and see if I can find copies. If possible, I'll get them both a complete set. You stay here if you like."

"Not a chance. I'm driving you."

Fury found a few of her books in a large Dublin bookshop. "At least they have my most popular titles. I'll split them between Evanne, Aunt Mary, and Mary-Margaret. I hope they don't shock Aunt Mary."

Mike laughed. "She'll probably enjoy them a lot more than she'll admit."

When Mike and Fury arrived back at the farm that afternoon, Mary was dressed in her Sunday best. Fury handed her aunt and cousin each a package containing two of her books. "I've ordered the rest for you both, but it may take a couple of weeks. They are a little on the spicy side, Aunt Mary, so I hope you're not offended."

"You wrote all of these?" Evanne asked, her tone revealing admiration.

Fury nodded.

"How many have you written?"

"Eight all together." Fury held up eight fingers.

Evanne shook her head as though astonished. "And I struggled to write a one-thousand word essay in my senior cycle at school. You've written thousands and thousands."

"They are just romance novels—not what I had planned to write. When the first one was published, I liked the money. Now I want to do what I set out to do."

"What's that child?" Mary asked.

"I want to write a book with social relevance. All of my books are just pure entertainment. Don't misunderstand. I'm happy that people enjoy them, but I don't think they learn from them. I want to produce a piece of work that has consequence."

"Do you know what that book will be about?" Evanne asked.

Here it was—her opportunity. Fury trembled a little before speaking.

"I think I do. It's part of why I'm here."

Evanne and Mary both looked puzzled. "You're in Ireland to look for a story of consequence?" Mary asked.

"I think so, Aunt Mary. I believe there's a serious story in what brought Granny O'Quinn back to Ireland when she was only sixteen."

Mary looked at Fury with a keen interest. "And what do you think that might be, my dear?"

"I don't know, but I suspect that it may have been connected to the commitment of Uncle Jim Dolan to a mental institution in Georgia."

"Who was Uncle Jim Dolan?" Evanne asked.

All the while, Mike was watching his sister with a serious expression on his face, as if he expected an explosion to erupt and he had to be ready.

"Uncle Jim was your great-grandmother's brother, luv. I don't know anything else about him," Mary said.

"My grandmother never talked about him?" Fury asked.

Mary shook her head. "Not that I recall. I only knew he existed when she took account of her family back in the States. Hers was a large Irish Catholic family like ours. I think Mam had the three brothers and three sisters. But none were known to us."

"Did my grandmother, ever say why she came back to Ireland?"

"No. No. She never talked of it. We all knew not to ask. I think that one night at the table, Ronan said, 'Mam, why is it that you are the only one who came back to Ireland? Wasn't it better in the States?' She cut him off with the sharp look that only Mam had. You remember that look, don't you, Mick?"

Mike nodded.

"I don't think that you were even born," Mary said, continuing to address Mike. "Ronan was probably no more than twelve or thirteen."

"Did she say *anything*?" Evanne asked, having become interested in a part of her heritage previously unexplored.

"She said that her reasons were personal to her and that it was in our best interests not to pry. We knew that to be the case, and neither of us ever asked again."

As Fury was about to inquire about family memorabilia in Mary's possession, Evanne broke into the conversation and changed the subject. "We should be getting to St. Bernadette's if we're to pick up Uncle Ronan and make the restaurant before the crowd gathers."

"You're right, child. Fetch me sweater," Mary said. "The place always has a chill."

"We should take the van. It has enough room for Uncle Ronan and his wheelchair."

Despite his age, Ronan O'Quinn brought forth a robust zest for life equal to Mike's. The reunion touched Fury's heart as the brothers recounted stories of tricks played on the sisters and the sneaking of an extra slice of pie when no one was looking.

"Why has it taken ye so long to make it back to see us?" Ronan asked at one point during dinner.

"Right now, I've got no excuse except to say that in the first years, the memories—they were raw. And then, raising the girls, Kathleen's sickness—it just never seemed to be possible."

After dinner, the men adjourned to a nearby pub where they were joined by Evanne's father, Casey, while the women returned to the farm. Despite speculation by the women to the contrary, the men came home early.

By the time that Mike and Fury returned to the inn, it was after ten o'clock.

"Did you talk to Mary?"

Fury shook her head. "I couldn't find the right time."

"If you don't ask her soon, we'll be back in the States."

"I know." She took a deep breath. "Tomorrow. I'll do it tomorrow. Evanne has a doctor's appointment in Dublin, so we'll be alone if you go to St. Bernadette's to visit with Uncle Ronan. I'll ask her then."

Mike smiled at her. "Banishing me, are you?"

"Of course not. But I know that you and Uncle Ronan have a lot more memories to talk about."

The next morning, Mike dropped Fury at the farm on his way to the nursing home.

"Tell me more about what Dad was like when he was a boy," Fury said to Mary as they had a cup of tea.

"Mick was the baby and had the personality that no one could resist. He never met the stranger, but could throw such a tantrum that would wake the dead. Mam knew he was to be her last and indulged him way too much. But it was hard not to. Mick had the charm, he did. It broke Mam's heart when he packed and took off for Dublin before his twentieth."

"What was she like, Aunt Mary?"

"Gentle and forgiving—a beauty to the day she died. But there was always a pain in her eyes that we didn't understand. As wee ones, we didn't notice it, but by the time I was fourteen or fifteen, I suspected there was something I didn't know that caused her heart to ache."

"And you never asked?"

"It wouldn't have been right to ask."

Fury took a deep breath and looked straight into her aunt's blue eyes.

"What is it, child?"

"Please forgive me, but I want to write Bridget and Jim Dolan's story. I think that something happened that caused both of them a lot of pain and definitely destroyed his life. Please know that my intentions are good. Even though it was a long time ago and they are all gone, I want to expose the person who may have put a member of our family through what was a life of torture."

Mary shook her head. "What is it that you think it could be?"

"I don't know, but I know that Uncle Jim was committed to a despicable place for most of his adult life because he supposedly threatened to kill a man by the name of John Graeme MacGregor. I can't find any evidence that he actually tried to kill the man and really none that he even made the threat."

"Who was MacGregor?"

"A very rich and powerful man in Georgia—the kind of man who could have made anything happen that he wanted. The Dolans worked for him. Your grandfather and your uncles were stonecutters in his marble factory. They carved statutes, architectural ornamentation, and headstones. Your mother, my grandmother, worked as a housekeeper or nanny in the MacGregor mansion."

"How do you suppose to find out about something that happened so long ago, child?"

"By trying to find any written papers that have survived. Do you know if my grandmother kept any letters or a journal?"

"I don't."

"Are there any trunks or storage boxes in your attic?" Fury held her breath.

Mary nodded, slowly. "Many."

"Would you consider allowing me to go through those trunks?"

Mary's brow pinched together in a slight frown. Fury sat motionless, eye-to-eye with the old woman. Mary's head moved slowly in a silent refusal.

"'Tis not that I would deny you, my child, but we are a simple family. We don't seek attention."

Fury's heart sank. *That's a no. Do I try to change her mind?*

"I know that you mean no harm, but—"

"Ms. Doyle," Nuala interrupted as she appeared in the doorway. Mary gave her a sharp look. "There's an emergency call."

"Who—"

"It's an officer of the Garda. He says to put you on the line."

"Oh my." As she attempted to rise, Fury stood to help Mary to her walker. The only telephone was in the small sitting room on the opposite side of the entry hall.

CHAPTER FIVE

Fury wasn't certain what to do. She was smarting from the apparent rejection, but was also concerned as to what kind of emergency would prompt a call from the local police.

Seconds later, Mary returned. "Fury, it's your da. The sergeant was not clear, but there's been an accident. Mick's car went off the road."

Fury's face went white. "Oh my God. Where is he? He's not—"

"No, child. He's alive. They've taken him to hospital."

"I have to go. Aunt Mary." Fury was seized with panic. "But we don't have a car. Evanne's in Dublin with yours. Dad had ours."

"Easy, child. I'll telephone Casey."

"I have me car. I can take the two of you," Nuala said. In the urgency of the moment, Mary and Fury had forgotten about the housekeeper. "Where's it that they've taken him?"

"The sergeant said he is on the way to Our Lady of Angels."

It took thirty minutes to reach the small hospital, located in a nearby town. Nuala drove. Fury thought they would never arrive, despite the car traveling at five kilometers an hour over the speed limit.

Bursting through the emergency entrance, a pale Fury fought back tears as she sought information about Mike's condition and location. Mary and Nuala trailed behind her, Mary on her walker.

"My dad is here. I need to find him."

The pert, young woman behind the window said, "His name, please."

Learning Mike's location, Fury ran the hallways to the unit

where he was being treated. The nurse on duty told her that Mike was undergoing tests and someone would give her information as soon as possible. The woman refused to comment further.

"Please have a seat in the waiting area. As soon as there is news, we will come for you. There's tea and coffee." She pointed down the hall to a sign over a doorway that read, "Family Lounge."

"Can't you tell me anything? Was he conscious? Was he injured in the accident?"

"I'm sorry; I have no more information available."

Mary and Nuala arrived minutes after Fury sat down on a straight chair in the waiting room.

"How is he, child?" Mary said, her eyes glassy.

"I don't know. They haven't told me anything. The nurse said that they are doing tests on him, and someone will come here to speak with me when they're done." Her voice cracked more and more as she spoke. "Do you know anyone here who can help us?"

Taking a seat on a small sofa, Mary patted the space next to her. "Come sit here, child. I can ask if my doctor is in the hospital today, but I'm sure someone will come soon with information."

The only visitors in the room, the trio sat in silence until Fury said, "I should call my sister."

Mary reached across and put her hand on Fury's arm. "Best wait until you speak with the doctor. No need to upset her before you know something."

Nuala nodded in agreement.

"If I don't tell her and something—"

"Don't think that. Mick's going to be fine. He's tough."

After what seemed to Fury like an endless time, although it was less than thirty minutes, a young doctor walked into the waiting area. All eyes turned to him.

"I'm looking for the family of Michael O'Quinn," the man said.

Jumping up, Fury said, "I'm his daughter. Are you his doctor?"

Nodding, he said, "I am Amit Patel. Your father is stable."

"What's wrong? How badly was he hurt?"

"He doesn't appear to have suffered any injury in the accident, but we're not sure about what happened. We found a bullet lodged in his chest cavity. Do you know how long it has been there?"

Fury nodded. "It's been there since I was a little girl. He was shot in the line of duty when he was a police officer."

"So, it's never caused him any problem?"

"None that I know of—not that he would tell me. Could something have happened with it?"

"We're going to need the results of more tests to know. It could have been a heart attack or cardiac arrest, he could have dozed off, or the bullet might have moved and caused a temporary blockage."

"Is he going to be all right?" Fury's expression pleaded for an answer.

"It's too soon to say for certain, but his vital signs are stable and he's able to communicate, which is good. However, he's groggy and tends to doze off. We'll know more later. He's being treated as a cardiac patient until something else is discovered. We'll be monitoring him closely."

"Can I see him?"

"I see no reason why not. However, don't encourage him to talk too much. He needs to rest to allow his body to settle down. It has undergone a substantial trauma."

"You go, child. We'll wait for you here," Mary said. "There's no need that Mick should have so many visitors at one time."

Fury leaned over and hugged the old woman.

"He's in room 312. Go left down the hallway, past the nurses," Dr. Patel said.

Mike's room was small with only one wooden chair. The bare walls were a pale shade of green. The late afternoon sun streamed through the one small window.

"Dad," she said, softly.

Mike opened his eyes. Seeing Fury, a smile crossed his face.

"You scared us to death, Dad," Fury said. "What happened?"

"Happened so fast, I hardly remember. Thought I'd been shot again. One minute, me and the car are rolling down the road, pretty as you please—the next minute, we're in the ditch." He took a deep breath. Despite the oxygen tubes in his nose, it was clear that the act of speaking exhausted him.

She leaned over the bed and kissed his forehead. He was connected to an IV and monitors, making any further contact impractical. "Don't talk now. I'll sit here for a while. Aunt Mary and Nuala are in the waiting room."

"You haven't called your sister, have you?"

"Not yet. Do you want me to?"

"No. . . . She'll be on a plane, and she doesn't . . ." His voice tapered off.

"Don't talk. I won't call her, yet."

"Good," he said, his eyelids growing heavy.

Fury stayed in the room with Mike for fifteen minutes after he fell asleep and then returned to the waiting room.

"How is he, child?" Mary asked before Fury had reached her side.

"His face is gray, and he's hooked up to monitors and an IV bag. It's hard to know."

"Can I get a sandwich for you?" Nuala asked.

"That's a good idea," Mary said, "if you wouldn't mind. We have tea here."

Fury smiled at the plump housekeeper as she rose to leave the room.

"You should go home, Aunt Mary. There's nothing you can do here."

"Nonsense, child. I'll stay with you until you're comfortable leaving. I'd like a glimpse of Mick, meself."

After nibbling on the sandwich Nuala brought, Fury made the call to Cory. As expected, her older sister wanted to leave for Ireland immediately.

"There's nothing you can do, and Dad is going to be furious with me for calling. I'll let you know the minute the doctor gives me more information. I promise."

By evening, Mary's family had learned of Mike's condition and joined the hospital vigil. Fury went into his room periodically, but he was always sleeping. Casey brought more sandwiches to the waiting room, but Fury could hardly eat. A few minutes past seven, Dr. Patel appeared at the door. Fury jumped up to greet him.

"Ms. O'Quinn, it appears from all tests that your father has suffered a sudden cardiac arrest. It caused him to lose consciousness for a moment. At this point, we are monitoring him closely and giving him medication to stabilize his heart rhythm. We are not certain as to the cause of his attack. He does have some buildup of plaque, but it doesn't appear to have closed an artery. A piece of plaque may have broken away and created a temporary blockage."

"Is he in danger?"

"I can't tell you that there's no danger, but at this time, we're optimistic that he will recover if he follows directions."

When Fury entered Mike's room an hour after her meeting with his doctor, Mike was awake and alert.

"You need to get out of this doom and gloom," he said. "Go to the hotel or with Mary. Come back tomorrow and pick me up. I'll be ready to leave by then."

"Right," she said, smiling with relief that he appeared improved. "You'll be here several days at the very least."

"I'll be a monkey's arse. They'll not keep me in this sterile asylum of medical experimentation."

"I know you're getting well—cantankerous as ever. Do you feel like seeing Mary?"

"If you tell her that there's to be no lecturing me about me lifestyle."

Fury grinned. "I'll tell her."

When Mary hobbled in on her walker, Mike's eyes betrayed his joy at the sight of her.

"Always did like the center ring, you ole faker," she said, easing to the side of the bed and affectionately taking one of his hands in hers.

"Love you, too, Queenie."

"You gave this sweet young thing quite a scare."

"I am sorry about that, but I didn't see it coming."

A nurse came in to check Mike's vital signs, which Mary and Fury took as their cue to leave for the night.

"Take her home with you, Mary. She doesn't need to be alone in that hotel."

"It has been my plan all along, Mick. Evanne can run her there in the morning to fetch her things. As long as you're here, she's to stay with us."

"Do I have a say?" Fury asked.

"No," the two said almost simultaneously.

When Evanne and Casey had arrived at the hospital earlier, Nuala had gone home, leaving Evanne to drive the women back to the farm. As soon as they arrived, Mary asked her granddaughter to make a pot of tea. When the young woman brought the tray to the living room, Mary directed her to bring a bottle of her Irish whiskey. Fury watched in awe as the gray-haired woman poured a generous amount of the liquor into the teapot.

"We both need a wee bit of the spirits to warm our blood and relax our minds, child," Mary said, pouring Fury a cup of the mixture. "But, this will be our little secret."

"I don't drink," Fury said, her eyes still dilated from surprise.

"It's not a drunkard that I intend to make you, child."

Reluctantly, Fury accepted the cup Mary extended and took a small sip. The taste was terrible, but the feeling of warmth that spread through her body felt good, and she drank her entire portion.

When she left her room at five a.m. the next morning, Fury expected to be the only one up; however, bacon was cooking and Mary and Nuala were already in the dining room and kitchen respectively.

"Have a cup of tea, child," Mary said, pointing to a pot and cups on the sideboard. "Did you sleep well?"

"Better than I expected. You are awake awfully early."

"Habit, dear. This is a farm. Chores begin early, and I knew you would want to go back to hospital. Evanne can drive you, and Nuala will bring me later. No need to be in a great rush. I spoke with Mick's nurse, and he is doing fine—slept well, the night."

"I don't want to continue to impose on the family, Aunt Mary. Maybe Evanne can help me pick up the rental car, wherever it is."

By ten a.m., Fury was in Mike's room, having obtained possession of the rental car that had suffered only the indignity of a mud bath in the accident.

"You're looking better today," she said as she pulled the chair up to his side after giving him a kiss.

"Feeling better, too. I hope you haven't stressed out your sister."

Fury blushed. "I did call her, Dad. I couldn't keep her in the dark when it was something this important. I've talked to her this morning and told her that you're doing okay."

"Wish you hadn't done that, but I knew you would." He made a slight face of dissatisfaction. "Did you get a chance to talk to Mary about the family papers before I upset the apple cart?"

Fury tipped her head slightly toward her shoulder. "I did. She's against it."

"Why, in the name of all I hold dear? What's her feckin' problem?"

"She doesn't want the family exposed to public scrutiny."

"Bull shit. We'll see about that."

"Calm down. You're causing your blood pressure to go up." Fury looked up at the numbers on the monitor attached to Mike.

"I need to get out of here," he said with determination.

"You're not going anywhere until the doctors say you're okay. So, just settle down and enjoy yourself."

"Right. There's nothing on that feckin' TV to watch, I don't have anything to read, and they don't serve pints in this place."

"I can't do anything about the TV, and you certainly can't have a pint, but I'll go see if I can find you something to read. What would you like?"

"A bloody good mystery or an American western."

As Fury looked up, all hell broke loose on his monitors. Before she could stand to call for help, a nurse burst into the room, grabbed

Mike's hand, and while looking at the monitors, pushed the intercom button. "Code blue. Room 312. Code blue."

"Dad—"

CHAPTER SIX

Nauseated from fear, Fury moved aside to allow the team converging on the room enough space to perform their tasks. Mike's color was growing more and more ashen as his heart failed to pump his blood sufficiently to oxygenate his blood. He gasped for air.

A nurse came from behind Fury and tapped her gently on the shoulder. "It would be best that you wait in the hallway or the family room. There's nothing you can do."

A stricken look on her face, Fury backed out of the room, fighting the desire to rush forward and hold on to her father. In the empty corridor, she felt desperate with only her panic for company. *Cory. I should have let Cory come. What if we lose him, and she didn't get to say goodbye? No, no. Dear God, no. We can't lose him.*

Bewildered, Fury staggered toward the family waiting room, her knees weak. It was empty. She went to the farthest corner where two lounge chairs flanked a table littered by a folded copy of the *Irish Independent*, two dirty paper cups, and the remains of a package of vending machine crackers. Alongside the trash was a lidless, wooden box, containing a rosary of black stone beads with a pewter crucifix. Shrinking down into one the chairs, instinct propelled her to take the rosary and begin reciting. "Hail Mary, full of grace," she whispered. The beads were cold in her hand but brought forth an instant calming effect as she lapsed into silently mouthing the words. It was there that Mary found her, still praying, thirty minutes later.

"We went to Mick's room; they turned us away. What's happened, child?" Evanne stood behind her grandmother, the question echoing in her eyes.

"He coded."

"Why didn't you call us?" Evanne said. "We could have been here sooner."

Fury shook her head. "I don't know. It happened so fast. One minute, he was fine; the next, everything went crazy. They made me leave."

"And they haven't told you anything?" the old woman said.

Fury shook her head. Evanne put her arms around Mary's shoulders, fearing the news would unsteady the old woman.

"No news is good," Evanne said. "It means they are taking care of him. Why don't the two of you sit over on the couch? I'll go check for information."

"I should call my sister," Fury said.

"Wait, child. She can't be here, and it's no good to put fear in her."

"She could begin arrangements to come. Her husband is a doctor. He could talk to the people here and understand exactly what is happening." Tears began running down her face.

"You're not alone. We're here for you. Mick is a fighter. He's to be fine. I know it."

Evanne was unable to learn any more about Mike's condition. Thirty minutes passed before Dr. Patel came into the waiting room. "Your father is resting well. He had a close call, but you can be very thankful that he was here when it happened."

"What happened?" Fury asked with urgency on her face and in her voice.

"His heart stopped. He has suffered an arrhythmia, which is probably what happened to a lesser degree yesterday. In layman's terms, his electrical wiring went wrong. He most likely blacked out momentarily because his heart rate was so high that it prevented sufficient blood flow to the brain. Today, it reached a point where his heart stopped, but we were able to resuscitate him successfully. He's stable now, and we can treat the cause. However, he needs to stay quiet for a while to make certain that the medication is working. Had this happened on your flight to America, it would likely have been fatal."

"Can I see him?"

"Just for a minute. He wants to see you as well and insisted that I tell you not to call your sister in the United States."

Fury smiled. "He would."

At Mike's request, Fury waited until late afternoon to place a call to Cory from his room. He persuaded his older daughter to stay in Georgia by agreeing to arrange for a telephone conference between Don Reynolds and Dr. Patel. However, he failed at persuading Fury to remain at the farm with the family.

Fury moved to an inn within two miles of Our Lady of Angels. It gave her the ability to go to her room when he was resting. She met his objections with, "It's not that I don't feel welcome at the homestead. I just prefer to have my private space." Mary received a different explanation. "I don't want to impose on you, and the inn is so close to the hospital." In the emotional turmoil of Mike's condition, Fury's request to Mary for permission to explore the family archives had been put aside.

On day four of Mike's hospitalization, he appeared much stronger. Fury spent the morning with him, but after lunch, she announced that she was returning to her room at the inn. "You need a nap. I need to work a little on my new romance novel, or I'll miss my deadline."

She worked longer than planned and did not return to the hospital until nearly dinnertime. Walking in, she found Mike sitting in a lounge chair, new to the room. His hair was combed and he appeared to have showered. "You've been busy since I left. I didn't mean to stay away so long," she said, kissing him on the forehead.

"I'm ready to go home now. Heart's just dandy—beating just fine."

"Right. You're not leaving here until Dr. Patel says that you are one-hundred-percent."

"You've already been around Mary too long. Taking up her bossy ways."

Fury rolled her eyes. "I'm just using common sense. Something I can't trust you to exercise." She walked over to the windowsill to check the water in a flower arrangement sent by Don and Cory. "These need water." She took a cup from Mike's tray table, filled it with water from the small sink in his room, and added the liquid to the vase. Turning back to him, she asked, "What have you been doing since I left, other than taking a shower and getting all dressed up?"

"I had a visitor," he said, with a mischievous look on his face.

Fury scrunched her eyebrows together. "What kind of visitor? You haven't gone and picked up some fancy lady when I wasn't looking?"

"'Twas a lady, but I wouldn't call her fancy. She might clobber the both of us."

"Okay, I give up. Who came to see you?"

"Me darling sister, Mary."

"And that's supposed to be news? Aunt Mary has come to see you every day."

"Aye. But this day is special." His blue eyes danced in anticipation of delivering his news.

Fury looked him in the eye. "*Why* is this day special?"

"It's special because she has agreed to let you into her precious attic."

Fury's face lit up. "You're kidding. How did you pull that off?"

"Wasn't so hard. I just told her that if she didn't, I was going to have me another one of those arrhythmias, and it would all be on her."

"You *didn't*."

"Course I did. I'm not letting my prideful sister keep you from learning whatever there is to learn. Mam and Da are long dead. Who's it to hurt? And who made her keeper of the gate? Whatever papers that belonged to our mother are just as much mine as hers. Ronan agrees with me."

"You told him about it?"

"I did. He said that he always wondered about Mam's past, but she would never tell. He agrees that it doesn't matter what it is. We'd just like to know."

Fury went over and hugged Mike vigorously. "You are unbelievable. I love you so much."

The next day was Saturday. Evanne was home and took Fury up

to the attic after breakfast.

"Have you ever been through any of this stuff?" Fury asked as they looked around the volume of boxes, trunks, old furniture, and shelving in the large attic.

"Only the trunks with old clothes and toys when I was a little girl. I was never interested in the books and the documents." She ran her hand over the dust on one of the boxes. "This is going to be a *big* job. There must be a ton of paper."

Fury smiled and nodded. "At least. But it gives me hope that there is something in here. There's a lot to be said for keeping a homestead. If this house had ever been sold, and the family moved, I bet most of this would have been trashed."

"Or maybe a sale in the yard. I hear they're popular in the States."

"This stash would make a monumental yard sale," Fury said, opening the drawer of a small dressing table. Now, all I have to figure out is where to start."

"Maybe you should have a fresh box to sort the stuff that looks to have promise."

"Good idea."

After sharing lunch with Mike, Fury and Evanne shopped for cardboard storage boxes, markers, labels, and a notebook to use for organizing and cataloging the items of interest. Before leaving the hospital, she told Mike that she and Evanne were going to work all afternoon, but she would come back after dinner.

"It's not necessary. You've spent enough time in this sterile institution. Come back tomorrow."

Taking him at his word, Fury spent the afternoon opening boxes, flipping through receipts, old bank statements, farm ledgers, and a slew of inconsequential documents.

"Look, Fury. Here is Uncle Ronan's Leaving Certificate, dated August 10, 1942."

"What's that?"

"It is his official completion of secondary school work."

Fury opened a box that was filled with American magazines. The publication dates were between 1968 and 1970. "I bet there are collectors who would want these," she said to Evanne.

Coming to take a look, Evanne said, "Those must have been Aunt Meggie's. She wanted to go to America to live when she was young. Da said that she thought that she could become an actress and make a lot of money."

"How is she related?"

"Da's sister—your cousin."

"Did she get there?"

Shaking her head, Evanne said, "Oh, no. She only made it to London. She took a job at Harrods and married her boss. She comes for holiday about once every two years."

The afternoon passed without discovery of any relevant items. When Nuala called them down for the evening meal, both were exhausted and covered with dust.

"This may have been a waste of your time," Evanne said.

"I'm not giving up. There are a lot of boxes and two or three trunks that we've yet to check."

Sunday morning, Fury attended an early Mass with Mary and Evanne before going to the hospital. Mike was watching TV when she walked into his room.

"How's the hunt going?" he asked as she entered. "Have you struck gold?"

"Not yet, but I will. With all the stuff that's in that attic, there's gold somewhere. Unfortunately, I'm not sure if it's the gold I'm looking for."

"Keep digging. Have you checked the little cupboard?"

"What little cupboard?"

"There is a narrow closet across the south end of the attic. It was always locked when I was a lad. Since I wasn't supposed to play there, I never asked about what was in it."

Fury's eyes grew large with interest. "Do you think Aunt Mary has a key?"

"Probably not. So many years have passed. If Mam kept the key to herself, it is likely lost. Take a hammer and break the lock. Shouldn't be too hard."

"Do you mind if I go now?" Fury was obviously excited. "If Granny had a secret to keep, what better place to keep it?"

"Go, luv. I'm getting used to the place, and there's a pretty young colleen in charge of me for today. I'll do just fine. But, would you get me the newspaper before you go?"

"You bet." She picked up her purse and then reached for his hand, giving it a squeeze. "I'll be right back."

Driving to the farm, Fury had butterflies in her stomach. *This could be it. Why didn't he mention it before? Why didn't I notice the closet?*

When she got there, Evanne had taken Mary to visit Ronan. Nuala was the only one in the house. Fury bounded up the stairs to the attic two at the time. Her heart was pounding. *South end. Dad said it's at the south end.*

Stepping onto the floor, she paused to orient herself. *The sun was shining on the front of the house when we arrived the first afternoon. Therefore, the south end is to the left of the entrance.* Walking to the left, she saw why the closet had been missed. The door was hidden by a large chest of drawers. She was able to pull the piece of furniture far enough from the wall to see that it concealed a small door. *I can't move it far enough to get into the closet by myself.*

Turning around, she hastily retreated down the stairs, calling out for Nuala.

"Nuala, can you help me?"

"If I can. What be it that you need?"

"I need help moving a large piece of furniture, but I also need some tools. Is there a large hammer and screwdrivers that I can use?"

Between the two women, they were able to pull the heavy chest away enough for the door to clear. The lock was ancient; however, it gave up with one swift blow of the hammer. Fury was trembling as she eased the old door open. It was dark inside. Illuminating the area with a flashlight, the sight of a small, trunk-like box of polished wood took her breath, but another lock obstructed her access. She considered smashing it with the hammer, but did not want to damage the piece. Using the smallest screwdriver, she removed the tiny brass screws securing the hasp. It was hot in the confined space and perspiration rose on Fury's forehead as she gently pulled the barrier away from its host and eased open the container.

CHAPTER SEVEN

As the contents came into view, Fury's heart stopped. *I've found it.* The box was full to the brim. On top, an antique rosary lay across a thick packet of yellowing letters that were held together with faded, blue ribbon. The first envelope was addressed to Bridget O'Quinn. *She kept memorabilia. Her story has to be in here.*

Closing the lid, she flashed the light around the narrow closet, looking for any more evidence of her grandmother's past. Other than two hatboxes, only old clothing, shoes, magazines, dishes, and several oil lanterns occupied the space. She looked inside each of the millinery containers on the chance they had been used to store other items but found nothing of interest.

"Are you still there?" she called out to Nuala.

"Aye. I am."

"I've found something, but I think I need a little help getting it through the door with that chest still in the way."

The housekeeper stepped over to help as Fury emerged.

"It's a heavy one," Nuala said, taking the box as Fury wriggled through the narrow opening. "Are there more?"

"I don't think so, but I may come back later to double-check. For now, I want to take this downstairs and have a look. I need to cool off," Fury said, lifting her hair off the nape of her neck.

"Maybe we should wait for Casey to carry it down the stairs?"

Shaking her head, Fury said, "No. I can manage. You go back to what you were doing when I interrupted you."

"I'll bring tea up for you."

"Could you make that something cold?"

51

Nuala smiled. "You Yanks and your cold drinks."

Once Nuala was out of the attic, Fury had second thoughts about transporting her find. *I hope I haven't bitten off more than I can chew. All I need is to go tumbling down those stairs, head first.*

Playing it safe, she went down the stairs backwards, working the box down three stairs at a time. Once on the second floor of the house, she took it to the guest room and put it on top of a small chest. Her heart was pounding in anticipation.

Opening the lid once more, she began lifting out the contents. The rosary was exquisite with faceted beads of deep blue and tiny brass spacers between each. The larger pater beads were of filigree brass as was the triangular flat piece on which the crucifix rested. *How many times did you pray, holding this in your hands, Bridget? Did you keep it locked away for security or for secrecy?* Fury held the traditional symbol of her faith reverently, feeling a mystical relationship with her grandmother.

Flipping through the packet of bound letters, she saw that all were addressed to Bridget. They appeared to be from different people, but all bore U.S. postage. Some had return addresses; others did not. She placed the rosary and the packet of letters on the bed. Beneath the letters was an assortment of photographs intermingled with prayer cards. In the corner of the box was a small, gold button, the approximate size of a nickel, with an insignia bearing an embossed eagle. Examining the piece, Fury could read the words "Riverside Military Academy" circling the bird. *Why would Bridget save a button from RMA among her collection of memorabilia?*

Among the photographs was an image of a family: two light-haired girls of about four and twelve, a toddler boy, and their parents. The clothing worn by the family appeared typical of American styles of the 1920s. The mother had a gentle face; the two girls appeared annoyed. Although a black *X* had been marked across his face, the father's stern expression and rigid posture suggested that he was not a warm and fuzzy man. *O'Quinns? Dolans? Why is there an attempt to X-out the man?*

As Fury sorted the items and laid them out on the bed, she heard the front door open and slam shut. She cringed, realizing that she would not be comfortable sharing her discovery with Mary. "Is that you, Aunt Mary?"

"It's the both of us," Evanne responded. "We're to have tea, would you like to come down and join us?"

Fury looked at the array of memorabilia and wanted to continue delving but felt courtesy and respect required that she go down and speak to her aunt. Taking a deep breath, she contemplated what to say about the discovery. While Mary had granted permission for the investigation, it was not without reservations, and Fury felt a discussion might be awkward. *I'm not going to bring it up.*

"Sounds great. Be down in a minute," Fury called out. Going to the one bathroom on the second floor, she washed her hands, splashed cold water on her face, and ran a comb through her hair.

Mary and Evanne were sitting in the living room, waiting for Nuala to serve tea when Fury came down.

"How was Uncle Ronan?" Fury asked as she went over to hug her aunt.

"He's good today. The arthritis is behaving. More than I can say for meself."

"He was in good spirits. I think he was relieved to hear that Uncle Mike is doing well," Evanne added. "We had lunch with him."

"Terrible food," Mary interjected. "Just give me a gun and let me make it end before your da ever puts me away in one of those God-forsaken, storage vaults."

"Granny. What a horrible thing to say," Evanne said, looking at her grandmother with a hard frown. "Uncle Ronan likes it there."

"He's got no sense. I think he likes eyeing the young nursemaids, in their way-too-short skirts, and telling his tall tales to the other old reprobates."

Fury smiled.

"Sure it must be good that there is still a bit of the fire in his furnace. Don't you think?" Evanne added as Mary scowled.

Before either could answer, Nuala came in with a tray. "I thought you might be hungry, so I made tea sandwiches."

"You are a saint, Nuala. I hadn't realized how hungry I am," Fury said, taking an egg salad sandwich from the tray.

The conversation focused on the weather and complaints of the elderly. Neither of the younger women mentioned Fury's scavenger hunt. After finishing her tea, Mary excused herself for an afternoon nap, eschewing offers of assistance to her first-floor room. As soon as she was out of earshot, Evanne turned to Fury.

"Have you had any luck in the attic?"

"I have. I can't wait to show you."

Evanne's face lit up. "Really?"

"Come on." Fury stood up. "You can help me organize it."

The two women went up to Fury's room like a pair of children headed to the tree on Christmas morning.

"Oh, my, gosh. The leprechauns have left you the gift. Are these all things that belonged to the great-grandmother Bridget?"

"They appear to be."

"Where in the name of Patrick, himself, did you find all this? And why didn't you say earlier?"

Fury pointed to the box. "That was in a closet at the end of the attic. We couldn't see it because of a chest of drawers. I didn't want to bring it up because you know that Aunt Mary is not so keen about me doing this."

Evanne nodded. "You be right about that. But she said you could. Have you read any of the letters?"

"Not yet. I wanted to get everything out and lined up before I begin reading."

"Mind if I do?"

"Go for it. I'm going to finish emptying the contents."

Evanne looked through the envelopes without immediately taking out the letters. She read several of the postcards while Fury separated photographs, newspaper clippings, greeting and religious cards into discrete stacks.

At the bottom of the box, there was a brown leather diary with gilt-edged pages. It was large, approximately seven by ten inches, and unusually thick. Fury could see that it contained insertions, causing the pages to bulge. However, she was once again blocked. A lock secured the journal.

"There's so much here; how do you know where to start?"

"This is where I want to start," Fury said, holding up the journal. "Why don't you read the letters? Maybe sort them according to whom they're from; they appear to be from various people. If you come across anything interesting, let me know."

After compromising the lock, Fury opened the journal and first fanned the pages to see if there were many entries. It was nearly full. Pressed flowers and several cards, mostly religious, were wedged between the pages. The last entry date was July 21, 1935. Beginning on the title page, Fury read an inscription in an elegant and precise hand:

To Bridget,

> Happiest of birthdays to a sweet and kind young woman who has been a Godsend to our family. May you record in this book your joys, sorrows, dreams, and prayers.
>
> Emma MacGregor
January 23, 1925

"Evanne, I was born on Bridget's birthday. No wonder they gave me her name." Fury turned the page; the entries began on yellowed paper in handwriting less grand and not easy to read:

January 24, 1925

Dear Beautiful Diary,

> I've never had such a lovely thing as you. Mrs. MacGregor says I should write often so that when I am old, I can look back to see who I was. I'm not sure that I will like what I see. I'm sixteen now. According to Father McManus, I've been responsible for my sins for four years. Then I must surely be going to hell. I pray daily for forgiveness, for not only what I have done, but also what I think about doing. It's not a good life that I have.
>
> Bridget

The first entry ended abruptly. However, the entry picked up three weeks later, lower on the page.

February 14, 1925

Dear Amelia,

I hope you don't mind being called Amelia, but I can't seem to talk as well to a book as I can a person. Amelia is my favorite name. There was a very beautiful Amelia at school. I would have liked to be her.

Today was St. Valentine's Day. It's a day for sweethearts but mine is denied to me. He says that we will find a way, but even he doesn't know how impossible that is. Power is against us. Miss Emma is so kind to me. It breaks my heart that I have so many secrets from her. I tried to confess to Father McManus, but the words wouldn't leave my mouth. I was to my home yesterday. Mary was preparing for her wedding. She will be a beautiful bride. I know that our mum would have been proud. If Mum were still alive, I might have been able to go to her, but never Mary. She is too sure of what is right and what is wrong. Life is hard. How can one girl be filled with so much love and so much hate at the same time? I may not live to be twenty!

Your friend,
Bridget

Fury read and reread the two pages, trying to speculate as to what was torturing the young girl. "Listen to this, Evanne." She read the two entries to her cousin.

"That's so sad," Evanne said when Fury finished.

"It breaks my heart. She was so young and so unhappy. Have you found anything that could give us a clue?"

"No. Not yet. The letters I've been reading were from Bridget—Granny's—sisters, Mary and Rebecca Dolan. They're mostly news about what they were doing. Mary was having a baby; Rebecca was teaching children's Catechism classes. They do mention Jim, but no details. They only say that they had visited him in Milledgeville and that he had lost more weight. Rebecca said that she did not understand what happened to cause him to be committed to that dreadful place."

Fury bent over the bed and spread the photographs around. A head-and-shoulders shot of a young man in a military uniform caught her eye. "Evanne, look at these." She held up the photo of the cadet along the side of a snapshot of a boy and girl sitting on the ground in a park setting. "Does Aunt Mary have any pictures of Bridget?"

"I'm not sure. I know she has a photograph of her as an old woman. There's an album in the credenza cabinet in the living room. I haven't looked through it in years, but it might have old photos in it."

"Can we look?"

"Sure."

Downstairs, Evanne pulled the shabby old album out of the cabinet. "Careful, it's falling apart."

Fury took it to the sofa and began turning the pages. There was a photo of a young bride and groom on the second page. "Evanne, could this be my grandparents?"

"You'll have to ask Granny. I really don't know. But why don't you try slipping the photo out of the corner tabs. It might have something written on the back."

Fury eased it out, corner by corner and then turned it over. "Conor and Bridget O'Quinn" was written in pencil on the back of the image. "I'm going to compare this with the one of the couple upstairs."

Taking the snapshot and the wedding portrait to the light of the upstairs window, the two women tried to decide if it was Bridget in both. It had no writing. However, the light-haired, young man was clearly not Conor O'Quinn.

"It definitely could be her in both," Evanne said as Fury studied the photos, looking back and forth between them.

"It's her. I'm sure of it. She looks to be young, maybe sixteen. I bet the guy in the snapshot is the one she referred to in her diary."

CHAPTER EIGHT

The room was quiet while Fury read from Bridget's journal and her cousin read various letters. Evanne broke the silence.

"Fury, listen to these two letters to Bridget." She read the two short missives aloud.

"The first is dated '5 May 1925.'"

> My dearest Bridget,
>
> I will finish school on the thirty-first and come home. We will have time together but only for a few days. They are sending me to Europe. I sail from New York on the eighth day of June. Father says that to experience Europe broadens a young man. You must know that I do not want to go. I will be away for the entire summer, and then I leave for Harvard. I do not know why Father demands that I obtain a university degree. He became rich and powerful with none.
>
> How long must I wait to proclaim to all that you are my own?
>
> Forever yours.

"Is there no signature?" Fury asked.

"No and no envelope. The second one is dated '14 June 1925.'"

For my dearest love, Bridget,

I found this in a small shop on my first day in London. It was made in Germany. I knew that you must have it. I used my food allowance, but it was worth it. The blue stones reminded me so much of your eyes. Say a prayer on each that we can be together soon and forever.

I wish that this could be a wedding ring.

Forever yours.

As she finished reading the second note, Evanne handed both to Fury. "Could he, the writer, be talking about that rosary?"

Fury nodded. "Maybe. I think that some of the journal entries I read directly relate to these." She pointed to the diary. "Read between the pages I tabbed."

Evanne took the book and began silently reading.

May 9, 1925

Dear Amelia,

Today was sunny. A letter came in the post with news that is happy and sad. I choose to concentrate on the good. HE will be here but a few days.

Knowing HE is in the world and loves me is all that I live for.

Your friend,
Bridget

June 6, 1925

Dear Amelia,

My heart left today. I cannot bear it. HE will not return until the end of summer, and then HE must leave for Boston. My heart is swollen. We had so few moments together, but we sealed our love. It was so different. We pledged ourselves as only true lovers can. I shall work and pray each day until HE returns.

Your friend,
Bridget

June 10, 1925

Dear Amelia,

The Devil is home. I told him that I have my monthly visitor. He backed away. I don't know where I got the courage, but I told him it could happen no longer, because I was pledged. He said awful things. I wanted to stab him. I have an evil plan. Pray for me, Amelia. I may do the unspeakable.

Your friend,
Bridget

June 15, 1925

Dear Amelia,

I have done something terrible. I am going to prison and to hell. You're my only friend. I didn't mean it to happen. What am I going to do? Please pray for me. I think God would not listen to me now.

Your friend,
Bridget

June 16, 1925

Dear Amelia,

Jim knows. He went to Forglen. I don't know what's going to happen. My life is over. I am so scared. Miss Emma is in the Atlanta hospital. I pray that she will recover. What have I done?

Your friend,
Bridget

June 17, 1925

Dear Amelia,

Men came for Jim in the middle of the night. They said he is crazy and took him away. Father said that they took him to Milledgeville. Jim is not crazy. Why are they doing that? I can't tell Father about me. It's because of me. I know it is. Everyone works for the evil one.

Your friend,
Bridget

June 19, 1925

Dear Amelia,

They are sending me to Ireland. Mr. MacGregor told Father that I was lucky that I wasn't going to prison. I don't understand. Father did not ask me what happened. He is not one to talk much. He said that Mr. MacGregor is taking care of the arrangements for my travel and that I will receive some money. I have to ride a train to New York to get on the boat. I am so scared. I know it is my fault that Jim has gone to that place.

Your friend,
Bridget

June 25, 1925

Dear Amelia,

You're all I have now. I am on the boat. They say we will be in Ireland in six days. I am so scared. Father said that his cousins will take me in until I can take care of myself. They sent a wire. Mr. MacGregor gave money to me to pay for my keep until I get work.

I am in the second class on a lower deck of the boat. It is not good but far better than the steerage endured by my parents. The room is like a cupboard, and the ship rocks. I've been sick to my stomach and threw up last night. I'm inclined to stay in my room but may walk around later.

> Your friend,
> Bridget

June 25, 1925

Dear Amelia,

I'm writing again today because I must tell you of a young man I met. He is from Ireland and traveling home. He was walking on my deck, taking a tour of the boat. His room is on an upper deck in first class. Conor O'Quinn is his name, and he comes from Kilkerran. He was at Cornell University to do a study in agriculture. His family raises sheep in Ireland. I think he likes me. I'm not of a mind to like another man, but he is nice and quite easy to look at with his black hair and eyes as blue as my own. He towers above me, some six feet and three inches. I cannot betray my love, but I'm never to see HIM again. It's just a folly to look at Conor O'Quinn with thoughts of more than conversation.

> Your friend,
> Bridget

June 27, 1925

Dear Amelia,

Conor O'Quinn says that he loves me. Can that be? He says that he wants to bed me and make me his own. That's never to be again without the ring on my finger. Of that, I am certain. What do you think, Amelia? Should I even consider it? Conor says that the captain could marry us. He says that a captain can do that when his ship is at sea. I would then move into his beautiful cabin. He promised that we can have a second wedding in Ireland, a proper church service with a gown and veil. Is this crazy? Have I truly lost my mind? But what better can there be for me? I haven't had my visitor this month. I am so scared.

Your friend,
Bridget

June 28, 1925

Dear Amelia,

I did it. I accepted Conor O'Quinn's proposal. We are to be married tonight. Please don't judge me. There is so much wrong, but it may be my only opportunity for having a real life. I know I cannot undo the things that I have done, but they are left behind in Georgia. I'll never see Georgia again. It's like I'm being reborn with a second chance, even though I don't deserve it. Pray for me, Amelia. I never meant anyone harm. Well, maybe one despicable person.

Your friend,
Bridget

June 28, 1925

Dear Amelia,

Tonight was my wedding night. The captain was very kind. I think that Conor was so excited that he did not notice anything missing. It was bearable, and it will get better. I know it will. I will grow to love him. But, I'll never forget HIM. A girl has to know what is possible and what isn't. Conor is handsome, and I do have some feeling for him as long as I don't let myself think of HIM.

Your friend,
Bridget

August 4, 1925

Dear Amelia,

You probably thought I had forgotten you. I just have not found a place where it is safe to write. We live in a big house with Conor's parents and his two sisters. Today, I found this small place in the attic where no one comes. I can't be gone for long. They laugh at the way I talk, but they are nice to me. Our church wedding was lovely. I felt pretty. Conor was handsome in his suit. I am trying to forget HIM.

Your friend,
Bridget

September 30, 1925

Dear Amelia,

A package came today from Rebecca. It was from HIM, whom I can never think of again but cannot forget. HE sent it from London, but I was gone when it came to the Post Office at home. Rebecca picked it up. It cost her too much to send it to me, but I'm so glad that she did. It is the most beautiful rosary that I have ever seen. I'll never be able to show it to anyone, except the local priest when I ask to have it blessed. But, I will treasure it forever, no matter how much I cry when I look at it.

Your friend,
Bridget

Evanne finished reading the selected pages within five minutes. "What do you think this means?" she said, closing the journal and handing it back to Fury.

"I think that my grandmother, your great-grandmother, had a hidden past, and there's no telling how much more there is to the story. Who was her American love? What did she mean by sealing their love? What did she do that could have sent her to prison?"

"She was obviously in love with the lad she calls HIM. But how could she just turn and marry my great-grandfather a few weeks later?"

"Desperation. My, God, Evanne, she was hardly more than a child."

"I couldn't imagine going to America at sixteen to live with people I didn't know."

Fury nodded. "Didn't you want to wrap your arms around her and protect her?"

Evanne nodded. "I also believe that beneath that vulnerable surface was the core of a tiger."

"Absolutely. . . . Do you know when Uncle Ronan's birthday is?"

"Fury, you're not thinking that Uncle Ronan isn't really an O'Quinn, are you?"

"And the thought hasn't occurred to you?" Fury said, tipping her head slightly and raising her eyebrows. "Not to change the subject but it's getting late." She looked down at her watch. "I need to go back to the hospital to check on Dad."

"I'll see if Granny is awake. She may want to go as well."

Mary elected to stay home, saying she was still tired. Evanne and Fury walked into Mike's room at four-thirty.

"Well, here are the two prettiest women on the Emerald Isle," Mike said as they entered. He was sitting erect in the lounge chair, minus the IV. "Doctor Patel has signed me out. I'm fit as a fiddle and ready to fly."

"I doubt that, but it's great that you can leave the hospital." Fury leaned down, squeezed his shoulder, and put her cheek next to his. Rising, she said, "I'll go down to the office and check you out. Evanne can help you get your things together."

"Granny and Da have prepared a downstairs room at the farm for you. She says that you are not to go to the inn," Evanne said.

"That was so thoughtful," Fury said.

"I hope it's not close to hers. I can only take me sister in small doses."

Evanne smiled, nodding in agreement.

"Dad, show some gratitude. I had no idea that she was planning for you to stay at her house."

Mike rolled his eyes. "I can tell that my convalescence is going to be miserable with a bunch of bossy women."

"I'll take up for you, Uncle Mick."

While Fury took care of the paperwork, Evanne gathered Mike's clothing and personal items. When everything was packed and ready to go, she called the farm to let them know of his release.

"How is the scavenger hunt progressing?" Mike asked as Evanne ended her call.

"I'm sure that Fury will want to share those details with you."

On the trip back to the farm, Evanne drove, and Fury sat in the back with her father.

"I hear that you made a discovery in the attic," Mike said, looking at Fury.

"I did. After we get you settled, I'll show you what I've found. You can look through it for yourself," she said, squeezing his hand. "By any chance, do you know Uncle Ronan's birthday?"

Mike thought for a minute and then shook his head. "Can't say as I remember. He's seventeen years the older, which makes him eighty this year, but I don't know the date."

"So, he was born in 1926."

"Either '25 or '26. Is that important?"

"Maybe."

Dinner was ready when they reached the farm. Although ambulatory, Mike walked slowly but insisted on sitting with the family to eat. After finishing the meal, he admitted to being tired and went to bed. Mary went to her room to watch her favorite television program, leaving Fury and Evanne to return to the research.

Among the photographs and greeting cards, Evanne found six envelopes, each with the name of an O'Quinn child written on the front and each containing a lock of hair. "Fury, look at these."

Fury took the envelopes and gently opened them. "Ronan's hair was a strawberry-blond and Saoirse's was red, like mine and Bridget's, but the rest are all brown. These are her treasures as well as her innermost secrets."

"Makes one wonder whether we're honoring her or intruding," Evanne said.

"Probably a little of both."

Evanne put down the card she was looking at. "I feel like I've grown so close to you in the past days, but I know so little about you other than you're a famous writer in the States."

"I'm only semi-famous, and there's not much to know."

"Have you ever been married—engaged? Is there someone in your life?"

"No, no, and no. I'm not good at relationships. How about you?"

"I was dating a lad when I was at university, but it didn't work out. He wanted me to move to the North. I couldn't see myself there, so we broke it off. Have you ever been in love?"

"I've tried."

Evanne looked puzzled. "Tried?"

"I never have chemistry for the guys you would label Mr. Right. The guys I'm attracted to always turn out to be Mr. Wrong. Since I won't settle for Mr. Right-Now, my life-plan may not include a man. But, don't get me wrong. If I were to find a sexy guy who could make me feel like his queen, I would marry him in a heartbeat. But, I don't think he exists."

Evanne looked at her intently. "What about children?"

"If all else fails, when I'm thirty, I will either adopt or have artificial insemination."

Evanne's eyes grew large. "You'd have a stranger's baby and go against the Church?"

Fury nodded. "Yeah . . . I don't personally believe that it's a sin to conceive a child without sex. And as for fear of the child's father being an unacceptable person, I've looked into it. Sperm banks screen and categorize their donors. It's not random."

CHAPTER NINE

"I hated to say goodbye," Fury said as she buckled her seat belt on the jumbo jet for the non-stop journey back to Atlanta.

Mike nodded and patted her knee. "It was a good trip—all but me little hiccup."

"That's behind us. Thank God you're okay now." Fury settled in, taking her leather portfolio and Bridget's diary from her carryon and placing them in the seat-pocket in front of her. "It meant a lot to me to meet the family, but it was especially moving to see photos in Aunt Mary's album of you, Mom and Mickey. I know it was hard for you to visit his grave, but it made him so much more real to me. Thank you." She took Mike's hand and squeezed.

"I'll be honest. It broke down the wall that has boxed me heart in for way too—"

"Ladies and gentlemen." The flight attendant interrupted, beginning her litany of instructions.

Once airborne, Fury removed her items from the pocket to begin studying the journal. "I am so grateful that Aunt Mary allowed me to bring home your mom's memorabilia. Did you have to blackmail her?"

Mike laughed. "I didn't. She said, 'Why would it be that I'd want to store away the vessels that I never had the interest to examine after the contents have been spilled? I can do just fine with me memories of Mam.'" He connected his earbuds, preparing to watch a movie. "She saw what it meant to you. Mary's not the dummy."

The flight was smooth and on time. When they cleared customs in Atlanta, Cory was there. Seeing Fury and Mike come from the concourse, she rushed to hug her father.

"I have been worried beyond belief," she said, holding on to him.

"I'm just dandy. No need for you to be upset. Just a little bleep of the ticker, but it's all under control."

"You're going straight to a cardiologist."

"I'll be doing no such thing. I'm good." Mike frowned.

"Dad, Cory's right. It wouldn't hurt to touch base with someone here—just in case you have something come up in the future."

Mike gave her a sharp look but offered no further protest.

Once the luggage was in Cory's SUV, she drove them out of the Hartsfield airport. "I'd like you to come home with me, Dad—"

"I want to be in me own bed tonight, thank you very much," Mike said. "Drop me at the apartment house before you take your sister home. You can come 'round tomorrow and fuss over me 'til you have it out of your system; but tonight, I just want to kick me shoes to the corner and watch me TV with a pizza and a cold pint."

"I think he's had his fill of women clucking over him, Cory."

"I'm right here. No need to talk about me like I wasn't."

Fury smiled, but Cory frowned. "I understand, Dad, but Cory didn't talk to your doctor or see how far you've come."

"Come out to Redbridge Sunday afternoon. Don will grill steaks, you two can fill us in on the trip, and Don can talk to you about your follow-up care, Dad."

"That will work," Fury said. "I can pick up Gypsy. The worst part of traveling is missing her."

"I would have brought her today, but I was afraid your plane might be late, and she would be stuck in the car too long. But I warn you, there may be a fight with the girls. They're attached to that little cat. She's even charmed Don, the quintessential dog lover."

When Mike and Fury arrived at the Reynolds' house on Sunday, Cory had the side dishes prepared. Don greeted Mike with a bottle of Guinness and led him out to the patio. The girls brought Fury's calico Persian out from their bedroom and reluctantly handed her to their aunt.

"I wish we could keep her," Suzi said.

"Sweetheart, I would give you a kidney, anything I have—except Gypsy. Maybe your mom and dad will let me look for a kitten like her for a 'best nieces in the world gift.'"

"Really?" Suzi's eyes lit up, and Sandy's face bobbed up and down, a big grin revealing a missing tooth.

Cory looked down at her daughters with a smile and, patting Sandi on the top of head, said, "Why don't you guys go outside and help Daddy and Granddad? Aunt Fury and I want to talk."

Giving Gypsy one final stroke, the pair skipped out the backdoor, singing, "We're getting a kitten. We're getting a kitten."

Cory shook her head. "You better produce, or you're going to be tarred and feathered."

"I can produce. I've been thinking about it for some time. Gypsy's breeder has a litter that will be ready to go soon."

Cory shook her head and then, her smile vanishing, handed Fury a soft drink. "Now, tell me straight. How bad was Dad's attack?"

"He was lucky. The first one was mild. The second could have been extremely serious if he had not been in the hospital, but he understands now what he has to do and has medication. But I do want Don to hook him up with a cardiologist in Atlanta."

"I'll make sure of it. Now, tell me what you found."

"Enough to convince me that there is a story, but the journals and letters only hint at the scandal. I need more. I want to interview J. Graeme MacGregor, maybe get a look at his family papers."

"Good luck with that."

"Don't dismiss it that casually. I'm calling his office next week to ask for an appointment."

Cory looked at her sister with an astonished expression on her face. "You're going to barge into his office and demand access to his family history? Are you crazy? He's not going to let you do that—if he even talks to you."

"He'll talk to me. I'll make sure of it."

Cory shook her head. "I could feel sorry for the guy. He probably doesn't have a chance with you after him. Do you know *anything* about him other than he's got more money than the U.S. Treasury?"

"I Googled him yesterday and pulled a few articles. He runs the empire now and has actually expanded it. He lives in the family home but has a condo in Atlanta. The Arabella paper carried a profile on him three years ago when MacGregor Enterprises made a huge donation to the hospital building fund. The writer said that he is somewhat of a recluse who keeps a low profile. At that time, he was thirty-four and never married."

"I should have known that you have done your homework."

"I'm not even half finished. I'm going to invite the gal who wrote that piece to have lunch with me this week—before I make an appointment with MacGregor. I'm betting that she knows a lot more about him than she printed. He probably owns the paper."

"Why would I ever underestimate you? But, do you think that she'll meet with you?"

Fury nodded. "I'm not a real celebrity, but I have sold my share of books. When she finds out that my family has roots in Arabella, I think she'll be interested. Not only that, scratch the skin of any writer, and you'll find would-be novelist in the blood. She'll see me as a possible conduit to an agent or editor."

"Are you going to tell her that you're looking for information about MacGregor when you contact her?"

"Not right off. I'm going to say that I'm working on a novel that is set in the area and want to learn more about the culture, which is absolutely true." Fury cocked her head, a mischievous expression on her face.

"Sly move. It's a shame that our cousin in Arabella didn't know the family better."

"That would have been nice. I asked Colleen if she thought her sons knew MacGregor the fourth when I was going through her trunk. She said that she was sure they didn't. They're older, and neither came back to live in Georgia after college. Colleen's husband worked for the MacGregor bank, and she remembered going to annual picnics in the summer but said she never really knew any of the family. The MacGregors only put in a brief appearance each year."

"Sounds like they were Arabella royalty."

Fury nodded. "Duly crowned and reigning over the Kingdom of Mercy County."

The kitchen door opened and the girls burst through. "Daddy said to tell you the steaks are ready," Suzi squealed.

"Tell Daddy that Aunt Fury and I are putting the potatoes and salad on the table." Cory turned to Fury and said, "I'm coming to Atlanta one day this week. If you have time, I'd like to have lunch and look at what you've gathered. You've piqued my interest. I'd love to be a flea on the dog's back when Fury O'Quinn meets J. Graeme MacGregor, IV."

CHAPTER TEN

Arranging for lunch with Caroline Elliot, *Arabella Gazette* reporter, was as easy as predicted. The young writer was approximately Fury's age and hungry for a story. Fury chose a private club on the top floor of a high-rise downtown building where the room was quiet and servers would not attempt to rush them. She could tell that Caroline was impressed with the ambiance.

"It's an honor to meet you, Ms. O'Quinn. I've read most of your books," Elliot said, extending her hand to shake as the maître d' seated her at Fury's table. "Your photos don't do you justice. You're much prettier in person."

"The pleasure is mine, and thank you for both reading my books and for the compliment."

"Didn't I see your picture on the cover of one of the tabloids with the actor Nicholas Colton?"

Fury smiled. "You might have, but don't believe any of the copy that went with it. I only had lunch with him to discuss a possible film option. I don't really know him."

"I'm still impressed—Nicholas Colton."

"Save being impressed until he actually makes the movie."

The waiter arrived, handed them menus, and took drink orders. Caroline ordered a Coke; Fury ordered hot tea.

"Your new novel is based on Arabella?"

Fury nodded. "I'm straying from my usual format and looking into my family's past for the story. I'm not sure what form it will take."

"That's fascinating. You do realize that you're talking to a journalist, and you're likely to become a story. I hope you don't mind."

Fury smiled again. "I appreciate press of almost any type. It sells books, and that's what I do. But, it's not the reason I invited you to lunch."

The drinks arrived and Fury began by asking Caroline some generic questions about Arabella and its inhabitants. By the time their food arrived, she was ready to ask questions about MacGregor.

"I read a fascinating article that you wrote a few years ago about one of the leading citizens of Arabella, J. Graeme MacGregor."

Caroline smiled. "Oh, yes. He's an interesting one."

"Really? How so?"

Caroline leaned forward and spoke in a lower tone. "He's like the Howard Hughes of Georgia. Doesn't like publicity and hard to get him to tell you anything about himself. It was a difficult interview. But all the major financial publications have written about what a genius he is."

"Really?"

"Oh, yeah. They call him the wonder-boy wildcard of the South because he has done some really unorthodox business deals. Four years ago, he bought what was thought to be a worthless island. It turned out to have tons of oil—as if he needed it. You won't see any articles about that in the *Arabella Gazette*. MacGregor Enterprises owns my paper, so nothing is printed about Gray MacGregor without his approval."

I knew it!

"Just about everything in town is MacGregor owned, isn't it?" Fury asked.

"Pretty much."

"I wonder why the town isn't named MacGregor."

"It is, kind of. Arabella was the name of Gray's great-great-grandmother in Scotland."

"Oh." Fury leaned in closer to Caroline. "From the photos, he looks quite handsome, if you like the type."

"Oh, he is. But, he is apparently a confirmed bachelor. Around Arabella, some say that he never takes more than two drinks and never takes a woman on more than three dates. I think they exaggerate, but he's not one to settle down. If he's ever had a long-term relationship, no one knows about it."

"Sounds rather narcissistic."

Caroline picked up a roll and spread butter on it. "Not exactly. He's more complex than that. Is your novel about a man like Gray MacGregor?"

Fury put a shocked expression on her face. "No, absolutely not. My story is set in the early 1900s."

Caroline looked relieved as if she was afraid she might have overstepped with something she said about MacGregor.

"Don't worry. You won't be quoted."

"I should probably be careful what I say, but I will tell you that the day I went to that house on Main Street to meet him, I was terrified. A butler met me at the door and took me to a room on the first floor that was referred to as his office. The house is huge. It's listed on property records as having over twenty thousand square feet. Why would a single man live in a house that large?"

Fury shrugged. "I saw photos of it on the Internet. Does he always work from home?"

"No. His official office is here in Atlanta. He agreed to meet me at the house because I live and work in Arabella. I was thrilled to get a look at the inside. I was new on the paper, but had lived my entire life there and seen that huge house almost daily. However, I had never been inside."

"Were you disappointed?"

"No. But even though it's a beautiful house, it's cold. There's no feeling of family in it. The furniture is antique and massive but well maintained. There were no papers on his desk and no family photos, only a portrait of his great-grandfather on the wall. I didn't go in the great living room, but I could see photos on the piano in there. The room that I was in had dark paneling and two ornately framed paintings of woodland scenes and the portrait. Three walls were covered with books. When I got there, I had to wait for ten minutes, alone, in that room before he came in. I felt like I was being watched by that old man. When Gray MacGregor came in, his dog was with him."

"Really. What kind of dog does he have?"

"It's a mix. Looks like golden retriever and something like Irish setter. It had short fur that was thick and reddish. The dog was friendlier than Mr. MacGregor."

"Was he rude?"

"Not quite. More cold, like the house. He offered me something to drink, and a housekeeper brought a tray of assorted soft drinks and snacks. He took a ginger ale and peanuts." Caroline paused to take a bite of her food. "This is delicious. I've never had lobster in a salad before. Actually, I have had lobster only once."

Fury smiled. "I never had it until I sold my first novel and was invited to join here. Did Macgregor give you a lot of information?"

Caroline shook her head. "I had a long list of questions. He responded to most but usually with a one or two-word answer—no elaboration. His voice is sort of medium deep, but he speaks softly, almost a whisper, *when* he speaks. He makes direct eye contact with a piercing stare that makes you almost afraid to look away—very intense. He dodged all personal questions about his family. I used more material from research for the story than from my interview."

"He sounds strange."

"He's different. I know a couple of women who have gone out with him, and they say he's the same on a date. It's not that he acts condescending; it's more like he's remote."

"I think I have the picture." Fury sipped her tea, deciding not to press for more information lest she lose her source.

"Tell me about you. Is Fury O'Quinn a pen name?" Caroline asked.

Fury chuckled. "No. It's the one on my birth certificate. You would have to meet my father to understand."

"I like it."

"Thanks. I'm not sure whether it sounds more like a romance writer or a stripper."

Caroline smiled. "What got you into writing romance novels?"

"Totally an accident. I wrote my first short novel, little more than a novella, in college. My professor liked it and had an old friend in publishing look at it. She bought it, and here I am. My sister says that

I made it because of my vivid imagination and pure Irish luck. It pays the bills."

The rest of the conversation centered around Fury's career and her suggestions on how to break in without a connection. She had been right. Caroline secretly harbored the desire to publish a book. Little more was mentioned about Graeme MacGregor, but Fury did learn that his gatekeeper in the Atlanta office was a secretary by the name of Gladys Stevens.

Fury began lobbying for a meeting with J. Graeme MacGregor the morning after her lunch with Caroline. It proved to be a daunting project. Gladys Stevens was indeed the steel door blocking access to the man. Repeated calls brought forth a series of excuses: "He's not available," "He's out of the office," "He's in a meeting," "He's not scheduling appointments today," "He's booked solid for the next three months, but thank you for calling."

After trying to set an appointment with MacGregor seven times over a three-day period, Fury decided a trip to his office was her only option.

"You're just going to walk into his office?" Cory asked, when Fury spoke with her on the phone.

"If I don't, it's not going to happen. That woman is never going to put me through to him or give me an appointment."

"Good luck. I almost feel sorry for *her*."

"You shouldn't—she's a witch."

On Monday morning at ten-forty-five, Fury entered the 34th floor lobby of MacGregor Enterprises. If the house Caroline had described was antiquated, his office was the polar opposite. Sleek furniture, mirrors, marble tile, and chrome adorned the area. One side of the room was glass from floor to ceiling, providing a view overlooking the city. Black and white dominated the décor with the only color coming from a large, abstract painting of hunter-green, burgundy, black, and white. Leading business periodicals lay fanned across the glass top of a chrome coffee table.

Fury wore a meticulously tailored suit of navy blue with a lime-green and navy-blue print blouse. Her skin had a fresh scrubbed, peaches-and-cream look, and her blue eyes appeared darker than usual. She was stunning and felt it.

She walked up to the reception desk where a dark-skinned woman, resembling Vanessa Williams in her Miss America days, sat sentry in front of an elaborate phone system. Fury drew to the full height allowed by her five-foot-three frame, supplemented by three-inch pumps.

"May I help you?" the almond-eyed beauty asked.

"I'm here to see Mr. MacGregor," Fury responded, wondering if this woman was the Gladys Stevens who had blocked her phone attempts.

"Do you have an appointment?"

"A pending appointment."

The woman looked at Fury as if she had missed the word "pending" and asked, "Your name please." A light on the phone board began blinking, distracting the receptionist.

"Ms. O'Quinn."

Without looking up, the woman pushed the blinking light and said, "Hold please," and then punched a second button. "Miss Stevens, Ms. O'Quinn is here to see Mr. MacGregor." There was a brief pause. "She says that she has a pending appointment."

Barely glancing up at Fury, the woman said, "She'll be right out," and then returned her attention to the waiting caller.

Fury debated whether to continue standing at the desk or to take a seat on one of the modern chairs that flanked a couch adjacent to the glass wall. She decided to remain standing. It was the position of strength, which she anticipated needing.

Within seconds, a trim woman, approximately sixty years of age, emerged from the hallway leading to the inner sanctum of the company. She was dressed in no-nonsense black with her gray hair cut in an unbecoming bob. She wore horn-rimmed glasses. Fury took the initiative.

"You must be Gladys Stevens," she said, extending her hand.

"Caroline Elliot told me all about you."

Stevens was caught off guard but immediately resumed her position of authority. "Caroline Elliot?"

"Of the *Arabella Gazette*."

"Oh, yes. Are you a reporter?"

"No. I'm a novelist."

Stevens' expression took on a fleeting glimmer of either recognition or interest. However, she quickly extinguished it in favor of her staunch defense of her employer.

"I'm in the process of research for a book that I'm writing involving events that took place in Arabella in the early part of the last century. I'd like to speak with Mr. MacGregor. I'm sure you know that his family played a significant role in the history of the town."

Nodding, the secretary said, "I'm sorry, but he's not in today."

"Well, when will he be in?"

"It's difficult to say. He's very busy. I'm not sure that he can work you in, but I'll send him a memo. Give me your card, and I'll get back with you."

When hell freezes over, you will.

"Miss Stevens, I'll be perfectly frank with you. I'm not going away." Fury tipped her chin to one side and raised one eyebrow. "All I'm asking is for fifteen minutes of his time. I know how to be brief. And, you might be surprised to know that I'm a busy person as well. My last book sold somewhere north of two million copies. You might have seen me on the cover of the *Every Day News* with Nicholas Colton."

Did I really just say that? But, it got the witch's attention.

Fury whipped a card case out of her $3100 Prada handbag, making certain the brass ID nameplate on the bag was clearly visible. "Give this to Mr. MacGregor, and see if he can find fifteen minutes in his busy schedule."

The following Monday, a message from "gstevens1945" appeared in Fury's inbox.

"Ms. O'Quinn, Mr. MacGregor instructed me to tell you that he will be at his home in Cashiers, North Carolina, this week. If you want to speak with him, you can come there. If you choose to go, please notify me by reply to this email. I will then provide you with directions and contact information."

YES!

When Fury met Cory for lunch at the Lennox Mall the next day, Cory was apprehensive about her sister's anticipated journey.

"North Carolina? You're going to drive to North Carolina to meet this strange man? You're not going to meet with him alone, are you?"

"If that is how I get to talk to him, then so be it. Don't look so shocked. He isn't a serial killer, but I'll make sure he knows my dad is a cop when I make the appointment."

"Retired cop."

"Whatever."

"Why don't you fly?"

"There's no convenient airport, and according to the Internet, it's only a three-hour drive."

"Are you going there and back in one day?"

"No. He won't set a time until I get there. There is a lodge in the vicinity. I'm going to stay there."

"Fury, you've never driven in the mountains."

"So? We have steep hills in Atlanta."

"The operative word in that sentence is *hills*. Totally different thing. Wait 'til you try driving on a narrow, winding road on the side of a mountain. And what if you are caught in a storm? When Don and I went on vacation to North Carolina two years ago, he had to do all the driving. I refused."

"That was you. When we were kids, you thought the merry-go-round was a life-threatening experience. As you must recall, I loved the roller coaster. I'll be fine."

Cory shook her head. "You're incorrigible, but there's no stopping you. Do you want us to look after Gypsy while you're gone?"

"No, but thanks. My neighbor is going to take care of her. I'll just be gone three, maybe four days. By the way, I talked to the breeder, and the kitten for the girls will be ready the week after next."

"Don't tell them until you've picked it up, or they will drive me insane wanting to know when it's coming."

The map to Cashiers, North Carolina, and Little Terrapin Mountain was clear, but the long stretches of unmarked road gave little reassurance to Fury that she was traveling in the right direction. Twice, she stopped to confirm that she had not strayed from the course. She arrived at the High Hampton Inn shortly before four o'clock. Driving onto the property, Fury met a scene that could only be described as a painter's paradise. Lush green lawns and shrubs sloped to a sparkling lake at the foot of a breathtaking mountain. Forests bordered the property.

What a fantastic retreat for an artist or writer.

She pulled her car up to the main entrance of the lodge and parked. Inside, the lobby of the main building was quiet as she walked to the reception desk. The quintessential mountain lodge exuded a rustic ambiance with rich paneling and chairs designed with arms and legs like unfinished tree branches. A focal point of the L shaped room was a huge, freestanding fireplace with openings and seating arrangements on all four sides. A large dining room was at the rear of the room.

"We've reserved Cabin 84 for you, Ms. O'Quinn," the desk clerk said, handing her a map of the property with her unit highlighted. "Would you like help with your luggage?"

"No, thank you. I'll be fine, but where do I leave my car?"

After parking in a large parking lot at the foot of the hill beneath the lodge, Fury noticed a building on her right as she walked up to her cabin. A sign indicated sandwiches were available.

I'll put my things in the cabin, go over to that shop for a Pepsi, and then make the call to Mr. J. Graeme MacGregor.

It was nearly six o'clock by the time Fury had picked up soft drinks, returned to her cabin, unpacked, and taken a shower. Given the time, she thought about postponing contact until morning.

You're stalling, Fury. Make the call. She sat on the screened porch of her building with her cell phone in one hand and a notebook with the important number in the other. *Maybe you're not as tough as you thought you were, Fury O'Quinn.*

Taking a deep breath, she flipped the notebook open and tapped his number into the phone. There was silence, and then the familiar beep and LED message that read, "Call Failed."

"Darn. I work myself up and can't get through." Starting over, she tried again. The result was the same. Frustrated, she walked outside and redialed. Still, no success. Since there was no phone in her room, she decided that her only option was to walk up the hill to the main building.

"Cell phone reception is not good here," the desk clerk said, when Fury explained her problem. "There is a spot on the deck of this building where most people are able to get a call to go through." He pointed in the direction of the right side of the structure.

Fortunately, no one was on the deck. She needed privacy to speak to him. After trying several spots on the deck, she found the right place and the call went through.

He answered on the second ring. "Gray MacGregor."

His voice was husky but little more than a whisper. Fury stiffened and forced herself to speak. "Mr. MacGregor, this is Fury O'Quinn. I'm here in Cashiers and would like to set up an appointment with you for tomorrow."

"Is there a problem with now?"

His response jolted Fury. She hesitated and then said, "No. Of course not, but I don't want to interfere with your plans."

"You won't." His abrupt tone indicated that interference would not have been tolerated. "Come on up." With that, he hung up, disregarding whether she knew the way.

Fury stood for a moment, stunned first by the timing of their meeting and second with his curt dismissal. *What a dichotomy? Arm's length hospitality.*

She walked back to her cabin on autopilot, mulling over and over the terse exchange that had taken place. *I didn't expect to like him, but he's even more arrogant than I imagined.*

After checking her hair and makeup, she debated about changing from jeans to business attire but changed her mind. *He stages a come-as-you-are and that's what he gets.* After checking her purse for the map to his house, the notepad, a pen, and her cell phone, she locked up the cabin and struck out for MacGregor's. She had no idea whether she would find a mansion or a log cabin. Despite Cory's admonitions, Fury had navigated the mountain roads with relative ease on her journey to Cashiers. However, she was not prepared for the path up Little Terrapin Mountain. It was barely more than a winding driveway. Periodically, mirrors were installed on trees at sharp curves. The posted speed limit was 17 miles per hour. *Where did they come up with that number?*

She was a little over halfway up the mountain when, all of a sudden, she could see no road ahead. It appeared to drop off. She slammed on the brakes. To her right was a drive that seemed to lead to a private home, but she had not traveled far enough, according to her odometer, for it to be the MacGregor house. Fury panicked. *I can't do this.* She was shaking, tears forming. *What am I going to do?*

Not moving for several seconds, she concluded that she had to call MacGregor—the last thing she wanted to do. *I don't have a choice. I can't leave the car here and walk.*

"Gray MacGregor," he answered, again.

"It's Fury O'Quinn. I'm sorry, but I can't drive up this mountain."

From the other end of the call came a throaty laugh. "You can't? Where are you?"

"I'm about halfway up, according to my GPS, but the road disappeared."

"It's there, but sit tight. I'll come down."

Waiting for him, Fury hated herself for being a coward. *This is not a good start.*

CHAPTER ELEVEN

It took Gray MacGregor less than five minutes to make it down to Fury. Parking his ATV in a small clearing about twenty feet behind her car, he walked up to the driver's side, opened the door, and said, "I'll drive."

"Mr. MacGregor, I presume," Fury said, looking at the six-foot-two, well-built stranger.

"Were you expecting someone else?"

My God, he's rude. But, bite your tongue, Fury. You're here to ask a favor.

"Touché. I won't bother to tell you that I'm Fury O'Quinn," she said, climbing out of the car and starting to walk to the passenger side. He made no attempt to escort her. The passenger door was locked, which he did not appear to notice. "Can you unlock this side for me?"

As soon as she was in the vehicle, he said, "Buckle your seatbelt."

She wanted to say give me a chance, but again bit her tongue. "I'm sorry to trouble you. I've never driven on a mountain, and I panicked. I couldn't see the road, but I see now that it took a sharp dip."

"Do you always rush in where you don't know what you're doing?"

"Only if it's important," she snapped, proud that she had not let him completely get the best of her.

The distance to his house was less than a quarter mile, and he drove like a movie stunt man. When they reached his drive, Fury took one look at the nearly180 degree incline and said a silent prayer of thanksgiving that he was at the wheel. She closed her eyes as they ascended. Feeling the car level out, she opened her eyes. In front of her was a two-story house, constructed of stone and wood shingles with a wood shake roof. It was not a mansion, but far from a log cabin. MacGregor parked in a paved area to the right of the semicircular, sandstone steps leading to the oversized entry. Fury considered waiting to see if he would come to open the door for her, but decided she did not want to feel awkward if he did not. She let herself out.

MacGregor, dressed in sneakers, jeans, and a subtle, blue-plaid shirt, paused at the base of the front steps. His sandy-brown hair was neatly cut, neither long nor short. His trim, tanned physique suggested that he either worked out regularly or was athletic. His eyes were deeply set under straight, brown-black brows that sloped down at the corners, giving him a serious expression.

His photos don't do him justice. He is handsome—very handsome.

Neither Fury, nor MacGregor, spoke. He gestured to suggest that she go up the stone steps first. Once they were on the landing, he reached around her to turn the knob of the unlocked door. Walking into the open-style floor plan, the view of the mountain range was immediately visible through the wall of tall, wood-framed glass doors and windows, running the length of living, dining, and kitchen area. It was breathtaking.

"Dinner is almost ready. You can set the table."

Stunned by the unexpected comment, Fury looked at him.

"The dishes are in the cabinet," he said, pointing to a huge breakfront on the wall opposite the windows.

Fury could smell an enticing aroma coming from the kitchen. "I'm eating with you?"

"It's dinner time, isn't it?"

"But, don't you want to know why I'm here, first?"

"No. Why would I want to take the chance on spoiling a nice dinner by saying no to whatever charitable donation you're soliciting?"

Of all the scenarios Fury had imagined would take place at their initial meeting, this was not one. *What is he all about?*

"That's *not* why I'm here."

"You'll find place mats and silverware in the drawers," MacGregor said, ignoring her response.

Speechless, Fury put her large handbag on the end cushion of the sumptuous suede sofa and walked over to the china cabinet. Opening drawers, she found an assortment of place mats and thought about asking which he preferred, but didn't. *He'll take what he gets.*

She chose two mismatched mats, placing them on the rich pecan wood table. She then took out heavy silver knives, forks, and spoons. Once the utensils were in place, she took plates from the shelves and completed the place settings. "Where are napkins?" she asked.

"I'm out. You'll have to use the roll of paper towels over here."

Okay. Expensive sterling and paper towels. He's a class act.

Taking a bottle of red wine from a thermal cooler, he uncorked it and began pouring it into one of two long-stemmed, crystal goblets, offering the first to Fury.

"No. None for me. I have to drive back to the lodge on that deathtrap you call a road."

"Take it. I'll drive you."

Looking at the wine, she said, "Forgive me, but that doesn't sound really reassuring to me—even if you know the road."

"Apparently you haven't done your homework as well as I expected. If you had, you'd know that I never drink more than two glasses of wine and never date a woman more than twice—or is it three times? Whichever, it is highly exaggerated." He thrust the glass toward her.

Reluctantly, Fury took the wine, but she avoided taking a sip, watching as he poured his and then held the glass up as if to make a toast.

"To a persistent, but lovely, woman with more than her share of guts."

Fury cut her eyes at him and gave a slight nod.

After taking a large swallow, MacGregor put the glass on the long bar that divided kitchen from dining room and turned toward the refrigerator. He took out a large bowl of Caesar salad and put it on the counter top, next to a set of salad tongs. He then took a pan of beef Wellington and a baking dish of potato florets out of the oven.

He must have some caterer. That smells delicious.

"Grab a plate," he said.

"Mind if I wash my hands first?" Fury asked.

"Not at all. There's a bathroom on this hall," he said, gesturing to his left. Then pointing down the long room, he continued, "And another on your left off the far hall."

Not wanting to walk by MacGregor, Fury opted for the guest bathroom at the other end of the first floor. It wasn't so much that she wanted clean hands as it was the desire to catch her breath and sort out what was happening. *Is this guy trying to seduce me? That would make no sense considering how rude he is. But what? Why is he wining and dining me? He doesn't strike me as being endowed with the Southern hospitality gene.*

As she reached the far hall, a large dog blocked her path.

"Are you going to let me pass?"

"Apache, come here," MacGregor shouted. "Let Ms. O'Quinn by."

"So, you're Apache," Fury said, reaching down to pet the dog as she got up to respond to her master's call.

When Fury returned, she served her plate and sat down at the table. MacGregor followed.

Taking her first bite, Fury said, "My compliments to your caterer. This is delicious." The beef was tender. The potatoes, roasted with butter, Parmesan cheese, and breadcrumbs were tasty.

"I hope you enjoy."

Few words were exchanged during the meal. If not for the new age music of Danny Wright playing softly in the background, the house would have been silent. When they had finished eating, Gray spoke. "We'll take our coffee on the deck, and you can tell me what it is that you want from me."

"Okay. That would probably be a good idea," she responded. While he prepared the coffee, she cleared the table but was careful not to move too close in proximity to him. He made her uneasy.

By the time they took their coffee cups outside, it was growing dark. A roof covered a portion of the deck where a seating group faced a stone fireplace. Along the uncovered section were several chaise lounges and a table with four chairs.

"Your view is spectacular. This would be a heavenly place to write."

He nodded and gestured Fury toward the table and then took a seat opposite her.

"The floor is yours."

She hesitated, almost forgetting how she had planned to begin. "I'm a writer."

"I know."

"I write romance novels."

He nodded.

This is not easy. I wish he would stop looking at me that way.

"And?" He took a swallow of his coffee.

"You're making me uncomfortable."

A close-lipped smile appeared. "How am I doing that?"

"Are you trying to seduce me?"

He shook his head. "What would give you that idea?"

"Dinner, wine, your reputation."

"Should I be insulted or flattered?"

"Neither one. I just want to get in front of any misunderstandings. I don't sleep around." *Oh, my, God. Did I just say that?*

He smiled. "That's quite an interesting fact, considering the erotica in your books."

Startled, she said, "How would you know about my books. You certainly haven't read them."

"I beg to correct you. I *have* read your books. Do you think that I would have allowed you to come here without research? I probably know as much about you as you know about me. I would suspect that we've both done our homework."

"You've actually read my books?"

He nodded. "Five, including your latest. Would you like to autograph them? But, before that, how the hell do you write such sexy stuff without experience? You write as though as you know your way around the bedroom."

"Is that why you invited me up here, fed me, and plied me with wine? You think I would be a good trick?" She stood up.

"Calm down, Ms. O'Quinn. I'm not about to take advantage of you. Regardless of the reputation that precedes me, I am not quite a womanizer."

"Your reputation as an arrogant chauvinist appears to do you justice."

He laughed. "I'm sure it does. The better you get to know me, you'll find out what a true son-of-a-bitch I am, but remember, you're the one who asked to see me. I invited you up here because you drove my assistant crazy, and after reading your novels, my curiosity was piqued. What do you want from me?"

"Your great-grandfather sent my great-uncle to the insane asylum in Milledgeville, and I think it was bogus." Blurting out her mission shocked Fury.

"My great-grandfather?"

"John Graeme MacGregor, the first—your great-grandfather."

"And you worked so hard to get to me to tell me that?"

"No. Not to tell you that. To ask you to let me examine any papers or diaries that you have in your family archives."

He stared at her before speaking, increasing her discomfort. "Let me understand you, Ms. O'Quinn. You want me to let you dig into my family history—and for what purpose?"

"Because I want to find out the truth. James Dolan spent forty-five years of his life in a torture chamber on a claim made by J.G. MacGregor that I think was false."

"What was the claim?"

"That my uncle threatened to kill him—not even that he tried—just threated."

He shook his head. "Let me see if I have this straight. You want me to give you access to my family's personal documents so that you can publically indict my great-grandfather for corruption or worse?"

Fury nodded.

"Why would I want to do that?"

"To right a horrendous wrong."

"What makes you think that I care?"

Fury was silent for a second. "You probably don't. But right is right, and wrong is wrong. Something was very wrong in 1925."

He took a swallow of his coffee. "What do you plan to do with any information you dig up?"

"Use it in a book."

"A romance novel?"

She shook her head furiously. "No. Either a history book or a historical novel based on a true story."

He waited before answering, watching her intently. "What are you not telling me?"

"Why do you think there's something I'm not telling you?"

"Instinct."

"I'll share with you anything I find before I use it. But I won't promise to allow you to censor it. Will you help me?"

"No. I won't help you."

Fury's face exposed her disappointment. But, before she could respond, Gray MacGregor continued.

"I won't help you, but I will let you go through whatever documents that are still around."

Her expression immediately changed. "That doesn't make sense. You say you won't help, but you'll let me search through your historical data?"

"I won't help you because I will not talk about my family. However, I won't stand in your way. When would you like to start?"

Stunned, Fury thought for a few seconds. He had agreed, despite the way he had behaved. "As soon as possible. You won't sanitize your files will you?"

He laughed. "If I were inclined to sanitize the files, I wouldn't be opening my door for you. You can start anytime you like. I'll define the areas of your access and make sure my staff knows that I've authorized you to explore. I trust that you would not attempt to violate your boundaries."

"Of course not. I hope you don't think that I would pry into your personal business."

"How large a leap of faith are you asking me to take?" He gave her an admonishing look.

With eye-to-eye contact, she contemplated his statement for a minute before responding. "You're right, Mr. MacGregor. You have no reason to trust me. If you like, hire someone to supervise, and I'll pay for it—just don't make me work with Gladys Stevens."

He laughed, stood up, and took her empty coffee cup. "No, my dear. You won't have to work with Gladys. But, I warn you, you will be dealing with Ella, my housekeeper at Forglen. She's more territorial than Gladys. I'll assure both of them that you have my full approval. Now, I'd better drive you back to Hampton Inn. My grounds keeper will pick me up."

By the time Fury was safely in her cabin, she was in a euphoric daze. She had accomplished her mission. He would let her into his family archives. She wanted to call Cory but remembered there was no cell service. However, the cabin was equipped with Wi-Fi, so she booted up her computer and sent an email.

"Had dinner with Gray MacGregor. One strange breed of cat. He's actually read my books, or so he said. There's no way to give you the total picture. There's a mysterious and enigmatic quality about him. Despite that he is unpredictable, arrogant, and domineering, he has a magnetic appeal and appears to pierce your mind with a look. Believe it or not, he agreed to let me read his family papers. I'll try to call you tomorrow. Cell service is scarce up here, and there's no phone in my room. Kind of scary. I guess if an intruder tried to break in, I would have to email 911."

CHAPTER TWELVE

A loud knock awakened Fury from a deep sleep at seven-thirty the following morning. The shock caused her heart to pound. Pulling on a robe, her first thought was her lack of access to communication. She tiptoed to the door and said, "Yes?"

"Desk clerk, Ms. O'Quinn. I have a message for you."

Fury eased the door open, keeping the security chain in place. The man put a slip of paper through the opening. Taking it, she thanked him and closed the door.

"I'll pick you up at eight for an early ride. Wear jeans." There was no name, but Fury knew it had to be from Gray MacGregor.

Unbelievable. But if I don't get ready, he could show up at my door.

She felt a strange excitement as she hurried to dress but questioned why she should comply with what was more like an order than an invitation. *I should tell him what he can do with his ride.*

The note said nothing about where they were to connect, but Fury decided to avoid the risk of his coming to her cabin by going to the main building. She moved like lightning to be ready before eight, taking a shower in record-breaking time, and throwing on makeup. She considered wearing anything but jeans, but again waived the impulse to defy him. Her short hair was still damp when she locked the door and walked to the lodge.

She was stirring a cup of coffee at the complimentary station when he walked into the building.

"Good morning. I hope this isn't too early for you."

Really? You're worried about that now?

"No. I'm always up early." Fury worked on staying nonchalant as she took a sip from the mug.

"The horses will be saddled by the time we get there."

Horses? Ride horses?

"I appreciate your invitation, but I can't. I need to get some writing done. My publisher is pushing for my next manuscript, and I've never ridden a horse." *Not exactly true.* "But, thank you so much for offering."

He moved closer to her. "I insist. A few hours out of your work day can't possibly hurt."

Fury backed up, discreetly. "Mr. MacGregor, I'm a city girl—Brooklyn, Atlanta. I don't ride, and I have to take advantage of my time in this exquisite atmosphere to write. I'm on a deadline."

"I considered you might lack expertise and made certain that the horse provided for you is accustomed to novices. As for writing up here, you can do that anytime."

She gave him a puzzled look. "Hardly."

"Not at all. You're welcomed to use my house. I think you would find it comfortable."

Fury frowned and said in a low voice, "You can't be serious."

"Of course, I am."

"There's no way I would stay in a strange man's house."

"Don't look so shocked. I'm not propositioning you. If I were, I wouldn't be that subtle. I don't have time for games. I'm merely suggesting that you enjoy my house when I'm not up here. Gladys can schedule it for you."

Right. I'm going to call Gladys Stevens and tell her to put me down for the house next week. "You are a perplexity. You met me yesterday, acted completely indifferent, bordering on rude—hospitality aside. Today, you offer me the use of your home?"

He nodded, a slight curl at the corner of his mouth. "Something like that. I've already given you the key to Forglen. I see no difference."

"Well, I do. Permission to visit for research and using for lodging are significantly different."

Despite herself, Fury's heart was pounding. There was an exhilarating feeling to the idea of being in his home. Was it the view—

or the man?

"We're wasting time. The horses are waiting, and we can argue about this later."

"I haven't accepted."

"But, you're going to."

She wanted to slap him. "Who the heck do you think you are?"

"The man who has something that you want."

"Are you blackmailing me?" She leaned her head to one side, her blue eyes growing larger.

"It's more in the nature of a business negotiation. You want access; I want the pleasure of your company for a morning ride."

"You wouldn't—"

"Want to test me?" His expression was smug and patronizing.

It was all she could do to restrain herself from lashing out at him. *What audacity! I didn't expect to like him, but he's making it very easy to dislike him.*

"You win this round, Mr. MacGregor, but don't think you've won the game."

"I look forward to the challenge. Don't you think you're mad enough to call me Gray?"

"You don't know what I would like to call you."

He laughed. "I probably do."

Gray had been right. The sorrel horse provided for Fury was calm and accommodating. However, as she initially approached the gelding, Fury fought to shake off her apprehension. *Think roller coaster. This can't be any harder. You did have riding lessons one summer at camp.*

Gray came up from behind as if to offer her help mounting. She immediately recoiled. "I can do it myself."

"As you like."

Three failed attempts later, she swallowed her pride and accepted his assistance.

Once in the saddle, they rode for about forty-five minutes. The weather was perfect and the scenery beautiful. As with the night before, conversation was sparse. Contra to Fury's usual personality, she said little during the ride as Gray's attitude had served to annoy her enough to keep her quiet. In the O'Quinn family, it was conventional wisdom that if Fury was silent, she was mad. About the only thing she learned about Gray MacGregor during the venture was that the white Hanoverian he rode was his own.

How appropriate. The Lone Ranger always rides Silver.

After returning to their starting point, Gray helped her dismount and then led the horses toward the stable where a groom waited to take charge. Watching him, Fury noted how confident his stride and how well he wore his tight jeans. It was hard to deny that the man had sex appeal.

Despite her dislike for his authoritarian attitude, Fury found herself fantasizing about a liaison.

What are you thinking? Have you lost your mind? That man is a weapon of mass emotional destruction.

Gray came back to where she waited and said, "I suspect you're hungry. There's a good restaurant between here and the inn."

She meant to say that she needed to work, but was shocked to hear herself say, "That would be nice."

Have I lost my mind?

The restaurant was a quaint little place with indigenous charm. The interior was snug with dim lighting and none of the chatter of a large restaurant. Classical music played softly in the background. The hostess greeted Gray with familiarity.

"We have your table ready, Mr. MacGregor."

He made a reservation? He is incredibly presumptuous. Does anyone ever tell him no?

As the woman led them to a booth in the back corner, Fury decided it was probably the standard order for seating J. Graeme MacGregor and guest. As she sat down, she resisted the impulse to ask how many women he had brought to the place.

Once settled, Fury took the initiative. "I'm going to confess that despite my misgivings, I did enjoy the ride. Thank you for insisting that I go."

He smiled. "The pleasure was mine." As he spoke, the waitress arrived with a pot of coffee, filled the cups already on the table, and took their orders.

"You said last night that you would like to begin your project on Monday, right?" Gray asked, watching the waitress as she walked away.

Distracted, Fury did not answer at first. *I might have known he would be all over a pretty woman.*

MacGregor turned and looked her in the eye, making her uncomfortable. Seconds passed and neither spoke.

"It will probably be best for me to introduce you to Ella. She knows more about the house than I do. She's been with the family since I was a child."

"Is she as difficult as Gladys?"

Gray smiled, and for a second, his guard seemed to soften. "Ella is the heart of Forglen. Without her, the walls would crumble. Step on her toes, or mine, and she'll have you for breakfast, but I think the two of you will get along fine."

"I'll keep that in mind."

Picking up his menu, he said, "I'll be in Atlanta on Monday. The morning will be hectic, but I could run you out to Arabella at lunchtime. It'll save time if you come to my office."

"Good enough, if you're sure Gladys won't have me tossed out."

Gray laughed. "I'll handle Gladys. Just be on time."

"I'll be there at noon."

There were so many questions that Fury wanted to ask, but her instinct told her to wait. He had offered more than she had hoped for, so to push him further was not worth the risk of overstepping.

As they finished lunch, Fury wondered what he might have planned next. She steeled herself to decline on the basis that she had to work. However, he returned her to the inn without additional comment. He failed to ask how long she planned to stay in North Carolina.

Saturday passed with no further word from MacGregor. She had expected to hear from him again, given the attention shown during her first twenty-four hours in the area. She told herself that she was relieved because no good could come from overexposure to the very carnal businessman. If honest, Fury was disappointed.

Despite the distraction created by thoughts of MacGregor, Fury was able to produce a substantial amount of text on her romance novel. Her latest hero began to take on a striking resemblance to the mysterious MacGregor. Sunday afternoon, she drove back to Atlanta.

"I'm so relieved to know you're home. I still can't believe you went to that man's house by yourself," Cory said when Fury called her from the condo.

"I'm fine. Physically, emotionally, and spiritually uncompromised."

"So, tell me. What is he like?"

"Physically, he's about six-foot-two, good build, with kind of golden-brown hair and tan complexion. His eyes are a translucent-amber and seem to see through to the core of your soul. He speaks with authority in a low voice, like a whisper on steroids. If he didn't award himself control of the universe, he would probably be considered handsome."

"That's certainly a confusing statement."

"If I describe the meeting, you still won't get the whole picture. When I made the initial call, he told me to come up to his house right then—just like that. When I got there, he had an amazing dinner waiting, as if he knew I was going to call—and would come."

"You're kidding?"

"I'm not. The next morning he sends me a message at seven-thirty that he's picking me up at eight, insists that we go horseback riding, takes me for a lovely brunch, and then I didn't hear another word from him. He doesn't ask anything; he tells you. If I didn't need to get into his family records, I would tell him to shove it."

"Wow! You said in your email that he is letting you do the research, right?"

"As far as I know. The last thing said was for me to meet him at his office here in Atlanta around noon tomorrow, and he would drive me to the house in Arabella. There's a housekeeper in charge. I guess that's still the plan. Would you believe that he had the nerve to tell me to be on time?"

"Fury, are you sure you want to carry on with this project? I have reservations about this man."

"I can take care of myself, but I'll be glad when I find what I need and can have no further contact with Mr. J. Graeme MacGregor, IV."

Fury spent Sunday night going through her closet, trying to decide what to wear on Monday. The professional attire of her first visit to MacGregor Global Enterprises did not feel right. She wanted to look good, partly for confidence, partly to keep the upper hand with Gladys Stevens, and partly to show Gray MacGregor what he couldn't have. By eight o'clock, her bedroom was a mass of clothing. The weather report predicted cool temperatures for the following day. After trying on and switching numerous separates, she finally decided on the town-and-country look with a white blouse, navy-blue slacks, and a crested, wool blazer of subdued navy, hunter-green, and burgundy stripes. To finish off the ensemble, she chose a pair of tasseled, luggage-brown loafers and a wine-red, Marc Jacobs handbag. Purses were Fury's guilty pleasure and primary indulgence.

"What do you think, Gypsy? Will this work?"

The calico had watched intently from her nest in the middle of a cashmere sweater on the bed. At the sound of her name, she got up and approached Fury, purring.

"I'm not trying to attract this guy, Gypsy. I just want to feel confident. He is so domineering in his quiet way."

As directed, Fury appeared in the lobby of the conglomerate at the appointed time. The reaction was dramatically different. The receptionist recognized her instantly.

"Good morning, Ms. O'Quinn. I'll ring Mr. MacGregor's office. He's expecting you."

Fury caught the young woman looking at her purse. Smiling, she nodded. *That's quite a switch in attitude. She and Gladys must have discussed my Prada bag.*

Almost immediately, Gladys Stevens appeared, looking exactly as before, only in a gray dress.

"Ms. O'Quinn, how nice to see you. Right this way. Mr. MacGregor is expecting you."

Okay. This is too much. She's being nice.

Fury's eyes sparkled as she graciously thanked the woman and followed her lead.

Gray's office was all Fury expected and then some. The walls were mahogany with heavy crown molding, chair rail, and raised panels. His desk was enormous. At one end of the room, there was a built-in wet bar with a tray of cut crystal, six glasses and three decanters. Lighted shelves showcased leather-bound books and collectible figures of dogs and horses in porcelain and bronze. The room exuded masculinity, wealthy masculinity.

I can smell the money, old money.

Gray rose upon his door opening. In contrast to his surroundings, he was dressed in jeans, a white dress shirt, and loafers.

"It's good to see you, Ms. O'Quinn. You're looking lovely today." Addressing his assistant, he said, "That's all Gladys." As the gray-haired woman closed the door, he turned to Fury. "We *have* reached the point where I may address you by your given name, right?"

Fury turned her head to one side, raised her eyes without lifting her chin, and said, "I think you could say that we have reached that point."

He smiled. "Very good. I hope you're hungry. Ella is expecting us for lunch."

Of course she is, not that you mentioned it before. Fury smiled. "How nice."

He paused for a moment before speaking and looked Fury up and down. "Unless you've brought a change of clothes, I wouldn't recommend you rummaging through the ninety-year collection of dust and dirt that goes with whatever is stored in my attic today."

"I can wait."

"Good decision. Then, you'll ride with me."

She nodded. "Thank you. And, thank you once again for allowing me to do this."

CHAPTER THIRTEEN

It took forty-five minutes to make the drive to Arabella. As she had come to expect, he said very little. Unlike North Carolina, the Georgia scenery was too familiar to hold her attention, so she found herself watching him drive. He had the strong hands of an outdoorsman, and every move he made was controlled and precise. She noticed "Harvard, Business School" underscoring the shield-shaped panel on a gold, class ring that he wore on his right hand.

Breaking the silence, she said, "I read where you have a law degree from Harvard, but your ring says business."

"Joint degree program."

"Are you a lawyer?"

"Nope."

"Surely, that's not because you couldn't pass the bar."

He laughed. "You are the impertinent one, aren't you?"

"I try to be."

"A thoroughly independent woman, right?"

"Again, I try to be."

"I don't quite put you in the Gloria Steinem category. I think you're more like Shakespeare's Kate—before Petruchio tamed her."

"Well, you just might be thinking wrong, Mr. MacGregor." *And I certainly hope you don't think that you're my Petruchio.*

His comment was enough to put Fury back in silent mode.

As they arrived in Arabella, Forglen was straight in front of them. It sat majestically on top of a hill. A horseshoe drive, bordered on one side by manicured shrubs, served as ingress and egress to the estate.

The house reigned over the small town.

"I've seen your house when visiting in Arabella and wondered what it would be like to live in a place that large."

"Probably not what you imagined."

"Where did the name 'Forglen' come from?"

"The house is modeled after a mansion in Aberdeenshire, Scotland, near where J.G. grew up. The word is Gaelic for 'hollow of the vale.' Thank God, the old man left the turrets off. It's enough of a monstrosity without them."

"I'm surprised that it's not covered in marble, since that's where he made his fortune."

"Wait until you get inside."

He parked the SUV at the top of the drive. The Tudor-styled entry was on ground level with tall, double doors set inside an archway. Columns flanked the portico, topped with dome-shaped caps. A plaque over the door read "FORGLEN," with 1919 etched beneath the name.

Gray unlocked the door and stood aside for her to enter. As she stepped across the threshold into the large entry hall, marble greeted her on both floor and walls. Even the steps on the central staircase were marble topped, softened slightly by an oriental runner, and held in position with brass rods.

"I see what you meant. There's more marble here than at the Lincoln Memorial."

"For the record, that shrine is made of Georgia marble."

"And why didn't I know that?"

Out of nowhere, Ella appeared. A short, stocky woman with white hair, she wore a plain blue dress with a pink, bib apron. Her hair was swept up in a soft bun with a few tendrils hanging loose. Her shoes were the type nurses typically wore.

"Come meet Ms. O'Quinn, Ella. She's the one I told you about who is going to do research in our attic."

Fury made note of how he referred to the attic as "our."

"Happy to meet you, Miss O'Quinn, and welcome to Forglen. Lunch is ready, Gray. But would you and Miss O'Quinn like a cup of tea or coffee before eating?"

She calls him Gray. That's interesting.

"We'll get right to lunch. I have to return to the office after I show Ms. O'Quinn the attic. She'll be coming back on her own as I told you. You can give her a tour of the house then."

"I'd be delighted."

Ella turned and headed back to the kitchen. Gray shepherded Fury to a breakfast room just off the kitchen that had a large bay window overlooking the backyard. A gardener was working in the flowerbeds that surrounded a large swimming pool.

"Where's Apache?" Fury asked.

"At the office."

"I didn't see her."

"She was probably auditing the accounting department. The staff spoils her egregiously."

The table was set and waiting for them. No doubt Gray had given advance instructions.

"I hope you like chicken. I took the liberty of telling Ella to make one of her special casseroles for lunch."

"I do."

During the meal, Fury hesitated to ask many questions, although her curiosity was raging. Finally, she broke the silence. "This house is so large for one person."

"No one lives here."

She looked at him, quizzically. "No one lives here? This is your house."

"I don't choose to live in the museum. It's an address. My time is divided between a condo in Atlanta and the house in Cashiers."

"You never stay here?"

"I have a room, and Apache likes the yard, but no, I don't stay here. Ella and Edward take care of it. I come out maybe once a month."

"Who's Edward?"

"Ella's husband."

"They live in?"

"In a cottage on the other side of the property that was a carriage house in the early days."

"I've read that you're an only child. Are your parents living?"

The conversation came to an abrupt halt. He didn't answer for a minute or two, and Fury realized that she had broken the rule.

"My father died in an accident the year I finished my graduate work at Harvard. I lost my mother when I was seven. I believe I told you that I will *not* talk about my family." There was no mistaking the warning tone of his voice.

"I'm sorry for your loss and apologize for intruding."

He just looked at her without responding, and she felt a knot in her stomach.

Stay off the grass, Fury. He was acting almost human, and you've driven him back into wherever he goes.

The rest of the meal was quiet. As Fury took her last bite of the homemade, chocolate pie, Gray stood up.

"Let's get you to the attic. I have a meeting back in Atlanta."

The stairway to the top of the house was off the butler's pantry and was wide enough for passage of two, but Fury trailed behind as Gray led the way. She had expected a trap door and was surprised to find a small landing with a standard entry. He went in first.

"There's no electricity up here, only the window light. Edward can pick up a few of those cordless lights."

"I could do that. You don't have to bother."

"No bother."

Walking in, Fury was overwhelmed. The O'Quinn attic was paltry compared to the volume of stuff in the MacGregor storage space.

Even in the dim light, it was easy to see dismay on her face.

"Sure you want to get into this?" he asked.

Nodding slowly, she said, "Absolutely sure. But, it may take longer than I thought."

What bodies are buried in all of this?

"If you need anything, just tell Ella. If she can't help, she'll get Edward or Sam, the gardener, for you."

Boxes were stacked on top of boxes, five and six deep. There were several old trunks immediately visible and a number of open boxes of toys and household items.

These people never heard of cleaning out, but I should be happy.

Once back on the road to Atlanta, Gray's mood lightened.

"Will you work every day?"

"I wish. Unfortunately, I'm committed to having a manuscript to my editor by December, and it's already October."

"Take your computer up to my place and write to your heart's content. I'll be in New York for meetings the last week of this month. The leaves should be in full glory, and the cabin will be empty."

"You never cease to amaze me. First, I would hardly call that house a cabin. And, you know nothing about me, have known me less than a week, and you're offering to let me stay in one of your homes without you there?"

He took his eyes from the road for an instant to give her a patronizing look.

"Let's see, Ms. Fury Bridget O'Quinn. You think I know nothing about you? You were born in Brooklyn, New York on January 23, 1980. Your parents were Irish immigrants, although your father had American citizenship. Your one sister is married to a doctor and has two daughters. They live in Redbridge. You attended Catholic schools in Brooklyn until your mother died when you were fifteen. Your father, an NYPD detective, then moved you and your sister to Atlanta. You were a rebel in high school and got into trouble for kidnaping the statute of a rival school's mascot, which your father got you out of and should have blistered your bottom for—but probably didn't because he adores you. You went to Agnes Scott on scholarship and graduated Summa with a degree in English. Since then, you've been churning out racy novels for women to read on the beach—and you do quite well with it. You've never been arrested, although you have collected several speeding violations. You're single with no known relationship. Oh, and by the way, you're a virgin, or so rumor has it."

"Wow. You're good. I didn't know you could string that many sentences together."

"My guess is you know almost as much about me, which you

don't need to recite. So, the offer is on the table. Take it or leave it."

"You don't fool around, do you?"

"I don't have time. I told you; I don't play games."

"I'll take it. Heaven help me. My sister is going to freak. Is there cell service at the house?"

"There's a tower near my property. I'll give you Robert's number. He's my grounds keeper and has keys to the property. He can help you with the drive if you still can't manage it."

"I will conquer that."

What have I just said I would do?. . . It's okay. I can always cancel out.

*****

"You're doing what?" Cory said, almost shouting.

"Quiet down. You're scaring Buttons," Fury said, holding the Persian kitten she had brought for the girls.

"Fury Bridget O'Quinn, you're not going to stay in that man's house alone. You have no idea who lives on that mountain, and what kind of man gives a woman the keys to his house after knowing her a week? There's something going on."

"I've been in his Arabella house three times so far, trying to sort and organize the boxes of papers that I'm going to search through. His housekeeper has known him most of his life, so I don't think he's dangerous. He said that she's protective of him, and I can see that. She treats him more like a son than an employer. But I knew you wouldn't like it."

"Not like it? It scares me to death. Does Dad know?"

"Not exactly, and you don't need to tell him. I'm over twenty-one."

"See. You know you shouldn't be doing this."

"Maybe, but how could I resist? The leaves will be changing, and the view will be even more spectacular." Putting the two-month-old, calico kitten on the floor, Fury changed the subject. "What time are the girls getting home? I can't wait for them to see this baby."

CHAPTER FOURTEEN

A week after delivering the kitten to the Reynolds, Fury arrived back at Little Terrapin Mountain. The sky was overcast, and she held her breath that it would not begin raining before she tackled Gray's driveway. She had not yet begun her excavation of the MacGregor storage.

I acted tough with Cory, but I am a little nervous.

Luck was with her, and the rain did not complicate her chore. It took all the courage she could muster, but determination trumped fear, and she made it up the steep incline. She had spoken with Robert, and as promised, he had left a key under the mat on the side entrance and told her to call if she had any problems.

Entering through the side door, she passed through a laundry room and into a small hallway. To the left was a bedroom with a bath. To the right was the kitchen end of the great room that ran almost the length of the house. The ceiling in the huge area was twenty-feet high, which combined with the wall of windows and doors to create an illusion of being even larger. Although alone in the building, she had an inclination to walk quietly.

Before bringing in her things, or choosing a room to camp in, she went out on the covered part of the deck to enjoy the view. Even with a gray sky, the foliage was extraordinary with all the brilliant hues of fall spread over the multiple mountains. It had begun to rain and the temperature was quite cool.

Being here is like having a mental massage.

After five minutes outside, she toured the house. He had not specified a room for her to use. She walked to the opposite end of the house where another hallway led to the master suite. She passed the small guest bath she had used before and walked into the master bedroom on the right. It was a big room with a ceiling height of about fifteen feet. A large armoire of golden wood housed a large-screen TV behind closed doors. It faced a king-size bed that was covered with a plump comforter and multiple, complimentary pillows. All were color-blocked in tones of burgundy, green, beige, and brown. Like the great room, glass doors comprised one wall, continuing the architectural design and providing a sensational panorama of the mountain range.

What a place to sleep!

The bed and view were so inviting that she wanted to plunge into the pillows and soak it in but decided that would take her presence one personal step too far.

That bed has probably logged mileage I don't want to know about.

The door was open to the bathroom where a garden tub, stall shower, and vanity counter with dual sinks exhibited MacGregor marble. A door next to the lavatory was closed. Fury told herself that she had no business opening it, but couldn't resist. Inside was a walk-in closet, neatly filled with Gray MacGregor's clothing and shoes. She could smell his presence. A built-in chest of drawers presumably stored his underwear and socks. She did not turn on the overhead light and stood for a moment in the dimness. Yielding to a naughty temptation, she opened the top drawer slightly. It held socks and a package of condoms. She closed it quickly and instinctively looked back at the bed whereby an imaginary image of a nude MacGregor and an anonymous woman flashed through her mind. Fury retreated from the suite.

Of course, this is his love nest. I should be ashamed for trespassing.

It was growing dark as Fury left the master suite. She needed to find the light switches, the thermostat, and to choose a room for her stay. The bedroom on the opposite end of the house seemed to be the most convenient, but had no view. She went to the second floor to check what was available. There were three bedrooms, each with an adjoining bath. The first faced the front of the house and was rustic in nature with paneled walls and only a dormer window for natural light.

It had twin beds, a small loveseat, and offered little access to the beauty outside.

The second room faced the mountain range. Windows went wall to wall on one side, providing an outstanding view. It was painted off-white with natural-wood moldings and decorated in a feminine motif with a double bed covered by a floral spread of ivory, brick-red, and green. Two upholstered chairs were positioned under the window. A small entertainment center with TV faced the bed. A walk-in closet had shelves and rods for hanging clothes on three walls. There were sheets, blankets, extra pillows, towels, and washcloths stacked neatly on one side.

This is the best choice.

Returning to her car for the remainder of what she had brought, she struggled to keep her belongings and supplies sheltered from the rain. After transferring contents of her ice chest into the large refrigerator, she stored the staples in a box in the laundry room. It was still raining when she made a cup of hot tea in the microwave. Her cell phone rang before she took the first sip.

"Are you there?"

"I am."

"Are you alone?"

"As far as I know. Cory, you don't have to be concerned about me."

"Well, I am. I promised Mom I would look after you."

"You take that too seriously. I was fifteen then. I'm twenty-six and have traveled over most of the country—alone. Stop worrying. How is Buttons?"

Cory's tone changed immediately. "She's wonderful. The kids adore her; even Don is captivated. She sleeps with Suzi-Lee. But don't change the subject. I want you to call me every day while you're there."

"You're acting like Gray MacGregor is an axe-murderer. He's not here. He's in New York on business. I have a security system, a landline, cell phone, internet, and TV. What more could I want?"

"Strangely, I almost wish that he was there. I don't like you so alone."

"I'm fine. Go take care of your real children. My tea is getting cold, and I want to make a sandwich."

When she finished eating, Fury cleaned up and turned out the lights, with the exception of one in the kitchen. She went up to her room and set up her laptop on the bed. After taking a shower, she climbed under the plump spread and flicked on the TV, meaning to watch one show and then write, but fatigue took over. She was sound asleep by nine o' clock.

Waking at six the next morning, Fury resolved to finish at least twenty pages of her novel each day. With four days to work, and two-hundred pages already written, it was possible to finish the first draft by Friday.

She was downstairs in the living room by six-thirty, drinking a cup of coffee and organizing her thoughts for the day's writing. Sitting adjacent to the fireplace, she stared out through the expanse of glass on the opposite side of the room. Although a veil of light fog obscured the mountain-view, the mood was peaceful and seductive.

What am I doing in this strange man's house, and why is he on my mind? He's arrogant and controlling, with far too much money and too much sex appeal. What am I thinking?

As the sun rose higher and the fog disappeared, the day appeared to be perfect. Sunshine and blue skies replaced the clouds and rain of the day before, and the mountains were ablaze with the autumn foliage. She took her laptop to the deck and wrote all morning. The weather was cool but a sweatshirt shielded her. By late afternoon, the book was going well. Her iPod was playing elevator music, and she was deep into a steamy scene where her characters were about to consummate their relationship when something touched her foot. Fury jumped, emitting a semi-scream.

"Where did you come from?"

As she reached out to pet the dog, her eyes cut around to the house. The glass door from the kitchen to the deck was ajar and obviously where Apache had come from. Shaking off her initial shock, Fury smiled. "How did you get here, girl? Do you stay with the caretaker?"

The words were barely out of her mouth when Gray MacGregor walked through the doorway. "Apache, leave our resident author to her work."

Fury stared at him for a moment, disbelief on her face. "You're supposed to be in New York."

"Plans change. One of my key men came down with shingles, and we had to postpone. Go on about your work. We won't bother you."

"We?"

He pointed to Apache. "She and I."

"But, I can't stay, now that you're here."

"Of course, you can."

She shook her head. "And wake up with you in my bed?" *Whoa. Might not have been good to say that.*

"Don't be sophomoric. I don't go where I'm not invited, and frequently, not even then. Your space and virtue are safe. Stay on your side of the house; I'll stay on mine. We can meet for meals in the middle. I think the house is large enough to accommodate us both."

Fury had an incredulous expression on her face. "I beg to differ with your analysis. I'm going to gather my things and move down to the lodge."

He walked closer to her. "You'll do nothing of the sort. Pretend that I'm not here. I'm hungry. What were you planning for dinner?"

She stared at him for a second. "Ramen noodles."

"You can't be serious." He frowned with disapproval.

"I am deadly serious. As serious as I am about leaving."

"Neither is going to happen. Come on in. We'll cook together."

"I don't cook."

He looked at her as if he didn't understand. "What do you mean you don't cook?"

"Read my lips. I don't cook. Never have, and probably never will."

"You don't know how to cook?" He seemed genuinely shocked.

"Mr. MacGregor, Gray . . . I write books."

"What do you eat?"

"Ramen noodles."

"Well, you're not eating a box of noodles in my house." He looked her up and down. "Get yourself in here." He motioned toward the kitchen. "I'll give you a cooking lesson. Ramen noodles!" He made a face.

"I haven't said that I was staying."

"But, you are."

Who the hell does he think I am? An employee?

As he turned his back to reenter the house, she looked at him for a second, debating her next move. Closing her computer, she followed him into the kitchen.

Gray opened the freezer compartment and took out two steaks. From the refrigerator section, he removed potatoes, butter, an onion, and a package of yellow squash. From a kitchen drawer, he took out a utility knife and handed it to Fury, along with a wooden cutting board. "You chop the onion. I'll take care of the rest."

Fury took the items and thought for a minute. "You really cook?"

"Of course I cook. How else do you think I eat?"

"Takeout, restaurants, a chef."

"*B.S.* If you want a good meal, you prepare it yourself."

Fury looked at the onion as if it were an alien intruder and then laid it down to wash her hands. After drying on a paper towel, she attempted to peel the vegetable. She cut away the top and slit the side to get rid of the skin. Her eyes began to burn. Gray was busy cleaning the squash and peeling the potatoes. By the time he noticed, tears were flooding her face as she tried to cut the onion into pieces.

"Oh, my, God. You really don't know anything. Give it to me and learn." He took an onion, split it, put the pieces cut-side-down on the cutting board, and chopped it into pieces within seconds.

"I can see that I have my work cut out for me," he said as he chopped.

"Why do you think that I want to learn to cook? I've lived twenty-six years without knowing how."

"Well, by the time you're twenty-seven, you're going to have a new skill to add to your bio."

She looked at him for a moment, and then asked, "Did you cook the food you served the last time I was here?"

"Of course."

She closed her eyes and took a deep breath. *This is crazy. I should go.*

"Make yourself useful and set the table. You know where everything is."

Just order me around like I'm your servant.

"Do all of your dates help you cook?"

He stopped and looked at her. "First of all, you're not my date. And, second, I don't bring dates here."

"But, why—" She caught herself. *Oh, my gosh. I was about to ask him why he has condoms?*

"But what?"

"Nothing. Forget it. I'll set the table."

Gray grilled the steaks on the gas barbeque on the deck. He made the squash into a tasty casserole with onions, cheese, mayonnaise, and milk. Fury watched in amazement. Mike had never cooked anything more than scrambled eggs and hamburgers. Cory and their mother, Kathleen, had done all the O'Quinn cooking and excluded Fury—not that she wanted to bother.

As they finished the meal, Fury looked at him and said, "I still haven't said that I'm staying here."

He smiled. "Hard as it is for you to admit, you know you are. You'll lock your door and be safe from temptation on either side. Keep in mind, I'm not about to make headlines in two states."

"I'll stay, my door locked, if you'll answer one question."

"You'll stay if I don't, but what is your question?"

"Where did you learn to cook?"

He waited a minute before answering. "I'll tell you, but no more questions. Agreed?"

She nodded.

"Ella. I hung out in the kitchen with her a lot when I was a kid."

I wonder why he wouldn't want more questions about that.

CHAPTER FIFTEEN

After dinner, they washed the dishes together as though it was the normal course of behavior. Fury noted that Gray was methodical in his actions as well as his speech. Each move, each word seemed thought out and carefully executed. When the last dish was put away, he made a pot of coffee, and they went out on the deck.

"It is so beautiful that I can understand why you want to spend as much time as you can here. It is kind of you to let me take advantage."

"Not a little crack in your usual armor, is there?"

"You're mocking me."

"Not really."

"I'll say this, and then I'm going upstairs. You're a difficult man to understand. Just when I think I'm getting to know you, you disappear. With me, it's what you see is what you get, but there are more sides to you than a Rubik's cube."

Gray smiled. "The key is that I'm far more simple than most. What I say has no subtext, and I *don't* play games."

"I'm beginning to see that." She tipped her head toward her shoulder and cocked an eyebrow. "And what is your *astute* take on me?"

"A wild mustang." He grinned and shook his head, slightly. "Beautiful to behold but difficult to master."

"I'll take that as a compliment, even though I'm not sure that you meant it as one. And, with that, I need to say goodnight."

She left him on the deck, collected her laptop from a table in the living room, and went up to her room. Although she did not fear him, she locked the door. *I don't know why I'm bothering. If he wanted to force his way in, he probably has the key. It is his house.*

She slept well and dreamed about the dinner they had shared. The next morning, she got up at six again, showered, but took more pains with her hair and makeup. When she came out of her room, she could smell bacon and coffee. *He's already up.*

As she walked into the great room, she saw grits boiling on the stove and a bowl of cut melon on the bar.

"I'll give you another chance to conquer the onion," he said as she walked toward the kitchen end of the room.

"Are you sure that you trust me with a sharp knife?"

"No. But, you need to learn. Respect the blade and try not to cut yourself."

She took the knife and walked around the island bar to where the cutting board and onion were on the counter, her competitive nature outweighing her rebellious side. Remembering his action the night before, she carefully made the necessary cuts. Pleased with the result, she laid the knife down and walked to the china cabinet before he could give additional directions.

"I see there's hope for you. You're a quick study."

She smiled. "You might want to keep that in mind. But, right now, I'm in need of a cup of coffee."

"Help yourself."

Gray made Spanish omelets to go with the bacon, grits, and toast. They had just begun to eat when Fury's phone rang. She wanted to ignore it, but knew that if it was Cory, not answering could have serious consequences.

Noting her hesitation, Gray said, "Answer it."

She stood up and walked away from the table before taking the device from her pocket. *Darn it, Cory. Do you have to hover over me like a bee over a blossom?*

"Good morning." A cheery voice came from the other end. "Did you sleep well?"

"I did." Fury wanted to say more but wasn't ready to let Cory know that Gray was in the house.

"Are you going out for breakfast?"

"No. I don't think so."

"You're very quiet. Is everything okay?"

"Of course. It's just that I am in the middle of developing a scene. Can I talk to you later?"

As she sat back down at the table, Gray smiled. "Boyfriend checking up on you?"

"No," she snapped. "My sister."

"You lied to her," he said, putting his coffee cup down.

"You listened?"

"Hard not to. You were only fifteen feet away."

"If you must know—"

"I don't."

"If you must know, I don't want her to know that you're here."

"Told you. I don't need to know." He stood up and began removing the dirty dishes. Fury said no more, but helped him with the cleanup.

As he put away the last pot, he said, "I'll be in my office if you need anything."

She looked at him with a blank face, not wanting to admit that she had toured the house and seen no office.

Reading her expression, he said, "It's downstairs."

"There's a downstairs?"

He motioned toward the back entry. "There's a stairway behind the door opposite the laundry room and an outside entrance on the north side of the house. The phone rings there as well."

Gray then walked back to his bedroom; Apache followed him. Within seconds, he returned with a large brief case and disappeared through the door in the back hallway.

As the door closed, Fury took her cell phone out of her pocket and dialed her sister, dreading the conversation.

Cory answered on the second ring.

"I am at a good breaking point and thought I'd take a minute to give you a ring." *It takes five lies to cover up for the first one.*

"I'm glad you did, but I can't talk now. I have a meeting of the school carnival committee. Catch you later."

Perfect. I'm golden with her and don't have to lie any more.

Although thoughts of her host peppered her concentration, Fury was able to turn out ten pages of rough text—again working on the deck. At fifteen minutes past twelve, the door from the living room opened.

"Take a break, and we'll run down to the Wild Flower Café for lunch."

Fury smiled, hit the "save" icon, closed out her laptop, and followed him outside.

As she climbed in the front seat of Gray's SUV, she said, "Do I really get to have a meal without having to chop an onion?"

He chuckled. "You are one smart-mouthed woman."

"It's probably why I'm still single. What's your excuse?"

He grinned.

Fury noticed a few flecks of silver in his hair as he slid behind the wheel.

"My complete lack of social skills."

With a coquettish tip of her head, she quipped, "Don't expect me to disagree with you."

He laughed. "I never thought for a second that you would. Now come on, Kate, let's get moving. I'm starved."

"Kate one of your girlfriends?"

He shook his head. "I'll let you figure that out."

The lunch had been pleasant with conversation devoted to neutral subjects like the frustrations of city traffic, media concentration on questionable celebrities, and the lack of convenience in commercial air travel. Neither ventured into personal territory, nor did they talk of her mission. Fury had been to Forglen three times, which she was certain that Gray knew, yet he made no inquiry as to how the search was progressing. As she started into the house upon their return after lunch, he called out to her.

"We'll be starting dinner at six o'clock. Have your apron."

She turned and made a face. "I *don't* cook."

"You do now. Be on time."

Damn, he's infuriating. Just when I start to like him, he goes all "lord and master" on me.

As she waited for her computer to boot up and then configure updates, her mind wandered to Gray. *Does he like me or is he keeping an enemy close? Do I care?*

With military punctuality, Gray appeared in the kitchen at six with a bag of groceries. Despite her rebellion toward following his instructions, Fury was waiting, a towel wrapped around her waist as a makeshift apron.

"I'm happy to see you take directions. I may keep you around."

"Don't depend on it. I may be cooperating just because you've been generous."

"Didn't think for a second that it was anything else."

"Where is my onion?"

Gray laughed. "I'll take the onion detail tonight. You're on peel-potato duty to start."

Fury not only peeled the potatoes for the au gratin casserole, but Gray also had her grate cabbage and carrots for the coleslaw, after first demonstrating how to use the grater. He grilled ribs with his homemade barbeque sauce. Again, the meal was excellent. Fury fell automatically into her role of setting the table. Throughout the evening, Gray's temperament was the most congenial she had seen. When the post-dinner cleanup was complete, he made the usual coffee but took his cup to the living room area. "Why don't we watch a film tonight?"

Panic seized Fury. *Am I supposed to sit on the sofa with him? What film will we watch?*

"What do you have in mind?" she asked, keeping her tone steady.

"You choose." He tossed her the remote. "Push the top button for the menu."

I'm actually getting to make a choice. This is a first!

Fury scrolled through the available films, eliminating many, based on sex, violence, and her personal distaste of sci-fi and supernatural plots. *Where is* Mary Poppins *when you need her?* She finally settled on *Walk the Line.*

"Oh, so you're a country music fan," Gray said.

Fury smiled. "Not in general, but I do like Johnny Cash's music." She put the remote on the coffee table and made herself comfortable in one of the armchairs flanking the couch where Gray sat.

When the film was over, he stood and started for the kitchen to put up his coffee cup. "You're welcome to continue watching TV if you like, but I'm going to bed."

She shook her head. "I'm going upstairs, but thank you for the offer." She started up the stairs and was halfway when she remembered her computer. Turning quickly, to go back down, her feet tangled and she tumbled.

"Oh!" she cried out, landing on the floor with a sharp pain shooting up her leg.

Apache came running with Gray close behind.

"What happened?" he asked, reaching down to help her.

"I don't know. My feet got scrambled." *How dorky I feel.*

"Let me help you up."

"No." She pushed his hand away. "I can't stand. I think something popped."

He knelt down and pushed her jeans up to expose an ankle that was already swelling. "It looks bad. We better get you to the ER."

"No. No, I don't want to go to a hospital."

"That's not an option. You're going. Put your arms around my neck."

"I'm fine, really. I'm not going to sit around an emergency room all night to hear that I sprained my ankle."

"You are going. End of story. And this isn't Atlanta. You won't sit around all night. Do as I say."

"You can't carry me."

"Well, you can't sit there indefinitely." He gave her patronizing look. "I most certainly can carry you."

"I'll just hold on to you. I can hop to the sofa."

"Don't put any weight on that foot. You could cause more damage.

Do you have a jacket upstairs?"

She nodded.

He helped her up onto her good foot. With her left arm around his shoulders, he got her to the couch.

"I don't need to go. It's just a sprain."

"Do you always have to be so difficult? You're going to get it checked out tonight."

Collecting her jacket and one from his room for himself, he came back to where she was rubbing her injured ankle.

"If we're going to a hospital, I'll need my insurance card, which is in my purse. I'm sorry that I didn't think to ask you to get it."

"You won't need it. I'll cover the bill."

"I wouldn't let you do that. It was my fault, not yours. They will probably want proof of my identity."

He went back up the stairs, two at a time, and returned with her purse.

"Like it or not, Kate, I'm going to carry you to the car. You hopping down the front stairs could cause us both to fall."

She looked at him for a moment and then nodded in submission.

Gray scooped her up effortlessly. Fury felt awkward but secure in his arms. When they reached his SUV, he put her down to open the door and then assisted her onto the passenger seat.

The emergency room was quiet. Fury was the only patient and received immediate attention. The x-ray showed no fracture or break. Gray insisted on an MRI, which showed a tear in one of her ligaments.

"You should put no weight on that foot for a while," the ER physician said. "For the next seventy-two hours, you'll need to apply cold compresses every few hours. After that, you can soak the ankle in hot Epsom salts several times a day and apply a cold compress afterward. I'll give you a prescription for pain and have my nurse bring you crutches. You should see an orthopedic physician when you return to Atlanta."

"You mean that I'm going to have to use crutches?"

"That would be the best course to follow. You will likely require surgery to repair the tear. This type of injury can take longer to heal than a broken bone."

"Looks like you'll have to spend a bit more time at the cabin," Gray said, smiling.

"You just want a poor cripple to chop onions for you."

He chuckled. "Don't forget the potatoes."

When they reached the house, he carried her up the front steps, into the house, and deposited her back on the couch. "You can't safely navigate the stairs. I'll move your things down here."

"I can't let you do that."

In a fatherly manner, he said, "Again, you don't have a choice. As much as this goes against that independent nature of yours, you are going to have to let me help you. Now give it up."

As Gray walked up the stairs, she leaned back and closed her eyes, taking a mental inventory of what she had brought. *He is going to be handling all my things, including my nightgown and underwear. This is embarrassing.*

Gray got her settled in the bedroom near the kitchen and prepared a plastic bag of alcohol and water to freeze for her cold compress therapy. She managed to get undressed and in bed by two a.m. Even though the ankle hurt every time it moved, she refused to take a pain pill. She slept until eight.

When she hobbled into the living area, Gray was sitting at the bar with a cup of coffee.

"How did you sleep?" he asked.

"Fine. It only hurts when I move it."

"Have a seat on the sofa, and I'll bring you a cup of coffee—cream and sugar?"

"Both, thank you. I'm sorry to be so much trouble."

"You're fine. I'm just glad it was only your ankle. What would you like for breakfast?"

Having an invalid to care for certainly brings out the best in him.

"Whatever you're having is fine—as long as it doesn't involve an animal Walt Disney featured in a movie."

"Do *The Three Little Pigs* count?"

"Whoops. I guess I'm caught on that one. I'm okay with bacon, ham, or sausage."

When breakfast was ready, he served her on a tray in the living room, and then brought his own.

"I should go home today," Fury said between bites.

"I'll hear of no such thing."

"No, really. I can drive. My car is automatic, and my right foot is fine. You can't be waiting on me here. That's too much to ask."

"You are not driving back to Atlanta. I forbid it."

Forbid it?

"You will stay here until Monday morning. I'll drive your car to the city."

"But, you'll need your car, and how will you get back up here?"

"I have another car."

Of course you do.

"I'll get a rental to come back up. Quit fussing over details. Where's your cell phone?"

"In the bedroom on the charger."

He picked up her breakfast dishes and dropped them in the hot, soapy water he had prepared when he took his own plate to the kitchen. Going into her room, he retrieved the cell phone and returned to the living room. Before handing it to Fury, he added the house number and his cell number to her contact list.

"I'll be in my office. Call me if you need anything. And don't leave this couch without the phone. Do you want your computer?"

She nodded. "It's easy to tell that you're accustomed to being in charge."

He turned his head, smiling, and said, "Occupational hazard."

After bringing her the laptop, and a tray with a bottle of water, can of soda, a glass, and an ice bucket, he asked if there was anything else she needed. She assured him that she was more than comfortable.

"Keep your foot elevated, and I'll check on you later."

Gray was hardly out of the room when Fury's phone rang. *Oh, my, gosh! Cory.*

"We didn't get to talk yesterday. Did I catch you at a bad time, today?"

"No. I'm just about to get started writing."

"Well, what's going on?"

Fury hesitated. *Can't tell her about the ankle. She'll be on her way up here.* "Not a thing. Just write, write, write. How about you guys?"

"We're good. You're coming home Friday night—right? Don and I thought we'd have you and Dad over for barbeque on Saturday."

Great! What do I tell her now? "That sounds terrific, Cory, but I don't think I want to plan anything for this weekend. I don't know what time I'll get in Friday, and I'll have all my laundry to do. Could we make it later?"

"What about Sunday?"

Damn.

"I really don't want to plan anything. Let me have a rain check for this weekend."

"Is there something wrong? You're acting strange."

"No. I'm not acting strange. I'm just under a lot of pressure to finish this draft."

Fury's excuse seemed to placate Cory, and the rest of the conversation centered on the girls and the new kitten.

I hope I'm off crutches before I have to see her, or she'll drive me crazy with questions.

Gray called at midmorning and came up at lunchtime. He prepared hamburgers and seemed to enjoy his new role as caregiver.

The rest of the week passed without incident. Day by day, Fury felt more and more comfortable with her host. He could not have been more accommodating. Only his domineering attitude detracted from his appeal.

By Saturday afternoon, she had finished her first draft. On Sunday, Fury began to feel pangs of regret that the week was about to end. Despite the pain and inconvenience of her injury, she had been happy and productive in Gray's home.

"How are you going to navigate the stairs at Forglen?" he asked on Sunday afternoon. "You might want to postpone your research."

"Trust me. I'll manage."

He leaned back in the chair next to the sofa where Fury was sitting, put his hands behind his head, and his feet on the ottoman. "I shouldn't even question you. If there's a way, you will find it, but I don't want you to risk reinjuring that ankle."

"You have a sturdy railing by the stairs. I'll be fine."

"You are going to see a specialist."

"I am. I promise. I'll have my brother-in-law recommend someone."

CHAPTER SIXTEEN

"I need Don to recommend an orthopedic doctor. I twisted my ankle on the stairs," Fury said to her sister in their first phone conversation after the writing retreat in North Carolina.

"How did you do that?"

"Good question. One minute, I was skipping down the steps, and the next minute, I was sitting on the floor with pain shooting up my leg." *No need for you to know when and where.*

"Do you need some help? I can come over this morning for a couple of hours."

"No. I'm fine."

"But how are you getting around?"

"I'm just limping—barely putting weight on the bad foot." Her phone beeped, signaling another call. Fury glanced at the caller ID and saw that it was Gray. "Cory, I have another call coming in. Can you get that referral for me? You can leave it on my voice mail." Fury hit the "call waiting" button.

"Good morning, Kate. How is the ankle?"

"It's fine, and thank you for all you did last week."

"No thanks necessary. Have you contacted a doctor here?"

"I just talked to my sister. She's going to get a name and call me."

"Let me know if you need anything. I'll be in town this week."

With that, Gray wished her a good day and ended the conversation.

Later that morning, Fury saw Don's colleague. She gave him her North Carolina test results, and he told her that if she continued the plan she had been following, the ligament tear should successfully heal without surgery.

"That's a relief. How long will I be on crutches?"

"I'll see you for a follow-up in two weeks. If all looks good, you should be able to discard the crutches at that point, provided you are careful for a couple of months."

Leaving the office, she thought about calling Gray, but decided against it. *If he wants to know, he'll call.*

The days following her return from North Carolina were spent on the tedious job of editing and revising her manuscript. She wanted to make a trip to Forglen but knew that getting the book to her editor would free her mind to concentrate on the MacGregor-Dolan research. Although she would not admit it, even to herself, she was disappointed that Gray did not call again. In contrast, Cory did what Cory did best—smothered Fury with attention. Late Monday afternoon, sister and nieces showed up at the condo, laden with food, including chicken soup, spaghetti sauce, and a container of Irish stew.

"What were you doing using the stairs when you have an elevator?" Cory asked.

"I was in a hurry." Fury felt guilty allowing her sister to believe that the accident happened in Atlanta, but she was not about to open the Pandora's Box that would develop if Cory knew the truth.

"I guess your ankle rules out your plundering through the MacGregor attic for a while."

"No, it doesn't. As soon as I send my manuscript to New York, I'm going back out there."

"How? You're on crutches."

"I'm not a paraplegic. I have a sprained ankle."

It took Fury nearly three weeks to have her manuscript in shape. Before Thanksgiving, the draft was on its way to New York. Considering the holiday, she expected it would take over a month before the markup would come back from her editor, which would allow her time for the MacGregor research. Swelling in the ankle had subsided, and she was able to wear a regular shoe and walk with only an elastic brace.

The minute she hit "send" on the email bearing the manuscript, her thoughts went straight to Forglen. She had not heard from Gray again. Although it bothered her, she chided herself. *I don't have a personal relationship with him. I'm just a person who wants information from his history. He said it himself, "You're not a date." Disliking that man is a whole lot safer than liking him.*

Slipping into jeans, a bulky turtleneck, and athletic shoes, she collected her notebook, attaché case, and a fresh legal pad. She had called Ella the night before to say that she would be coming. It was raining when she rang the door chimes at shortly after ten. Edward answered.

"Good morning, Miss O'Quinn. I hope you managed to stay dry."

"Thank you, Edward. I did. It was pretty nasty leaving Atlanta, but it looks like it's clearing."

"Can I have Ella get anything for you before you go up to the attic?"

"I'm fine. I brought a bottle of water. I don't want to be any trouble."

"Ella said to tell you that lunch will be ready at twelve. Mr. MacGregor, Gray, will be joining you today."

Really. Three weeks and not a sound, and today he's joining me for lunch. Is he here? It is his house. I just never think of him in it. Why would he want to have lunch with me?

"He said for you to wait for him in case he is tied up in traffic getting out of the city."

Fury nodded. "Of course." *So, he is coming out from Atlanta.*

Once in the attic, the endless chore of opening box after box and leafing through reams of documents, clippings, and assorted other items took Fury's full attention. None of the boxes she had gone through contained items from the 1920s. She wanted to skip some and attempt to reach the relevant materials sooner but was afraid she might miss something important. There was not much organization to the storage. At ten minutes to twelve, her phone alarm rang. She marked her place in the box she was working on and went down to wash her hands in the closest bathroom on the second floor. She put on fresh lipstick and combed her hair.

When she walked into the breakfast room, he was already there.

"Hello. You look as though you've been busy. I see that you're off your crutches."

"Just off, but the ankle is doing well. No surgery needed. By the way, there's a mountain of stuff up there. It's like eating a bowl of oatmeal. You take a bite out and the cavity fills back up."

He smiled. "No one is forcing you."

She gave him a sarcastic smile. "Thanks for reminding me of that."

Before he could respond, Ella came in with a tray of baguettes, roast beef au jus for French dip, and two Caesar salads.

The food was delicious, and Fury ate more than she expected. Ella finished off the meal with a dessert of angel food cake, hollowed out and stuffed with bourbon-laced vanilla ice cream and pecans. The surface was covered with whipped cream.

"Have you received your invitation to my Christmas party?" Gray asked as Ella poured coffee for the two of them.

"Invitation? No, I don't think I have."

"Well, you will. It's an annual affair here at Forglen. All employees and some of our primary customers are invited. Make sure you add it to your calendar for Saturday, the sixteenth."

"Is it a plus one invitation?" *Why did I ask that?*

"It's not. I'm your plus one."

She looked at him and frowned. "You're my plus one?"

"I believe that's what I said."

"Does that suggest that we're having a date?"

"I believe it does."

"And you assume that I'm accepting?"

"You are."

"What if I have to be in New York?"

He smiled. "You don't."

She shook her head. "You can't know that."

"Your book isn't due out for several months. December 1st is the deadline for your first draft. Have you forgotten that you were writing it at my house? I may not know a lot about publishing, but I know that the big houses don't turn a manuscript around in two weeks. The party is the sixteenth. You'll enjoy it. Everyone is happy because bonus checks are distributed."

"You are unbelievable. I don't hear from you for three weeks, and then you announce that I'm to be your date at a big party at your house."

"The phone works both ways. I didn't hear it ring for me."

"I'm not in the habit of calling men unless it's for a business related matter."

"No sense dwelling on yesterday. By the way, you might want to check the storeroom at the plant."

"What are you talking about?"

"MacGregor Marble. If you want to see correspondence that went between my great-grandfather and his associates, you might want to peruse the storage area for his old office."

"Why would you tell me that?"

"Damned if I know, but I have to get back to Atlanta now."

"Will I have a clue as to how to dress for the party?"

"Cocktail attire. The troops like to dress up, but it's not formal."

"Should I drive myself?"

"You will not. I will be talking to you between now and the party. In fact, we'll be having dinner this Saturday night—that is, if you're free."

Her eyebrows squeezed together in a frown. "Nice of you to take that into consideration."

"What time shall I pick you up?"

"Did I say that I would go?"

"You will."

"Are you always so domineering and so sure of yourself, or is it just with me?"

"*Probably* domineering and *definitely* sure of myself . . . but not exclusively with you. If I couldn't read people and make quick decisions, I wouldn't survive thirty minutes in the piranha tank that

I swim in."

"Are you saying that you're psychic?"

He laughed. "Absolutely not. There's nothing supernatural about it—purely scientific."

"Scientific?"

"Google Dr. Paul Ekman. You might learn something you could use in one of your books. Now. I repeat. What time shall I pick you up?"

"Seven."

He smiled, got up, and walked toward the door. Turning back, he said, "I'll see you then."

What just happened? She sat at the table for at least five minutes after he left, gazing out the window, and trying to analyze their conversation. Ella had not come back in to remove the dessert plates. *We're dating now?* In a town like Arabella, the MacGregor Christmas party would be newsworthy. *With his two-date custom, it'll be over before the ink is dry on the newsprint. He won't be around for New Year's.*

Snapping out of her reverie, she picked up the dishes and headed for the kitchen.

"You shouldn't do that," Ella said. "I can take care of it." The older woman all but snatched the dishes from Fury's hands.

"It was such a delicious lunch. The least I can do is take the dishes into the kitchen."

"It's my job, Miss O'Quinn."

As she left the kitchen and headed back to the attic, she thought about Ella's attitude. *Was she concerned that she had not done her job, or does she dislike me?*

Fury dug through box after box in the attic until five o'clock. She found some family photos and tossed them into one of her file boxes to examine later. But most of the items she saw related to the more recent family members. As she looked through the boxes of the past twenty-five to thirty years, Gray's mother was conspicuous by her absence. There was no wedding album, no family vacation photos—it was as if she had not existed. *I probably haven't found the boxes with those items, yet.* As she thought about it, she realized that she had not seen a photo of his mother anywhere in the house. She had not taken an inventory but did remember paintings of Emma MacGregor and Gray's grandmother, Dorothy MacGregor. All the MacGregor men were memorialized in rigid paintings, scattered through the house—all but Gray.

Why isn't there a photo or painting of his mother? She may have died young, but surely, there were photographs, if not a painting. I can't ask him, and something tells me that I'd better not ask Ella. Something is wrong here, but I don't know what.

Driving back to Atlanta, Fury made a mental list of things she wanted to search for in public records—none related to her work on Bridget, Jim, and J.G. She was haunted by the question of why Gray's deceased mother didn't appear to have a place in the home. Even his father was barely acknowledged. If not for the large oil painting over one of the fireplaces in a sitting room and a couple of photographs, he would have been a nonentity as well. The grand piano was covered with antique photographs. She made another note to check for signs of Gray and his mother among them. *I should be able to tell the generation by the style of clothing on the images.* The only person she felt she might ask about Gray's mother was her cousin Colleen in Arabella. *I don't even know his mother's name, but I certainly know his father's. I'll look for marriage records in newspaper archives.*

By the time Fury reached her building, her ankle was aching. She started to go straight to her unit from the parking garage, but thought about the MacGregor invitation and pushed herself to walk to the bank of tenant mailboxes instead. It was there. Among the advertisements, including Christmas catalogs from Saks Fifth Avenue and Neiman Marcus, the ivory vellum envelope stood out. She made a mental note to keep the upscale wish-books for shopping for a special dress to wear to the Christmas party.

A large manila envelope protruded from between the catalogs, revealing the postmark of Ireland.

CHAPTER SEVENTEEN

Once in the condo, she tossed the mail on the coffee table in front of her couch, wriggled out of her coat, and sat down to examine the correspondence. Like an expensive wedding announcement, the MacGregor invitation was engraved on a thick card with gilded edges. Below the standard language, it listed the order of events: Cocktails at Six, Dinner at Seven-thirty, Announcements and Presentations at Nine, and Music and Dancing until Midnight. Fury held it for a minute, mentally picturing Forglen filled with guests, Gray in a dark suit, and herself at his side. *Stop it. Don't think of him that way.*

Laying the invitation down, she tore into the envelope from Evanne. They had not communicated since she returned. On top was a handwritten letter.

November 29, 2006

Dear Fury,

I hope this finds you well. Granny has been ill. I thought that Uncle Mike would want to know. She was in hospital for more than a week. The doctors called it congestive heart failure. She's home and recovering well. You know what a tough old soul she is.

The second reason that I write is the enclosed letter that I found when going through Granny's drawers. Her trip to hospital was sudden, which caused her to ask me to bring her personal items. I probably should not have taken the letter, but I know how hard you are working to find out what happened so many years ago. I'm not even sure whether Granny put it in the bottom of that drawer, or whether her mother put it there. I think it proves one of your suspicions. I have to warn you, it is hard to read.

In closing, I hope that your family has a happy holiday season. God bless you all. One day, I hope to visit you in America.

With great affection,
Evanne

P.S. Granny does not know that I took the letter.

Fury picked up the aged envelope that bore no writing. Inside, there were three pages of thin parchment, also yellowed from time. She gingerly unfolded them.

My dear son, Ronan,

The end is near for me. Do not mourn, for I had a fine life with Conor and you children. But, I cannot go without telling you the truth, as painful as that may be for the both of us. You are my firstborn and have always held the special place in my heart. There is probably a right place to start, but I know not where that is. Does it start with the day that Mrs. MacGregor told me that I had the job of nanny to her wee ones? I was but barely past my fifteenth birthday and had just lost me mum.

I was so thrilled. It would mean money to buy new shoes, ones without holes that had not been worn before me by elder sisters. Da and my brothers made little wages, working as stonecutters in Mr. MacGregor's quarry. The MacGregors were rich beyond my understanding. They lived in the huge house in the middle of town. With the new job, I would live there too. Imagine that! Bridget Dolan, a little red-haired, Irish Catholic girl from an immigrant family, living in that grand house and being paid as well. I was to earn three dollars a week. It was a fortune for a girl like me.

It all began well. The children were dear. There was a son, just older than me, who was away at boarding school most of the time and a daughter of twelve. But it was the little ones that I was to care for. I even sat with them for classes with their tutor. I wanted to learn. I wanted to read the books that lined all the shelves in the giant library room. Maybe it was my fault that the bad things started.

Mr. MacGregor said that it was. He was nice at first. One day, he called me to his study. It scared me. I thought that I had done wrong because that was where the children were called to be punished.

But, he asked me if I was happy and if there was anything that I wanted. I told him that I loved the children and was very happy working for the family. He asked again if there was anything I wanted. I thought about it, and he seemed really interested, so I told him that I wanted to read and write better, like his children.

He said that he admired my ambition and offered to tutor me. That's where it all started to go wrong. Mr. MacGregor called me to his study every night for my tutoring. He always locked the door. I thought it was to keep the little ones from disturbing us. The first few times, Mr. MacGregor sat behind his giant desk with me in a chair on the other side. Then, one night, he came around the desk and said we should sit side by side on his leather sofa where he could see the page I was reading.

I still hate the smell of leather. That first night, he put his hand on my leg. I wondered why, but I dared not ask. After that, he never tutored me that his hand was not on my leg. It moved up more each time until it reached a forbidden place. I knew it didn't feel right that he should be touching me like that, but I was afraid to tell him to stop. And then, one night, his hands went under my skirt and his fingers found their way inside my panties. I tried to pull away, but he held me tight. His face had a funny look, and he was breathing hard. I said, "Please Mr. MacGregor, Miss Emma wouldn't want you to do this." Even though I didn't know what he was about to do. I knew it was wrong.

He became angry. Very angry. He said, "And who do you think you are? If you even think about telling Mrs. MacGregor, you'll leave this house, and your father and brothers will be without work."

I was trapped. If he threw me out, I would never see my love again, and I couldn't let him fire my brothers and Da. I let him have his way. I cried myself to sleep every time. The tutoring stopped, and he began coming to my little room at night. He was evil. I hated him—hated his cigars. But, it doesn't excuse what I did. I have to confess to Father O'Malley before I die, or I shall surely go to hell.

Oh, Ronan, I can't tell you the rest. I thought I could. I pray to the Virgin Mary to intercede for me, but I can't tell you. I know that I should, but I cannot.

The writing ended with no signature, but there was no mistaking who wrote it. Fury's blood went cold in her veins. Rereading the missive, nausea set in.

That vile man was Gray's great-grandfather. Is Uncle Ronan J.G. MacGregor's son?

Fury sat paralyzed for nearly thirty minutes. She knew that in spite of herself, she was attracted to Gray MacGregor. But, his great-grandfather had perpetrated a heinous act upon her grandmother—and gotten away with it.

The bastard raped an innocent fifteen-year-old! There has to be a connection between the abuse and Jim Dolan's incarceration at Milledgeville.

Fury's heart ached for what her grandmother had endured and wanted more than ever to avenge the wrongs committed against her family in the only way she could. *Should I show this to Gray? No. He may have never thought I would uncover such despicable information. He could shut me down.*

She had a fitful night, waking several times. Her ankle was hurting more than it had since the accident, but what kept her awake was the cloud hanging over her, created by Bridget's letter. She felt guilty being excited about attending the Christmas party in the MacGregor house, knowing what she knew.

What would Dad and Cory think? Did Aunt Mary know and hide the information? Could the letter have been hidden and unread for thirty years? How much of J.G. MacGregor was in Gray?

She drove to Forglen the following day with a different perspective, feeling as though she was traveling to a haunted house. So many questions swam around in her brain. Bridget's letter had stalled her Internet search for information about Gray's mother, which still posed unanswered questions. How evil was that family?

Looking up as she stepped out of her car, the house seemed larger, the door more sinister. As usual, Edward answered with his cordial greeting. However, before going to the attic, Fury felt compelled to visit the study.

Over the fireplace, the huge painting of J.G. presided like the chairman of the board. A leather couch anchored a grouping of wing-backed chairs and a marble coffee table in front of a fireplace. An ornate antique desk with gilt trim was angled in a corner. Three walls of the room were floor to ceiling shelves, filled with books. *Is that the same sofa where Bridget was first violated?* Fury was drawn to sit on it. Looking up at the painting, she could almost feel the offending hand creeping up her leg.

This is where it started. I hate the pompous bastard.

Out of nowhere, Ella appeared. She had not made a sound as she entered the study.

"Will you be having lunch today, Miss O'Quinn?"

"I didn't hear you come in, Ella. No. I don't want you to go to any trouble for me. I'll run out for a hamburger."

"I can't let you do that. If you'd like a hamburger, I'll make it for you."

"No—really. I'm sure that you have other things to do."

"Gray would be furious with me if I didn't make certain that you had lunch."

Seeing a no-win situation, Fury submitted. "That would be very nice of you. But, please don't cook. If you have cold cuts, any sandwich would be perfectly fine."

She doesn't like me. I see it in her eyes.

"Is there anything that I can get for you now?"

"No. I'm fine. I was just admiring the portraits of the family. This is the original Mr. MacGregor, right?"

"It is."

"And the beautiful painting over the parlor fireplace is his wife?"

Ella nodded. "She was beautiful."

"Is there a portrait of Gray's mother?" Fury held her breath.

"No." It was an abrupt answer. "I have to get back to the kitchen."

She made that clear. I've overstepped my bounds. There was no mistaking Ella's tone. There would be no further discussion about Gray's mother with her.

Determined to see if there was any sign of Mrs. John Graeme MacGregor, III, Fury went into the formal parlor. In a ball gown of red velvet, her white hair swept up in a queenly cluster and held in place by a tiara, Emma reigned supreme in the room.

The diamonds in her hair are probably real.

The grand piano had a Victorian shawl draped across it. A dozen or more antique-framed photographs were randomly scattered on the lid. Walking closer, Fury tried to match each with the MacGregor names she knew. Of the ones that appeared to be the most recent, she recognized Gray in a graduation cap and gown. There was another casual photo of Gray, and presumably his father, standing in front of MacGregor Marble. Gray looked to be about sixteen or seventeen. A very old photo took Fury's eye. It was also of the company, but much, much older. A dozen employees were scattered around the scene in work clothes of the era. A man in a stiff suit, a cigar in his hand, was at the center of the photo. Looking closer, Fury recognized J.G.

Were any of those men my relatives? Uncle Jim?

Nowhere among the photos did she see a female in sufficiently modern attire to have been Gray's mother. It was becoming more and more clear that signs of the woman were nowhere to be found in the house and that Fury would not be permitted to delve into why.

If she died, there would surely be photos.

Pouring over the contents of boxes that afternoon, Fury found a small, brown leather journal. Carefully opening the cover, she saw that it had belonged to Dorothy Vanderlin MacGregor—Graeme's wife, the daughter-in-law of J.G, and grandmother of Gray. Many of the pages were blurred, as though someone had spilled liquid, maybe tears on the pages. As Fury read, she felt the grief and depression oozing from Dorothy's pen. Skimming through the pages, she skimmed through lines written by the deceased woman.

"I pray that he will learn to love me. I cannot abide his coldness much longer." "He comes to my room to relieve his needs but it's only his body that he offers, not his heart." "He loves our children. Why can't he love me?"

There's no joy here. No happiness.

Fury tucked the journal in her briefcase to examine later more closely. Farther down in the same box she came across an old newspaper. The front page carried the headline:

ARABELLA MOURNS THE UNTIMELY DEATH OF MRS. JOHN G. MACGREGOR, JR.

Into the briefcase went the paper. *This family seems to be a curse for the women who marry into it. Emma's husband was a philandering rapist, Dorothy's apparently didn't love her, and Mrs. J.G., III is among the missing and unaccounted for. Maybe it's a good thing that Gray MacGregor has shown no interest in bringing another innocent woman into the lair. Keep that in mind, Miss O'Quinn. Let not thy hormones run amuck of thy common sense.*

That night, Fury settled herself on her bed with her laptop. Into the browser's search bar, she entered the term: Arabella Gazette archives. *They might purge Mrs. MacGregor from the house, but they couldn't purge her from public records and newspaper files—or could they? The MacGregors owned the paper.* Once on the home page for the periodical, she typed in "John Graeme MacGregor, III wedding/marriage." Up it came on the first try.

WHO'S WHO OF MERCY COUNTY ATTEND NUPTIALS OF JOHN G. MACGREGOR, III AND ZAIRA AYITA ROSS

There was her image in the formal wedding photograph—Zaira MacGregor.

She's stunning.

The face smiling at the camera was extraordinarily beautiful. Zaira MacGregor was slender with dark completion, dark hair, and an air of elegance. She had the same facial bone structure of her son—high cheekbones, deep-set eyes. She was without doubt his mother. Fury printed the story and then returned to the search bar. This time, she inserted only the first and last names. Articles appeared describing charity events that Zaira had hosted, her drive to build an art center in Arabella, the annual MacGregor Christmas parties, and Gray's birth. There were no articles published after 1977. Fury printed them all and then went to the obituary page where she typed in Zaira's name in all of its permutations—no results.

She can't be dead—can she? But, if not, where is she—Milledgeville?

Giving up her research for the night, Fury closed the computer and began reading the articles. The Ross-MacGregor wedding had been held in the Presbyterian Church with more than one hundred guests attending the service and two hundred attending the reception held on the grounds of Forglen. According to the article, the radiant bride wore a hand-beaded gown of tulle and satin, imported from France. For their honeymoon, the couple, described as charming and popular, went on a six-week tour of Europe. Typical of small-town journalism, the article was rife with editorial opinion.

Gray's birth announcement contained only basic statistics. "Mr. and Mrs. J. Graeme MacGregor, III welcome the birth of John Graeme MacGregor, IV, February 18, 1970. The couple's first child was born at the Wesley Memorial Hospital of Emory University, Decatur. The happy parents, Jack and Zaira, are prominent members of Arabella society. Mother and child are doing well."

Creating a file for the articles, Fury's instinct told her that Gray would not appreciate her digging into his mother's background. *There's more to know about you, Zaira Ayita Ross MacGregor*, Fury thought as she put the research in the cabinet, which was filling fast. *Your mysterious disappearance has to be part of what goes on behind Gray's inscrutable eyes and audacious behavior.*

CHAPTER EIGHTEEN

Instead of going to Forglen the following day, Fury drove to the Mercy County Courthouse and then to the Arabella Library. She found that the name Zaira had Celtic origin, while the woman's middle name, Ayita, was Cherokee Indian. The license application in Public Records for the Ross-MacGregor marriage gave the names of Zaira's parents. Researching through genealogy records, she discovered that Zaira's father was half-Cherokee and half Scottish. Ayita had been the name of her paternal grandmother, a Native-American. Zaira's maternal ancestors were Irish.

Gray is part Irish!

For some reason, the knowledge that Gray had Irish ancestry was comforting to Fury. If the cloud over their budding relationship was not lifted, it was at least beginning to disburse. She could look forward to the dinner date, knowing that Gray's heritage was less a blend of Bluebeard and Roman Polanski.

Saturday evening, Gray was on time, but Fury was on the phone with her agent.

Does he always have to be so punctual?

"I'll just be a minute," she mouthed, pointing to the phone as she let him into the condo.

He smiled, nodding, and walked to her couch. Fury went back into her office to finish the conversation. When she came out, Gray was browsing through the Saks catalog lying on her coffee table. Gypsy was in his lap. As she came closer, she saw that the book was open to a page that she had tabbed. It displayed an expensive, designer chemise, in a floral print of tomato-red, green, and tan, that was barely longer than a teddy.

Holding it up and grinning, he said, "I like your taste. I'm sure you would melt stone in this."

Reaching over and closing the book, she said, "*You're* not likely to ever find out."

He looked at her with an expression that suggested she might be wrong, but said nothing.

Changing the subject, she apologized for keeping him waiting. "I was talking to Sarah Anderson, my agent."

"Does she often call on Saturday evening?"

"Rarely, but Nicholas Colton is optioning my fourth book for a film. The contract had just been messengered over to her from his American representatives."

"Congratulations. We'll have to toast your success tonight." Looking her up and down, he added, "Better wear a warm coat. It's getting colder tonight. Will it bother your ankle?"

"The ankle's doing fine, but I'm still wearing flat shoes as a precaution."

"It needs to heal before the party so that I can show you off on the dance floor."

"As clumsy as I am, I might trip over you."

He smiled. "I'll make sure that I have a good grip."

"I'll hold you to that, but first, I better get a roller so you can remove the fur gift that Gypsy left on your coat."

When they reached the guest parking area, Fury got her first look at Gray's primary car—a beige Aston Martin Vanquish. "Well, this is quite a contrast to your practical Highlander."

"You could say that."

He held the door, while she slid into the bucket seat. The motor made barely a sound as he turned the ignition.

"This is another side of Gray MacGregor. How fast does this motorized magic-carpet go?"

"It'll get you there on time."

"You can probably program it for your scheduled time of arrival."

He laughed.

"So. We're actually on a date."

"We are."

"Are you as domineering with a date as you are with those seeking a favor?" she asked.

"Of course."

"And didn't *I* know that? I'll have you know that no other man has ever been able to tell me what to do."

"And didn't I know that, Kate?"

"Why do you keep calling me *Kate*?"

"I think you know why."

"Shakespeare's shrew?"

He nodded. "That and O'Hara's Kate in *The Quiet Man*. You remind me of her, a petite version—same scarlet hair, flashing blue eyes, and fiery temperament."

"I'll take that as a compliment, whether you meant it as one or not."

He slowed the car, stopping at valet parking in front of an Irish pub. "Thought you might enjoy some of your native atmosphere."

She smiled. "I love it here. It's one of Dad's favorites."

Gray had made a reservation, so the hostess led them to a booth in the back of the restaurant where it was considerably quieter. He ordered a Guinness; Fury ordered hot tea.

"You're a beer drinker?"

"Not really. But when in Rome."

Gray's manners were impeccable, causing Fury to wonder who trained him with no mother in his formative years. Despite his reticence, she relaxed and all but forgot the sinister information she had accumulated about his family.

"You said we would talk more about the party, tonight. I did receive the invitation. It's impressive."

"I had nothing to do with it. Gladys takes care of all the arrangements. I put on my suit, comb my hair, and hand out checks."

"I appreciate your offer to pick me up, but I can drive myself."

"Nonsense. I'll pick you up at lunchtime. You'll stay over, and I'll drive you back Sunday."

She looked at him. "You want me to have a sleepover date with you? Whoa. I didn't see that on the invitation."

"Calm down. I'm not asking you to share my room, only my house. As you recall, it's quite large—larger than the house in Cashiers. Did I cross any boundaries there?"

Fury thought for a minute or two. "You're right. You were a total gentleman. That was an overreaction on my part, and I apologize. However, in North Carolina, it wasn't planned, and no one knew we were in the same house. It's got to cause speculation in Arabella—Ella, Edward."

"Irrelevant."

She frowned and thought for a minute. "Okay. Here's the deal. I'll drive my car over on Saturday and drive myself back on Sunday." *I'm not ready to be trapped in that house without my car.*

"I would prefer to pick you up, but that's a fair enough compromise."

He actually gave in to me on a point. That's a first.

After dinner, Gray drove to Piedmont Park where they walked the paths, stopping to rest on an occasional bench. Leaving the park at closing, they reached the door of her condo at midnight. "There's touring production of a hit Broadway show in town next weekend. Would you like to go?" Gray asked.

She smiled. "Sounds enticing. But, if I'm going to be your date for the party, that would violate your two-date rule."

Gray shook his head, his eyebrows pinched in a frown. "You really believe that BS?"

"Why shouldn't I?"

"Because it's trash. I'll admit to never having a long-term relationship, but there's no written or unwritten rule on how many times I take a woman out."

"Isn't it true that you have a string of broken hearts the length of I-85 in your rear-view mirror?"

"Hell, no. I've never said or done anything to lead a woman to believe that a relationship was permanent."

Having said that, he took her key and unlocked the condo. She thought he might attempt to kiss her goodnight. He did not, and she did not invite him in. As he walked away, she reopened her door and called out.

"Do you still want to take me to the show, or have I totally pissed you off?"

Without turning around, he semi-shouted over his shoulder, "Yes to both. Curtain is at eight. I'll pick you up at seven. Be ready."

The next afternoon in her condo, after attending Mass and having lunch with Mike, Fury took Dorothy MacGregor's journal out to read more carefully. On page after page, the unhappy woman expounded on her misery. Graeme had not abused her physically; rather, he seemed to have emotionally abandoned her. Most of the entries were redundant. Growing bored, she almost stopped reading. However, the last entry gave her chills.

November 14, 1950

Today, he finally admitted what I've always known. He doesn't love me—never did. Our marriage was a sham. J.G. forced him to marry because the family needed an heir.

I was a good wife. I begged to know what it was that prevented him from giving me his love and affection. He tried not to tell me but finally confessed. Tears ran down his face as he admitted that for all these years, his heart has been elsewhere—with a girl he fell in love with when he was seventeen. He wouldn't say her name, only that she was a blue-eyed, red-haired, Irish girl. She left Arabella and went to Ireland to live while he was away on a summer holiday. He never saw her again, but her memory haunts him. He is still in love with her. Graeme begged my forgiveness but was adamant that he could never love me.

Now that J.G. is dead, he wants a divorce. I can't live as a discarded wife. I could never face anyone. But, I can't stop him. There is no hope.

I want to hate him, but I can't. I love him with all my heart. Without him, I am nothing. My heart is as dark with clouds as the dreary winter sky. I cannot say goodbye to my children, but Graeme will take care of them. I will use the pills that Dr. Pritchard gave me to sleep. It will be peaceful, and my heart will ache no more.

There were several blurred sections on the page, but the entry was legible. Fury closed the journal and dug into her briefcase for the newspaper that announced Dorothy's death. The date on the masthead was November 16, 1950.

She killed herself. Her husband was in love with my grandmother. Gray's grandfather and my grandmother were in love, maybe lovers. I need to see a photograph of Graeme.

She booted up her computer, went back to the *Arabella Gazette* web site, and ran the permutations of John Graeme MacGregor, Jr. While there were many articles in which he was mentioned, there were only three photographs—their wedding photograph, in which he was looking down at Dorothy and shown only in profile; one when he was about thirty and not facing the camera; and the last, his death notice, a formal headshot taken when he was at least fifty. None helped in comparison to the photos of the young Bridget with her companion that Fury discovered in Ireland.

On Monday, Fury returned to Forglen with a mission: find a photo of Graeme MacGregor, Jr. when he was young. For comparison, she had pulled the image of the young mystery cadet and the one of Bridget with a young man from her Ireland files. Her search took all day, but at four-thirty, when she was about to give up, she struck gold. In a trunk on the opposite side of the attic from where she began, Fury found the family history as collected and preserved by Emma MacGregor. Her hands were trembling as she removed the volumes of leather-covered albums and journals spanning the length of the Emma and J.G. marriage.

Emma had been methodical and thorough in saving her family's history. It would take a great deal of time to examine all the material that Fury painstakingly cataloged. To satisfy her immediate curiosity, she flipped through the photo albums until she found images of the family from the mid-1920s. There he was in a family portrait: J.

Graeme MacGregor, Jr. She did not have to pull out the photos found in the O'Quinn attic to know that Graeme was Bridget's secret love— his father, her demon. Questions flooded her mind. *Who was Ronan's father? Bridget's lover or her abuser? What made Bridget feel guilty? Did Emma know about Bridget and her husband—her son?*

Since it was late, she transferred five of Emma's journals and three photo albums to one of the plastic containers she had bought for the project, laid her briefcase on top, and started for the door. A figure appeared in front of her, causing Fury to let out a small sound of shock.

"I'm sorry, Miss O'Quinn. Ella sent me to ask if you would be staying for dinner."

Breathing a sigh of relief, Fury said, "No, Edward. I was just leaving for the day, but thank her for me."

The butler nodded and then reached out to take the box from Fury. "Allow me to assist you. Gray would not like it if you were to injure your ankle, again."

Instinctively, she wanted to decline his offer but thinking about the threat to her balance that carrying the heavy container could create, she relinquished it. "Thank you, Edward. That would be a huge help."

CHAPTER NINETEEN

Fury did not return to Forglen the next day. She had accumulated more than enough material to keep her busy at her condo, and it felt nice to work at home. While she was always alone in the mansion's attic, there was a stifling effect from the house. She was not certain whether it was the ghosts of past inhabitants, the ambiance of the building and its décor, or Ella. Although the housekeeper was never rude, she kept Fury at arm's length, never letting down her guard. The temperature in the room dropped ten degrees when Ella entered.

Fury started leafing through Emma's journals. They revealed primarily a mix of entries about her garden club, the historical society, the women's auxiliary at church, and her quilting group. In the early volumes, Emma expressed her desire to work in the suffrage movement and for prohibition. Both activities were forbidden by J.G.

Her writings portrayed a gentle, anxious-to-please matriarch who loved hosting the annual Christmas parties for the family business. She made certain that there was a toy and a sweet for every child of a MacGregor employee. Entries revealed that workers came to Emma when there was a sick child or an accident. She would make certain that medical care was provided. In 1924, Tom Dolan, Fury's great-grandfather, came to Emma.

June 30, 1924

I was surprised to have a visit today from Tom Dolan, one of MacGregor Marble's finest stonecutters. He came to ask my help with his young daughter, Bridget. Tom said that since her mother died earlier in the year, the girl has been despondent and has withdrawn from even her beloved schoolwork. I told him that I could use an extra pair of hands with the two little ones. Graeme is off to military school; and Sissy is shamelessly spoiled by Mr. MacGregor and will not help with her siblings. Of course, I had to clear the proposal with Mr. MacGregor. He remembered the girl from Christmas parties and was quick to approve. I hope to be of help. The Dolan men have long been faithful and loyal employees. I believe that four of them work in the quarry.

If Tom Dolan had only known that he was placing his daughter in jeopardy.

The MacGregors had married in 1906. Reading entries of J.G.'s autocratic control over his wife made Fury's blood boil.

What a patriarchal ass he was. I hate him. She was a kind and gentle woman.

When Fury reached the diary dated 1925, she held her breath as to what it would reveal.

Skimming through the first half of the year, nothing jumped out to indicate Emma had knowledge of her husband's secret behavior. The entries stopped abruptly in June and didn't pick up until the middle of July.

July 17, 1925

It is so good to be at Forglen again. They were good to me at the hospital in Atlanta, but I missed my home and my children. Graeme is still in Europe, learning the ways of the world, according to Mr. MacGregor. I wish that he were here. I still don't know how I got so sick. The nurse said that I nearly died. When I asked about my malady, the doctor said only that it was a disorder of the digestive system. He assured me that I shouldn't fret about it, but he had a peculiar look on his face. I lost a lot of weight, and I am still weak and pale, but the pain is gone. I can hold down my food. The pain in my belly was worse than the birth of my babies.

When I arrived home today, the children and the servants greeted me with joy at my return to health. I was sad to find that Bridget was gone. According to the housekeeper, Bridget went to Ireland to live with relatives. How strange. I thought she was happy working with the children. She was such a young thing to make such a move. I shall miss her. Mr. MacGregor refused to discuss the matter. He bristled when I asked after her, and I knew to inquire no more.

Fury closed the book and sat thinking about what she had read. *Lecherous tyrant! She never called him by his first name, much less a term of endearment. He ruled the house. If she knew anything, she would have stifled or denied it.*

Much to Fury's disappointment, the diary gave no clue as to the event that sent Bridget across the Atlantic and Jim to Milledgeville. Instead, it presented another question. What was wrong with Emma that summer?

Do I keep going through the attic, or should I act on the tip Gray gave me about the office storeroom? Is that where the bodies are buried?

There were about twenty more of Emma's journals back in the attic, which would take countless hours to review. Would it be a waste of time? Would Emma ever recognize the evil in her husband, or discover his dark side?

I have to resist the temptation to leave the attic before I've done a thorough investigation. There could easily be something in the later diaries. Bridget didn't write her revealing letter until she was close to death.

Fury closed the book and took it to her file cabinet. Her MacGregor research was taking a life of its own. She could hardly fit the journal into the dedicated drawer, and her computer already stored hundreds of pages of notes and dozens of scanned images. Despite his being media-shy, her collection of articles on Gray was an inch thick.

For a moment, his file distracted her, and she removed it. A clipping from the *Atlanta Constitution* slipped out. It pictured Gray with Scarlett Kavanagh. Fury knew Scarlett. They had both been on staff of the literary magazine at Agnes Scott. When she first saw the article, Fury had thought about contacting her former classmate, who was now an attorney in Atlanta. In school, their relationship had fallen somewhere between acquaintance and friend.

After pinning the article to the bulletin board above her desk, she wrote on her to-do list: "Call Scarlett."

Returning Gray's file to the cabinet, she turned her attention to a packet of Emma's pictures. Flipping through them, Fury noted that no one smiled when J.G. was in a photo. Sissy MacGregor had the look Fury recognized from a coterie of spoiled, rich girls—snobby and condescending. In contrast, the younger girl, Louisa, had a gentle look like her mother. Louisa married young, but according to an article in the *Arabella Gazette*, she and her first child died during childbirth.

By the end of the day, Fury felt like she was a member of the family. She felt their pain, their intimidation by the patriarch, and some of the joy in their accomplishments. She liked Graeme and Louisa, disliked Sissy, and was ambivalent about Martin, the youngest. Later she would discover that he died in the invasion of Normandy. Curiosity about what other relatives Gray might have arose when she realized that neither Louisa nor Martin had progeny.

Did Sissy marry and have children? Could she have been another victim of her father?

Returning to her computer for a search of the *Arabella Gazette*, Fury found Sissy's death notice. She died unmarried with no surviving children.

So, only the union of Graeme and Dorothy produced MacGregor grandchildren.

Later that night, Fury found Scarlett Kavanagh's number in the latest alumni directory and placed a call.

"What an unexpected treat to hear from you, Fury. I don't have to ask what you've been doing. I see your name all over the bestseller lists."

After exchanged pleasantries and updates, the two women made plans to meet at the same private club where Fury had entertained Caroline Elliot.

As soon as they were seated the following Thursday, Fury said, "Scarlett, I know you were shocked to hear from me, and I should be subtle, but you know I'm not. God forgive me." She crossed herself. "I'm Irish and missed the memo on social subterfuge."

Scarlett laughed. "I've got a bit of the Irish in me, too. My sisters got that memo, but I was absent at roll call as well."

"It is great to catch up with someone I spent so many hours with in college. I'm in awe of your law degree from Harvard, but what I really want to talk about is Gray MacGregor."

"Gray? Why would you—ohhh, you're dating him." Scarlett gave Fury a knowing look.

Fury nodded. "Sort of."

Scarlett smiled. "Hasn't everyone 'sort of' dated him?"

"That's what I guess I'm asking. I don't want to invest in worthless stock."

"Fury, Gray is the stray puppy that follows you home and then disappears when you're preparing his dinner."

"That bad, huh?"

Scarlett hesitated for a second. "I'm probably exaggerating. He was a nice date. I went out with him not long after a bad breakup. I was pretty damaged. If we didn't work out, it was as much my fault as his." She took a sip of water.

"We met at Harvard," Scarlett continued. "He had come back for a student-alum affair that I was chairing. It was about the time that he was building his reputation for being a financial maverick with incredible instincts."

"Maverick?"

"Oh, yeah. One of the big financial publications dubbed him 'a genius maverick with supernatural vision who always gets what he wants despite the odds.'"

"That's interesting. I knew that he was wealthy with multiple interests, but I had no idea that it was on that scale," Fury said.

"Believe me. It is. We linked up because we were both Georgians in New England. The dialogue led to dinner. I cannot say anything bad about him. He was quiet, not much personality, but you knew that behind those mysterious eyes was a blue-ribbon brain." Scarlett nodded as if to confirm her statement. "His personality was the opposite of my ex, but they are both smart and both damned good looking. We dated a few times when I was home for holidays, but never anything serious. I was in Cambridge, trying to extinguish a king-sized torch; he was in Atlanta. My mother was a lot more excited about him than I was. She saw a photo of *the* mansion—what is it called?"

"Forglen."

"Right. Mom had visions of her Scarlett ensconced in a pseudo-version of her beloved Tara. Mother is nuts about *Gone with the Wind*. But I knew that Gray wasn't permanent. We probably had only about six dates. It was a relationship of convenience. And no, I didn't sleep with him. I know girls who did, but I didn't join the club."

"So, you had more than the legendary two dates?"

Scarlett laughed. "I did. Trust me—they were never serious. I had the feeling that Gray MacGregor was looking for something and running from it at the same time. Of course, he's older now. That was five years ago."

"Soul sister to soul sister, would you advise me to run?"

Scarlett thought for a minute. "I can't say that I would. If you're still the Fury O'Quinn I knew at Agnes Scott, you can handle it. If it were to work out, I have the feeling that Gray MacGregor could be a good mate. Just keep one part of your heart locked up in case he pulls the disappearing act."

That night, Fury was taking her evening meal out of the microwave when the phone rang. It was Gray.

"What are you doing?"

"Making mad, passionate love to a frozen dinner."

"God, that's disgusting."

"Don't ask, if you don't want to know."

"You're going to learn to cook, Kate."

"Kate may learn, but I doubt that Fury ever will. What's on your mind tonight?"

"First, I want to firm up our plans for Saturday—dinner and the theater—and, I want to schedule time on your calendar for a tour of the quarry. Thought you might like to see where your ancestors worked."

"You know, I would. When do you have in mind?"

"Sunday. It's quiet out there on weekends."

"That sounds a little ominous—quiet at the quarry."

"The writer never rests."

"Could be the title of my book."

"That'll likely be the one that I don't read."

More than she wanted to admit, hearing his voice brought excitement to her evening.

The Saturday night date went very well. After the show, they dined at an upscale restaurant. When they reached the entry of her condo, Gray turned her around as she started to unlock the door, pulled her close, and kissed her—far more than a friendly goodnight kiss. Fury succumbed completely, but then pulled away abruptly.

"Relax," he whispered. "That was not the prelude to seduction. I won't muscle my way into your boudoir."

She looked up at him for a second, and then he pulled her back and kissed her again. The second time, she did not pull away. His hands roamed her body, but did not seriously breach decorum. She felt tears arise. Against her best judgment—she wanted him.

It was Gray who drew away the second time. "I'd better go before I do compromise you. Be ready at eleven, tomorrow morning. Dress comfortably." He brushed a tear from her cheek and the hair away from her forehead, quickly kissed the top of her head, and left.

Where is that protected section of my heart? And where the hell did the tears come from?

CHAPTER TWENTY

Sunday morning, Fury awoke at seven. *We crossed the line—platonic relationship gone.* She closed her eyes and tried to recapture the moment when he pulled her against his body with one hand, gently took her face in his other, and pressed his lips against hers, slowly and then passionately. *What am I doing? He is home delivery heartbreak.*

As she dressed, her heart raced. She fought the conflict of the growing attraction she had and the fear of ultimate rejection. *Scarlett said go for it but only seventy-five percent. How is that done?*

Gypsy jumped on the bed, and Fury scooped her up.

"I don't have the option of walking away, Gypsy-cat, not with the research at stake. What was it Dad once said about a case of his where the husband was murdered by his secretary-slash-lover? 'Don't dip your pen in the company ink.' Too late now. The ink is over my head and blinding me."

Once with Gray, the apprehension disappeared. The day at the quarry was delightful with breathtaking scenery and perfect weather. They dined on the way at a homespun café with great soul food and then again on the way home at the Irish pub. As they entered, a jovial man of about sixty-five stepped away from the bar.

"Fury. Fury O'Quinn. How's it going?" He threw his arms around her and gave her a bear hug.

"Shawn. I haven't seen you in forever."

"Saw your dad a few weeks ago. Said that his ticker took a dip in the homeland this year. Is he doing okay?"

"He is, and thank you for asking. I'll tell him that I saw you. Shawn Sullivan, this is my friend, Gray MacGregor."

Gray extended his hand. Shawn clasped it and shook vigorously. "Glad to meet you, Gray. This is a special little lass. Her dad taught me everything I know."

"Gray, Shawn and Dad were partners at the NYPD. Dad talked him into moving to Atlanta when he retired from the force."

"Fury. Is that you?" The female voice came from behind Fury.

She turned to face a bleached-blonde holding a mug of beer. "Maeve! You look gorgeous."

"Getting old, but staying the course. Say, hon, I read your new book. Great stuff, gal. How do you do it?"

"You're too kind. Cory says I have an imagination on steroids."

"Well, whatever, don't let it stop. Frank says they're the female equivalent of Viagra. Whenever he's in the mood, he sticks one of your books in front of me and says, 'read.'"

"You're making me blush. Where is Frank?"

"He got a call. Shawn and Kat are stuck with me."

Gray stood patiently, watching Fury interact with the patrons. After she introduced him to Maeve Carter, they went to their booth at the back of the pub.

"You seem to be well known."

"Remember the venue. Take an Irish girl to an Irish pub, and she is going to find people she knows. They are really my father's friends. I told you that I've been here with Dad."

Running into her father's friends made her nervous. She had kept so much from Mike and Cory about the route her relationship with Gray was taking and wasn't sure why. Up until that night, it had been compartmentalized, but with Maeve and Shawn meeting Gray, there was a possibility that Mike would find out. As Gray took a forkful of shepherd's pie, Fury watched, trying to analyze her feelings.

Why am I uneasy about my family knowing? We're not the Hatfields and McCoys or Capulets and Montagues.

After dinner, Gray returned her home. At the door, he laid out plans for the following weekend before repeating the intimacy of the preceding evening. She accepted that they would go out Friday and Saturday nights and drive to a horse show, south of Atlanta, on Sunday. During the week, he would be in New York for the meetings.

The two-date myth of Gray's reputation was broken, but Fury cautioned herself not to expect his interest in her to endure. Regardless of how many dates Gray had with previous women, he remained unmarried.

Enjoy his company while it lasts, but heed Scarlett's warning.

December 16th dawned, and Fury had still not told her sister that she was seeing Gray socially. Fortunately, Cory was distracted by wife and mom duties during the holidays. Fury awoke that morning, excited about the big party but nervous about the public disclosure of their relationship.

Stop obsessing. It'll be history before Cory finds out. She hardly knows Colleen and knows no one else in Arabella.

Her foot had healed to the point that she could wear high-heeled shoes. Her dress was Christmas green—a Neiman Marcus extravagance. She had wanted Cory's opinion but wasn't about to ask. Each time they spoke, Cory monopolized the conversation with talk about Christmas shopping, planning a holiday party for Suzi's class, and a staff soiree for Don's office.

"Why don't you come to the office party? You know most of the crew, and I haven't heard you mention any social events this month."

"It's just too much trouble with my ankle," Fury had lied. "Gypsy and I are going to have some quiet time. I have so much more reading of the journals and papers that I found at Forglen to do, plus I need to get ready for my book tour in February."

There is nothing to be gained by opening up something that will probably be history in a couple of weeks. With all the negative things I've told her about him, she would drive me crazy.

"We'll all be together for Christmas Eve. What can I bring?" Fury said.

"The same thing you always bring—your sparkling personality."

As Fury packed for the stay-over at Forglen, her mind wandered. After three pleasant weekends with Gray, she was falling into a comfort zone with him that frightened her.

I'm spending the night there—the house with many faces, dead and alive. Surely, there's no possibility that I will be put in J.G. and Emma's room or Bridget's. I feel like I'm wandering into a scene from a Bronte novel.

She felt butterflies birthing in her belly as she pulled out of the parking garage. She had not been to the house that week. Ella had made it clear that the staff would be overworked with party preparations, even though an Atlanta chef was catering the event. Fury was not about to push the envelope.

Hardly a block away from her condo, Gray called.

"I hope you slept well. It'll be a long night."

"I did, but maybe I'll take a power nap after I get there."

"Good idea. Just avoid Ella and the kitchen. She's armed with sharp knives and dangerous on party day."

Fury laughed. "I have no trouble believing that."

"This is her big moment every year. Be sure and tell her how beautiful the house is. If you think it's gaudy—lie. She thrives on glory."

"Gray, does Ella know that I'm your date?"

"I haven't given it much thought. She should have figured it out when I instructed her to prepare a room for you."

If Ella chose my room, I may be sleeping in the basement. Fury paused, still mystified by the nature of his relationship with the old woman. *She knew him first as a child. Now, he gives her instructions—yet, she calls him by his given name.*

"I hope I didn't add to her workload."

"Hardly. Drive carefully. Holiday traffic is bad, and you have a reputation for having a heavy foot."

She glanced down at the speedometer. It was registering ten miles over the posted limit. She immediately let up on the accelerator. "I'll try to keep it under a hundred. See you shortly."

Once at Forglen, Gray greeted her with enthusiasm. Showing her to her room, he said, "If you need anything, ring for Edward."

I wouldn't disturb anyone in this house, today, if my hair caught fire.

"Thanks."

"I'll come for you at six-twenty."

"But, I thought—"

"I let the majority of guests fill the house before going down."

Of course. Grand entrance. It's nice to be with the king. Please, God, don't let me trip on the red carpet. Fury immediately had a mental image of herself lying at the foot of the central staircase, her designer dress crushed, and Gray's guests standing around laughing. She almost laughed, but stifled it.

He leaned forward, kissed the top of her head, and left her to prepare.

Fury was ready at six-twenty. She had been ready since before six—time enough to second-guess every choice she had made: dress, shoes, and accessories. However, the expression on Gray's face eradicated her doubts when she opened the door.

"Perfect," he said, giving her a seductive look.

Fury was beautiful. The shade of green emphasized her red hair and actually made her blue eyes bluer.

He presented his elbow and said, smiling, "I would say 'break a leg,' but you might."

"I have a response for that, but I left my street vocabulary at home."

He laughed. "All kidding aside, you could not be more beautiful." Patting her hand, he said, "Let's give Arabella something to talk about."

Walking down the hall, Fury could hear the clamor of conversations coming from downstairs. When they reached the head of the steps and started down, a hush came over the house. Fury felt herself shiver. Every eye below stared up at the couple. As they neared the bottom, Fury caught a glimpse of Gladys. Still austere in her choice of clothing, she wore a black silk sheathe dress with a double strand of pearls. Her expression was not pleasant.

The other woman who hates me.

Reaching the floor, Gray dropped his arm and took Fury's hand.

People immediately began to cluster around him. As each person captured his attention, he introduced Fury, absent any explanation as to how she fit into his life. No one had the nerve to ask. Some recognized her name and commented on her career. After disengaging himself from the masses, Gray spotted his aunt.

"Come over this way. You can meet one of the few relatives I have."

The woman was about the age of Gladys. She was dressed in a purple dress that screamed for a red hat—the stereotypical, female senior citizen, distinguished only by the diamonds that dripped from every body part available.

Queen Elizabeth had better check the Tower of London. Some of the crown jewels have to be missing.

"Valerie, I'd like to introduce you to someone special. This is Fury O'Quinn, the author."

Special to him or special because I write?

"Delighted, my dear. I believe I've seen one of your books," the woman replied.

"I'll see that you have a full set under your tree for Christmas," Gray said.

Fury blushed. "I'm not sure that she would like my books."

"Nonsense," he said. "Valerie is a progressive woman, aren't you?"

The older woman, nodded.

I don't think so.

"Excuse us, Valerie. I believe that Fury needs a drink."

"It was very nice to meet you," Fury said.

Valerie nodded as the couple walked away.

"You didn't tell me her last name."

"MacGregor. She changed it back after her divorce."

It was obvious to Fury that he needed to work the room without her tagging along. "Gray, go ahead and do your thing. I'm a big girl and don't have to hang on to you."

He looked at her, obviously giving thought to her proposal. "Tell you what. I'll circle the crowd and catch up with you at dinner. It's only about five more minutes."

"Take your time." A waiter passed by with a tray of canapés. Fury took one and started toward the side of the room, hoping to find a seat, when she ran into Caroline Elliot.

"Hi, there," Caroline said. "I didn't expect to see you here. You're with Gray MacGregor?" Her tone registered genuine surprise.

"Good to see you," Fury responded, smiling. "I guess I am." She was glad to see a familiar face.

"When did that happen?"

"It's a long story."

"It can't be that long. You didn't know him when we had lunch a couple of months ago."

Fury thought she detected a dissonant note in Caroline's voice.

"Long story on fast forward, I guess you might say."

"Let's have lunch again, and you can share your secret weapon with me," Caroline said.

"That would be great. I think you have my number. Give me a call after the holidays."

Never happening. Talk to a reporter at this point? I don't think so. There was resentment in her tone. Was there more between her and Gray than she said?

A chime rang and everyone stopped. Gray walked to the staircase and went up a couple of steps. All eyes were on him. The house grew quiet. "I believe that we have been summoned to dinner. As usual, it's buffet. Fill your plates and enjoy. Edward will announce the guests who will join Ms. O'Quinn and me at the host table and those who will be seated with Aunt Valerie."

Everyone looked around for Fury, who stood by the piano, not sure of what her next move was supposed to be. *Am I supposed to know where the host table is? Wait for Gray? I needed to read the manual before I came.*

Her confusion did not last long. Gray separated the crowd and found his way to her.

No one tampered with the buffet until Gray and Fury reached the huge dining room. The room had been cleared of the usual furniture and filled with round tables. Serving tables lined two walls.

"The music room has also been set up with tables. Some of the guests will take their plates and disperse through the house," he said as he led her to the buffet.

When their dinner companions were finally seated, it turned out that Caroline and Gladys had been chosen for the host table. *Just my luck. Over one-hundred people here and I get to sit with those two. Is Ella joining us, too?*

CHAPTER TWENTY-ONE

Dinner went well. With Gray at the table, Gladys was exceedingly polite to Fury. Caroline was quiet. Shortly before nine, another bell chimed, signaling that the important phase—distribution of Christmas bonuses—would begin shortly. It was the cue for guests to take a break while the ballroom was cleared. Band members took their places where the instruments had been setup at the end of the room. The crowd appeared to know the procedure.

Gray presided over the presentations, assisted by Gladys. Once the coveted checks had been distributed, the music started and young couples began to fill the dance floor. The crowd thinned as a number of the elders departed, including Aunt Valerie. As earlier, Gray was kept busy with guests clamoring for his attention, leaving Fury to make small talk with strangers. She would have preferred to retreat to her room.

Once word spread as to who she was, readers in the crowd began to seek her out, which helped fill the awkward time. At one point, Gray broke free of his contingent and asked her to dance. It was a pleasant moment, but short-lived. When lights blinked at eleven-fifty-five, signaling the close of the evening, Fury was more than ready to escape the small talk. The band played "Goodnight Ladies" and guests began collecting coats.

When the last guest was gone, Gray took Fury's hand and led her to the study. As they entered the room, the memory of Bridget's letter flashed across her mind, causing her to briefly tense.

"I have something for you," Gray said, taking a gift-wrapped box from the lower drawer of the massive desk.

"It's early for a Christmas gift," she said as he handed it to her.

"It's not a Christmas gift. Open it."

Fury tore away the wrappings and lifted the cover of the box. Inside was the Saks Fifth Avenue chemise that she had tabbed in the catalog.

She looked up at him with a puzzled expression. "I hope this isn't a subtle way of inviting me to your room tonight."

"You should know by now that nothing I do is subtle. So before you assume that I'm attempting to violate your sacred boundary, look closer."

Pushing the tissue away, she saw a small velvet pouch with a gold drawstring nestled in the silk. Inside was an exquisite marquis-cut diamond solitaire. The size and brilliance of the stone was breathtaking. She held it for a second, not sure what to say.

"You didn't steal this from Aunt Valerie, did you?"

He smiled, took her left hand, and as he slid the ring on her finger, said, "Can you stop being a smart ass for a moment? I'm asking you to marry me."

She looked at the ring and then at him. "You've got to be kidding, and I'm not being a smart ass."

"I'm asking you to marry me, Fury O'Quinn. The gift—it's for our wedding night. I want to wakeup Christmas morning with you beside me."

"Are you serious? Marry you? Before Christmas? We only met three months ago. I'm not even sure that I like you."

He smiled. "You probably shouldn't—but you do."

She shook her head slowly. "This is surreal. You've dated at least half of Georgia's most beautiful women, and you ask me to marry you after a handful of dates? Are we on *Candid Camera*?"

He frowned. "Have you not learned, *yet*, that I don't play games? I want you for my wife, and my instincts say that you want me." He took both of her hands and looked into her eyes. "What I've known since the day we met is that you are different. You stirred something inside of me that scared the hell out of me and still does. I've never had this feeling before. For the record, this is our seventh official date, plus a few lunches. And don't forget, we spent nearly a week together in North Carolina under some pretty intimate circumstances."

Her blue eyes opened wide; her heart raced. "Well, you managed to conceal your thoughts very well."

"When I want something, I don't tip my hand until I know the key to making it happen. From the moment you walked into my house, everything about you captivated me. Not only are you beautiful and sexy as hell, you're smart, clever, successful, witty, annoyingly independent, unpredictable, brutally honest, totally committed to whatever you sign on for, and the only woman I've ever dated who would have the guts to call me out if needed."

"Really?"

"Really."

"What if I want a traditional wedding—the white dress, parties, family, and friends?"

"You don't."

"How would you know that?"

"I know you. You have more attention than you want in your career. I've hungered to take you to bed since North Carolina. It isn't going to happen until vows are exchanged, which I respect and is all the more reason that I feel the way I do."

"If you loved me, and I don't recall your ever mentioning that you do, you would be willing to wait a respectable length of time."

Gray was silent, his gaze holding hers.

Then he spoke, even softer than usual. "I love you. . . . I'm in love with you. I will wait, if I have to, but do you really *want* to wait?"

Again, the room was silent as she looked him straight in the eye. "No."

"Could you say that a bit louder?"

"I said, no. I don't want to wait."

"Good. We'll drive to Cashiers on Tuesday. There's no reason we can't be married by Thursday."

"Why not here—or Atlanta?"

"I want our marriage to begin where I first laid eyes on you."

"Hold on for a second. Before we do this, and I can't believe that

I'm actually considering it, we need to address a serious issue. Does this proposal package include children?"

He grinned. "Absolutely—as many as you're willing to have."

"Then, there's only one condition to my accepting."

He looked at her, turning his head slightly and frowning. "And just what is your condition?"

"You tell me about your family."

He was silent.

"It's a deal breaker, Gray. If I'm going to marry you and have your babies, I need to know what happened to your mother and why won't you talk about your father? It's as if you want me to believe that you dropped on the planet from Krypton. If you can't talk to me about this, how can you be my husband? Is your mother dead or alive?"

He looked her straight in the eye, pausing for a second before speaking. "I don't know."

"Just like that—you don't know?"

"Just like that."

"With your money and resources, you could find out with a snap of your fingers."

"I could, but I have no interest in knowing."

"Talk to me."

"I don't believe I'm doing this—but—you do have a right to know."

She watched him, completely entranced by his words.

"I was a marital asset, bought and sold like a piece of furniture."

Fury shook her head in disbelief. "You're going to have to explain that."

"Fifty-thousand dollars. That's all it took—all I was worth."

"I don't understand."

"Neither did I. One day, I had a mother. The next day, I didn't."

"What happened?"

"My father caught her in bed with the Forglen gardener. I was seven at the time and at school. When I came home, she was gone. I never saw her again."

"What made you believe that she sold you?"

"Oh, he made sure that I knew—showed me the $50,000 check with her signature on the back."

"That was cruel. Maybe it was a divorce settlement."

"A settlement that included leaving Arabella without me."

Fury looked at him, thinking before she spoke again. "Why do you blame her? Maybe it was as much your father's fault as hers."

"Without a doubt, but she didn't even try to fight him. She never tried to contact me as a child—never said goodbye. She walked away with her money and never looked back. She knew what an asshole he was and still left her child. Lord Jack only wanted to demonstrate his power and parade his trophy son around on state occasions. He didn't even like me. He looked at me and saw her. His hatred consumed him."

"But, he left you the estate."

"He had no one else. It had to stay in the hands of a MacGregor, even a half-breed MacGregor."

"Gray, I'm sorry. It must have been horrible for you when were just a little boy. But, you've only heard one side of the story. You're smart enough to know that there's always another side."

"Look. This is not a poor-little-rich-boy fest. I've said all I'm going to say, which is more than I've ever told anyone. People assume that Zaira is dead—that she died in 1977. I like to keep it that way."

"And your father—your relationship with him?"

"That's definitely a story you don't want to hear, and one I'm not going to tell. Drunk, abusive Jack MacGregor—king of the colony. You would be smart to run. This is one hell of a dysfunctional family you are fooling around with. I shouldn't even think about inviting you into the fray."

It was the only sign of vulnerability Fury had seen in Gray. It brought forth a realization that beneath the surface of the man who appeared to have everything was a man lacking in the most fundamental need of all—the love of a family. "You're not them. You're your own person."

"I'm a product of at least four generations of self-centered, ruthless men, and an adulterous woman who was willing to abandon her only child. Not a good gene pool to perpetuate."

"You are not responsible for the acts of your ancestors. I couldn't feel the way I do about you if you didn't have character and a conscience." Reaching up to touch his face, she added, "Don't forget, if we have children, they will be half Irish."

He smiled. "Yes." He nodded. "Yes, they will. But, I caution you, this is a no escape contract. You sign on with me, have my child, and it's for life—no loopholes. I will not subject a child to a broken home. Can you do it with that knowledge?"

"Absolutely."

He smiled, took her in his arms, and held her tight. As they separated, she asked, "How did your father keep the story about your mother quiet?"

"He owned Arabella. No one dared cross or question him."

"And you own it now."

He shook his head. "I don't look at it that way."

"It was pretty obvious to me from the party tonight. Eighty percent of the town works for one of the MacGregor businesses."

"They are what they are. My focus is the global divisions—the network that I've created."

"What about prenuptial agreements?"

"I don't need one, but if you feel that you do, have it drawn up."

"Well, don't think this ring is a free pass into my bedroom tonight. You're going to have to tough it out a few more days."

He smiled. "I wouldn't have it any other way." He took her face in his hands, gently pulled her closer, and kissed her."

Fury left Forglen after breakfast the morning after the party. Her thoughts were going round like laundry on the spin cycle. *We're getting married. What am I doing? Am I insane? What will I wear? What about Gypsy?*

She stopped for a traffic light and dug her cell phone out of her purse. Gray answered on the second ring.

"Where are we going to live?"

"Hello, Kate."

"Gray, where are we going to live?"

"Where would you like to live?"

"I get to choose?"

"We have four residences between us. If none of those works, we can buy a new one. I think we can figure something out."

"I'm serious. What if Apache and Gypsy aren't compatible? Apache is huge; she could kill Gypsy. I won't give my cat up or put her in jeopardy."

"Calm down. We'll figure it out. I expect that we'll spend as much time as possible in North Carolina, but, to start, I'll move in with you and Gypsy at your condo until we decide. Apache can stay at Forglen until we learn how to make it work with them."

"My condo is probably the smallest place of all."

"I think you have room for me. A bed, a shower, and a decent kitchen should take care of it. Now hang up. You're driving."

As they hung up, sunlight caught the diamond on her finger, dispersing streaks of light. Dropping the phone in her open handbag, her mind raced.

I can't believe that it is happening, but I've never felt this way before. I pray that I'm not making a mistake, but I can't help myself. I want him.

CHAPTER TWENTY-TWO

"Are you sure you don't want your family at the ceremony?" Gray asked on Sunday evening as they made their final plans for the trip. "I will arrange for a car to drive them up and make reservations at the inn."

"No. I'll tell them afterward."

"Are you sure?"

"Gray, this is my wedding week. I want to enjoy every second of it. As much as I love my sister, I don't want her making the week miserable by trying to talk me out of it because she is over protective and can't choose which roll of paper towels to buy without a Congressional investigation."

With a local magistrate officiating, the ceremony took place on December 21, 2006 at five p.m. in front of the stone fireplace. Robert Wilson, the groundskeeper, and his wife, Jeanette, served as witnesses. At Gray's request, Jeanette had arranged for the flowers and the catered dinner.

Fury wore a winter-white, wool sheath dress. Gray wore a navy suit, white shirt, and striped tie. They made a handsome couple. Anyone looking at the photos, taken by the Wilson's teenage son, would never have guessed that the service was put together in five days.

After dinner, the Wilsons and the magistrate left. Gray took off his jacket and loosened his tie. He then prepared a tray with a bottle of chilled champagne, two long-stemmed, crystal flutes, a plate of caviar, crackers, strawberries, and a small bowl of assorted nuts. "May I escort you to the honeymoon suite, Mrs. MacGregor?"

"Why don't you give me a few minutes to freshen up and change into something more comfortable, and I'll meet you there?" she said, tipping her head in a coquettish manner.

He smiled, giving her a look that generated a rush of heat through her body.

As Fury climbed the stairs to the room where she had stayed before, her knees felt weak.

This is it. For better or worse, I'm his wife. With her hands trembling, she took the gown he had given her out of the closet and stroked the fabric. Putting it over her arm, she took a silk peignoir from a hanger and a pair of slippers from the shelf, and then went into the bathroom for a quick shower. The warm water ran down her body, enhancing the sensuous feeling that encompassed her. When finished, she dried off and stepped out onto the soft mat. Slipping into the chemise, Fury stood for a second, gazing at her reflection in the mirror on the back of the door and then looked down at the ring on her left hand. *I'm about to go downstairs and go to bed with my husband.* She shuddered with anticipation. Brushing her hair and spraying a light mist of fragrance, she put on the negligee and the satin mules.

The heels of her slippers made a slight clicking sound when striking the wood floor as Fury approached the staircase. The memory of tripping on the stairs that night weeks before flashed across her mind. *Take your time and hold on to the bannister. Don't spoil the evening by falling again.* As she reached the top of the stairs, she heard the passionate sound of "This is the Moment" coming from sound system below—was it coincidence or design?

He stood at the bottom, sleeves rolled up and shirt unbuttoned. As she descended, he raised his arm to take her hand. As she stepped onto the floor, he led her into the living room that was now illuminated only by candles and the crackling fire. Swirling her in front of him, he grasped her around the waist and pulled her tight against his body, swaying, and then dancing to the music. Fury felt as though she had dissolved in his arms, his grip was powerful, his scent musky. As the momentum of the song built, he swept her up and carried her to the master bedroom.

The champagne tray sat on the dresser, but Gray ignored it. Approaching the king-sized bed, he eased her gently to her feet. A candle on the night table and one on the dresser gave a soft glow to the room. An arrangement of roses infused the air with a fragrant aroma. Fury stood in front of him, waiting for his next move. He untied the belt of her peignoir, and it fell open. His eyes held hers as he slowly dropped the garment from her shoulders, letting it cascade to the floor. For a minute or more, he looked up and down her motionless stature, covered only by the wispy floral silk. Candlelight backlit her red hair, creating a halo.

"Exactly as I imagined," he whispered and slowly he moved one of the tiny straps off her shoulder and then the other. Her heart beat as though she had run a marathon; she quivered. Gray dropped his shirt to the floor and unbuckled his belt, whipping it out of the loops and discarding it to the floor as well. Fury instinctively reached for the button of his trousers, easing the button free and sliding the zipper down. As his pants fell, he pulled her close and she could feel his desire separated from hers by only a thin layer of fabric.

It was then that he picked her up and laid her on the bed, positioning his body over hers. The music swelled to a crescendo.

His hands caressed her body gently, while his lips kissed her with intense passion. Fury wanted him—wanted him like she had never wanted anyone. His hands were everywhere, stroking and teasing her senses. His fingers found places no longer forbidden and stimulated every nerve ending in her being. Without releasing her, he maneuvered deftly out of his briefs.

When she thought she could stand the anticipation no longer, she felt him—taking her to an unimagined euphoria.

Afterward, they lay relaxed for several minutes. Then pulling her close, he whispered, "Till death do us part, my love."

Fury was spent. She couldn't speak. The nerves in her fingertips pulsated. She had wanted to scream.

After several minutes, Gray said, "Are you okay?"

She nodded.

He brushed the hair away from her face. "I didn't hurt you, did

I?"

She shook her head, still unable to speak. He took her chin in his hand and kissed her, long and hard. Her body automatically conformed to his, and they lay together until each fell asleep.

In less than an hour, Gray woke, slipped off the bed, put on a black terry robe from his closet, and poured a glass of champagne. One candle had burned out. The music loop still played. Fury opened her eyes. "Can I pour you some barely chilled champagne?" he asked.

She smiled and nodded, clutching a sheet for modesty. He picked up her lingerie from the floor, handed it to her, and then turned toward the dresser. Bringing the tray to the bed, he put it down, and they nibbled on the snacks and sipped the champagne. "To my beautiful wife . . . Fury MacGregor," he said, raising his glass to hers. "May our union always be as perfect as our first night."

They each took a swallow. He leaned toward her, kissed her, and then whispered, "I truly love you, Fury MacGregor—as I've loved no one before. Never doubt that."

She looked down at the rings on her finger. "I believe you."

The following day, they slept in. When they woke, Gray made love to her again before getting up and preparing a gourmet brunch of eggs benedict with crabmeat and Canadian bacon, potatoes with cheese, and fresh fruits.

"Would you like to go sightseeing or stay in?" he asked as they finished the meal.

"I'm okay with staying in. We're got a full weekend ahead."

He smiled, obviously pleased with her response. "We'll relax all day and then go into Highlands for dinner. I made a reservation earlier this week."

As they drove back to Atlanta on Saturday morning, Fury said, "It was a perfect wedding, intimate and personal to us. I know Cory is going to be upset that she didn't know and wasn't included, among other things, but I'm glad we did it the way we did."

Gray reached across the console and patted her leg. "You won't hear any argument from me."

Before going to Fury's home, they stopped by Forglen for Gray to pick up the clothing and possessions he would need. Although his Atlanta condo was well stocked, he wanted a few items from the house.

"Are you going to tell Ella and Edward?"

He smiled. "Not yet."

After taking the luggage into the condo, Gray kissed Fury and said that he needed to check on a few things at the office, but would be home by six."

As soon as he left, she dialed Cory. After the usual amenities were exchanged, Fury said, "I'm bringing someone with me tomorrow night, if it's okay with you.

"That takes me by surprise, but of course it's okay. Who are you bringing?"

"I want it to be a surprise."

"Fury. You can't leave me in suspense."

"I just did."

"Come on. Tell me. You've never brought anyone to our Christmas Eve celebration."

"Give it up, Cory. I'm not saying, but don't go to any extra trouble—just set another place at the table. I know you'll have plenty of food."

Cory made one more attempt to pry the name of the mystery guest out of her sister, but Fury was steadfast. "It's only one day. You'll survive," Fury said as they hung up. *I know you're frustrated, Cory, but I'm not going to be engaged in a telephone interrogation.*

CHAPTER TWENTY-THREE

Gray and Fury arrived at the Reynolds' house at six o'clock on Christmas Eve. Mike's car was in the driveway.

"Here we go. I hope you're prepared to face the music," Fury said as Gray pulled the SUV in behind her father's vehicle.

"I'm pretty tough. I just hope that your dad isn't carrying a gun tonight."

"It's not my father you have to worry about. Cory is the one that you had better fear. Watch your back; she's sneaky."

The house was aglow with Christmas decorations. A life-size nativity stood on the front lawn, illuminated by spotlights. Clear lights outlined the roof of the home; and a cedar wreath, accented with a large, red-velvet bow, hung on the entry. The bell had barely chimed when Cory, flanked by the two girls, opened the door with a big smile on her face. When she saw Gray, her expression changed instantly.

"Cory, I would like you to meet my husband, Gray MacGregor." Disregarding the shock on her sister's face, Fury leaned forward and put an arm around each child, pulling them close. "Suzi, Sandi, this is your Uncle Gray."

Gray had extended a hand to his shocked sister-in-law, whose manners denied her the ability to decline his gesture.

"He's our uncle, Aunt Fury?" Suzi said.

"He is. We were married on Thursday."

Turning toward the living room, Cory called out, "Dad. Come here. Your younger daughter has something to tell you—she's married."

Mike put down the cup of cider he was drinking and moved quickly toward the entry hall.

"Do you mind if we come in out of the cold?" Fury asked.

Cory shook her head in contrast to her response. "Of course. Come in." Watching the couple pass into the foyer, her face had the judgmental look of a great horned owl—dilated pupils and V-shaped brows.

Gray was silent, observing Fury as they slipped off their heavy coats and hung them over hooks on the hall tree.

"This is such a shock that I don't know what to say," Cory blurted out.

Turning around to face her sister, Fury said, "For a starter, why don't you try, 'Best wishes, Fury. I'm so happy for you.' And, 'Congratulations, Gray, you've got a great gal.'"

"Right. But don't you think you might have told us, maybe even included the rest of your family in your wedding?"

Mike had reached the group, with Don trailing behind. "What am I hearing, me girl? You're married?"

Fury's head bobbed up and down, a huge smile on her face. "I am, Dad. I'm Mrs. J. Graeme MacGregor, IV." She extended her left hand for him to see the diamonds blazing across her finger like Christmas lights.

Gray extended his hand to shake Mike's. For a moment, Fury held her breath as to what her father's reaction would be.

"Damn. That's *great* news, me boy," Mike said, vigorously shaking Gray's hand with his right, while holding Fury's with his left. "Welcome to the O'Quinn clan."

"Fury, how could you do this without us? You two have known one another less than six months."

"Hush up, Cory. This is a grand occasion. Don, do you have anything we can toast these kids with?" Mike asked as Don shook Gray's hand, introducing himself.

Don retreated to the small refrigerator in the den bar and returned with a bottle of champagne. "Just so happens that the parents of a patient gave me this for Christmas. How timely was that?" He popped the cork. "Cory, could you find us some glasses?"

Still in a daze, Cory went to the breakfront in the dining room and returned with five champagne flutes.

"Mommy, can we have some?" Suzy asked.

"Not on your life."

"I'll get them some of their champagne. You get glasses," Don said.

"Theirs will be ginger ale," Fury whispered to Gray.

Mike hugged Fury and then turned and slapped Gray on the back. "You think you can handle this one, son? She's a handful."

Gray smiled. "Couldn't agree with you more, but I think I have it under control."

When all the glasses were filled, Mike raised his toward the newlyweds. "To me baby daughter and her new husband: 'May your mornings bring joy and your evenings bring peace. May your troubles grow few as your blessings increase.' Your sainted mam is looking down with her smile for the two of you." As he spoke the last sentence, he raised his chin and gazed upward.

"Amen," Don said. "To Fury and Gray, may your future be filled with love and prosperity."

Cory was silent but clinked her glass with the others and drank the champagne. Finishing the liquid, she turned to her sister.

"How about helping me out in the kitchen."

"Sure." Fury squeezed Gray's hand. "Dad and Don can entertain you with crazy stories about me while I'm gone. Believe only half of what Dad says." She winked and followed Cory.

Closing the kitchen door, Cory turned to Fury. "What in the name of God have you done?"

Fury shrugged. "I got married. It's what you've been telling me that I should do for a long time."

"Don't be obtuse. You don't know this man. I've never heard you say that you've even had a date with him. You've said yourself that he's a controlling womanizer—and with everything that you've found out about his deviant family. I thought you disliked him. What were you thinking?"

"Slow down. I know him a lot better than I've shared with you. And those were my *first* impressions. They were not accurate. And, yes, it appears crazy. But, trust me on this. It felt right. It still feels right."

Cory shook her head. "It can't be true. You can't really have done this. It must be a prank. You're going to say, 'gotcha' in a second or two."

"I really did it, Cory. Look at the rings. Read my lips. He's my husband—signed, sealed, and consummated."

"You're Catholic."

Fury crossed herself. "I'm also free, over twenty-one, and Irish. I think I know all that. Gray is willing to convert. We'll have a religious service, or renewal of vows, whatever; you can even plan it."

"Fury, what do you know about him?"

"Cory, do you think I'm completely stupid?" Cory was nodding as Fury continued. "I know more about him, good and bad, than you knew about Don when you got married. I've spent time with him that you don't know about. I've dug into his past; I've been in his home—three of them as a matter-of-fact. He's a good guy. I know it. And incidentally, I'm head over heels in love with the man."

"That's what I'm afraid of. Hormones are driving the boat; common sense be damned."

"Can we table this? It's Christmas Eve. The girls are waiting to open gifts, and we should be celebrating. I know you're hurt that I didn't tell you, but we wanted it low key and private between the two of us. A traditional wedding would have attracted more attention than either of us wanted. This was the best way."

"Be honest. You knew that I would try to talk you out of it—talk some sense into you." Cory took a deep breath. "It's going to take some getting used to, but I suppose there's nothing to do about it now but hope for the best. You do look happy."

Fury embraced her sister. "Thank you. You know I love you."

When they returned to the living room, the girls were showing Buttons to Gray. He took the kitten and gently scratched the little head. Buttons purred and thrust her face against his hand.

"She likes you, Uncle Gray," Suzi said.

"And I like her as well. She reminds me of Gypsy," Gray said, smiling at the two children.

"She's Gypsy's little sister," Sandi said.

"Now, which of you is which?"

"I'm Sandi. I'm the oldest. She's the baby, Suzi."

"I'm not a baby," the little one said.

"Girls, take Buttons back to your room. We're almost ready for dinner." Cory turned to Gray. "They'll drive you crazy, if you let them."

"They're fine," he replied, smiling at the sister-in-law who was far from ready to make him a member of her family.

"The house is beautiful, as always," Fury said, hoping to put the focus back on the holiday and not her husband.

"Just the usual," Cory responded. "Does anyone want anything else to drink before we have dinner?"

Everyone agreed that they were fine, knowing that the girls wanted to get to their gifts. Cory asked Mike to say grace, and the family stood and joined hands. Gray was between the two girls, who were obviously captivated with their new uncle.

Fury watched her husband with a warm feeling, seeing his positive interaction with the children. Cory's eyes followed, suspicion written all over her face.

Finishing the blessing, Mike said, "Father, bless this family and especially the marriage of these young people. May they live long and have healthy little ones. Amen and happy Christmas."

The family echoed the last sentence.

The Reynolds' dining room table was covered with the traditional Irish dishes. A large ham anchored the south end with a turkey at the north. Roasted potatoes and assorted vegetables lined the sides. On the credenza, Cory's best china, silver, and cloth napkins were waiting. A teacart held the Christmas pudding, Bailey's Irish Crème cheesecake, and mince pie. Don carved the turkey; Mike carved the ham. A platter of spiced beef was already sliced. Sandi turned on the audio system, and the soft sound of holiday music filled the house. The festivities had been choreographed many years before, and everyone fell into their respective roles. Fury handed Gray a plate.

"The food looks delicious, Cory," Gray commented.

"Don't be expecting your *wife* to cook," Cory replied. "She doesn't know the difference between an egg beater and a can opener."

Gray smiled. "We've talked about it. There have been no misrepresentations."

"Full disclosure, Cory. You can't tell on me. He knows all my flaws."

As the family scattered with their plates filled, Fury relaxed. Cory seemed to be reconciled to the situation. However, the bride knew that there would be another interrogation down the road.

When everyone had finished eating, the family gathered around the tree in the den. Gray went to the car and brought in gifts. He had added a gift certificate to each one chosen by Fury. She insisted that he offer their gifts to the girls, who were more than thrilled with the dolls found in their packages. Both threw their arms around Gray and Fury.

If only adults were as accepting as children.

"Gray, we would have had gifts for you if my sister had bothered to let us know she had a husband," Cory said.

He smiled. "Marrying your sister is the best and only gift I need."

By the end of the evening, although he was reticent, Gray had won the approval of all but Cory. He had exceeded Fury's expectations with his social skills, in contrast to her initial interaction with him.

Fury did not speak with Cory again until Tuesday morning. Her cell phone rang at nine-thirty.

"I'm coming to Atlanta to have lunch with you," Cory announced when Fury answered.

"Did I hear an invitation in there somewhere?"

"Don't fool around with me. We are going to talk."

"As if I didn't know this was coming. Okay. Let's get it over with. I'll meet you at Cheesecake at one-thirty. The crowd should have thinned by then."

"Where are you living? I don't even know where you are."

"I'll bring you a list of all my addresses and phone numbers. Right now, we're staying in my condo."

Cory was at the restaurant when Fury arrived.

"You're late."

"My God, Cory. It's one-thirty-five. Fine me."

Before Cory could say more, the waitress arrived with Cory's glass of tea and asked for Fury's beverage order. When she walked away, Cory fired her first question.

"What the hell have you done?"

Fury held up her left hand. "Isn't that a little redundant?"

"What possessed you? Did he drug you?"

"He did not. I fell in love. Totally in love, and I took the brass ring . . . maybe not quite brass . . . ," she paused, looking at the diamonds on her finger, "and ran with it. Why can't you be happy for me?"

"Because I'm terrified. For months, you've been digging into this man's background. You've shown me page after page of information— all of it negative. You've complained about how arrogant, rude, controlling he is, and now you've married him? It would have been bad enough to marry a choirboy you knew only a few months—but Gray MacGregor? Has it occurred to you that he might have married you to prevent you from exposing his deviant family?"

"No, it has not. He has done *nothing* to discourage me from writing my book. He opened his house to me—even clued me in on a place to look that I had not thought of. He could have stopped me at any time."

"He may be just too smart for you."

"Cory, I know you love me. I know you want to protect me. That's the only reason I'm sitting here listening to you bash my husband. Don't push it. Try to trust me."

Cory played with her silverware, contemplating her next response.

"Tell me one reason that gives you cause to trust him."

"I sprained my ankle at his North Carolina house, not at my condo, in October. He was there. I didn't tell you, because you would have thrown a fit. When it happened, he picked me up gently, like I was a baby, and carried me to the car, demanding that I receive immediate medical attention. He waited on me for five days, preparing my meals and delivering them to me. He never made an inappropriate move."

Cory looked at her sister with disbelief written all over her face.

"I wanted to tell you when I got home, but something kept me from talking about it. I think that I was falling for him and was even afraid to admit it to myself. I know he can be annoying, but there's a kindness behind that thick skin and curt personality. I've seen his tender side. Didn't you see how he was with the girls and Buttons?"

"I don't know what to think. I don't know the man, and I'm not convinced that you know him well enough. You have to promise me that you will always be honest with me. If you suspect anything, if he is in any way abusive to you, you have to promise to tell me. Promise."

"That's an easy promise to make. You have my word."

"And you have my prayers that I am off-base and that you will have a wonderful marriage. Have you talked about children?"

"We have. He wants children, and he is committed to the idea that his children will never suffer a broken home."

"That begs the question of would you publish a book that blemishes your children's name with his family history?"

CHAPTER TWENTY-FOUR

As she drove back to the condo, following lunch with Cory, Fury mulled over the conversation. Although she refused to give credence to Cory's comments, her sister's attitude toward Gray cast a shadow on the bride's marital bliss and carved a nick in their sisterly relationship.

Why can't she be happy for me? Gray marrying me to block my writing the book is ludicrous. With her negative attitude, I don't think I want to talk to her for a while.

Despite her faith in her husband's motive, by midafternoon, she had resolved to have a serious conversation with Gray about her book. It was nearly six o'clock before he arrived at the condo. She was in her little office, reading some of the MacGregor articles.

"How was your day, Kate?" he said, bending over to kiss her.

"Unexceptional. How was yours?"

"Rather calm for the last week of the year. Why don't we go out for dinner? I have a craving for a glass of wine and good Italian food. How does that sound to you?"

"As long as I don't have to help cook, it sounds perfect."

"I'll let you off the hook tonight. But, you *are* going to learn how to cook my dinner, Mrs. MacGregor."

"As long as you realize that it could be dangerous to your health."

He grinned, "A risk I'll have to take." He then squeezed her shoulders affectionately. "Be ready in ten, after I grab a quick shower and shake off the CEO mode."

"Should I change?" she asked as he walked out of the room. She was wearing a pair of burgundy corduroy jeans and a bulky, cream-colored turtleneck sweater.

"You're fine," he shouted, without turning around.

Looking at the piles of notebooks, files, and papers scattered around the room, she became acutely aware of the awkwardness of her delving into the scandals of his family history. He had not appeared to pay any attention to the voluminous data she had collected. However, living in the condo gave him full access to her work, including her files on him and his parents. Would he go through the office? If he did, would he be angry that she had dug so deeply into his personal life? *Maybe I should lock my file cabinet.*

They went to a cozy restaurant in the neighborhood for dinner. Fury wanted to bring up the subject of her research all through the meal but the words kept refusing to come out.

"Where are you, Irish?" Gray asked as they waited for the server to bring the order of tiramisu they planned to share.

"What do you mean?"

"The sparkle is absent from your eyes tonight."

"Maybe it's the lighting in here."

"Maybe."

He gave her a look that she had come to recognize as meaning that he knew she was not being completely candid.

"Or maybe you'll tell me what's on your mind when we get home."

She smiled. "You know, Gray MacGregor, your ability to read people can be annoying at times."

Returning the smile, he said, "Never said I was perfect."

When they reached the condo, Fury hung their coats in the hall closet and started to turn out lights. Gray came up behind her, put his arms around her waist, and whispered, "Tell me what's bothering you and don't try to deny it."

She turned and looked into his eyes for a few seconds before taking his hand and leading him to her office. Turning on the light, she made a sweeping gesture with her free hand. "See? All of this is research on our families—your family, even you. Some of it isn't pretty. Do you want me to stop?"

He drew her close, pressing her body against his, and then pulled her head against his chest. "No. No, my love. I don't want you to stop. It's who you are—part of the woman I fell in love with. Do what you need to do, just don't talk to me about it."

"Do you want to look at any of these papers?"

"No."

"I have a file on you—a"

"Of course you do."

"And one on your mother."

He stiffened slightly. "I would expect that."

"Do you have a problem with it?"

The room was quiet for what seemed like an eternity. Gray loosened her arms from around his back, took her by the hand, and led her to the sofa in the living room. Fury trembled, fearing she had pushed him too far.

When they were seated and facing one another, he held one of her hands in his and brushed away the tears on her cheek with his free hand. "There is no elephant here. You are free to investigate as you require. I will not interfere with your work. You do not need my permission to write your book. I will not censor or monitor you. However, I will not contribute, participate, or discuss it—especially anything about the couple responsible for my birth. I do not want to read any of the material that you collect and cannot promise you that I will ever read what you write or publish. As far as I'm concerned, the data in your office is research on the sex life of South African bullfrogs." He pulled her close and hugged her tight as she clung to him. He stroked her hair for a few seconds and then began to caress her body. "Now, go put on my favorite gown," he whispered, "so I can exercise the privileges of marriage."

As she stood to prepare for bed, she looked at him and said, "I've been meaning to ask. How did you get so good at those privileges?"

He grinned. "By following your manuals."

"What manuals?"

"Your novels. They are handbooks on how to please a woman, aren't they?" He slapped her playfully on her rear. "Now, hurry up and get ready for bed. I need more practice."

It was a good night, and Fury woke the next morning with a sense of relief. Gray was already in the kitchen, making coffee. She put on the silk negligee, stooped to pet Gypsy, and walked to the kitchen.

"You're up very early," she said, taking a mug from the tree on the counter. "It's only five-fifteen."

"Yesterday was calm, but I'm going to be with accounting today, tying up the year. Don't wait to have dinner with me. I probably won't be home before bedtime." He put his coffee cup down and pulled her to him with one hand while running the other down the silk covering her naked body. "I'll try to make it up to you when I get here."

"I'm going to hold you to that."

Gray was gone by five-thirty. When he left, Fury curled up on the sofa with her coffee and the morning paper. The thought of Cory crossed her mind. She wanted to call her sister and describe the conversation with Gray but knew that it would only create a debate. *She's not ready to accept him. Why give myself more stress?*

Gypsy jumped up onto her lap, purring.

"You want your breakfast, don't you, girl? What do you think of Gray?"

The cat thrust her face against Fury's hand, her paws kneading her mistress's leg.

"You don't have to answer. I've seen you make yourself at home in his lap. I just hope that you and Apache are compatible." Putting the cat on an empty cushion, Fury got up and took her cup to the kitchen. Gypsy followed.

As the cat sprang up onto the kitchen bar, Fury rinsed out the feline's water bowl and refilled it. "I think I'll call Dad and invite him to have dinner with me. I need some family TLC."

Fury and Mike met that evening at Patrick's Pub, the place where she and Gray had run into his friends. After a bear hug, they sat in one of the rear booths—Mike with a glass of Guinness and Fury with a cup of tea.

"So, my baby girl is a married woman," he said, grinning. "I like your man."

"Do you, Dad? Cory's giving me a hard time."

"Cory's got your mam's edge of suspicion and feels she has to look out for you. She'll come round."

"She suggested that Gray married me to stop the book from being written."

Mike shook his head. "I hardly think that would be the case. There would be many less drastic ways to keep his family secrets. On the soul of St. Paddy, I swear the man could buy up all the copies and use them for kindling if he wanted to end it. Besides, I saw the way he looks at you. The man loves you. I've no doubt."

Fury grinned and reached across the table for his hand. "Do you know how much I love you?"

"I have a bit of a notion. But tell me, lass, when will you let the world know that you're married?"

"I ordered engraved announcements today. We're going to tell Gray's people after New Year's and send announcements to the press right after that. I'm staying away from Forglen until the staff there knows. I don't think that Gray's housekeeper likes me. She's a little intimidating."

"Since when has my feisty daughter been intimidated by anyone?"

"Both Ella and Gray's executive secretary make me uneasy. They both think he's their property. Ella has been at Forglen since he was a little boy. I think she was a surrogate mother to him. Gladys, his secretary, is used to shielding him from intruders. They both feel like they ride the inside rail. I don't think that I've done anything to either one of them, although I was a little pushy with Gladys at first. But, I believe it's more of a territorial issue."

"You'll handle them. And if you can't, I think Gray will take care of it. You're the wife, which outranks secretary, housekeeper, and even mother."

"Speaking of mothers, Gray's mom may be alive."

"May be?"

"He hasn't seen her since he was seven years old. It's a complicated story, but I want to find out what happened to her."

Mike gave her a quizzical look. "And how does the husband feel about you looking for his mum? I would expect that he could have found her a good bit ago, if he had wanted."

"He didn't and doesn't want to now."

Mike frowned. "Are you sure you want to go there? Might cause trouble in your marriage."

"We talked about my research. He says that he does not care what I do as long as I don't involve him. He said that if I were a medical examiner, he would not want to hear me describe an autopsy."

"He may say that, but it still makes me uncomfortable. It sounds like it's a raw spot in his life."

"It is. But, Dad, she is the only grandmother our children will have. I need to know what really happened that drove her away from Arabella. Will you help me?"

"You want me to help?"

"You're a cop. You've done PI work—tracked down bail jumpers. You know private investigators. I can't find a trace of her after 1977. I want to hire you."

"I'll not be taking wages from me daughter."

"You will, or I'll hire someone else."

Mike muttered something under his breath.

"What did you say, Dad?"

"I said MacGregor's got his hands full with you."

Fury laughed. "I'm a chip off your block as Mum used to say. So don't go throwing stones."

He nodded. "When do I start?"

"I'll put together a packet of the information I have on her and send it over to you. We're going to squeeze in a honeymoon trip to Paris before I start my book tour. We'll be gone about ten days in late January. You can take your time. There's no deadline."

"Paris. Nice."

"I know. We're going to make a stop in Ireland on the way back. I want to introduce Gray to Evanne, Aunt Mary, and the rest of the family. We're also going to make a quick trip to Scotland to see the original Forglen."

"Sounds like you've got it all covered."

"Dad, please don't say anything to Gray about this. I don't feel like I'm going behind his back, but he doesn't like talking about his family. So, please, please be discreet."

"Like the CIA, I'll be."

New Year's Day, Fury and Gray drove to Forglen. He had called ahead and asked Ella to prepare lunch for four. He had driven over twice during the week to check on Apache. Each time, he made certain that Gypsy had been on the clothes he wore, hoping that the dog would become familiar with her scent and thereby ease the eventual introduction.

When they entered the kitchen, Ella greeted them with her usual cool reserve. "When will your guests be arriving?"

"They're actually here, Ella. You and Edward are joining Fury and me for lunch."

The old woman's forehead furrowed. "Joining you and Miss O'Quinn?"

"That's what I said. Call us when you're ready."

While Fury freshened up, Gray took out a towel from her tote bag that Gypsy had slept on the day before. When Apache came to him, he held the fabric out for the dog to sniff, while petting her and reassuring her that she was a good dog. She nuzzled the material.

Shortly after Fury returned to the bedroom, Edward came to announce that lunch was ready. While Gray had shared informal meals with his staff in the kitchen, it was the first time Edward and Ella had been invited to dine in the formal room. It was obvious to Fury that they both felt a little uncomfortable. Both stood until Gray took his place at the head of the table. He motioned for Fury to join him to the right and Ella to the left. Edward took the remaining seat next to Fury.

"You're both wondering why we're all having lunch together, I can tell."

Ella nodded, while Edward remained motionless.

"It's because I have an announcement."

Before he could say more, Fury could see that Ella was knowingly anticipating his announcement. Her expression was less than pleasant.

"Ms. O'Quinn did me the great honor of becoming my wife on December 21st. I'd like you both to welcome her as the new mistress of Forglen."

Edward's expression was a combination of shock and pleasure. Ella's was forced acceptance.

"Congratulations, Gray, and welcome, Mrs. MacGregor," Edward said.

"Call me Fury, Edward. I'm looking forward to spending a lot of time here."

Ella sat frozen. Fury had not expected a welcoming hug, but Ella's reaction left her speechless. After a minute or so of silence, Gray said, "We haven't decided where our primary residence will be, but we'll likely be spending more time here than in the past."

Fury turned to Ella. "I'll try not to be any trouble for you, and I hope you'll help me learn a thing or two in the kitchen. Gray wants me to learn to cook, and you are so talented."

"You really have no need. I'm sure writing your books keeps you busy," Ella replied.

Throughout the meal, Ella remained quiet. When they finished eating, the older woman rose to clear the table. Fury stood as well. "Would you allow me to help?" Fury asked.

Shaking her head, Ella said, "No ma'am. I can take care of it."

CHAPTER TWENTY-FIVE

"She hates me, Gray," Fury said as he led her into his bedroom.

"No more than your sister dislikes me. They'll both come around. We have the rest of our lives to convince them."

"I suspect I'm going to receive the same warm embrace from Gladys tomorrow."

"Gladys is an employee. If she doesn't like it, she can be replaced."

"I can't believe you just said that. How long has she worked for you?"

"Not so long that she has authority to interfere with my personal life. Not even Ella has that right. They both know it."

"Don't say anything to them, Gray. That would only make it worse. Let me try to win them over."

He grabbed her by the waist and pulled her close. "Wise beyond your years, are you?"

"We Irish are underestimated."

"Well, Irish, let's put our brand on this bed."

"Gray. It's three o'clock in afternoon."

"I don't remember reading time restrictions on the marriage license."

"Ella and Edward are in the house," she said in slightly above a whisper.

Brandishing his arm around the room, he asked, "Why are you whispering? The walls of this house are a foot thick."

"Someone might come in."

"We'll lock the door, if it makes you more comfortable. But I can assure you that no one would barge into my bedroom, with or without you here—Apache, maybe, but not Edward or Ella."

An hour later, Fury woke. Gray was asleep on his stomach with his arm across her chest. It was heavy but comforting. Looking around the room, she wondered about its history. She took comfort in the fact that the furniture was contemporary.

Is this the master suite, where all the patriarchs slept?

It was a large room with a private bath and walk-in closet, but not as large as Fury would have expected the lord and lady of the manor to occupy. The overall décor was definitely representative of Gray. The walls were hunter-green with beige moldings. The artwork was comprised of photographic scenes of horse pastures. Although it depicted his personality, it seemed commercially designed and sterile, lacking a lived-in feeling. Gray stirred, opened his eyes, and smiled.

"I've heard it said that what you do on New Year's Day is what you will do all year," he said, a twinkle in his eyes. "I think we've made a good start for 2007."

She returned his smile and changed the subject. "This is a very pleasant room. Is it the master bedroom?"

"No. You can relax. You're not in my great-grandfather's chamber."

"I would have thought that you would have occupied it once your father passed away."

"Well, you would have been wrong."

"Was this your room growing up?"

He shook his head. "It's just a room I drew out of the hat when I graduated from law school. It holds no history for me. I'm not sure who may have occupied it in the past, but I believe it was a guestroom." His tone indicated that it was not a subject for further discussion. "I feel like a steak. Want to head back to town?"

"We're not staying here tonight?"

He shook his head.

As predicted, on Tuesday morning, Gladys Stevens took the announcement with the same enthusiasm as Ella. Although she quickly approached Fury, fawned over the rings, and welcomed her as the first lady of MacGregor Enterprises, there was an unmistakable chill in her demeanor. Fury glanced around the gathered staff and felt that she could read the disappointment on the faces of some of the younger, female employees. *I bet at least some of them harbored fantasies of capturing the heart of the boss. Why wouldn't they?*

A week later, the MacGregor marriage story hit the press. The *Atlanta Constitution* gave it an expanded announcement in the weddings section, noting that Fury was a best-selling novelist and Gray an international financier and entrepreneur. The *New York Times* gave it similar coverage. However, the *Arabella Gazette* made it a front-page story written by Caroline Elliot. Fury's heart stopped. *Caroline didn't seem happy that I was Gray's date at the Christmas party. What has she said in the article?*

Fury's apprehension was well placed. Caroline had described how the couple met through the author's research for a book about the MacGregor family.

Showing the paper to Gray, Fury said, "I never said that to her. I told her I was researching my family. She twisted it."

"Relax, angel. It's not fatal. You must have learned by now that half of what you read in print is either fabricated or spun for sensation. Remember the myth about my two-date limit."

"Point well taken. But, I hate that everyone in Arabella will be thinking that I'm writing an expose on the first-family dynasty."

"Aren't you?"

"Maybe. Maybe not."

"Maybe, maybe not?" Gray looked at her with a puzzled expression on his face.

"I want to know what happened, but I don't know for sure what I'm going to do with it. I could use part of it—all of it—to write a novel. I don't know."

Gray's eyes questioned her statement, but he said nothing more about it.

"We're leaving in a few days. By the time we return, that article will be forgotten."

The European trip was all that Fury could have asked for. Despite the limited time in the Paris, they managed to take in the major tourist attractions. On the fourth and final day, they lounged in their rooms, shopped, and enjoyed a show at Maxim's in the evening.

Paris had been chilly, but Scotland was cold. While Forglen remained a private residence and not open to the public, tourists were allowed to walk on the grounds, and cottage rentals were available. Gray and Fury spent two nights in the lodge, which had been the gatekeeper's home at one time. It was an amazing architectural design with a warm and homey interior.

"I'd like to come back when it's not so cold, and we have more time," Fury said to Gray as they boarded a plane for Ireland.

Evanne was excited to see Fury again and clearly fascinated with Gray.

"He is the handsome one, but I can't believe you met and married so quickly," she said to Fury when they were alone in Evanne's room on the pretext that she wanted Fury's opinion about some new clothes. "Is he really the grandson of the "Him" that our Bridget wrote about?"

"Try not to hold that against him. I know how crazy our marriage must seem to everyone," Fury said. "Cory is giving me a really hard time."

"It was no faster than the O'Quinn wedding."

"You're right. Do you think that I'm subconsciously trying to channel Bridget?"

Evanne smiled. "You are supposed to look like her, and from what I can tell, you have her spirit. What does Uncle Mike think of Mr. MacGregor?"

"He is so cool with it. Thank goodness. I would hate to be dealing with opposition from both of them. I had the feeling this afternoon that Aunt Mary likes him."

"She does. I'm not sure she realizes who he is. But then, she never talked about her mother's history in America. Since you've married into his family, are you still going to write that book?"

Fury paused before answering. "I've had some questions, but how could I not? Bridget and Jim deserve it. I'm still digging into

MacGregor archives, and I even have Dad working on a piece of the puzzle."

"I didn't want to mention it in front of Granny, but I've found something else that you will be interested in reading. It was in Uncle Ronan's house. I was helping clean it out, because he is never going to be able to live there again and wants Dad to sell it. I found a travel journal that Conor O'Quinn kept on his trip to America."

"Did you read it?"

Evanne nodded. "I did. He wrote about meeting Bridget and the wedding on the boat. Dad said that I should give it to you." She went to her dresser and took out an old, black leather book that was small enough to fit inside the lapel pocket of a man's jacket. It had worn, gold lettering. "Here. Tuck it in your purse."

Fury hugged her cousin. "Thank you. You are the best." Drawing away, she said, "We'd better get back out to the living room. I shouldn't leave Gray alone with Aunt Mary for too long."

As they started to walk out of Evanne's room, Fury stopped. "Evanne, I need a big favor. Could you get me a sample of Uncle Ronan's DNA?"

"How could that be done? And what could you do with it?"

"A hairbrush might be all I would need. And there's probably no hope of doing anything with it, but you never know. When I was on genealogy sites on the Internet, there were advertisements for DNA testing to discover a person's ancestors."

Evanne snapped her fingers. "You want a hairbrush; I'll get you a hairbrush."

Hugging her cousin, again, Fury said, "I'm not sure whether to call you a literary assistant or a partner in crime."

"I'm actually enjoying playing Watson to your Sherlock."

By the time the honeymoon was over, Fury was exhausted. "I never thought I would dread a book tour, but I really don't want to do this one," she told Gray on the plane. "For some reason, I am so tired. It's probably a mental block about having to disrupt our time together."

He took her hand. "While I wish you didn't have to go, I

understand your career obligations. I'll join you on weekends as often as I can."

She smiled and turned to take a nap.

Monday morning, after they had landed in Atlanta on Sunday, Gray left very early. Fury was not completely awake when he kissed her goodbye. Through bleary eyes, she read "4:45" on the clock and then went back to sleep. When she woke a few minutes before eight, she got out of bed to go to the bathroom but was overcome with a rush of nausea. *Oh, no. Is this a stomach virus?*

She sat back on the bed and then rolled over on the pillows. *Don't throw up.*

After a minute or so, she rose slowly and walked to the bathroom. However, despite retching over the toilet, she did not throw up. *Strange. There's no stomachache, and nothing comes up, but I'm miserable.* Suddenly, a thought hit her. *My period! I haven't had one. How could I be so stupid? I'm pregnant.*

Her instinct was to call Cory, but with her sister's attitude toward Gray and the marriage, that did not seem like a good idea. She dragged herself to the kitchen and made a cup of hot tea. Sitting at the bar, sipping the tea, she began to feel better. *What is Gray going to think? The ink isn't dry on the marriage license.* Gypsy jumped up on the bar.

"You're hungry, aren't you, girl? Can you believe what I've done— we've done?"

The nausea began to subside after she nibbled at saltine crackers and finished the tea. As soon as she felt decent, she dressed and went to the closest pharmacy for pregnancy tests. Back at the condo, her suspicions were confirmed. She looked down at her abdomen. "There's a tiny MacGregor growing in there. I'm going to have a baby," she whispered.

As Fury disposed of the test wrappings, the phone rang. Looking at the caller ID, she saw "Donald Reynolds." *Great timing, Cory.*

"I thought you might call when you got back in town," her sister said in a sarcastic tone.

"I was going to call you today, but I've been tied up with unpacking."

"I assume your European honeymoon was fabulous."

"If that's a sincere comment, the answer is that we had a really good trip, but it was very short."

"Ten days in Paris, that's not so short."

"We weren't in Paris for ten days. We were there four days and then two days in Scotland, two in Ireland, and two spent traveling. How are the girls?"

"They've both had a bug, but they're back in school. Are you free for lunch this week?"

Fury paused, trying to decide whether she felt physically like meeting her sister for lunch or emotionally ready for Cory's attitude about Gray. Their last meeting had left her depressed, and this was not a good time for an encore. "I have to set a couple of appointments before I leave on the tour, but I can probably work in a lunch later in the week, if you promise not to bash my husband."

"I promise. Dad and Don have reprimanded me about my attitude. I'll try to be positive."

"Thank you. I'll call you tomorrow, and we can set a date."

As soon as she hung up the phone, Fury called her gynecologist and asked for the first available appointment.

When Gray came home that evening, he brought Chinese takeout. "I didn't think that I would get home in time to start dinner."

"Chinese is good," Fury said, but the aroma of the food ignited her nausea.

She tried to eat, but found the food repulsive.

"Is something wrong with your lo mein?"

"No. I'm just not hungry. I had frozen yogurt not long before you came home," she lied.

I'll tell him after I see the doctor.

CHAPTER TWENTY-SIX

Fate was kind. Fury's doctor had a cancellation for the following day. The exam and lab work confirmed what she already knew. According to the physician, her projected due date was mid-September. Armed with nausea-coping strategies, pregnancy vitamins, and brochures on birth options, she left the office with thoughts of how and when she would break the news.

When Gray arrived home that evening, Fury had all of her nausea remedies lined up on the kitchen bar.

"What's all this?" he asked as he went to the kitchen for a cold drink.

"We have to talk," she said, taking his hand and leading him back to the living room sofa.

He feigned a frown. "This sounds serious. Did you wreck the Vanquish?"

"Not hardly, since you won't let me drive it."

"Your foot is way too heavy for that machine, my love. What's going on?"

"I have some news, and I hope you're going to be okay with it."

"Best way to find out is to spit it out."

She hesitated, searching his face for reassurance when he had no idea what she was about to say. "I went to the doctor today."

His expression turning serious, he said, "And?"

"It seems you got me pregnant on our wedding night."

His face relaxed, and a broad grin appeared. "You're pregnant?"

"That's what I said."

"You couldn't have thought for a second that I wouldn't be okay with it?"

"Well, it happened pretty fast, don't you think?"

"Come here." He pulled her to him. "Nothing could make me happier. Of course, I'm okay with it." He hugged her tight, and she began to cry. "Are you okay with it?"

She couldn't talk. She just moved her head up and down on his chest. They sat for several minutes, Gray holding her and stroking her hair. Breaking the silence, he said, "And all that stuff you have lined up on the bar is related?"

"To help with morning sickness."

He laughed.

"It's not funny."

"I'm not laughing about the nausea; I'm laughing at your pathetic excuse for failing to eat last night."

"If you only knew how revolting that food smelled to me."

"I guess this tables your cooking lessons for a while," he said, cocking one eyebrow.

"You know how disappointed I am about that," she said, playfully pounding on his chest with her fist.

He laughed and hugged her again.

On Friday, Fury had lunch with Cory. The tricks Dr. Albracht provided had worked to tame the nausea. Sitting across from her sister in a cozy tearoom in an old section of the city, she desperately wanted to share the news of her pregnancy, but, not wanting to risk a negative reaction, she decided to wait.

"So, tell me what all you saw and did in Paris," Cory said as the waitress took their drink orders and left menus.

"The usual tourist attractions: the Louvre, Versailles, the Eiffel Tower."

"With money no object, I'm sure you traveled first class. Or did you take Gray's private jet?"

"I don't think you're exactly starving," Fury said, choosing a tea bag with cinnamon from the chest left by the server. "We took his plane to New York but flew commercial to Europe."

"We're not in the financial universe with a Gray MacGregor—to say nothing of all the money you make on your books."

"Don't make me feel guilty that we had a good time."

"I'm sorry." Cory reached across the table for her sister's hand. "I didn't really intend to sound mean or jealous. I'm glad you have what you do."

Fury smiled, squeezed Cory's hand, and said, "We've always been close. Please don't let my marriage come between us. I know you love me and want to protect me, but you have to trust my judgment."

Looking at Fury, Cory's eyes were misty. "I've felt terrible these past weeks. I knew you were mad at me. All I want is for you to be safe and happy."

"I know that. Just give Gray a chance. Don't judge him on what you've heard about his family, or the things that I said about him at first. Okay?"

Cory nodded.

Fury almost told her at that moment about the baby but decided to wait. *It's going well. Don't mess it up.*

The rest of the lunch conversation focused on the impending book tour, Cory's daughters, and Mike's health.

"Dad told me that he spent last Sunday at your house. Does Don think he's doing okay?"

"He does. Dad's color is good, and he's lost a little weight. I think the scare in Ireland has made him take better care of himself. He still likes his Guinness, but he's not drinking near as much."

Fury smiled. "That's good to hear. I'm having dinner with him Monday night to tell him about our trip."

Fury was at the pub twenty minutes before Mike arrived. "Sorry, lass. I got a call at the last second and traffic was snarled on 85."

"You're fine." She stood up and put her arms around him. "I'm so glad to see you."

He reciprocated and then took off his overcoat. "I've got some news for you."

Fury's expression perked up with anticipation. "Did you find her?"

"Your mum-in-law is alive and well and living in a small town called Foxgrove in the Kentucky Bluegrass Country."

"You're kidding. You really found her? Are you sure?"

"I did. Never underestimate your old dad." He grinned and winked at the waitress who had walked up to take his order. "Hello, Sierra. What's best on the menu, today?"

"You know it's all good, Mike. You having your usual Guinness?"

"Don't think my warden here would allow it this early in the day. How about a cuppa of your strongest, hottest tea? It's cold out there."

"You got it. How about you, honey? Can I bring you more tea?"

"Sierra, this is me daughter—the younger one, Fury O'—MacGregor. Just got married, she did—last month." Turning to Fury, he whispered, "I can tell it now, can't I?"

Fury nodded. Observing the waitress, who appeared to be about forty, she wondered how well her father knew the woman.

As soon as Sierra was out of earshot, Fury spoke up. "What else? What else about Gray's mother?"

"She's a nurse. Works at the local hospital in labor and delivery and has a little house nearby. Quite a handsome woman she is."

"How do you know that?"

"I've seen her. That's how."

"You've been to Kentucky?"

"Aye. That I have. She goes by Zaira Ross. Seems like she's been there quite a long time."

"Is she married?"

"No. No record that she ever remarried. Lives by herself with a little dog—one of those lap dogs with a lot of fur in his face."

"You found all that out?"

"I did. Have had a couple of conversations with her."

Fury's face filled with awe. "You've talked to her? What did you say, and how did you manage that? Ring her doorbell?"

"Did me turn in undercover back in the day. I still know a thing or two."

"But, how?"

"Several nights a week, she stops for dinner at a little diner. My guy in Lexington got me that intel and a current picture. I just hung out there for several days until she came in. It's a small town but close enough to Lexington so that the locals are used to outsiders with all the tourists that pour into the area for the horse sales. But I didn't approach her until after I'd been there a few times. Managed to walk by her table and let some coins fall out of my hand as I passed. Some of it rolled under her table, like I knew it would. Her being a nice lady, she helped me pick it up. Perfect way to start a conversation."

"Dad, what did you say to her?"

"I told her that I was a retired New York cop, my wife died, and I was looking for a new place to live because I didn't want to live in the city any more. It was easy as could be—all true."

"True over ten years ago."

"True, just the same. Told her I had a daughter who might come with me and help me make up my mind. Do you want to meet her?"

Before Fury could answer, Sierra was back at the table with Mike's tea. "What can I get you to eat, Mike?"

"Give me the corned beef sandwich."

"Fries?"

Mike looked at Fury, who was frowning. "No. Better pass on the fries. What are you going to have, missy?"

Fury ordered potato soup. As soon as the waitress walked away, Fury leaned across the table toward her father. "Of course, I want to meet her."

"What would you tell the husband?"

"I'm not sure. I have time to think of something because I can't go until after my tour. But, I'm definitely going."

"Never doubted that for a minute. How's it going with the senior warden?"

Fury smiled. "You're talking about Cory, I presume."

"Of course."

"It's an armed truce at the moment. I don't think she's changed her mind about Gray and my marriage, but at least I've put a gag order on her."

Mike laughed. "Good luck with that. She's my Kathleen all over."

When their food arrived, the conversation took a break. Fury finished her soup first. "Dad, there's something I have to tell you as well."

"Something good, I hope."

"We think so."

"We? That'd be you and Gray?"

She nodded. "I know I've managed to shock the family with the marriage, and I hope this isn't a bigger shock, but . . . we're going to have a baby."

Mike put his sandwich down. "You don't say." His eyes twinkled. "That's a dandy bit of news," he said, reaching for her hand. "When's it to be?"

"September. Before you start doing the math, it probably happened the week we got married."

"It be God's will, lass. I'm more than pleased for the two of you. You'll make a crackerjack mom. I wish Kathleen could be here to see how you and your sister have turned out. Three grandchildren! 'Tis grand indeed."

"I haven't told Cory, so don't say anything. She'll be furious if she finds out before I tell her, but I'm just not ready to hear a lecture on how we should have waited."

"Don't have to tell me. I get my ears full of her lectures." He took a drink of water and then changed the subject. "And the rest of your research—how's that going?"

Fury looked at her lap, smoothed the napkin, and hesitated before responding. There was a lot she had discovered that she hadn't told Mike about, but somehow, she didn't want to share. *Am I wanting to shield Gray? Has our relationship put a damper on my book?*

"It's slow, but I am finding more and more information about the past," she said, without looking up. "I'll catch you up later."

The rest of the week was hectic for Fury, putting things in order for the tour. Gray wanted her to cancel because of the baby, but Dr. Albracht convinced him that she was healthy and capable of the travel if she rested whenever she felt tired. New York was the first stop, and they would travel there together on his company jet. He made a point to arrange his schedule of business meetings in the city to coincide with her commitments. He had become nearly as protective as Cory.

"I have something for you," Gray said, walking into the bedroom.

She looked up from the clothing she was folding to pack as he extended a small, velvet ring box. Inside was a plain gold band.

"I'll store your rings at the bank. I don't want you to be a mugger magnet in those big cities."

"Gray, sweetheart, have you forgotten that I grew up in New York? But, I agree." She pulled the diamond rings off, handed them to him, and slid the band on her finger.

"I would rest easier about your traveling alone, if I thought you would be sensible. But that headstrong, Irish streak in you is not to be trusted. You'll keep going long past when you should stop to rest. So, I'll be in New York and Boston, like it or not. If you behave, I'll trust you for the remainder of that week, but I'll catch up with you when you head to Chicago. We'll avoid O'Hare by taking the corporate jet."

"Yes, sir!" She gave him a mock salute. "As if it would do me any good to argue."

"Thank you, Kate, my love. You're learning." He grinned and turned to go to the kitchen to check on the pasta he had on the stove. "When you're done packing, you can help me finish up dinner."

"I thought you said I was to take it easy," she said in a mocking tone.

"On the road, my love. On the road."

As he left the bedroom of the condo, Fury took a purse down from her closet shelf. It was the one she had taken on their honeymoon and had not used since. As she started to put it in her suitcase, Conor O'Quinn's journal fell out. *My gosh, with the pregnancy and morning sickness, I forgot all about this.* She slid it back in the purse and closed the zipper. *I'll read it when I'm alone in a hotel.*

CHAPTER TWENTY-SEVEN

The tour lasted three weeks. By the time it was over, Fury was able to start the morning without ginger in her tea. She had met with her agent and her editor while in New York and had been pressured by both to turn out another romance novel.

"I'm pregnant, newly married, and tired. Give me some time. My current contract says I have to produce three books by June of 2008. Two are out, so I have plenty of time to be in compliance."

"Are you still working on the historical novel? Sarah asked.

"I am."

"I'm sure it will be a very good book, Fury, but I'm not sure how it will fit into our line," her editor, Miriam DeSantis, said.

"I'm not counting on you to publish this one, Miriam. Of course, I'll give you first refusal, but if you pass, I'll either have Sarah market it elsewhere, or I'll publish it myself."

"Sounds like this one is a labor of love," the editor commented.

Fury thought for a moment. "Love or hate."

Both professionals looked puzzled, but neither responded.

In the end, Fury had won her point. She would take time off.

"I can produce a romance in three months," she told Gray, when recapping the meeting in their hotel room that night. "I've worked nonstop since I began. I know the momentum for my brand has to be kept fueled, but the movie will give me exposure this coming year."

"I'm not interfering in your professional life. I told you that I am here to give you support and help, if needed, but the rest is your decision."

"You've never had any fear that my career would rob you and the baby of a wife and mother?"

He shook his head. "I know the woman I married. You love your career and deserve to pursue it, but you'll never let it seriously interfere with the family. If it pinches me a little, now and then, I'll survive."

Fury moved closer to him on the sofa and took his hand. "And that's why I fell in love with you. You may try to boss me around, but I know in the things that really matter, you will always encourage me to be me."

"Not here to clip your wings, Kate, only to help you keep them preened."

The Saturday morning after her return to Atlanta, Gray prepared a full breakfast.

"I feel like our real life is beginning today," Fury said, sipping her tea. "Honeymoon's over, everyone knows we're married, tour's over, morning sickness is gone."

"And my wife is back in my bed."

"That *would* be the first thing on *your* list."

"So what is my red-feathered canary going to do on her first day out of the cage?"

"I have to bite the bullet and tell Cory about the baby. We have to decide where we are going to live and hopefully integrate our pet population." She was looking at Gypsy. "I think we should start with the latter by bringing Apache over here—soon. We have to test it eventually, and I think that it's better that Gypsy have the home-court advantage since she's smaller."

"Want to try it this afternoon?"

Fury nodded. "We can ride over to Forglen and pick up Apache, but we should soak our clothes in Gypsy's scent."

"You have a plan for that?"

"We just rub something we're going to wear on her coat. You can come up to the condo first and hold Gypsy. I'll bring Apache in. That way, neither will feel she has to protect her person."

"I see that you've got this all figured out, Dr. Doolittle."

"Stop mocking me."

"Why? It's such fun." He got up and went around to her side of the table, bent down, and turned her face up so that he could kiss her. "I'm giving you a hard time, but it sounds like a good plan. Get dressed, while I clean up the kitchen, and we'll head out to Forglen."

The phone rang just as Fury finished dressing.

"You're back." It was Cory. "When did you get in?"

"Last night about eight-thirty. I was going to call you later. Gray and I are heading out to Forglen to pick up Apache."

"Apache? Is that his dog?"

"Yeah. We're going to try introducing her to Gypsy. If you and Don don't have plans, we would like to come over for a visit tomorrow afternoon."

"Not doing a thing. Why don't you come for lunch?"

Fury hesitated and then said, "That's sweet of you to offer, but give us a rain check on lunch. I want to sleep in and have a leisurely breakfast. That'll put us in different time zones for eating. We'll come out about three, if that's okay."

"See you then. The girls are going to be thrilled."

Fury entered the condo with Apache, apprehensive as to how the animals would react. Eying the big dog from the safety of Gray's lap, Gypsy stiffened, her pupils dilated, and her claws dug into his jeans. Apache, seeing her master across the room, strained at her leash, her tail lashing the air. While Gray appeared calm, smiling at his dog, Fury was terrified.

What if they never get along?

The closer the dog came, the more the cat's fur rose. She was poised for battle and emitted a warning hiss.

"It's not going to work, Gray," Fury said, pulling Apache back.

"Give them a chance, Irish. I'd spit, too, if a strange creature five or six times my size invaded my domain. Let Apache come forward, slowly."

Gray continued stroking Gypsy with one hand, while the other kept a grip on her. Reluctantly, Fury followed his directions. By the time that Apache reached her master, the cat had relaxed, slightly, but watched the dog with a steady gaze.

Apache was so happy to see Gray that she barely paid attention to the cat. With his free hand, Gray alternated stroking the animals for several minutes. At one point, Apache swiped the cat with her tongue. Gypsy looked at her as though she was crazy but did not react. Gray eased his grip on the cat, and she jumped to the floor. He took control of the dog, allowing the cat to move freely. At first she retreated, then slowly moved forward to check out the dog. By the end of the introduction, they were not yet bedfellows, but no blood had been shed. "They're going to be fine," Gray said as Fury retuned from putting the cat in their bedroom. "We'll keep putting them together for short intervals until Gypsy is comfortable."

"Can it be that easy?"

He grinned. "It can, especially if we keep catnip handy."

On the way to Redbridge, Fury was nervous. They had dropped Apache at Forglen after nearly twenty-four hours without a dog and cat incident. "I hope Cory behaves as well as our pets when I tell her about the baby."

"I would be concerned, but I happen to know that you and your sister are equally matched. She may have the claws, but you have the bite."

"Well phrased, Shakespeare. Trouble is I've given her two fronts to fight on. One, she's not going to like us having a baby before she's given the marriage the COQ stamp of approval; and two, she's really not going to like being told over a month after Dad."

When the couple arrived at the Reynolds house, the girls opened the door before Fury rang the bell. They had been waiting by the window and saw the SUV pull onto the driveway.

"Aunt Fury," Suzi squealed and threw herself against her aunt.

"Don't knock her down, Suzi," Don said, coming up behind the girls. "Come on in. Cory's made one of her desserts and has a fresh pot of coffee and a fresh pot of tea ready for you—something stronger, if you like." He reached out and shook Gray's hand, then hugged his sister-in-law.

Cory came out of the kitchen, a large tray in her hands that she put down on the coffee table as Fury and Gray took off their coats.

"You haven't been here since Christmas dinner," she said as she met Fury with a hug.

Fury held her breath, wondering how Cory would react to Gray, but was relieved when her sister turned and hugged him as well.

Don immediately began talking to Gray about the upcoming season for the Atlanta Braves. Cory began pumping Fury for details about her tour.

"Before we lose track of time," Fury said, "Gray and I have an announcement."

The color drained from Cory's face as though she had read her sister's mind.

Fury took Gray's hand and said, "We're expecting a baby in September."

Don's face lit up with a big smile. "Congratulations," he said, getting up to give Fury another hug and shaking Gray's hand.

Cory was speechless. She put her teacup down on the table. After a second or two passed, she got up and walked over to her sister, motioned for Fury to stand, and wrapped her arms around her. "I'm so happy for you." Releasing her, Cory turned to Gray, who was standing, and put her arms around him. "I trust that you will always take care of my little sister and your baby."

"Cory, I plan to prove that. You have my word."

"Why are you crying, Mommy?" Sandi asked.

"I'm crying because I'm happy. You're going to have a new cousin."

During the ride back to Atlanta, Fury said, "Cory's reaction to the baby news has got me freaked. Do you think she's really happy or faking me out for the next attack?"

"If I were you, I would stop trying to analyze the situation and accept it at face value. 'All's well that ends well.'"

"You're the expert at reading people. Did she seem sincere to you?"

"Kate, I'm not going to be sucked into the relationship known as the O'Quinn Sisters, Limited. You two have history that's beyond my knowledge. But, my advice is that until she shows something different, enjoy the moment."

After Gray left for the office on Monday morning, Fury called Mike.

"When can we go to Kentucky, Dad?"

"You want to leave so soon after your tour?"

"Gray has a business venture that's going to keep him working late for at least two weeks. He will hardly miss my being gone three or four days. I feel like I can't dive into getting us settled in our full-time home until I make the trip."

"Have you two decided where that home will be?"

"It seems only practical for it to be Forglen—even with the voodoo there. My condo is out of the question for a family. Gray's is not much larger, North Carolina is not practical for fulltime, and I don't think we want to deny our child the advantages of a house and yard when there's one standing there waiting for us."

"I didn't think you liked it."

"Neither of us likes it. But, how can we walk away from a house that has been in his family for over eighty years? I think that if we change some of the décor, it will be an entirely different atmosphere. Those spooky portraits are moving to off-site storage."

"Are you planning to tell Gray where you're going?"

"I have to tell him *where* I'm going, but not why. I plan to say that I'm traveling with you to see some property that you've been looking at."

"Fury, my girl, don't lie to Gray. That's no way to start your marriage."

"You're right. It's not that he would stop me. He has said that I am free to do whatever I feel I need to do. It's just that he's so adamant about denying his mother even exists that it would be awkward for me to say that I'm going to meet her."

"You say that he never asks you questions about your research and doesn't want to discuss it. Tell him that you're following a lead, and you know he wouldn't want to be involved so I'm going."

"All true. That will work."

Fury and her dad arrived at their hotel in Lexington on Wednesday afternoon of the following week. According to Mike, Zaira was a regular at the café.

"Do you want to drive over to Foxgrove today or wait until tomorrow, lass?"

"Let's do a practice run tonight."

"Probably a good idea. One never knows; she might change her pattern this week."

Within the hour, they were on the road for the twenty-minute drive. Mike was behind the wheel of the rental car.

"You're mighty quiet, me girl."

"I'm a little nervous."

"My Fury—nervous? That's not like you, lass."

"I know. But, what if she's not alone?"

Mike reached across the console with his right hand to take Fury's left. Squeezing it, he said, "Then, we'll have to improvise. Leave it to me, love."

"What if she doesn't want to be found or doesn't like me?"

"How could she not like you? Just be yourself. What's the worst that can happen? She tells you to go back to Georgia. You'd be no worse off, and Gray apparently doesn't give a fig."

Kathy's Diner was located in what appeared to be a converted house—a one-story, white frame building. The Foxgrove Hospital, a two-story, brick building, was visible on the block behind the little restaurant. The café parking lot had room for approximately twenty cars in the back, but only five spots were occupied when the O'Quinns arrived at five-thirty-five.

"Don't see the lady's car," Mike said, pulling their vehicle into a space. "She's usually here by five-fifteen—comes straight from work."

"I don't know whether to be disappointed or relieved."

The front door of the café was decorated for St. Patrick's Day with a poster of a leprechaun. As Mike held it open for Fury, she pointed to the picture. "That should make you feel at home."

Inside, there was a short-order counter, six or seven tables covered with gingham tablecloths, and high-backed booths lining two walls. A cardboard sign on a flimsy easel directed patrons to seat themselves. Following suit with the door decoration, there were green streamers draped around the ceiling and shamrock-themed candleholders on each table.

"What's the food like here?" Fury asked as Mike led her to a booth.

"It's really very good. Typical Southern-style cooking with chicken and dumplings, country-fried steak, and lots of greasy vegetables."

A waitress came over to the pair soon after they settled in. "Hello, Mr. O'Quinn. It's your time of year."

Leave it to Dad. He's already established himself with the town waitress.

"That it is, Helen. And how's your young lad?"

"Doing better since you had the talk with him. My husband and I are grateful for your help. What can I get you tonight?"

"To start, I could do with a cup of coffee and some of that homemade bread you make here. How about you, love?" he asked, looking at Fury.

"I'll take a cup of hot tea."

"We don't have fancy teas here, Miss. Just plain tea," the waitress said.

"All the better. I prefer simple black tea with sugar."

When Helen left, Fury leaned across the table. "You sure get to know people in a hurry."

"Well, how could I socialize with the target without being obvious, otherwise? Besides, Helen's boy was acting out, and I just told him about what could happen to a young man who goes down the wrong path."

Zaira did not come in that evening. After having a cholesterol-laden meal, they drove back to Lexington with nothing accomplished.

CHAPTER TWENTY-EIGHT

The following day, Fury and Mike toured some of the local attractions and drove out through horse country. "I wonder if Zaira came here because of the horses. Gray loves to ride. Maybe his passion came from her," Fury said, snapping a picture of a pair of horses through the window of the car.

"Could be, love. There's much to be said of the gene pool. Here's hoping he got more of hers than those scoundrels on his father's side. I like the lady. Can't see her being the one who messed up. But, who knows?"

That afternoon, they didn't get to the restaurant until nearly six o'clock. Fury was on edge. "Do you see her car?" she asked as Mike turned the corner of the parking lot.

"No. It's not here."

"Oh, no. What if she doesn't come? Or, what if she came early and has gone? Maybe she's sick, or maybe she's out of town."

"Calm down, missy. Panic will change nothing. We'll go in, have a nice dinner, and see what happens."

They stretched dinner out to seven-thirty without a sign of Zaira Ross.

The second night was a mirror image of the night before. Mike even ordered the same entre. Fury decided on a chef salad. "That's not enough to nourish you and the wee one," Mike said.

"It's plenty and leaves my conscience free to have some of that banana pudding you had last night."

By seven-forty-five, there was still no sign of Zaira, and they prepared to leave.

Just as Mike stood up to take the check to the register, the door opened, and in walked a tall woman with salt-and-pepper hair. As she took off her coat to hang on the restaurant's rack, Fury saw that she wore a nurse's uniform.

"Hello, Mike. You're back in town?"

"That I am, and you'd be running late tonight."

"I know. I'm exhausted. We had an emergency with one of our staff, and I had to stay until someone could come in to cover. I started to go straight home and have a sandwich for dinner."

"Well, I'm glad you changed your mind. We were just about to leave, but if you'd like some company, me daughter and I would be obliged to stay a while."

"I don't want to impose on you, but I would like to meet your famous daughter. I assume that this is Fury from your description and the photos on her books."

Fury smiled. Thankful that no more was required of her yet. This was Gray's mother, the woman he despised. *She looks like I expected, but her personality is much warmer. Apparently, she's familiar with my books.*

"Come on; sit at our booth," Mike said.

Fury nodded in agreement as Mike slid into the booth on her side, leaving the opposite clear for Zaira.

"I'm so impressed to meet a best-selling author," Zaira said.

"Please, don't be. I'm just lucky."

"Don't be modest. All the nurses where I work have read your books."

"Your work is far more important than mine" *She's so nice. How am I going to tell her who I am?* "How long have you been a nurse?"

"Oh, my. I lose count." Zaira paused as if doing the math. "It's been over twenty-five years." She rolled her eyes. "Time flies."

"Have you always been here in Foxgrove?"

"No, no. I've been here not quite twenty years. I did my training in North Carolina."

Helen came to the table. "Evening, Zaira. You're late tonight."

After Zaira repeated what she had told the O'Quinns, the waitress took her order and left the table.

"So, how long will you be in Kentucky, Fury?"

When do I let her know who I am? "Only a couple of days. Dad and I got here yesterday and will probably go back to Atlanta on Friday." She tried to see if the mention of Atlanta stirred any reaction from the older woman, but if it did, she kept it hidden. "Have you ever been to Atlanta?" Fury asked. *I shouldn't have asked that. When she finds out who I am, she'll know I was baiting her.*

"No." The answer came swiftly.

"You should come for a visit. There's a lot of the craic to be found in our city," Mike said.

Helen brought Zaira's coffee, a fresh pot of hot water and teabag for Fury, and refilled Mike's cup.

"Fury O'Quinn. That's such an unusual name."

"Actually, she's now Fury MacGregor," Mike said.

Both women froze. Zaira might have concealed her reaction to Atlanta, but she couldn't hide the impact that the MacGregor name had. Fury trembled. This was the moment.

I wasn't ready for him to out me. What do I say? What is he going to say if I don't speak?

Zaira broke the silence. "Fury MacGregor. Does that mean you're married?"

Fury nodded, smiling, unable to think of what to say next.

"Not only is she married, she's to have a wee one come September."

The two women locked eyes. Fury tried to read her mother-in-law's thoughts, but they were inscrutable. *I have to tell her. Stalling will only going to make it worse. She's either going to throw her coffee in my face or accept me.*

"My husband is Gray MacGregor, John Graeme MacGregor, IV." She paused, while Zaira stared, a blank, uncomprehending stare.

"I believe you're my mother-in-law—Gray's mother."

Still, Zaira did not speak. When she finally broke her silence, she said, "I'm sorry. That's not possible. I don't have a son."

Fury grabbed Mike's hand under the table and held it tight. "I know something happened a long time ago in Arabella, but I don't believe that the story Gray was told is true or is the whole truth. Please don't hate me for having my dad find you. I just want to talk to you. You're the only grandmother my child will have."

At the word grandmother, Fury could see that Zaira was moved but instantly resumed the stoic expression seen in historical photos of Native Americans. No one spoke. Fury couldn't think of anything more to say, and Mike seemed to sense that it was best that whatever happened had to be in the hands of his daughter. His role was done.

After several moments of silence, Zaira lifted her chin and once again looked Fury in the eye. In a voice barely above a whisper, reminding Fury of Gray's speech, she said, "I wish that I were the person you think I am—but I'm not. I'm sorry." A tear rolled down her cheek.

Fury wanted with all her heart to press, but something told her it was not the right thing to do. Instead, she took out her wallet and removed one of her business cards. On the back, she wrote the name of their hotel in Lexington, and then put it down in front of Zaira.

"I understand your shock and maybe how you feel, but I assure you, my intentions are honest. I want to know you, and I want my child to know you. If you change your mind, Dad and I will be in Lexington through tomorrow. Call my cell or come to the hotel—anytime. And, Zaira, I apologize for our deception. We didn't know any better way to approach you."

Zaira picked up the card and held it. Fury thought she saw the older woman's hand tremble.

Zaira did not make further eye contact with Mike or Fury. They gathered their coats and prepared to leave. Mike put a twenty-dollar bill on the table before taking the check to the register. As he started to walk away, he reached down and rested his hand on Zaira's for a second.

Fury left the restaurant ahead of her father. She didn't even pause to use the bathroom. Once in the car, tears flooded her face. *She hates me. We trapped her like an animal. She'll never talk to me now.*

The car was silent all the way to Lexington. Mike knew better than to try to console an inconsolable daughter. When they reached the hotel, they took the elevator to their floor without exchanging a word. At Fury's door, Mike put his arms around her and hugged her close. "You've done what you could. It's up to God and Zaira to do the rest. Don't torture yourself, my little one."

Frequently during the night, Fury would wake and grab her cell phone, hoping for a text or voice mail from Zaira. It was blank.

The next morning, Fury was downstairs for the complimentary breakfast when Mike caught up with her. "How did you sleep, lass?"

"Just like you know I did. I think we messed up, Dad. She's not going to contact me. She isn't going to admit she's Gray's mother, but she knows that I know it. He looks like her. His eyes have the same piercing gaze."

"Give her time, lass. I know we aren't known for our patience, but some things you can't rush. Let her get used to the idea. You may hear from her, yet."

"I don't think so. She and Gray are different from you and me. I think she has the same ability to freeze her feelings that he has. We might as well head back to Atlanta today."

"I don't think that's a good idea. Let's go shopping for the baby."

"Shopping for the baby? Since when were you interested in shopping for anything?"

"I've got me a craving. Humor me."

Fury rolled her eyes. "You're trying to distract me, but I love you for it. Just for that, I'm going to call your bluff. Let's go baby shopping. Maybe get him a little jockey outfit."

She gathered up her trash and took it to the receptacle. "Have something to eat while I go upstairs for my purse and our coats."

As Fury entered her room, she felt the cell phone in her pocket vibrate. Taking it out, her heart paused. It was a Kentucky area code—Zaira?

The voice on the other end of the line was shaky. "I couldn't sleep last night. Do you still want to talk?" Zaira asked.

"Of course. Where are you? I'll drive over to meet you."

"I'm downstairs in the lobby."

"You're here in Lexington? Come on up to my room. It's 419."

Waiting for Zaira, Fury called Mike and told him what was happening.

"You two have your chat. I'll be fine."

When the knock came at the door, Fury's adrenaline went into overdrive. "Please, God, give me the wisdom and patience to handle this properly."

Zaira was dressed in navy slacks, a light-green sweater, and loafers. She had a photo album in her hands. As she sat down on the edge of the bed, she handed the volume to Fury. "I thought you might like to see what he looked like when he was a little boy."

"I would love to."

"It's all I have of him, except a few newspaper clippings."

Fury laid the package down and went to her suitcase. "I thought you might like to see what he looks like now. I'm a terrible photographer, but I think you can get the idea. He really resembles you."

Tears welled in Zaira's eyes as she took the packet of photos Fury handed her.

"They're yours. I have duplicates."

After leafing through the album, Fury looked up at the older woman. Zaira was mesmerized by the photos of her adult son.

"You really loved him, didn't you?" Fury asked.

"With all my heart."

For a few minutes, both women were silent. Fury spoke first. "I know Jack MacGregor's version of what happened. I hope you'll tell me yours."

It took Zaira several minutes to begin. Her hands trembled as she laid the photos on the bed. "In the world according to MacGregor, everything they say and do is right. What you've probably been told is completely true and completely wrong. I made a mistake—a mistake that cost me everything. Did I wrong Jack MacGregor? Absolutely not. Did I break my marriage vows? How can you break a vow to something that doesn't exist? There was no husband-wife relationship. It was a master-servant contract. He owned everything, including me. He was free to use and abuse. I was free to be quiet and obey."

Fury watched as years of pain were clear in Zaira's eyes.

"Does he know you're here—know where I am?"

"Jack is dead, Zaira."

The woman nodded. "I know. I meant Gray. Does he know?"

Fury shook her head.

"I didn't think so."

"He doesn't even know whether you're alive. I'm sorry."

"He hates me."

Fury didn't respond.

"I tried to contact him when I heard that Jack was dead—about twelve years ago. He wouldn't take my calls and wouldn't respond to my letters. Someone who worked for the company said that I was an imposter—that Mr. MacGregor's mother was deceased, and if I called again, they would report me to the police. Whatever his father told him, he believed."

"He thinks that you sold him."

Zaira's chin moved up and down, her face bearing an I-knew-it expression.

"Sold him for fifty-thousand dollars, right?"

Fury nodded. "I suspect that is not true."

"Look at me, Fury. You're carrying a child. As a mother, do you believe that I could sell my son?"

Fury moved across from the bed that she was sitting on to sit next to Zaira. Reaching over to put her hand on top of Zaira's, she said, "Tell me what really happened."

"What good would it do? It was nearly thirty years ago. Nothing can change the past."

"It's never too late for the truth."

"There are times when the truth can be dangerous."

"You are Gray's mother and the grandmother of my child. Both of them should know you." Fury squeezed the older woman's hand. "To answer your question: No, Zaira, I don't believe that you sold Gray."

CHAPTER TWENTY-NINE

Zaira looked at Fury with unspoken gratitude in her eyes. "You want to know what happened? Okay, I'll try.

"I met Jack MacGregor at Chapel Hill. I was a freshman and his sister Valerie lived in my dorm. He was five years older than me and a graduate student at the University of Georgia."

"Did Valerie set you up?"

Zaira shook her head. "No—I wasn't in her league. Jack had come up with some of his friends for a football weekend and was waiting for Valerie in main reception. I was a scholarship student and working the desk. When he flirted with me, I was flattered. Before they left, he had asked me for a date."

"Did you and Valerie become friends?"

"No. She never approved—I was part Cherokee, which Valerie considered synonymous with savage. When Jack took me home to Forglen to meet his father, I was mesmerized by the house and the lifestyle. Graeme was a widower and a kind, gracious man. Looking back, I've wondered how he could have raised Valerie and Jack."

For a moment, Zaira stopped and looked down as if reflecting. "I was young, naïve, and thought I had captured the heart of the most eligible bachelor in the South. Only, what Jack had in terms of looks, money, and power was offset by a heart of stone. I was just another trophy. In those days, I was considered by some to be somewhat attractive."

"You still are."

Zaira smiled. "I think I knew within a few weeks of the wedding that Jack didn't love me, but I couldn't admit it. We lived at Forglen, and he was decent enough to me while his father was alive. But, he changed after Graeme died of a heart attack. Nothing I did was good enough. He was in control and treated me with contempt and worse. He liked throwing in my face what *he* considered to be my lack of breeding."

"Why didn't you leave him?"

"Gray—I had no way to support us."

"Jack would have had to pay alimony and child support."

Zaira shook her head. "I had no money for a lawyer, and what chance would I have had in a Mercy County court? But, as it turned out, I lost everything anyway. With Graeme gone, Jack began drinking and staying away. When he was home, he was angry and critical. I knew he was seeing another woman—or women—lipstick on his shirt collar, strange cologne on his clothing. If I complained, he became angry and violent. A wife didn't report being slapped around by her husband in those days, especially if he owned the town. I was miserable. The only bright spot in my life was Gray. And then Roberto, our gardener, began flirting with me. It was innocent at first, but I started looking forward to the days he worked. He made me feel attractive, intelligent. Roberto gave me back everything that Jack had stripped away." She put her face in her hands for a moment. "It was wrong. Two wrongs never make a right."

"And Jack caught you."

She nodded. "He ordered me out of the house immediately. He said that he could kill us both and no jury in Arabella would convict him. He was probably right."

"And you left without Gray."

She nodded. "I told Jack that, if I left, I was taking Gray. He said, 'Just try that and see what happens.' He slapped me." She choked up, looked away from Fury for a few seconds, and then continued. "He knocked me to the floor, kicked me, and shouted, 'You will not so much as try to see my son again if you know what's good for you.' I cried and begged him just to let me leave with Gray—that Gray loved me. He sneered at me and said that I should have thought about Gray before I screwed the help." She wiped an eye. "His face was filled with hatred when he said, 'I can do worse to you than you can imagine.'"

Seeing how distraught Zaira was becoming, Fury said, "Take your time. I didn't mean to upset you."

"It's all right. I'm fine." She took a tissue from her purse, blotted her face, and blew her nose, softly. "Fury, you've got to understand how close Gray and I were. He wanted love and respect from his father, but it wasn't there. All Jack could do was criticize. Gray was a sensitive child, intuitive, and very smart. In fact, sometimes, he frightened me with how smart he was. But, he didn't interact well with his peers. He told me once, not long before I was thrown out, 'Mommy, the kids at school hate me. They say that I'm rich and stuck-up.' It broke my heart. I put my arms around him, and he clung to me. 'You're the only one who likes me, Mommy.'"

Zaira looked away as if she couldn't face Fury any longer.

"How could I have done that to him? He needed me. Why did I give in to stupid temptation? I'll never forgive myself. There's no telling how Jack treated Gray after I was gone."

"You were in a terrible position. It would have been easier today, but I can see how, thirty years ago, it would have been hard to go up against the MacGregor money on your own. Don't beat yourself up."

"When I picked myself up from the floor, I pleaded one more time, begging Jack to let me take my son—that Gray needed his mother. His response was, 'Valerie and I grew up just fine without a mother. Gray will too. Leave peacefully, and on Monday there'll be a check at my office, along with papers for you to sign. Now, get out of my house—you're dead to us.'"

Fury cringed.

Zaira was trembling uncontrollably by the time she finished. Fury felt tears running down her own face. She put an arm around the shoulders of the older woman, knowing how much courage it took to tell the story.

Zaira composed herself and said, "I should have tried to fight him."

"You did the only thing you believed that you could."

Zaira nodded.

"What happened to Roberto?"

"I have no idea. I never saw him again. I had a few dollars saved from the allowance Jack gave me, so I went to a cheap motel. I spent three nights, crying—not eating. When Monday came, I did as Jack had commanded. I signed the papers without reading them, picked up the check, and caught a bus home to my family in North Carolina."

"I understand. You had no choice. Neither did my grandmother."

Zaira looked at Fury with a confused expression. "Your grandmother?"

"I'm sorry. It's a long story. Suffice it to say that my grandmother worked for the MacGregor family in the 1920s. I'll tell you the whole story some other time."

Fury was about to say more when her phone rang. She jumped, pulled it out of her pocket, and read the screen. "It's Gray," she said, looking at his mother with an expression of warning.

The color drained from Zaira's face.

"Good morning. How is the weather in Atlanta?" She grimaced. "Oh, I bet Apache didn't like going out in the rain." Smiling, she said, "I miss you, too. We'll be home tomorrow afternoon about six if the plane is on time. Give Gypsy a hug for me. See you then."

"That was him?" Zaira said, her eyes betraying her eagerness.

Fury nodded. "You're going to see him, soon. I promise."

"Don't make promises that you can't keep. I probably should never have come here."

"I *don't* make promises that I can't keep, Zaira. Somehow, I'll find a way to reach him. Give me time." She tossed her phone on the bed and threw both arms around the proud woman's shoulders. "It'll happen," Fury whispered.

Zaira's head moved slightly side to side. "He's a MacGregor— raised by a MacGregor. You're not likely to change his mind. I just pray that he's a better husband to you than his father was to me."

"You can be sure that he is. I think he's more Ross than MacGregor and doesn't even know it."

A wide grin broke across Zaira's face.

Fury was quiet on the plane back to Atlanta. Mike's attention had been on the morning edition of the *Atlanta Constitution* that he picked up in the airport. Finishing his perusal of the newspaper, he turned to Fury and said, "Penny for your thoughts, lass."

She smiled. "You wouldn't get your money's worth." As haunted as she was by the meeting with Zaira, her thoughts had turned to Conor O'Quinn's journal. His entries made it clear that he knew Bridget was pregnant when they met. If Ronan was not Conor's child, was he the love child of Bridget and Graeme? Or, was he the result of the rape of her grandmother by J.G.?

"Thinking about your mother-in-law?"

She smiled and nodded. It was easier allowing him to make an erroneous assumption than to reveal her true thoughts.

"How is the book coming? Will you be done anytime soon?"

"I'm still accumulating and organizing the material. I haven't started writing."

"You talk about it at all with Gray?"

She shook her head. "No. He will not talk about it, even though he insists that he's okay with me writing it."

Fury and Mike parted at the airport. When the cab let her out, she was disappointed to find that Gray wasn't at home. He had warned her that a meeting at the office could make him late. Gypsy met her at the door. The condo was as neat as when she left. There were no dishes in the sink, not even a glass. A note on the counter said, "Apache at Forglen."

Her mail was positioned neatly on the desk in her office. Gray had removed the bulk-rate junk, leaving a stack about two-inches thick for her to sort.

When she went into the bedroom, a green envelope was lying on the pillow on her side of the bed. Picking it up, the outside read: "This spot reserved for the sexiest redhead in Atlanta." The card inside was for St. Patrick's Day. On one side was a traditional Irish blessing, on the facing side a handwritten note.

Happy St. Patrick's Day to my favorite Irish gal.
Thank you for bringing meaning to my life and warmth
to my bed. Meet you here after dinner.

Love,
Gray.

P.S. Wear my favorite gown.

Placing the card back in the envelope, she smiled. *He's not like his father or great-grandfather. He's Zaira's son.*

She couldn't wait to put on comfortable clothing. It seemed that her mid-section had increased in size considerably during the few days of the Kentucky trip. *Must have been that calorie-laden cuisine at the café.*

Once in a cozy velour warmup suit, she settled down on the sofa with a soft drink, Gypsy in her lap along with the stack of mail. Sorting for priority, she opened envelopes from Sarah and Miriam first and then moved to acknowledgement cards for gifts made to charities in lieu of weddings gifts. A letter from Scarlett Kavanagh caught her eye. Scarlett expressed her surprise and delight at the marriage and asked to meet for lunch in the near future. Among the pieces of mail was an envelope with no return address. She assumed it was a solicitation and nearly tossed it.

I better not assume it's trash, she thought, sliding the letter opener under the sealed flap.

Inside was a single sheet of paper with a short, typed message.

"Writing about the MacGregor family can be VERY DANGEROUS."

As she read the last word, she heard Gray's key in the door. Quickly folding the paper and returning it to the envelope, she buried it among the rest of her mail. A sick feeling gnawed at her intestines.

Fury made it to the door before he could enter. "I am *so* glad to see you," she said, throwing her arms around his neck.

He withdrew his key from the lock with one hand and slid the ring into his coat pocket, while his other arm encircled her waist. "Nothing like a warm body to erase the chill," he said, pulling her tight against his coat and running one hand down her back. "The only thing that feels better than velour is bare skin," he whispered as he kissed her.

She molded her body to his, clinging like molasses on bread. The emotions of her meeting with Zaira, exacerbated by the anonymous note, were culminating in a mini-meltdown.

After a few seconds, he pulled away. "Not that I don't want to take this all the way, but I'm detecting more than carnal vibes. What's wrong?"

She looked at him. His amber eyes mirrored those of his mother. "Nothing. I've just missed you."

He cocked his head to one side, an eyebrow raised. "You're not telling the truth, Kate . . . but you will. I can wait." And then he pulled her back to him. "Now where were we?"

"I thought you wanted me to put on the Saks gown."

He nuzzled his face in the nape of her neck and whispered, "I don't need any more provocation." With that, he scooped her up and headed for the bedroom.

After they made love, Gray said, "I hope you know that you destroyed my elaborate plan for your homecoming."

"Excuse me. Who seduced whom just now?"

Without answering, he grabbed her and tickled her bare ribs. She squealed. Pausing, he said, "You'd better put your clothes back on before I lose control again."

"Don't hold back on account of me."

"You little tease. I'm going—"

"Going to what? You love it and you know it."

"I think I've married a nymphomaniac."

"No. You created one."

For the time, pleasure and desire overcame the emotions invoked by the anonymous note. She wanted to tell Gray—but something held her back.

Later, as they ate dinner, he inquired about the trip.

"It was good. When Dad wasn't working, we drove through beautiful horse country. I think you would have enjoyed it."

The weekend passed without further drama. A few days later,

when she met Cory for lunch, there was an initial moment of strain.

"I seem to have lost my place in your life. You were nearly three-months pregnant before you told me?" Cory said as soon as the waitress took their orders and left.

"I didn't want to hear you tell me what a mistake it was to have a baby with Gray when, as *you* think, I hardly know him."

"Under the circumstances, it would have been hard for me not to feel that way, regardless of *who* you married."

"But especially since I married Gray MacGregor."

"You said that, I didn't. Maybe you ought to remember that you were the one who went on a mission to uncover what you suspected was the nasty truth about his family."

"His family—his ancestors—not him."

"Fury, it's not that I believe Gray is a bad person. I just don't think that you knew him well enough. You were a girlfriend for about thirty minutes. And what I don't believe you understand is that you haven't had enough time to adjust to marriage to be bringing a child into the picture."

Fury frowned. "You're—"

Cory raised her hand, signaling Fury to stop. "Listen. I promised I wouldn't bash Gray. I want to keep that promise. You mean too much to me to let a man compromise our relationship. You're pregnant, and that's more permanent than marriage. So, I'm going to be happy for you and pray that you and Gray have a wonderful life together—and that he turns out to be a great husband and father."

Fury smiled and reached across the table for her sister's hand. "Thank you."

"I know *you'll* be a good mom, in spite of that impetuous personality." Cory winked.

Relieved that the moment was over, Fury wanted to tell her sister about the Kentucky trip, and the anonymous note, but resisted out of desire to avoid any further tension.

After lunch, they shopped for summer clothes for the girls, and Cory bought a sleeper for the baby.

"I'm a pushover for baby clothes," she said, handing the bag to Fury.

CHAPTER THIRTY

Three weeks went by. Gray was busy with work. Fury had immersed herself in the organization of her research. While time had dimmed the anxiety over the anonymous note, she had not yet accessed the archives at the Arabella office of MacGregor Marble. She told herself not to allow the note to impede her work on the book, but subconsciously, she had avoided working outside of home and couldn't help but take an inventory of those who might be responsible.

As much as she fought the idea, she had even included Cory and Gray in the pool of potential suspects but quickly reprimanded herself for such thoughts. *If Gray wanted me to stop the project, he's had plenty of opportunities to say so. Cory may not like my marriage, but she wouldn't do anything like this.* Mike was the only person she excluded from the list of suspects, but she did not mention the note to him.

Concerning Zaira, Fury had not found an opportunity to maneuver a conversation with Gray to include any reference to his mother. However, she stayed in contact with her mother-in-law through email and was feeling increasingly closer to the woman. As estranged as Gray and his mother were, the relationship between the two women made Fury feel closer to her husband. Stories that Zaira shared about Gray's childhood were precious to Fury. While Ella knew much about his youth after Zaira was gone, she avoided personal conversations with Fury.

On the first Monday in April, Fury received a packet of documents maintained by the Milledgeville asylum on the commitment and confinement of James Dolan.

It took them long enough.

The old records were sketchy but showed that his commitment papers to Georgia State Sanitarium were signed by a Benjamin Carlson, MD of Arabella, Georgia. According to the registration form, James Dolan was identified as criminally insane because of infective-exhaustive psychosis and manic depression.

According to Carlson: "Patient diagnosed as result of violent behavior, arising from manic episode in which he stated he would kill his employer." The doctor recommended that Dolan be treated as psychopathic and extremely dangerous. The notes indicated that Jim was brought in bound, gagged, and sedated.

Fury cringed as she read.

It took most of the day to review the old papers. The more she read, the angrier she became. According to descriptions in the records, Jim had been hostile, claiming that he was railroaded into the institution to cover up crimes committed by his employer.

October 14, 1925: Patient continues to rant that his commitment is fraudulent. He suffers from delusions. Extreme measures may be necessary.

December 23, 1925: Patient is chained in room. Must be continually sedated to reduce manic outbursts.

October 21, 1927: Malaria treatment implemented.

Fury made notes as she read for terms to research.

August 3, 1929: Today, Jim appeared calm. Weight loss significant. Purging appears to be working.

June 10, 1935: Insulin therapy begun on patient. Coma induced each day for four weeks. Patient has seizures. Therapy not effective. Still insists that he was falsely admitted.

No one listened to that poor man.

August 14, 1941: Patient uncontrollable today. Screamed that boss should go to prison. Dr. Longino authorizes electroshock therapy.

Nowhere in the records was there a reference to a physically violent act committed by Jim prior to admission. His only recorded violent behavior had occurred when resisting treatment.

I would have fought that torture, too.

According to the records, Jim was frequently placed in a straitjacket with tape over his mouth. He spent the first few years of his confinement chained to the floor of his room.

Oh, Jim. What pain and humiliation you must have endured.

It wasn't until an entry made in 1946 that Jim was labeled as docile.

> **March 8, 1946:** Patient docile and responding well to treatment.

He had to either adjust or die. His brain was probably so fried by the "Georgia Power cocktails" that he didn't know or care where he was.

The final entry was made the day of Jim's death in 1970. It simply read:

"James Dolan found unresponsive at 6:15 a.m. Attempts to resuscitate the patient were unsuccessful. Family notified to claim the body. Cause of death: Natural causes. No autopsy ordered."

Fury's fingers flew across her legal pad while tears smeared the ink. "Forty-five of Jim's sixty-six years of life were spent in a torture chamber because of the crimes of another man. My grandmother repeatedly raped and denied the love of her life. Even his own son's life ruined—his daughter-in-law committed suicide—all because one man had too much money, too much power, and no moral compass."

Filing the documents, Fury's initial fire was re-ignited. *He lived a life in hell on earth because of J.G. MacGregor. I have to write my book.* She made up her mind to make the trip to MacGregor Marble.

When she arrived at the company office a few days later, Fury received a royal welcome. Although the officials had been present at the Christmas party, she remembered no one. Several referred to meeting her, which she deflected with a perfunctory nod, saying, "Of course. Nice to see you again."

"Gray said to show you where the ancient company records are stored. I have to warn you, it's pretty danged dusty and dank down there," the senior vice president, Elijah Benson, said as he led her to the basement.

"I'm completely accustomed to foraging around in dusty records. I'll be fine."

"I'm going to send Thomas, our new intern from the college over in Atlanta, to help you. We have to take care of our first lady."

Southern charm oozing by the bucketful. They must sell it at the local Walmart.

Fury's impulse was to reject the offer of assistance, but remembering the volume of material in the Forglen attic, coupled with her desire to spend as little time as possible in the company cellar, she smiled and thanked the man.

Thomas turned out to be a Godsend. The second pair of eyes, plus the young man's physical strength, allowed Fury to reach the boxes with records from 1925 in far less time than she could have accomplished alone.

"What are you looking for?" Thomas asked. "I might be able to help you find it." He had stacked three large boxes labeled 1925 by a dusty library table in the center of the space.

"Problem is, Thomas, I don't know what I'm looking for. It's a case of know-it-when-you-see-it."

The young man appeared disappointed.

"But, you can certainly help me sort the papers. I'd like to separate the personal documents from the strictly company business."

While Thomas began his assignment, Fury decided to wander around the dreary space. She wasn't sure why, but something told her to explore. The boxes of old records were stacked neatly on metal shelving. She noticed that 1950 was the last year stored there. "I wonder if there are rats in here," she said as she perused the shelves.

"What did you say?" Thomas shouted.

"I was just thinking that there might be rats down here."

"I hope not."

When she reached the back wall, there was a row of metal cabinets, approximately six-feet-tall with padlocks. Two were secured.

"Thomas," Fury shouted. "Can you come here?"

"Are you okay?" he responded as he hurried back to her.

"I'm fine, but look at those locked cabinets. I want to see what's inside."

"How would we get into them? Those are sturdy locks."

"Whatever is inside was not intended to be seen."

Fury drew her cell phone out of her pocket and hit a number.

"Gray, I'm in the basement at MacGregor Marble. Are there any keys to the metal cabinets in here?"

Thomas's jaw almost dropped. Seeing the shocked look on the young man's face, Fury remembered that Benson had introduced her as Fury O'Quinn. *This kid didn't realize that he was working with the boss's wife. I wonder why that wasn't made clear?*

"If he doesn't have any keys, do you have any problem with our having the locks broken?" Fury said to her husband.

Fury glanced over at Thomas.

"I was referring to a nice young man from Atlanta Metropolitan College assigned to help me. He's interning here. Can you call Mr. Benson and let him know that you're okay with us breaking into these cabinets. I don't want any hassle."

When she hung up, Thomas said, "Were you talking to *Mr. MacGregor?*"

Fury smiled. "He's mortal."

"But—"

"I'm Mrs. MacGregor. Apparently, Mr. Benson didn't tell you."

"No, ma'am. He didn't."

Seeing instant awkwardness develop in their relationship, Fury reached out and patted the young man's shoulder. "I'm mortal, too. Relax."

Thomas tried, but Fury could tell that it would take him time to adjust. *Poor kid. He is probably hoping to get a job with the company. Now he's as nervous with me as a mouse at a cat convention.*

"Would you mind asking Mr. Benson if he knows where the keys are to these cabinets? If he doesn't, we're going to need a locksmith."

Before Thomas could walk upstairs, they heard Benson calling, "Ms. MacGregor. Where are you?"

Fury looked at Thomas. "That didn't take long." Turning toward the stairs, she called out, "We're against the back wall."

Finding his way to them, Benson said, "Gladys called from the Atlanta office and said that you need keys for some cabinets and that I was to make sure you get them."

"I do, but only two are locked. They're right here." Fury pointed to the metal cupboards.

"I don't think we have the keys."

"Then, would you be so kind as to call a locksmith?"

Thomas was watching the exchange, mesmerized.

As Benson returned to the main floor, Fury invited Thomas to have lunch with her while they waited.

Over sandwiches, the pair discussed Thomas's studies and his hopes for his future. He was working on a degree in business administration and hoping to interview Gray for a major finance paper but had not thought he would have a chance. Pastrami and Swiss on rye, with mustard and pickles, at the Arabella Deli seemed to loosen the barrier that Fury's position had created.

"Thomas, you will have your interview. I promise."

"Are you serious, Ms. MacGregor?"

"Dead serious. I have a little pull with the boss."

He grinned and wiped mustard off his fingers with a paper napkin.

The locksmith had just arrived when they got back to the office. With Thomas leading the way, they returned to the basement. It took half an hour for the man to breach the barriers. Opening the doors of the first cabinet, they found old newspapers, a few ledgers and three large, metal boxes, plus a smaller one. All were locked. Inside the second cabinet was a single, wooden box secured by a padlock.

"Someone wanted whatever is in those boxes kept secret," Thomas said.

"No doubt."

As the technician began packing up, Fury said, "Don't leave yet." She pointed to the boxes. "The job's not quite finished."

Popping the remaining locks was accomplished quickly. Fury

waited until the locksmith was gone before opening the containers.

The first one she attempted to pick up was heavy, so she bypassed it in favor of the smaller one. Thomas watched as she opened the container. Her heart raced as she saw the collection of carbon copies bearing the heading: "MacGregor Marble." Under the company name was printed: "J.G. MacGregor, President." Other letters appeared to be originals to J.G. from a law firm, Dr. Carlson, and even the Sheriff of Mercy County.

"I've found it, Thomas." As he looked down in the box, she said, "This is what I hoped to discover." She carefully leafed through a few of the yellowed papers. "Could you find me some empty banker's boxes? I don't want to carry those heavy metal ones home."

"Yes, ma'am."

You didn't want anyone to see these, did you, J.G.?

As Thomas left, Fury turned to the heavy box and raised the lid.

Oh, my, gosh!

CHAPTER THIRTY-ONE

Stunned, Fury stood motionless in awe and disbelief at what she was looking at.

Gold! You old bastard—you squirreled away a secret fortune.

The box was packed to capacity with solid gold ingots. Catching her breath, she looked inside the remaining boxes and found more of the same, plus several cloth bags. Opening three of the pouches, she found gold coins. The fourth held what appeared to be diamonds. Her hands trembled as she put the bags back in the box, and picked up an ingot.

What do I do with this? I can't just leave it with broken locks. I have to talk to Gray.

She closed the boxes, glad that she had been alone when the contents were exposed.

Still in shock from the contents of the metal containers, she opened the wooden box. There was no gold. Instead, it contained letters, a few documents on MacGregor Marble letterhead, and an enameled jewelry box with a chinoiserie motif. Fury immediately noticed that several letters were addressed to J. Graeme MacGregor, Jr. or simply Graeme MacGregor.

These belonged to Gray's grandfather, not J.G.

Taking out her cell phone, she made another call to Gray.

"Can you come over here before this office closes? There's something here that you need to address, and I can't tell anyone else or talk about it right now." As she spoke, she could hear Thomas coming back down the stairs.

"I'm busy right now. Is it urgent?" Gray asked.

She lowered her voice to a near whisper. "It's pretty important, Gray."

"I'll be there by four."

As she put her cell phone back in her pocket, Thomas walked up with a package of unassembled banker's boxes. Ripping the cellophane wrapping off, he put one together and handed it to Fury. She took the contents of the smaller, metal box and stacked them in the paper container.

"That will be much easier to carry. Thank you, Thomas." She labeled it "II" with a magic marker. "If you don't mind, assemble the rest of the cartons."

"What about the other boxes, Mrs. MacGregor? Should I transfer the contents?"

Fury didn't respond. She wasn't sure what to say. Until Gray arrived, she did not want anyone to know about the gold. "Actually, Thomas, there are some family items in those that I want Gray to see before a decision is made about what to do with it. He's coming over."

"Mr. MacGregor?" The young man's face lit up. "Is he coming here today?"

Fury smiled. "He is." *I'm not that much older than this kid, but I feel like his mother.*

"If you don't mind me asking, how old are you, Thomas?"

"Almost twenty-one."

She smiled. *How long it seems since I was twenty-one.* "Maybe you can ask Mr. MacGregor about the interview when he gets here."

"Are you sure that he wouldn't mind?"

"I'm sure. While we are waiting, let's look around on the open shelves—just to be sure that we haven't missed any of the records from 1925."

Gray arrived at the office fifteen minutes before four. Apache was with him. Fury and Thomas were sitting in the reception room, looking through photo albums of marble pieces made by the company over the century it had been in operation. When Gray entered, Thomas sprang to attention like a private giving respect to the general. Almost as quickly, Benson appeared as though he had radar.

"Mr. MacGregor, to what do we owe the honor of your visit today?"

How the heck did he know Gray was on site?

"Relax. Please. I just came to check on my wife and to see if she needs any help."

"I assigned young Thomas here to assist her. Do you need anything else, Ms. MacGregor?"

"I'm fine," Fury said. "Gray, I'm craving a latté from Starbucks. Would you like something? I bet Thomas wouldn't mind running downtown for us."

"I'd be glad to, sir."

Gray pulled out his wallet and handed the eager young man a fifty-dollar bill. "Pick up a medium coffee, black, for me and a decaf latté for Mrs. MacGregor. Benson, would you like a coffee?"

"That's very kind of you, but I've had my quota for the day."

"Get yourself something, too, Thomas," Gray said as the young man left. He then turned to Benson. "Don't let us interrupt you, Eli. Fury can show me down to the archives."

Knowing he had been dismissed, Benson said, "If there's anything you need, don't hesitate to shout out."

As soon as the man was out of earshot, Gray said, "Okay, Irish, show me what has you so alarmed, but please tell me that it's not body parts."

"Not quite." Fury led him down into the cellar and back to where the cabinets were. Removing the lighter box, she raised the lid of the heavy one.

"What the fuck?"

Nodding her head, she said, "See why I called."

Gray whistled, reached in, and picked up an ingot. "Do you know what these damn things are going for?"

"No, Mr. Financial Genius, I have no idea, but I know they're worth a lot."

"If I recall right from the listings on Friday, these are going for about seventy-thousand a piece, give or take a few thousand. Have you counted how many are here?"

257

"No. But that's not all. There are two bags of gold coins and a bag of diamonds. Someone in your family had quite a piggy bank. I'm guessing it was your great-grandfather."

"If so, he must have planned to coat the roof of Forglen to match the dome of the Georgia State Capital. Is there anything in the boxes to identify the time or source?"

"I don't think so, but I didn't take everything out."

Gray moved some of the ingots around, searching for clues in the boxes. "Irish, I think you've just uncovered a nightmare."

"It doesn't look like a nightmare to me—more like a dream-come-true for most people."

"Sweetheart, the Gold Reserve Act in1933 forced private citizens to sell their gold to the Treasury. From then until 1974, it was illegal for private citizens to own gold. If old J.G. squirreled these away, how that would play out—I have no idea. I'm not even sure who owns this stuff now, but I'm pretty sure the IRS will want a cut."

"You own the company, don't you?"

He nodded. "It might not be that simple. I think the lawyers will have to look at the chain of inheritance, unless there is evidence that it was my father's treasure chest, which I doubt."

"That's the big picture. What do we do with them now? We can't very well just close up the cabinet and leave them."

Gray shook his head with a puzzled look on his face. "I thought you might dig up something interesting, but this exceeds my imagination."

"What do we do?"

"I'd like to seal them back up and forget they exist."

"Would you do that?"

"No, as tempting as that thought is. I think the MacGregors are going to have gold under their mattress tonight." A mischievous look crept across his face. "I can't say that I've ever made love on a bed of gold."

Fury balled up her fist and rapped him on his shoulder. "That's not funny."

He smiled. "I'll get a vault tomorrow—and put my legal team to work."

"How do we get them out of here?"

"With the help of the young man we sent for coffee. Good that I'm driving the SUV."

"Do we just carry them up the stairs?"

"I'm sure there's a dolly in the building that we can use."

Fury started back to where she had left the documents she had tagged to take home. "Thomas is a nice kid. He wants to interview you for a paper he's writing in school. You will do it, won't you?"

"Do I have a choice?"

"No."

"I didn't think so. Tell him to call Gladys."

They had barely closed the boxes when Thomas called down to ask if they wanted their coffee in the basement.

Gray walked to the stairwell. "Keep it up there. We're coming." He motioned to Fury.

When they reached the waiting room, it was empty, and the building was quiet. As he handed Fury her drink, he said, "Thomas, check to see if everyone has gone for the day."

"Yes, sir. I'll be right back."

Gray took his paper cup and went to the small couch. Sitting down, he stretched his legs out on the magazine-covered table in front of the sofa.

"Make yourself at home," Fury said.

"Come sit here with me and catch your breath." He patted the cushion next to his.

"This is making me nervous. I feel like a thief," Fury said as she sat.

Gray smiled and put an arm around her shoulder. "Relax. It'll make a good story to tell our grandkids."

"I'm almost afraid to keep digging—afraid of what I might find next."

"Just don't dig in the garden at Forglen. I can't deal with the dead bodies you might find." He smiled and squeezed her shoulder.

You think you're kidding.

By the time Thomas came back, Gray had finished his coffee.

"Only the security guards are left in the building, Mr. MacGregor."

"Fine," Gray said. "Drink your coffee, and then find me a hand truck. There must be one around here."

Thomas nodded. "There's one in the supply room, sir."

"We're going back downstairs. Bring it to us when you find it."

Gray and Fury spent the night at Forglen, although he did not put the gold under the bed as he had threatened. The containers were stacked in the corner of their bedroom. When they had unloaded, Edward had offered to help, but Gray refused.

"We've got it covered. You can hold the door open for me." Even with the hand truck, it took three trips because of the weight.

When they were alone, Fury put her hand on the top box and said, "Surely, you trust Edward."

"Trust him not to steal the gold? Absolutely. Trust him not to let it slip that we have it? Absolutely not."

"I hadn't thought about that."

The next morning, Gray kissed Fury goodbye and promised to have the gold transferred before the day was over.

"If you don't mind, I'd rather you stayed here today. No one will go in our room without your permission."

"Sure. But, please have it moved as soon as you can. I feel paranoid, even though we're the only ones who know about it. I'm sure that thieves have gold-detecting GPS devices for something of this caliber."

At eleven-thirty, Gray arrived back at Forglen for lunch. Fury was in their bedroom reading. "There's an armored car coming to transfer the gold. I'll take the stones and coins to a bank deposit box."

"Are you staying until they arrive?"

"I am. I don't want you responsible for the inventory."

"I'll be relieved when everything is gone. I feel like a CIA operative, and I think Edward and Ella suspect something is amiss. Did you talk to your lawyers?"

"I'm about as paranoid as you are. I decided to wait until everything was in a vault before speaking to anyone. I did have Gladys make an appointment for Frank Lowell to come to my office tomorrow. I'll brief him then and let him delve into the legalities."

"I'd better collect the documents that we scattered between the boxes before the car gets here."

"While you're doing that, I'm going to make some phone calls." He kissed the top of her head and went downstairs.

After the security people removed the gold, Fury took the box of documents to her car while Gray completed the paperwork. When the armored vehicle pulled away, Gray said, "Want to have dinner here or go back to Atlanta?"

"Atlanta. I didn't expect to stay over last night. Thank goodness I left Gypsy plenty of food, but I'm sure it's running low by now."

Gray met with his lawyer the next day, and the investigation began as to who held title to the valuable property.

"At first blush, I would say it's all yours, Gray, but I can't suggest that you act on that until I do the research," Lowell said.

"I imagine that you need to look into any ramifications involved regarding the ownership during the prohibited time period, as well as the chain of inheritance, and the taxes that might be involved."

"That would cover it. Too bad the original owner didn't leave a clue as to when it was stashed away."

"We might could tell by identification of the containers, but that would only work if the containers are reasonably current."

Fury was anxious to delve into the documents she found in the company cellar but waited until she was back in the condo and Gray was at work. She had become so emotional when reading the asylum records that she was afraid to review J.G.'s papers with Gray present. Checking her email, she was relieved that there was no message from Zaira. Fury was beginning to feel guilty that she had not tried to talk to Gray about his mother. She knew how anxious Zaira was to make contact with Gray, but the time had not yet presented itself for that discussion.

On Friday morning after her trip to MacGregor Marble, Fury spread the documents out on the dining room table and began sorting them. Picking up one letter with J.G.'s signature, she could almost feel his presence.

As she had all of her stacks in order, her phone rang. She recognized Mike's number on the caller ID.

"Hey, Dad. What's up?"

"I've got a spot of the flu, lass. Could you fetch some supplies for me? I hate to ask, but the fever's a little high, and my pantry is low."

"Say no more. I'm on my way."

It was after four o'clock when Fury got back to the condo. Mike had promised that if his fever went higher, or he didn't improve within twenty-four hours, he would call his doctor.

It's too late to spread everything out now. I'll have to wait until Monday, darn it.

Turning to the day's mail delivery, her heart stopped.

On top was an ominous envelope like the one she received before. She stood paralyzed for a minute—not wanting to know the contents.

This is ridiculous. I have to open it.

CHAPTER THIRTY-TWO

Her fear was justified; the plain paper inside read:

"SECOND WARNING: STOP INVESTIGATING THE MACGREGOR FAMILY."

Fury trembled, causing the paper to shake. *What should I do?*

The awkwardness that surrounded the potential book kept her from taking the notes to Gray. She had started to throw the first one away—wanted to burn it—but as the daughter of a police officer, she knew better. After looking at warning number two, she returned it to the envelope, took it to her study, and filed it with the first one.

Who is sending these and why? Is there a relationship between my trip to the company and this one?

Both notes had been mailed to the condo. Gladys certainly knew the address, and Ella could find it easily enough.

I don't care who is doing this. I'm writing the book. Bridget and Jim deserve for the truth to come out, and J.G. deserves to go down in history as the horrible man he was.

The weekend was uneventful. Fury checked on Mike and was pleased to find him better. She tried to forget the anonymous notes, but a reminder would flash through her mind periodically. She wanted to begin reviewing the MacGregor documents, but Gray did not leave their home without her. She was never comfortable working on the research when he was around.

Sunday morning, the couple relaxed on the condo balcony, drinking coffee and reading the papers. "This being tax week, I'll be working late every night. How about my making it up to you with two weeks in Cashiers at the end of the month," Gray said.

"Can you afford that much time away from the office?"

"I will stay in touch electronically but should have plenty of quiet time for us. We can figure out our domicile. We will need more room when the baby comes."

"You are right. As long as Dad is okay, I'd love to get away. Maybe you can give me riding lessons while we're there."

He shook his head. "Not this time, sweetheart," he said, reaching for her hand. "That will have to wait until after September. I don't want you to risk taking a fall."

She looked at him for a second as if assimilating his statement. "You're right. I hadn't thought about the baby."

"You've got the rest of your life to ride—between pregnancies." She jerked her hand away and sat up straight. "Exactly how many babies are you expecting me to have?"

He started laughing and pulled her back to him. "I'm teasing you, Irish. But, I hope we have one or two more. An only child can be a lonely child."

After Gray left for his office on Monday, Fury cleaned up the breakfast dishes, made the bed, and dressed in record time. By seven-thirty, she had the files arranged on the dining room table. Choosing the Carlson file first, she flipped through the dates until she found correspondence exchanged in June of 1925. The first was written by J.G. to Dr. Benjamin Carlson.

June 17, 1925

Dear Ben:

I am told by Floyd Lawton that you have the authority to admit a patient to Milledgeville. For the protection of society, I believe that one of my employees, James Dolan, should be so confined. The man is out of control and dangerous. He has threatened my life. Time is of the essence. Advise at your earliest convenience as to what steps are necessary to accomplish this action.

It goes without saying that you will most certainly be generously compensated for handling this matter. Your discretion goes without mention.

>   Very truly yours,
>   J.G. MacGregor.

"I knew it," Fury said aloud. Without reading any more correspondence in the Carlson file, she dug through the records for the E.F. Lawton, Counselor at Law file.

It was substantially thicker and took Fury several minutes to isolate the relevant period. Pulling out a letter dated June 16, 1925, from Lawton to MacGregor, Fury shook as she read:

Dear J.G.,

Following our confidential conversation of last night, I reiterate my position that you should allow the authorities to arrest the girl. There was a serious attempt on your life that resulted in the perilous condition that your dear wife is experiencing.

Of course, my greatest sympathies are extended, and my prayers are being said for the rapid recovery of Mrs. MacGregor.

Understanding your concern for the delicacies of the matter, and your desire to make certain that allegations remain private, I recommend that you assist the girl in relocation to an area as far from Arabella as can be managed.

As for her brother, he said that someone should kill you. It is my legal opinion that such a statement is grounds enough to declare the man criminally insane. Consult with Ben Carlson. No doubt, he has the forms necessary for admission to Milledgeville. In my view, from that position, young Dolan can do you no harm.

As always, I serve at your pleasure with the utmost discretion and confidentiality.

>   Floyd Lawton.

Oh, Bridget. What did you do?

Fury sat for a few moments, looking at the two letters side by side. There was the smoking gun—evidence of the conspiracy that sent an innocent man to a brutal life of torture and forever changed the course of life for the abused teenager.

You must have felt so helpless and so desperate, Bridget.

Staring out the window in thought for several minutes, Fury decided that she had to know what Bridget had done. Emma's condition would be a clue, but the hospital where she was treated had not been named in any of the documents. Taking a fresh folder from her supplies, Fury put in the two letters and labeled the file "CONSPIRACY."

I need to find out where Emma was admitted. Either I can search through all those papers from 1925 for payment of her medical expenses, or I can try calling around to the hospitals that existed in 1925.

She decided on the canvass, gathered up all the files, and returned them to her office cabinet. With a quick search of the Internet, she found six hospitals in operation in 1925. One was easy to eliminate, because it had treated only crippled children. That left five. Would they have the archives? Was Emma admitted under her real name?

What hospital would J.G. take Emma to? Probably not Georgia Baptist or Grady. He wouldn't want her in a big facility, much less one that treated the poor. Maybe the old Emory University Hospital—Wesley Memorial?

She began calling. After being passed around the medical records departments of each hospital, she finally got promises from three that they would delve into archives and get back with her. Each warned her that the records might be confidential.

"I think you can release them if they are over seventy-five years old," she replied, basing her assumption on discovery that the Milledgeville records were open access after three-quarters of a century.

This is not going to happen today or tomorrow, I bet.

On Wednesday, Emory called to say they had no record of an Emma MacGregor being a patient in the year 1925. Thursday, Saint Joseph's Hospital of Atlanta left a similar message on Fury's voice mail.

This may be an exercise in futility.

She was wrong. On Friday morning, as Fury was packing for North Carolina, she got the message. Saint Luke's, a small, private hospital, had found the records of Emma's stay. They were making copies from the microfilm, which Fury could pick up the following week.

"I'll be out of town, but let me give you my credit card information. Charge the copies to me, and I'll pick them up as soon as I return."

Fury had everything packed and the luggage lined up by the front door by the time Gray came home on Tuesday afternoon. She had taken Gypsy to Cory's house. Apache would go with them. The minute Gray walked in, Fury could see from the relaxed expression on his face how happy he was to be leaving Atlanta.

"You would love to live on the mountain, wouldn't you?" she asked, watching him change into jeans and a sweatshirt.

"You got me. It is my favorite place to be."

When they got to Cashiers, the majority of their time was spent relaxing; however, both did a little work. Gray spent about an hour each day in his downstairs office. Fury worked on an outline for the historical book and made notes for her next romance novel. On the first Thursday, they debated the matter of where they would make their primary home.

"I think we agree that we want to raise our family in a house, not a mid-town condo," Gray said.

Fury nodded. "I grew up in a Brooklyn apartment and always wanted to live in a house with a yard."

"Then our first consideration is whether to live in Atlanta or Arabella."

"It would be a lot better for you if we live in Atlanta."

"If you're thinking about the commute, it doesn't bother me. In fact, it gives me time to get my head in and out of the business."

"Then why do you have the condo?"

He waited a minute before responding. "To avoid Forglen."

Fury reached across the table where they were sitting and took his hand. "Then why have you kept it? It's yours to do with as you like."

"Maybe I've just been too busy to bother with selling it."

"You're always reading my mind. I'm going to read yours, my love. I think you've kept it because despite all the evil voodoo there, there are some good ghosts, too."

He crinkled his brow and cocked his head slightly askew. "You'd better leave the mind reading to me." He got up and went to the refrigerator. "Want something to drink?"

"Come back here, Gray MacGregor. You know I'm right."

"Water or Pepsi?"

"Not going to work. We're going to figure this out today, and Forglen is a big piece of the decision." She stood up and motioned for him to come back to the table. He obliged.

"I'm not as smart as you are, Gray, but I'm smart enough to figure out that you don't want to live in Atlanta and that something ties you to Forglen. It's just a house. The house didn't do anything wrong, and the people who did are dead. I agree that there are things about it that will conjure up negative feelings, but I think we can paint them out of the picture. Buy new furniture, change the overall atmosphere, and the bad memories will be abolished—poof!" She snapped her fingers in the air. "I have my demons there, too, but believe I can redecorate them away. I don't see you disposing of a home that's been in your family for four generations, and I really don't see us keeping it while living in another house in Arabella."

Fury wanted to remind him of the good memories—of the smiling child that he had been with his mother. However, she was afraid that to bring up Zaira would risk spoiling their holiday.

"If we can table any talk of the history of the estate, then I'll agree that we try your idea. Do whatever you like, and we'll see what happens."

Toward the end of their second week, Gray had just returned from taking Apache for a walk and had gone into the kitchen for a bottle of water. Fury was at the opposite end of the house, watching TV. Suddenly, she cried out for him. He rushed to the bedroom with Apache close behind.

"Honey, what's wrong?"

She was standing by the bed, one hand on her stomach. "Nothing's wrong. The baby is wiggling. Here." She pointed to her bulging stomach.

His eyes lit up as he moved closer, and put his hand flat against her abdomen. She guided it to where the she felt the movement.

"Do you feel it?"

"I do," he whispered. "I feel it." He pulled her against his body, one hand still on her belly, the other around her waist. As she laid her head against his chest, he whispered, "I love you, Fury MacGregor. As God is my witness, I promise to do my best to be the husband and father that you and this baby deserve."

"You already are." She pulled back, put her arms around his neck, and they kissed. As they parted, she said, "I think he waited until we were here to make his move. We met here, married here, conceived him here, and he's reached out to us here."

Gray grinned and kissed her again. "*He*? What makes you think it's not *she*?"

"He's a boy. I know it. But, the sonogram will tell us for sure on May 3rd."

"Oh, really?"

"Yep. You'll be there."

He looked at her with a question on his face.

"It's on your calendar. I've already had Gladys mark it out."

"So, you're going to let them tell us the gender?"

"Of course. Did you think that I could wait another five months to find out?"

He shook his head—still grinning. "Why did I even ask?" Taking her hand, he said, "Let's go out on the deck, watch the sunset, and savor the moment."

Departing Cashiers at the end of their stay had been a mix of emotions. One part of Fury hated leaving the beauty and tranquility of the mountain. The other was excited about having the sonogram, starting the Forglen renovation, and picking up Emma MacGregor's medical records.

"I already miss the mountains," Fury said as Gray started to leave for the office the morning after their return.

"We'll go back soon. With summer months ahead, we'll squeeze in as much time as we can up there."

As soon as he was gone, Fury fed the pets, took a shower, and left for Saint Luke's Hospital. After obtaining Emma's records, she drove to the post office and picked up the mail held during their absence. Back at the condo, she opened the medical records, first. The faded writing was difficult to read, but the word "poison" stood out. Struggling to make out the handwritten narrative, she read:

> Female patient, age forty-two, admitted at one a.m. in a semiconscious state. Patient is said by her husband to have accidentally ingested rat poison. Patient has acute abdominal pain, nausea, and diarrhea. Skin is slightly discolored. She has suffered what her personal physician, Dr. Carlson, described as a seizure while en route here. Her breath has a distinct odor of garlic, consistent with arsenic commonly used in control of rodents. Protocol for arsenic poisoning begun.

You tried to poison him, Bridget. But—it was poor Emma who consumed it. Thank goodness she lived.

After returning the hospital records to the envelope, Fury was so absorbed by what Emma's medical reports had revealed that she ignored the remaining mail.

J.G. couldn't risk the threat of Bridget's motive coming out in a trial. He used his money and power to ship her thousands of miles away and to put Jim in the asylum.

Fury's heart was pounding. *The pieces fit.* Putting the mail aside, she went to the terrace door and stared out at the city while mentally reviewing all the information she had found. She could almost hear her grandmother say, "Now you know the truth."

Gypsy threw herself against Fury's leg, interrupting her

concentration. "I did it, little bit. I found the pieces of the puzzle." After petting the cat, she returned to her desk and flipped through the remaining correspondence, discarding the junk and sorting the rest. Halfway finished, she saw it—the plain, white envelope.

No, not another one!

She dropped the mail in her hand on the desk as though it were on fire, got up, and walked to the terrace. *I can't read it. This isn't a prank. Someone is seriously threatening me.*

The rest of the afternoon, Fury avoided her office. She tried to read but couldn't concentrate. She tried to watch television, but found her mind wandering to the anonymous notes.

I have to tell Gray. I can't ignore them any longer.

She was playing Solitaire on her Palm Pilot when she heard his key in the door at seven o' clock. Tossing the device aside, she sprang to greet him. Apache pushed through the opening first, but Fury ignored her, throwing her arms around Gray.

"I'm so glad you're home." She clung to him.

"I like the enthusiastic welcome, but why are you shaking?"

"I thought you would never get here. There's something I have to tell you." She took his hand and led him to her office.

"What is it, honey?"

Pointing to her desk, she said, "Open that plain envelope with no return address."

He looked at her with a puzzled expression.

"Just open it. I can't."

He picked up the brass letter opener and sliced through the paper. Taking the single sheet out, he read the words aloud.

"CONTINUE DIGGING WHERE YOU DON'T BELONG AND SUFFER THE CONSEQUENCES."

Looking first at the front of the envelope and then up at her, he said, "What the hell is this about?"

"Someone doesn't want me to write about your family."

"And they sent you anonymous notes? I'm assuming this isn't the first, since you couldn't open it yourself."

Fury nodded.

"How many?"

"This is the third."

"Why haven't you told me before?"

"I thought it was a harmless attempt to make trouble and wouldn't happen again. But, now it's scaring me."

She trembled as tears began to run down her face.

"Come here, sweetheart." He reached out and pulled her to his chest. "I'll get to the bottom of this."

"What are you going to do?"

"First, we're going to take the letters to the police. You have the others, don't you?"

She pulled away from his embrace. "I do. But, Gray, if we go to the police, it could get in the papers. We don't want publicity."

"We're going to the police." His expression was resolute. "Let me see the others."

She opened a drawer, took out an unmarked file, and turned it over to him.

"Have you told your father?"

She shook her head. "I don't want to worry him. I haven't told anyone."

"That's probably good."

Fury watched as he took each note out and read it.

"Who would do this, Gray?"

"It depends on the objective. If it's what the notes say—your book—then I think we have to start with people around me. But, if that's just an excuse to harass you or to cause trouble, then it could be anyone. I see that all the envelopes are postmarked 'Atlanta.'"

"I don't know of anyone in Atlanta who knows that I'm working on a book about your family, except Dad and Scarlett Kavanagh. Of course, Dad talks a lot at the pub."

"Scarlett Kavanagh?" He frowned as if puzzled.

Fury looked him in the eye. "Scarlett Kavanagh. . . . Harvard. . . . You dated."

"Oh." He tipped his head with a puzzled look on his face. "You know Scarlett?"

"Yeah." Her voice drew the word out as she nodded. "You should know that she gave you a four-star rating back when we first started dating."

"Four stars? Checked me out, did you?"

"Of course. Just like you did me."

He chuckled. "Back to this situation. Try not to worry about it until we talk to professionals. I'll take care of hiring protection for you."

"*No*, absolutely not. I don't want that."

"Fury, I want you protected. We don't know what kind of kook we're dealing with."

"Well, I don't want strangers hanging around my every move— unless it gets worse. I'll be extra cautious."

Tuesday morning, Gray and Fury met with a detective at the Atlanta Police Department. Given Fury's public status and Gray's wealth and position, the detective took the notes seriously but was skeptical about being able to trace the sender.

"These are extremely difficult and frustrating cases. Isolated episodes of anonymous letters are often unresolved. Have there been any other unusual happenings in your life, Mrs. MacGregor?"

Fury thought for a minute and then said, "I have had some hang-ups on my phone, which I thought were strange, but did not connect them to the notes."

"We'll pull a log of calls from your carrier, have you identify any unfamiliar, incoming numbers, and then we'll run those down. If anything else out of the ordinary occurs, let me know." He handed a card to both Gray and Fury.

As Gray put the card in his wallet, he said, "Detective Ryland, we want this kept quiet. I'm sure you understand that neither of us wants the media involved."

"I understand, Mr. MacGregor. It's not our policy to leak information to the press. I hope that we can solve it, but I have to warn you, again, that it might not be easy."

"Can't you test the notes for fingerprints?" Gray asked.

"I'll turn these envelopes over to our forensics lab, but it's a long shot."

"I'll pay for any sophisticated testing available," Gray said.

"I understand your concern, Mr. MacGregor, but I assure you that I'll do everything possible to determine who is stalking your wife."

Leaving the building, Gray was agitated. "I may need to hire my own people to investigate this business."

"It could go away," Fury said. "Maybe we're wrong to keep our contact with the police secret. If the culprit knew that law enforcement is involved, he or she might be afraid to continue."

He shook his head. "I'm not going to assume that. But for now, let's get lunch."

On Thursday, Gray and Fury met at her doctor's office. After her routine examination, Gray was called in for the sonogram. He sat in a chair beside the table and held her hand as the technician rolled the Doppler over her abdomen. "Can you see your baby?" the woman asked.

Fury squeezed Gray's hand. "I see him. Can you see him?"

Smiling, he said, "I think I do."

The technician grinned. "This is one of my favorite parts of the job. You were right, Fury. You have a healthy baby boy in there."

"See, I told you," Fury said, grinning at Gray.

"I should have known better than to doubt you."

Fury didn't return to her writing after the visit to the Atlanta Police. It was as if the notes had put a barrier between her and the accumulated research. She couldn't get the anonymous threats off her mind. Someone was serious about blocking the book. Regardless of her resolve not give in to coercion, she was nonetheless stifled.

Without the motivation to work on the book, Fury was lost. She met Cory for lunch one day and her dad another, but said nothing to them about the notes. As much as she fought it, there was a tiny possibility in her mind that Cory was the sender. Fury almost hoped that she was. Her sister would not pose a bodily threat. Her motivation would be to cause trouble between the MacGregors and potentially break up the marriage. *How am I even thinking for a second that it could be Cory? She would never do anything so disreputable. The person behind those notes is cruel, maybe dangerous.*

"I'm going to start on the renovation of Forglen, if that's okay with you," she said to Gray a week after their visit to the Atlanta Police station. They were having dinner at a favorite restaurant and planning to see a movie. "I'm really not ready to work on the book."

"I'm all for you starting the makeover, but I don't want you intimidated by those notes. You've worked too hard."

"I'm not giving it up, just taking a break."

Once she started, Fury was immersed in the project and spent the next few weeks selecting a decorator, reviewing catalogs, meeting with subcontractors, and shopping for new furniture and accessories. She tried to include Ella in some of the decisions but was met with a lack of enthusiasm. She ceased trying. Ella was never rude, but never embraced her new mistress. The housekeeper continued to be an unspoken suspect in Fury's mind.

By the end of May, no further anonymous communications had appeared, lulling the MacGregors into a comfort zone. Detective Ryland sent Fury the phone log. She marked the unknown numbers and sent it back. However, they were unable to trace the subject calls. All came from disposable phones, pointing to the probability that it was her stalker. Gray continued to lobby for hiring security; Fury continued to object.

"I haven't received any more messages. It may have blown over," she told him.

In early June, she resumed work on the book and created an outline. She remained conflicted over whether she would write it as fiction or non-fiction. Her original intent had been to write a novel, but she was plagued with a belief that only a non-fiction book would adequately avenge Jim and Bridget.

Fury and Zaira were communicating regularly, mostly by email. She regretted not having approached Gray about his mother but had not found the opportune moment.

"I know you're thinking that I'm never going to talk to Gray about you, but I am. It's just that he has been working so hard, and we've had a couple of complications in our life that I'll tell you about later," Fury wrote.

Zaira responded, "I've waited thirty years, a few more weeks won't hurt. I do hope that I can see you when the baby comes."

The second week of June, Fury remembered documents left in the company basement that she had not reviewed in the excitement over the gold. They had forgotten to take the banker's box that contained papers from the wooden container.

"I'm going back to MacGregor Marble tomorrow," she told Gray at dinner. "There's a box that I almost forgot about checking."

"Don't overdo it. If you wait until the weekend, I'll go with you."

"That's sweet of you to offer, but I feel great. It's just one box, and if it's too heavy, I'll get that nice young man, Thomas, to help me. You haven't mentioned giving him his interview."

"As a matter of fact, we're doing it on Friday. He's coming to the office."

"Good. He's a sweet kid. Have you heard anything from your lawyers about the gold?"

"Only that it's definitely mine to deal with according to the chain of inheritance. They're still working on the tax angle and the legalities of ownership during the prohibited time frame."

The next day, Fury arrived at MacGregor Marble and was again given the VIP treatment by the Vice President. Thomas accompanied her down to the basement, and she went to the banker's box that had blended in among the other storage boxes.

"What can I do to help you, Mrs. MacGregor?"

He is so eager.

"I tell you what. I think I would like to take this box to a more pleasant environment. Is there a conference room upstairs?"

"Yes, ma'am. It's down the hall from Mr. Benson's office."

"Can you check on whether it's available right now?"

Within ten minutes, Thomas had cleared use of the room and carried the box upstairs.

"I can take it from here, Thomas. But, if it's not too much trouble, would you pick up the sandwiches like we had last time and bring them to the conference room at noon?"

"Of course. Maybe you could give me some tips about my interview with Mr. MacGregor this week."

Fury smiled and handed the young man a fifty-dollar bill.

With Thomas out of the room, she began to empty the contents of the box on the conference table. There were some legal-type documents, a few photographs, and a small stack of envelopes. It did not take long to realize that she had personal documents that had belonged to Graeme MacGregor, Jr., not J.G.

That's why they were in a different type container. These are all papers written by or to Gray's grandfather.

Standing out among the majority of envelopes was a large one with foreign postage—Ireland. The postmark was partially obscured, but Fury was able to read January 7, 193. . . . The last number was too blurred to decipher. It was addressed to Bridget O'Quinn's sister, Rebecca Clarke, and contained a second envelope. Fury's heart raced as she saw the onionskin letter addressed to J. Graeme MacGregor, Jr. but without postage. Taking the three-page letter out, she began reading.

> My most dearest Graeme,
>
> This comes to you from a heavy heart. Forgive me, but I cannot allow you to have my address because you can never contact me. I asked my sister to see that you received this in person. She will not give you any information concerning my home. My name is no longer Bridget Dolan.
>
> Although my heart breaks with every thought of you, it is as it must be. I couldn't leave you forever without an explanation. As hard as it is to tell you some of the following, you deserve to know the truth.
>
> I did a terrible thing. Because of it, your mother,

the kindest person I ever knew, nearly died. I take full responsibility and have prayed every day, since, for forgiveness. It was an accident, but my true intent was evil. It was your father that the rat poison was meant to make ill.

CHAPTER THIRTY-THREE

Fury put the letter down and stared out the window for a few moments.

Poor Granny. She was horribly abused, denied the person she loved, and forced to live in fear and guilt because she tried to defend herself.

Taking a deep breath, Fury resumed reading. The next page described for Graeme the brutality Bridget had suffered from his father. When she resisted him, she was met with physical and verbal abuse. He had laughed when she told him that she was in love with Graeme.

"You can forget your fancy ideas about my boy. You're nothing but the hired help, and a whore at that, but I don't mind sharing you with Graeme," J.G. had said to the girl.

Reading J.G.'s words inflamed Fury. *What a bastard!* She tried to finish the letter.

> If I there had been a knife, I would have stabbed him. Instead, I told him I was in the lady way so that he would leave me be that week. The following night, I made his tray of coffee. You know how he always added the brandy. It was not Miss Emma's custom to take coffee after dinner. I only meant to make him sick with a little of the poison that Mrs. Monihan kept for the kitchen mice.

At that point, Fury couldn't go on. Tears were streaming down her face. She turned the letter face down, got up, and walked around the room to recapture her composure. *I wish he weren't dead so that I could kill him.*

Aware that either Thomas or Benson might come in at any time, she dabbed her face with a tissue from her purse and sat back down—still not ready to read further. Thomas arrived before she returned to the letter.

He put the food and Fury's change on the table.

"Thank you, Thomas. The corned beef smells awesome."

He smiled. As they unwrapped the sandwiches, he said, "Ms. MacGregor, when I interview Mr. MacGregor, is there anything that I shouldn't ask?"

Fury looked fondly at the eager young man. "Stay away from personal questions. He'll be candid about succeeding in business, but he won't discuss his private life."

When they finished eating, Fury said, "Now, if you'll get rid of this trash while I put the papers back in the box, you can help me by taking it to my car. I'm going to call it a day."

"Yes, ma'am."

Back at the condominium, she settled in a corner of the sofa with a glass of iced tea and   forced herself to continue reading Bridget's letter.

> I knew it was wrong, but the poison was my only means of escape. It went so wrong when Miss Emma drank the coffee meant for him and collapsed. Dr. Carlson was summoned. He said she was poisoned. While the doctor tended to her, your father came to my room. He found the poison and made me confess. I thought he would see me arrested that very night, but he didn't. He sent me home with a warning of not to speak of what happened.
>
> Jim found me crying and forced me to tell him the whole story. He became angry and went to Forglen.
>
> The next night, men came and took Jim away, and then two days later, a strange man came for me. He took me to the train station in Atlanta, bought me a ticket to New York City, and gave me a little money. The man said that there would be another man in New York who would put me on the boat to Ireland. If I protested, I

would go to jail and every Dolan would be fired.

Please don't hate me. I never meant to harm your most kind and gentle mum. I am grateful to God that she survived my foolish act.

I love you, still, dear Graeme. However, as I am older and wiser, I know that we could not be. Your father would never have let you marry me. That would have been the worst of all, because we have a son—a beautiful lad of seven years this February.

Oh, my God. Bridget! Your son Ronan is the brother to both Dad and Jack MacGregor!

Stunned by the revelation, Fury put the letter down for a few seconds, and then taking a deep breath, she resumed reading.

He has the eyes of you and Miss Emma and is a happy, loving boy. I am married to a good man, whom I do love, albeit different from my love for you. We have a bonny daughter as well. Although the husband and I never speak of it, he knows that he is not the lad's true sire, but he treats the boy as his own.

I think of you often, but I know that as a pregnant servant girl with no husband, I would have been sent away to the nuns to have the child, and our precious boy would have been taken from me. In a cruel turn of fate, it is as it had to be.

Please try to think of me with kind and forgiving thoughts and know that we will all meet again one day in the hereafter.

Before I close, there is a large favor that I must ask—if you have any feelings for me left in your heart. I beg of you. Please, have Jim released from the asylum. The Dolans have no money for a lawyer. Jim was never insane. It was your evil father's doing. Please help him. Jim did no harm, and he suffers there.

Eternally gratefully, I would be for your help.
Forever,
Bridget

Fury folded the letter and put it away, tears streaming down her face.

Gray and I are related. We share a common relative . . . but, thank God, no common genes.

Watching Gray as he read the *Harvard Business Review* after dinner and then as he undressed for bed, Fury couldn't get their newly discovered relationship out of her mind.

How different our lives would have been if Bridget and Graeme had been able to marry, but now they reunite in the child I carry. How the shadows of the past hang over us in ways we never know.

That night, she slept fitfully. The baby was busy working out in her stomach, and her mind was saturated with ghosts of the past. At one point, she dreamed she was on a boat, screaming, and reaching over the side toward the place that she was leaving. She woke suddenly and sat up in bed.

"What's wrong?" Gray said, reaching out to her.

Trembling, she said, "Nothing. Just a dream."

"It must have been a nightmare, judging from how you're shaking. Come here." He pulled her over and wrapped his arms around her. "Now, go back to sleep. Everything's fine. You're safe, sweetheart."

The dream haunted Fury all the next day. *Am I the reincarnation of my grandmother, and Gray of his grandfather? Is Bridget standing behind me, guiding me?*

Two days later, Fury returned to Forglen to meet with the interior designer. She was to make final selections of the wallpaper. In the beginning, she had believed that she needed to gut all the rooms in order to modernize.

However, the designer had insisted that she consider retaining some of the old furniture. "In my opinion, some of your priceless antiques, tastefully blended with modern pieces, will produce an interesting and unique décor," he said.

"The portraits go," Fury said. "That's not up for discussion. We'll put them in storage. Future generations may want them. Gray and I don't."

By the time they were done, it was after four o'clock.

"We'd both better get back to Atlanta. Traffic is going to be horrendous," Fury said.

It was after six when she reached the condo. Gray was home, watching television, with Gypsy in his lap and Apache at his feet.

"Where have you been, Irish?"

"Forglen. I told you. I was meeting with the decorator."

"Right. How's that coming along?"

"Good. I like what he's doing. Are we cooking tonight?"

"You look beat. Let's order in."

"I'm all on board with that. You take charge while I take a shower."

He smiled. "Done."

Fury started toward the bedroom but hesitated, going into her office instead. Booting up her computer, she opened her mailbox. As usual, it was cluttered with junk emails. Deleting them quickly, she stopped abruptly on an entry with a subject-line that read:

"FINAL WARNING."

Cringing, she considered calling out to Gray, but didn't. With a click of the mouse, the image of a dead canary appeared with the caption, "What happens to those who sing too much."

Standing up, Fury screamed, "Gray!"

He was at her side almost instantly. Shaking, she pointed to her computer.

"Damn. Why the hell can't they find this bastard?" He sat down in front of her computer. "I'll check for others."

As he scrolled down the remaining new emails, his fingers froze when "Zaira Ross" appeared in the address column. Pausing for a second, he clicked it open.

The message was brief: "Had you on my mind this morning. How is the renovation coming? Let me hear. Love, Z."

He turned around. "What is this?" he asked, pointing to the screen.

Looking at the screen, Fury was speechless. She took a deep breath. "What it looks like—an email."

"Damn it, Fury. What the hell have you done?" It was the first time that he had shown anger toward her.

"Can we talk about it later?"

He glared at her for a second or two and then turned back to the screen. "We *will* talk about it." Completing his review of the inbox, he pulled out his wallet and removed Detective Ryland's card. After printing and saving the offensive message, he forwarded it to Ryland with a brief message, "My wife and I will meet with you tomorrow."

Gray closed her computer out and turned. His expression was harsh. "We'll talk now," he said, rising and shepherding her toward the living room.

Once seated on the sofa, he spoke. "Out with it. What the hell is going on?"

"It seems pretty self-explanatory."

"Don't be a smart ass. You're corresponding with Zaira?"

Without blinking an eye, Fury replied, "She's my mother-in-law."

His frown intensified. "You don't have a mother-in-law. I repeat: What the hell have you done—lie to me?"

"Don't use your top-dog-in-charge tone with me. To answer your question, I've found a lovely woman, whom I like very much, and for the record, I have not lied. Or don't you recall telling me that I was free to investigate as I require and didn't need your permission?" Fire flashed in her eyes.

Ignoring her question, he said, "What, in the name of all you hold sacred, caused you to dig her up?"

"I wanted to know the other side of the story and the woman who is our child's grandmother."

"The other side of the story is that the woman who gave birth to me walked out with a check and never looked back. I have no mother and our child has no paternal grandmother. Why would you ignore my wishes?"

"You never *told* me not to look for her."

"Why would I have expected you *to* look for her? You know how I feel, and you most certainly did it behind my back, whether you overtly lied or not."

"Gray MacGregor, you did not limit my research. And if you consider *that* going behind your back, then every bit of research I do is behind your back, because *you* don't want to know about it."

"Zaira Ross is beyond the scope of your research into J.G. MacGregor."

"Maybe, maybe not. But, she is your mother—like it or not."

He glared at her, a steely look in his eyes. "This discussion is over." He stood and started walking toward the balcony.

"No, it's not, and don't you dare walk away from me. That woman loves you. She's been through hell since your father threw her out. She made *one* mistake. You listened to him. Why can't you give her the same opportunity?"

With a hand on the terrace door, he turned. "You're asking me to *talk* to her?"

"Ten minutes of your precious time, Gray. That's all—ten minutes."

"It will never happen. I won't forbid *you* to communicate with her because it would be useless, but don't expect me to condone it, and never mention it to me again." Sparks shot from his eyes, matching hers.

Fury watched defiantly as he walked out.

CHAPTER THIRTY-FOUR

The Chinese food Gray had ordered arrived shortly after he went onto the balcony. Fury paid the delivery boy and put the bag on the kitchen bar without opening it. For the next thirty minutes, she busied herself in the condo while resisting the impulse to approach him. She could see through the glass that he was standing at the railing, apparently staring into the night. Finally, she could stand the impasse no longer and went to the door.

"Should I put the food in the refrigerator, or are you coming in?"

He turned around, looked at her for a second, and said, "I'm coming in."

As he walked toward the bar, Fury said, "Do you want me to reheat it?"

He shook his head. "It's fine."

Nothing more was said about the angry exchange, but tension in the room was heavy as they ate and then watched TV. After the late night news, Fury stayed on the sofa while Gray went to the bedroom. On his side of the bed, a notebook was waiting. Five minutes later, when she walked in, he was sitting, turning the pages. She said nothing. He did not look up, although he had to have been aware of her presence. Taking a magazine from her nightstand, she sat down in a chair near the bed and pretended to read.

After ten minutes, without looking up, he broke the silence. "Where did you get this?"

"Are you sure you want to know?"

Raising his head and glaring at her, he said, "Cut it out, and answer the damned question."

"It's a copy of an album Zaira has."

He looked at the notebook and then back at Fury. "Are you telling me the truth?"

"You're the expert. Look at me and tell me whether you think I'm lying."

"She kept this?"

"It's the only thing she took away from Forglen, other than her clothes and the infamous check."

"And she's kept it all these years?"

"You're her son. She's grieved for you—just like you grieved for her, much as you won't admit it."

He closed the notebook. "Let's get some sleep."

"That's it? You're not going to make a comment or even ask when or how I got the notebook?"

"No."

"Gray, you're thinking something. I know you are. You looked at every photograph and every article."

"I have a long day tomorrow, and I need a good night's sleep. I think I'll have a glass of brandy. Can I get you anything?"

She shook her head.

"You can get ready for bed while I'm gone. Wear something sexy."

How does he switch gears like that? "Pregnant women aren't sexy."

"I beg to differ, my love. A pregnant woman is very sexy, especially to the man responsible."

As much as Fury wanted to press him about Zaira and the album, her inner voice told her to hold back. It had been a traumatic evening in which she had stood her ground. In the end, he had looked at all the photos of his early childhood and the media articles Zaira had saved from his adult years. After Gray was asleep, Fury was still awake, replaying the events of the evening.

He had to have remembered the good times.

CHAPTER THIRTY-FIVE

The next morning, Gray acted like business as usual. He had coffee made before Fury woke and was in the process of scrambling eggs when she stumbled into the kitchen, bleary-eyed. Despite passionate, make-up intimacy, she had not slept well. Waking intermittently during the night, both Gray's hostility over her relationship with Zaira and the fear of the anonymous stalker tormented her.

"Plain or with cheese?" he asked, holding up the whisk.

"Plain. . . . Ouch."

"What's wrong?"

Fury smiled. "Nothing. I think your son is trying out for the Dallas Cowboys."

"Really." He grinned, put down the whisk, and walked over to her—placing a hand on her stomach. The baby kicked again. "I feel him." Gray stood for a moment, obviously enjoying the idea of the baby, before kissing her lightly on her cheek and returning to his eggs.

Fury poured herself a cup of coffee and set the table, Zaira still on her mind.

Bringing their plates to the table, Gray took his seat and began spreading orange marmalade on a piece of toast. "I've given it some thought," he said.

Fury's heart stopped. *Is he talking about Zaira?* She waited anxiously for his next statement.

"I think we should bring your father into the loop on this stalker."

Darn it. "Not yet, Gray. I don't want to worry him. It hasn't been that long since his heart attacks. I'm sure the APD is doing all that can be done."

"Well, it's not enough. This should have been stopped before now. With all the sophisticated technology available today, they should have been able to find this fucking guy."

"Or fucking gal. It could be a woman."

"Why would you think it's a woman?"

"Maybe an ex of yours, or a wannabe, who would like to break us up?"

"I hardly think so. My money is on some kook, looking for attention."

What about Ella or Gladys? They don't like me.

The rest of breakfast was spent talking about Forglen and the changes that were being made. Fury knew that Gray wasn't interested in the details, but he listened patiently. She wanted to bring the subject of Zaira up in their conversation but kept choking on the words. As they cleared away the dirty dishes, she took the plunge. "Gray, what about Zaira? You saw the pictures she had saved for so many years. Doesn't that change how you feel about her even a little?"

"I'm not ready to talk about that."

"Does it mean that the door may be cracked to consider it in the future?"

"Don't push it. When I'm ready, I'll let you know."

The finality in his tone told Fury that it was time to table the discussion. She wanted to give Zaira hope, but knew that if she pushed him, he might retreat permanently.

When Gray went to the bedroom to shower, shave, and dress for work, Fury opened her computer and wrote a quick note to Zaira.

"Gray knows. He saw your last email and was angry at first, but I think there's hope. I left the copy of your album for him to find, and he took his time looking through it. Nothing for sure, yet, but he's thinking."

The reply was swift.

"It is easy to see how Gray fell in love with you. You are a very special person—a saint. No matter how it turns out, thank you for all you've done."

As Fury smiled, savoring the note from Zaira, her computer

pinged, indicating an incoming message.

Automatically, she hit "keep as new" and closed out Zaira's reply. Returning to "new mail," she opened the message bearing the ID of "A Devoted Fan" and subject line that read, "Thoughts."

"Not taking me serious is extremely poor judgment. Trash your project, or I promise, YOU WILL BE SORRY."

The font was at least 16 point and the last sentence in bold, red ink.

Fury froze. In an instant, her mood changed. *Who is doing this?*

She could hear that the water was still running, so she waited to call Gray, paralyzed by anxiety.

As he came out of the bathroom, towel wrapped around his waist, she was sitting on the bed, a sheet of paper in her hand.

"What's going on? You're whiter than an albino."

Fury held the paper out to him.

When he read the latest threat, he turned to her. "Get ready. We're headed to APD for answers."

While Fury showered and dressed, Gray called Ryland.

"Did you get my email?"

"I did and was planning to call you this morning."

"As I said, we're coming in. There's been a second email since the one I forwarded last night, which we'll bring. See you at ten."

Terminating the call to the detective, he called his office.

"Gladys, clear my schedule this morning. I won't be in until after lunch."

The consultation with Ryland did not appease Gray. While he contained his frustration, he made his position clear. "I'm not satisfied that this case has been given sufficient attention. I can assure you that I am not seeking special treatment, but I do expect better results than have been shown so far."

"Mr. MacGregor, I understand where you're coming from. I know it is disturbing to receive communications of this type, but believe me, we are exploring every lead."

"It's not working. I am willing to supplement your efforts with whatever you tell me will help. My wife is pregnant and does not need the stress that this type of action creates. The number of contacts that she has received certainly indicates that this is not a prank. Someone is posing a serious threat. I want this given priority. If that's not possible, then I will look into other options."

"It would help if you could give us a list of possible suspects who we can investigate. You've given us nothing but the anonymous notes. Of course, we'll have our cybercrime team work on tracing the emails."

"We'll put together a list tonight and have it on your desk by morning."

"I recommend that you consider anyone who has a grudge against you as well, Mr. MacGregor. This type of criminal can be motivated by many things."

"Gray, I don't know where to begin with a list of potential suspects. I don't want to accuse innocent people," Fury said as they drove back to the condo.

"At this point, everyone is a suspect."

"Why would anyone that I know want to stop me from writing a book about your family?"

"The book may be the excuse. Think of anyone who would want to disrupt your life or your life with me—old boyfriends, jealous females—everyone."

"But, they would need to know about the book to use it as a mechanism."

"Think about everywhere that you've done research on your project and anyone you're talked to."

"I've done more research in Arabella than Atlanta."

"Maybe we've been looking in the wrong place. I'll make a call to the police chief in Arabella."

After dinner, Gray and Fury made their separate lists of potential suspects and then compared the two. Fury was shocked to see that Gray had included Ella, Edward, and Gladys on his list. She had not.

"I can't believe you put them on your list."

"I don't think any of them is our asshole, but I'm not ruling anyone out."

She nodded. "Should I put my sister on the list?"

He smiled. "Cory is adjusting to me, but she's an O'Quinn and doesn't have the deviant gene necessary to cross this line."

"Thank you." Taking his list, she took them to her printer, made copies, and put a set in each of three folders.

"Let's get some sleep," Gray said. I will have these messengered over to Ryland tomorrow, and we'll take the third set to the Arabella Police Department."

The bedroom light was out by eleven-thirty, but at two-fifteen, Fury was still awake. Turning on her side, she looked up at the LED readout on the clock radio.

"What's wrong?"

Fury turned her face toward Gray. "Nothing. Just a little trouble sleeping."

"I'm *not* angry with you."

She looked at him and started to tremble.

"You want to tell me about her?"

"Really?"

He rose up on an elbow. "Really," he whispered, looking down at her and brushing a tear from her cheek.

"Okay. I don't know where to start except to say, I like her. I like her a lot."

"Take your time." He lowered himself to his side and pulled her close.

"She's a beautiful and proud woman. I saw so much of you in her. You have her eyes."

"You've met her?"

"I have."

"Where is she?"

"A small town near Lexington, Kentucky."

"That's where you and Mike went."

Fury nodded. "I'm sorry. It now seems like a sneaky thing to do."

"It's okay. I gave you no choice. Is she married?"

"No. She never remarried. She's a nurse. She went back to school after your father threw her out."

The next half hour was spent with Fury telling him Zaira's version of the MacGregor marriage—Jack's abuse, Zaira's infidelity, her anguish at leaving Gray behind, and the contract Jack had made her sign, agreeing that if she attempted to see Gray, she would have to pay back the $50,000, plus interest and a $50,000 breach of contract penalty. Zaira had shown Fury a copy of the document. Gray did not interrupt. When she finished, he said, "It's a credible story."

"Are you willing to see her?"

He was silent for several minutes. "I'm not ready for that, yet. Give me time to digest all of this, one piece at the time." He caressed her face. "You can be a challenge, Kate MacGregor, but I love you."

"I love you, too."

"The damn stalker is going to be caught. I'll make it happen."

She snuggled even closer to him.

Days went by after the list of suspects had been provided to both police departments. Tracking of the emails hit a dead end, and the stalker was in hibernation.

Fury continued to review the materials she had gathered. In the Graeme MacGregor documents, she found letters he had written to Bridget but had not addressed the envelopes. Most talked about his love for her, his disappointment in his marriage, and his regret that they were not together. However, in one, he spoke of Jim Dolan.

January 23, 1944

My dearest Bridget,

Today is your birthday. I wish I could tell you in person how I tried to right my father's wrong. I met with officials at the Georgia State Sanitarium at Milledgeville and was permitted to visit your brother, Jim. It grieves me to report that the poor soul does not have the capability of release. So many electroshock treatments have been performed on him that he is truly incompetent now. Only the sorrow of losing you outweighs my sorrow for his suffering.

While there, I funded an account to provide him with as many comforts as available. I was assured by the authorities that Jim would be reclassified as a private patient and accorded the best treatment available.

I am so sorry, dear Bridget, that I did not know so many truths in time to make corrections. My father was a powerful man, both in business and family. It grieves me to admit that while he lived, my actions were stifled.

How I pray that someday there will be a way to reach you and to meet our son—perhaps when this horrendous war is over. My marriage is difficult. It is my fault. Dorothy is a good woman and tries, but I am hollow. At least she has Jack and Valerie for comfort. I should never have allowed Father to coerce me into a marriage for which I knew that I could not commit. Dorothy deserves more than I have to give.

Kind, gentle, Bridget, I pray that you and yours stay safe in Ireland. Maybe someday, this letter will find its way to you.

Forever yours in spirit and love,

G.McG.

So much sorrow beginning with one evil man.

As Fury sat, internalizing the words that Graeme MacGregor had never been able to convey to the woman he loved, she reread the portion of his 1944 letter that spoke of trying to help Jim Dolan.

The headstone. Was it bought and installed by Graeme MacGregor, Jr.?

Fury began to dig through the remaining documents, searching for a receipt or work order for the large monument. While there wouldn't have been a receipt unless he bought it from a rival company, she tried to find a work order stating what the inscription was to say and describing the model.

It took her nearly an hour, but deep among the papers was the document she sought. It was a boilerplate order form but not from MacGregor Marble. The logo was that of a rival company. The information for the inscription mirrored that on the James Dolan monument. The purchaser was listed as Greg Johnson.

Pretty transparent, John Graeme MacGregor, Jr.

The remainder of the form specified that top-grade marble was to be used and the workmanship to be assigned to the best stonecutter at the company. It listed the cost at $9,500.00, paid in full with cash. The form was dated: November 10, 1970.

You did what you could, didn't you Graeme—never expecting to be acknowledged?

CHAPTER THIRTY-SIX

The remainder of June, through the first two weeks of July, Fury was busy with the Forglen renovation. She and Gray were spending weekends at the house in preparation for a move of their domicile. While it could not be said that Ella had extended a total "glad to have you here" to Fury, her near hostile attitude had been downgraded to a polite reserve.

Gray had said no more about connecting with his mother. Both Zaira and Mike had encouraged Fury not to pressure him. No word had come from either police department regarding leads on the case. The absence of any further contact from the stalker lulled the couple into complacency until the air was released from all four tires on Fury's car at a shopping center in Atlanta.

"It *could* have been intentional and carried off by the same person, but Atlanta is a big city with a lot of vandalism," said Detective Ryland. "There was no note, Mr. MacGregor."

"Am I going to have to put a private detail on my wife 24-7? You may not know it was her stalker, but you don't know that it wasn't."

On the morning of July 23, 2007, Gray left for work early. The landscape crew was performing weekly maintenance on the grounds of Forglen, and Fury was leaving for Atlanta to look at new pieces of furniture her decorator wanted her to consider. She was also having her seven-month prenatal checkup with her gynecologist. She had left her car on the circular drive in front of the mansion the afternoon before. As she walked toward the driver's side, she waved to one of the team who was trimming the front shrubbery. He gave her a military salute as she pressed the car remote, hardly looking at the vehicle.

As she grabbed the door handle, she emitted a blood-curdling shriek.

The gardeners looked up as Fury turned and started to run back toward the house. Her foot caught on the brick border of the driveway and she fell, still screaming.

"No, no, no. Please, God, no."

"Ms. MacGregor," Sam, the gardener, said as he rushed to help her up. "What's wrong?"

Fury kept screaming, "No, no, no," and shaking her head.

The assistant gardener ran up the stairs of the house and pounded on the door. "Mr. Edward, come, come," the man shouted.

"She's dead. She's dead. No, no, no." Fury was hysterical.

Edward and Ella came outside. "What's happened?" Edward said, while Ella went directly to Fury who was crying so hard that she was choking.

"She just went to her car and then started screaming and running. She fell over the brick," Sam said.

"What's wrong, Fury? Honey, what's wrong?" Ella asked, putting her arm around the distraught woman.

Fury struggled to talk, pointing to her car. "He's killed her. She's dead. There's blood all over the seat."

Ella grasped Fury tight, trying to comfort her, while Sam and Edward went to the car.

"It's not Gypsy, Miss Fury," Edward shouted. "It's not her."

Hearing him, Fury gasped for a deep breath. "Are you sure?"

"It's not a real cat. It's a stuffed animal, covered in either red paint or ketchup."

Fury's knees went out from under her, and Ella could hardly hold her. Bud, the assistant, stepped up to help.

"What kind of bastard would do a thing like that?" Ella said with fire in her eyes. "This poor thing—pregnant and all. Edward, get Gray on the phone and then bring some cold water. Help me get her to the steps, Bud."

Fury allowed them to take over, nearly carrying her to the front steps. Dazed, all she could think of was seeing Gypsy.

Edward was back in a flash with a bottle of water in one hand and a cell phone in the other. He handed the water to Ella. "She's right here, Gray. She took a fall. We're not sure if she's hurt. There's some blood on her arm and she is very upset. Yes, sir. Here she is." He handed the phone to Fury.

She took a deep breath and said, "I'm okay. I thought someone had murdered Gypsy. It was awful." Emotions overtaking, she couldn't say anymore.

Ella took the phone. "What do you want us to do, Gray? Take her to the hospital here or to Atlanta?"

"I don't want to go to the hospital. I'm fine. I need to see Gypsy." Fury was sobbing and shaking her head in protest.

"You've taken a fall, Fury. You've got to think of your baby," Ella said.

She looked down at her stomach. "Oh, no." Panic seized her face. "You're right. I could have hurt my baby."

"Don't get upset. I'm sure the baby's fine, but you do need to be checked."

Fury's chin went up and down in agreement. "But, I need to see Gypsy before I leave, please. Edward, will you take good care of her. This monster may really try to get to her for some perverted reason."

"You can be sure I will. She will stay locked securely in your room. I promise. Gray says he's sending an ambulance to take you to the hospital in Atlanta. Ella, he wants you to go with her, and he'll meet you at the hospital." He turned to Sam. "And he says for you to stay with the car but not touch it until the police get here. He's calling them."

"Edward, why don't you go upstairs and bring Gypsy down while we wait for the ambulance," Ella said. "Bud, help us into the house."

"I can walk. I'm okay now." Fury took a drink of the water and stood up. A thin stream of blood ran down her left arm from a cut.

They had hardly reached the living room when the ambulance and the police arrived. Edward had just brought Gypsy to Fury, who was hugging the puzzled cat against her face, tears flowing again.

"Thank goodness you're okay."

"Mrs. MacGregor, are you hurt?" Detective Sawyer said as he walked into the house behind the paramedics.

"I'm not sure. Did you see my car?"

"I did. We have a forensic team on it now."

"I'll take Gypsy back upstairs, if you like, Miss Fury," Edward said.

She nodded. "Just make sure she's okay," she said as a paramedic wiped the blood off her arm with an alcohol pad and then wrapped a blood pressure cuff around it.

"I'm okay. I just tripped and fell on the ground."

"Just need to be cautious, Ms. MacGregor. Can't take chances with your baby so close. When is your due date?"

"September."

"Early or late?"

"Early. The first."

"So you're about seven months?"

"Thirty weeks. I was supposed to have a checkup today."

"I think you're still going to have that checkup, but it's probably going to be at the hospital."

Gray was at the emergency room entrance when the ambulance arrived. Leaning over to kiss her, he said, "Are you sure you're okay?"

"I'm fine. I pray that the fall didn't hurt the baby. He's been quiet since it happened." She squeezed his hand.

"Let us take her into the examination room, Mr. MacGregor. It won't take long to do the initial workup." The speaker was a man in green scrubs.

Mike and Cory arrived shortly after Fury was rolled into a room in the ER. Gray had called Mike, who had in turn called Cory, who had been on her way to Atlanta to meet Fury at the Furniture Mart.

"What happened, son?" Mike asked.

"Fury has had a stalker for a while. It escalated today when a stuffed cat resembling Gypsy was left on the front seat of her car with red liquid poured on it."

"Oh, my, gosh," Cory said. "That must have made her crazy."

"I wasn't there, but Edward said she was hysterical. When she turned away in panic, she tripped."

"Why didn't she tell me this was going on?" Mike said.

"I wanted to," Gray said, "but she didn't want to worry you. Now, I think it's time we ask for your help. Neither the Atlanta nor the Arabella police have come up with anything."

"I'll get to work as soon as I know she's alright."

"Mike, I want you to do whatever is needed. Hire whomever you need to hire—if it takes a damn army. We're going to catch this bastard."

Mike nodded.

"Can you arrange for immediate security, or do I need to put my staff on it?"

"It'll only take a call. I'll have someone at the house before dinnertime. But, I suggest that we don't publicize that fact."

Gray looked at his father-in-law. "I see your point. Mike, I hope you understand that I want a full team—24-7—no blind spots."

"Don't worry. The crew that I set up will have off-duty officers with full detain-and-arrest authority."

As soon as the staff doctor walked out, Gray and Cory were on him like groupies at a rock concert.

"How is she?" Gray asked, his tone urgent. Cory was right beside him.

"She appears okay, Mr. MacGregor. The baby's heart rhythm is strong, there's no sign of tear, and Mrs. MacGregor shows no sign of concussion. Given that she did take a nasty spill and she's only six weeks from delivery, I would like to keep her overnight."

"Absolutely," Gray said.

"But, she wants to go home."

"She's staying here, and so am I."

Cory watched Gray's control of the situation, seeing her brother-in-law in a new light. The humility he displayed both times he visited in her home was absent in the ER. Gray MacGregor was in charge.

"May we see her?" Cory asked.

The physician nodded. "She's anxious to see her family."

Cory started toward the door, but Mike took her arm, holding her back. "'Tis her husband that should be first, love."

Gray immediately said, "She wants to see you, too." He motioned for Cory to go ahead, stepping aside to allow her to enter Fury's room first. She immediately crossed over to the bed and hugged her sister. "Are you okay?"

"I think I'm fine. I'm worried about the baby. Dr. Marks said he's fine, but there is a chance the fall could induce labor. Cory, it was awful. I thought someone had killed Gypsy. I'm still afraid for her. Did Gray tell you that someone has been sending me notes and emails, demanding that if I don't abandon the book project, I will be sorry?"

"And, of course, you wouldn't do that."

"I didn't know for sure how serious this person was until this morning. If he or she will do that, come on our property, they will do worse. I'm scared."

Gray stepped forward, and Cory moved to allow him closer access to the bed. "I promise you that this is the last time this person will harass you. I've authorized Mike to hire as many investigators and bodyguards as he feels necessary. Hell, he's free to hire a band of mercenaries if need be. We're going to identify this guy and put him behind bars."

"I'm afraid for Gypsy, even Apache. This person is insane."

"Why don't I take Gypsy home with me? No one needs to know where she is," Cory said. "Would that make you feel better?"

"Sweetheart, I think you have nothing to worry about with her at Forglen. There will be armed security on site from now until this is over, but if you're more comfortable with her staying at Cory and Don's, I'll have Edward bring her over right now."

Fury's chin moved up and down, while she fought back tears. "I think I would feel safer with her at Cory's. This is all horrible. I want to go home. "

"I understand, sweetheart, but you need to stay. I'll be here with you. We are not taking a chance with you or the baby."

Cory put her hand on Fury's. "I'm going to go get Dad. I know he's dying to come in. What can I get for you from the condo? I'll run over there and pick up some essentials while Edward is on his way here with Gypsy."

Gray reached in his pocket, took out a key, and handed it to her.

"That's sweet of you," Fury said. "If I have to stay, maybe my makeup, toothbrush, sleepwear, and slippers. This is not my favorite fashion statement." She pointed to the hospital gown and made a face.

Cory was hardly out the door when Mike came in and, like the others, immediately hugged his daughter. "Why didn't you tell me about this scumbag stalker, lass? I could've been on it at the start."

"I didn't want to worry you, Dad. I thought it was a prank, or at the worst, an attempt to cause trouble between Gray and me. But now, I'm really scared." She began to tear up.

"Not to worry. Sully will be all over this. His boy is with the FBI. We'll get this solved before you can kiss a leprechaun."

"But no Federal crime has been committed."

"Ah . . . I think there has. This SOB has used the postal service to threaten you, and, with what happened today, he has committed a crime that could fall under the Federal Unborn Victims of Violence Act. Wish we could go after the bastard for a threat against your little fur friend, but don't think that one's on the books until it happens."

"Who is Sully?" Gray asked.

"Shawn Sullivan. Dad's old partner that you met at the pub," Fury said.

"I'm going to go now and get started on this. You get some rest. Let us take care of everything else." Mike leaned over the bed, kissed her on the forehead, and left.

With the two of them alone, Gray moved to the side of the bed and took her hand. "I think we'll take a week or so off and go to Cashiers. Tell no one where we are but Mike and Cory."

"Maybe I should just make an announcement that I'm not writing the book."

Gray shook his head. "Even if that would stop this, and there's no assurance that it would, I wouldn't let you be coerced by a criminal. That book means a lot to you, and your choice to write it is yours and yours alone."

CHAPTER THIRTY-SEVEN

Cory brought a tote bag of essentials from the condo for Fury, along with a pair of jeans and a pullover for Gray.

"That was very considerate of you, Cory," Gray said as he hung his change of clothing in the cubby in Fury's hospital room. "Edward is coming to pick up Ella, and he'll have Gypsy."

"Thank you so much, Cory," Fury added.

"I'm glad to help. Like Dad, I wish you had let me know sooner."

"There's nothing you could have done but worry."

Cory stayed about thirty minutes, and then at Fury's insistence, left to take Gypsy and to get home in time for dinner with her family.

Later that evening, as they finished eating Guinness beef stew that Gray had delivered to the hospital, he asked, "Are you calming down, honey?"

"It's strange. I feel like I'm someone else—that this isn't real."

"It's going to be back to normal, soon. I expect with the all-out push to catch his bastard, they'll have him by the time we come back from Cashiers."

"That would be such a relief." She pulled the bedsheet back and started to stand. "Excuse me; I'm going to the restroom."

"Do you need any help?"

"No. I'm fine."

Two minutes later, Fury emerged from the bathroom, her expression changed.

"What is it?" Gray asked. "You are white as Georgia cotton."

"Please call the nurse. There's blood."

Gray grabbed the call button and pushed.

The door opened within seconds and Fury's LPN came in. "Can I help you, Ms. MacGregor?"

Tears were building in Fury's eyes. "I think something's wrong. I went to the bathroom and there was blood. . . ." She pointed in the direction of her crotch.

"I'll call for your RN."

"The baby can't come now."

Gray stood up, moved to the side of her bed, and took her hand. "Don't panic, darling. This is why we're here. It will be all right."

The nurse came and repeated the observation made by the LPN. "I've put in a call to your private physician, and Dr. Cordero is on his way up. Don't be upset. Worst case scenario, you'll become a mommy tonight."

"It's too soon."

"You're over seven months. Seven-month fetuses have an excellent rate of viability. It might be a little smaller than we would hope, but it should be healthy enough to be fine. Just stay calm," Fury's nurse said.

Calm wasn't in Fury's vocabulary at that moment.

The resident physian arrived within minutes of the RN. "What seems to be the problem?"

"She's thirty weeks and has some vaginal bleeding. Dr. Albracht is on his way. He said for you to call him on his cell when you reached her room," the RN said.

"Can you get him on the phone while I take a look?" He turned to Gray. "You're the husband, I assume."

Gray nodded.

"Do you mind stepping out for a minute? Jane will call you back in."

Gray looked at Fury.

"It's okay. Just don't go far."

With Fury's private physician on the phone, the in-house doctor relayed information. "Do you want me to do an examination?"

Dr. Albracht apparently answered in the negative.

"We'll do a sonogram immediately. You're how far out?"

Hanging up, he turned to the nurse. "Her private doctor should be here within ten minutes. Bring her husband back in."

Gray's face was ashen as he reentered. "What do you think?"

"It's too soon to tell. I see from her chart that she suffered a fall today. It could have precipitated this but maybe not. There are a number of things that can cause third trimester bleeding. The most obvious being the start of labor, but she shows no signs of that. All we can do is rule out the others. We're doing an ultrasound. Dr. Albracht has also ordered blood work."

"Gray. . . ." Her voice was weak. Fear was taking over.

"I'm right here. It's going to be okay. This is a state-of-the-art hospital, and you've got a good team."

"You're going to be okay, Mrs. MacGregor. Your gestational period is far enough along that if we have to deliver the fetus, there should be minimal risk. We're putting a heart monitor on the baby now and getting an IV started to keep you hydrated."

"Gray, call Cory. I want Don here. If the baby comes, I want him to be here."

"I've already called Mike. He's on his way and getting in touch with her." Gray's eyebrows were pinched together, exposing his concern.

By the time Cory and Don arrived, Fury's doctor was on site, and the ultrasonography had been performed, but the doctors had not given her a diagnosis.

"I'm sorry to bring you out this late, but thank goodness you're here," Fury said as her sister and brother-in-law came in the room. Her hands were clasped together in the prayer position, but fingers folded. "I wanted Don here in case the baby comes tonight."

"You couldn't keep me away, sweetheart," Don said.

"What has your doctor said?" Cory asked as she took one of her sister's hands.

"He hasn't."

Don had walked over to Gray and extended a hand. Mike stood up. Don turned and hugged his father-in-law.

"Don, go see if you can find anything—"

The door opened and two doctors walked in, interrupting Cory's statement.

"How are you doing, Fury?" her gynecologist, Stephen Albracht, said.

"You know better than I do."

The physician smiled and looked around the assembled group. Recognizing Don, he extended a hand. "Good to see you, Dr. Reynolds."

Don nodded and shook his hand.

"We'll wait in the hall," Mike said.

"No, stay, Dad. It will keep me from having to tell you later what was said."

"What have you found?" Gray asked with a solemn look on his face.

"We have ruled out everything but placental abruption, which we now have to assume may have caused the discharge," said Dr. Albracht. Dr. Cordero, the resident nodded in agreement.

"What exactly does placental abruption mean?" Gray asked.

"It's where the placenta detaches from the uterus too soon. While it is a serious condition, in your wife's case, we believe that it's a minor detachment and that with proper care, there will be no problems."

Fury's eyes were wide open as she listened to the doctors.

"There does not appear to have been any further bleeding, no pain, the baby's heart rhythm is steady, and there's no sign of hardening in her abdomen or uterine area. We want to keep her here for a few days as a precaution. She's free to move about, in fact, we want her to walk. If there are no further symptoms, then she can go home for the duration of her pregnancy, but absolutely no strenuous activity."

"What caused this?" Gray asked.

"Most likely—the fall she had."

"Is my baby going to be okay?" Fury was beginning to breakdown.

"We have every reason to believe that your baby is going to be fine. I think you were lucky that the fall was no worse. It probably caused a minute tear."

"Is there any likelihood of delivery tonight?" Don Reynolds asked.

Dr. Albracht shook his head. "While there's never a guarantee as to what Mother Nature has in mind, we see no scientific sign of labor. Her cervix is not dilated—no sign of contractions."

As soon as the two doctors left the room, Cory went back over to the bed. "We're going to go now and let you get some rest. I'll be back tomorrow."

"I'm so sorry to make you drive here tonight for nothing."

Don spoke up. "Fury, I am thankful that I wasn't needed. But, nothing would have kept us away." He turned to Gray. "Put both our house number and my cell in your phone and call if there's any hint of labor."

After hugs and supportive wishes, the family left, leaving Gray and Fury alone.

"It's going to be fine."

"I probably can't go to North Carolina."

"Don't rule that out. We can have a fulltime nurse, and I think you can rest more comfortably up there. Don't forget, you're already familiar with the hospital."

She smiled. "Yeah. Thanks for reminding me of that, but having a baby is a little more complicated than spraining your ankle."

To her chagrin, the doctor kept Fury in the hospital for five more days. Albracht agreed with Gray that the reduction of stress North Carolina offered was worth the minor risk, particularly if Gray arranged for medical supervision.

The night before her discharge, Gray told her that she had been approved to travel with a nurse and that he had rented a van, outfitted with a bed.

"Do I really need a nurse?"

"Yes, you do."

"But—"

"There are no buts, and I have a nurse in mind, but you will have to make the call."

She looked at him, crunched her eyebrows together, and said, "You're *not* thinking who I think you're thinking?"

He smiled a mischievous smile and nodded. "You've been dying for me to meet her, haven't you?"

"Gray MacGregor—you're talking about your mother?"

"Let's just say that I'm talking about Zaira Ross for now, okay?"

As they drove out of Atlanta, Fury felt the most relaxed since before the traumatic fall. She and Gray were in the van, and a security detail followed.

"Just an overabundance of caution, love," Gray had said when she asked. "I've rented the house below to accommodate them. Their vehicle will block the road to our home at all times."

"I still can't believe that you allowed me to ask Zaira to come."

"You need a nurse. She's qualified. It's strictly an employer/employee relationship."

"I don't believe that for a minute, but you keep telling yourself that. We'll take it."

"Well, if the *truth* be known, I wanted to make an honest woman of you so that you don't slip around behind my back again."

She popped him on the shoulder. "You, lie, Gray MacGregor. But if that's the game you *want* to play, go for it."

They stopped for lunch near the mountain, arriving at their house a little before three o'clock. As Gray began taking luggage out of the van, Fury reached for her makeup case, and he slapped her hand.

"No lifting."

"That case weighs less than five pounds. I'm not totally disabled, Gray."

"Well, pretend that you are. You don't lift anything heavier than a cup of tea until that little guy makes his debut."

Fury sighed, turned, and walked up the covered ramp to the backdoor. Once inside, she sat down and put her feet up on a footstool in front of the chair, waiting for Gray to finish unloading. Apache followed her and took her place in front of the hearth. The baby stirred. "Just move around all you want to, little one. That reassures me that you're okay," Fury said.

"What did you say, honey?"

"I was talking to your son, not you."

He smiled. "Did he answer you?"

"No, Jimmy Fallon, he didn't. Can you bring me my computer? I'd get it myself, but I'm afraid the roof might crash in if I dared lift it."

"Nice to see you're getting the hang of the rules, Kate." He brought her the laptop and put it on the coffee table. "Urgent business to attend to?"

"I'm going to email my nurse and let her know that we're here. You know how poor cell phone reception is at the inn."

"Tell her that we'll meet her in the lobby at four-thirty."

Zaira was sitting in front of the large fireplace in the Hampton Inn lodge when they arrived. Seeing Fury, she immediately stood. Fury went over to her and wrapped her arms around the stately woman. They remained in an embrace for at least a full minute. "I'm so glad to see you again," Fury said.

"Not half as much as I am." Tears were in Zaira's eyes as Fury moved aside to clear the way for Gray.

He stepped forward and extended his hand to shake Zaira's. For a second, Fury held her breath.

"It's nice to see you," Zaira said.

He nodded. Fury was unable to read the expression on his face.

"Do I call you Mr. MacGregor, given that I'm in your employ?"

He shook his head. "I think we'll start with Zaira and Gray, if you agree."

What is he thinking? Does he see the mother he loved?

For a moment, there was an awkward silence. No one seemed to know what to say next. Fury broke the ice. "I guess we better get back up to the house so that you can do what you need to do to be sure that all is well. We have dinner reservations for six. Right, Gray?"

"Right. The van is on the driveway. Do you need to get anything from your room?"

He can't bring himself to call her name.

Conversation in the car was limited to Zaira's flight from Lexington and the weather. Gray did not participate. Fury looked at him from time to time to try to see what he was thinking, but he wasn't revealing anything. She could tell that Zaira was nervous but did an admirable job of masking it.

What can it possibly feel like to be near a son you haven't seen in over thirty years and thought you would never see again?

CHAPTER THIRTY-EIGHT

The day after arriving, Gray drove Fury and Zaira to the hospital where Fury's ankle had been treated. "We have an appointment with the senior attending physician in obstetrics. I want him up to speed on the outside chance that a problem arises while we're here. Dr. Albracht forwarded a copy of all your records."

"He doesn't leave a stone unturned," Fury said to Zaira. "But, he's usually right, as much as I hate to admit it."

The next five days passed smoothly with Zaira coming to the house during the day, having dinner, which the security team delivered, and then returning to her room at the lodge at bedtime. Gray was polite and treated her as he would any guest. He avoided referring to her by name and spent a lot of time in his downstairs office. Fury could see that the situation for her mother-in-law was precious, uncomfortable, and frustrating.

"It must be like rubbing a sore muscle because the pain actually feels good. You're so close to him, and yet he won't let you be close."

"Am I that transparent?"

"Probably not to anyone but me. But, I think he's feeling the same way. He's just not ready to admit it."

"I don't know, Fury. He is doing a good job of concealing his feelings—if they exist."

"I believe they do. I know it must be hard. But, do you realize how far we've come in less than six months?"

The older woman nodded. "Thanks to you."

"Don't give me too much credit. There's a method to my madness.

We're going to need a good sitter when this little one is in the picture."

Zaira smiled. "You know where to find me. . . . Whoops. It's time to take your vitals. Is the baby active this morning?"

Fury nodded with a grin on her face. "He is, thank goodness. I panic every time he doesn't move for an hour or so. I tell myself, he has to rest, but it's such a relief when I feel that first flutter."

"It's not much longer now." Zaira went to her bag and took out a stethoscope, blood pressure cuff, and thermometer.

Gray had spent the morning downstairs. He came up to the first floor as Zaira returned the medical equipment to her bag. "Everything okay, today?" he asked as he walked to the kitchen for a cup of coffee.

"Perfect," Zaira responded.

Bringing his coffee to the sitting area, he took a seat in the chair by the fireplace, adjacent to the sofa where Fury and Zaira sat. "Do you ladies have any plans for today?"

"Right," Fury said. "As if I'm allowed to make plans."

Zaira remained silent as she usually did when he was around.

"Well, if Zaira thinks it's safe for you, I thought we might roam around the area—show her the horses and some of the countryside. What do you think?"

"You don't have to ask me twice. As much as I love this house, I would love to get out," Fury said.

They both looked at Zaira. She waited a few seconds before commenting.

"As long as Fury doesn't push herself, I don't see any medical reason standing in the way."

The weather was perfect, and the excursion proved to be a success. Gray and Zaira actually engaged in more conversation at the stables than had taken place between them during her stay. They had lunch at Fury's favorite café and browsed in a small bookstore. Fury giggled when Zaira pointed out a display of her novels. "You should tell the owner you wrote them."

Fury shook her head. "No way—maybe when I'm not looking like the Hindenburg zeppelin."

That night, Gray prepared dinner. It was the first meal he had cooked with Zaira there. "I am overwhelmed with your skill in the kitchen," Zaira remarked after finishing the curried chicken casserole he had made.

"Someone in the family has to cook," he said, winking at Fury.

"Ignore him, please. He gives me a hard time because I don't know anything about a kitchen."

"I put up with her because she has other talents."

"Uh . . . I think we won't go there," Fury said, kicking him under the table.

Zaira smiled, relaxing more than she had in his presence. "I think it's great when a man knows his way around the kitchen."

"If Gray hadn't inherited a marble quarry, I think he would have been a chef," Fury said.

Gray smiled. "Not a bad idea. I might try it eventually."

After the security detail took Zaira back to the inn, Gray sat down on the sofa next to Fury with a cup of tea for each of them. "I think it would be easier on the detail if we had Zaira stay here."

Well, aren't you the clever one, Gray MacGregor—easier on the detail?

"That sounds like a practical idea. I'll ask her if she would mind moving into one of our guest rooms." *As if that is going to be a question—but I'll play your game and raise you one.*

"Are you sure, Fury? I don't want to push him," Zaira said when Fury extended the invitation. "It was so nice, last night. He seemed to let his guard down a little."

"It was his idea. Get your things together."

The next week went smoothly. Gray spent a great deal of time in his office, which gave Zaira and Fury the freedom to talk about subjects they could not discuss in his presence. Fury told Zaira about her research in depth.

"You knew Graeme MacGregor. He and my grandmother were in love, but the old man, J.G. ruined it all."

"From all I've seen of Gray in the past days, he's more like his grandfather than Jack—thankfully," Zaira said.

Fury cautioned her to avoid mentioning the book in Gray's presence. The only reminder of the still-unidentified stalker was the presence of the security guards. Both women avoided that subject, because the thought brought back the terror, elevating Fury's blood pressure.

"I can't wait for you to meet my sister and her family. You know Dad. Don't be shocked though. Cory and I are as different as a bull and a cat. I charge forward with the angels on my shoulders and little consideration of consequences; she contemplates cautiously, consults every resource short of the Pope, and finally makes her move."

Zaira smiled. "I'm not sure that I can go to Forglen, Fury. The idea still puts knots in my stomach."

"Don't worry. You won't recognize it. I admit, it still has more marble than Michelangelo's closet, but everything else is changed. It's a new house. You left Jack's house. You'll be coming to Gray's. I decorated a room with you in mind. I hope you will like it."

"You're too much. I've said it before, but I'm going to repeat it. I understand why Gray fell in love with you."

Two nights before Fury and Gray were scheduled to return to Georgia and Zaira to Kentucky, the women were sitting on the deck when Fury grabbed Zaira's hand and squeezed tight. The color had drained from her face.

"What's wrong, honey?" Zaira asked. Gray turned around from the barbeque pit where he was grilling steaks.

"I'm not sure, but there's a sharp pain in my back."

Zaira dropped her hand and stood. "I'll get my case."

Gray put down the fork and sat down beside Fury. "Does it still hurt?"

"It's fading. But the baby hasn't moved in the last hour or so. I'm scared."

Zaira returned with her instruments, and Gray moved to give her room. She first put the stethoscope on Fury's abdomen. "The baby's heartbeat is good." She then put the blood pressure cuff on Fury's arm.

Gray went to the grill, turned off the gas, put the meat on a platter, and turned. "We're going to the hospital."

"I don't want to go if it's a false alarm."

"Staying here is not an option. I know Zaira is a nurse, but this isn't a hospital. We're going."

"I'll get her things," Zaira said.

On the way to the hospital, Fury's pains grew closer together. Zaira sat at her side in the back of the van. When they arrived at the emergency room entrance, they were met with a gurney.

"I can walk," Fury protested.

"You are a difficult patient, sweetheart. Will you let the professionals do their job?" Gray said.

Her labor was quickly confirmed, and she was taken to the obstetrical floor. Once outfitted in sterile gear, Gray was permitted in with her, as was Zaira.

"It's too soon. I wanted to carry him at least thirty-seven weeks."

"He'll be fine. There's a good neonatal nursery for preemies here," Zaira said. "I read about it on their web site."

"Just concentrate on what the doctors tell you and try not to stress, my love."

"Did anyone call Cory?"

"I did," Gray said. "She and Don are picking up Mike and driving. They will be here by morning."

"The girls?"

"They have a sitter."

"But, Don doesn't know the way."

"Stop stressing, sweetheart. He has a GPS, and you found your way up here. I think Don can, too."

Eight hours later, in the wee hours of August 18, 2007, Baby Boy MacGregor came into the world with both of his surviving grandparents and his aunt and uncle present. Although Don was not licensed to practice in North Carolina, he was afforded the professional courtesy of scrubbing in for the delivery and allowed to observe the baby's first examination. No one else could have given Fury more assurance that her son was healthy.

"He's a fine, healthy boy, Fury. At five pounds, six ounces, he's a rival for a full-term baby. We'll monitor him for a couple of days, but he's not in need of any extraordinary treatment that I can see." Don patted her on the hand. "Well done." He turned to Gray. "Congratulations, Dad. Life as you knew it just changed forever. But, I can assure you, they're worth it."

"Thank you, Don," Fury said.

"Yes, thank you for coming," Gray added.

"I would not have missed it for the world. Sandi and Suzi are going to be crazy to see that little guy."

"I can't believe that I'm a mom, now."

"When he cries at two a.m., you'll know it. I'm going to head back to Georgia. I think Mike and Cory are staying over until tomorrow. I'm taking a rental back. If you need anything, I'm just a phone call and three hours away."

When Don left, Fury and Gray were alone for the first time since she delivered. "We have to decide on a name. You know that—don't you?"

"I see no reason not to keep the tradition. John Graeme MacGregor, V. is a name of significance."

"I think it's time to retire that one."

"Gray . . ."

It's not happening. This is a new day and a new beginning. We're not starting it off with the shadows from the past."

"What if we're all a part of the past?"

He looked at her. Am I supposed to know the answer to that question?"

"I know you don't want to talk about my research or the book, but there's one thing you really need to know."

"Fury. You're taking advantage of me because you've just given birth to my son."

"A girl has to use what a girl has. Seriously, Gray, there is something you need to know. If I write my book, this is going to be a major fact. Please let me tell you."

"One thing." He raised an index finger, tipped his head, and cocked an eyebrow, silently admonishing her to limit her inquiry.

"Your grandfather and my grandmother were in love—lovers. I

318

think that we are the full circle of that relationship. Call me crazy if you want, but I think that I was guided to you by the spirit of Bridget Dolan O'Quinn."

"Graeme and Bridget?"

She nodded.

"And you know that, how?"

"It's in letters they wrote. My uncle, Ronan, is your uncle, too."

"Whoa. You're saying we're related?"

"No. We're not. We have an uncle in common, but no blood. Gray, I'm sure that we were meant to fall in love."

"Predestined—that's your theory?"

"Why not? Wasn't it crazy that we met and everything went at roller coaster speed?"

He leaned over and kissed her. "What makes us work, my love, is that you live in the clouds and my feet are always on the ground. You keep me from sinking, and I keep you from floating away." He stroked her hair, smiling. "If you want to believe that we are divine destiny, I'm not going to dissuade you, because it doesn't matter to me how we came together. What matters to me is that we stay together."

He kissed her again. "I'm going to let you get some sleep. I need to call the office to be sure there are no missiles roaming in search of a target. I'll be back in about an hour."

She nodded. "I am kind of tired."

As he walked down the hall, Gray stopped, turned, and went to the infant nursery. Zaira was there, looking through the window at the baby.

"Admiring your grandson?"

Startled, she turned. "Indulging in déjà vu. You may not want to hear this from me, but he looks like you when you were born."

"Only you would know." He put his arm around her shoulders and pulled her close. "So, what do you want your grandson to call you, Mom?"

Zaira stiffened, turned, and looked up at him. "What did you just say?"

"I said, 'What do you want your grandson to call you, Mom.'"

"You called me mom?" Tears flooded down her face.
"It's about damn time, don't you think?"

CHAPTER THIRTY-NINE

Choosing a name for the baby proved to be more difficult than had been anticipated. Gray was determined that there would not be a fifth John Graeme. Although Fury argued that a tradition nearly one-hundred-years-old should not be broken, Gray countered.

"This is not a European monarchy, and it's time to start fresh."

Gray gave into maintaining the family tradition when Fury came up with the idea of calling the baby Quin.

Fury and Quin stayed in the hospital three days as a precaution. To ready the mountain house for the arrival of the baby, Cory and Mike shopped for the basics.

"I've got you a car seat, bassinette, a few baby clothes, linens, toiletries, diapers, a baby monitor, formula, and bottles. I know you will want to pick out the rest, but this should be enough to tide you over," Cory said the night before she and Mike returned to Atlanta.

Zaira returned to Kentucky the day after mother and child were released from the hospital. As she was leaving, Fury hugged her and said, "We will come visit you in Kentucky and hope you'll come to Georgia soon."

Gray stood motionless, but said, "We would like to have you." Zaira started to get in the car but stopped, turned around, and went to Gray with open arms. He leaned forward and returned her embrace.

Fury watched with tears in her eyes. *God works in mysterious ways. Who could have predicted the way their reconciliation would occur?*

Later that day, Gray made an early dinner while Fury fed Quin and put him down. After they finished eating, the house was quiet with only the occasional sound of Apache's claws softly clicking on the wood floor.

"Shall we take our coffee out on the deck and enjoy the sunset?" Gray asked.

She nodded. "I'll grab the monitor."

As she leaned back against the sofa, outside, she said, "You know you suck at changing diapers, don't you?"

"Not a skill I've ever aspired to perfect. But, I can cook."

She laughed. "What are you going to taunt me with when I finally learn my way around the kitchen?"

"I'll think of something." He raised his arm, bringing it down around her shoulders, and pulled her close.

"I wish we could stay here forever—pretend that there's not someone in Georgia who wants to make my life miserable or worse."

"That's going to end. I promise."

A week later, the MacGregor family was back in residence at Forglen. Ella's reserve toward Fury had begun to thaw the day of the fall and melted even faster the minute she saw Quin. Without saying a word, her affection for the baby was clear.

"Welcome home, Miss Fury," Edward said. "That's a handsome boy you have."

"Thank you, Edward. And thank you both for all you did the day I fell." As Fury spoke, Ella actually smiled.

"Gypsy's upstairs. Your sister wanted you to have her as soon as you arrived. Where do you want her to stay now that the baby is here?" Edward asked.

"I think she'll be fine in our room. I don't believe the old wives' tale about cats taking a baby's breath away."

"Can I bring refreshments up to your room? Ella asked.

"That would be nice," Fury said.

"I understand that we will be interviewing nannies tomorrow," Gray said.

"Gladys arranged for about ten candidates. I met with all of them and narrowed it down to the four I felt were qualified and would fit into the household. The first one is coming at ten o'clock to meet with you," Ella said.

"That will be Fury's territory."

"I think you should be involved in the final selection," Fury said.

"We'll see, but right now, let's get the two of you upstairs," Gray said. "I'm going into Atlanta to put in a little time at the office."

Once in their bedroom, Fury laid Quin in his bassinette and turned to Gray. "How late will you be?"

He took her by the waist. "I'll be home by seven. You know I still have a job."

She tucked her chin as if ashamed. "I know. I'm spoiled, having you to myself for the last few weeks."

He lifted her chin. "I wouldn't have you any other way. I'll be home as soon as I can. Stay away from your computer unless someone screens it first. Your mail has been checked."

"Do you think that he will make contact with me again?"

Gray shook his head. "There's no way to know. But, you're safe. There are two men watching the house day and night. To be extra safe, stay away from windows."

"You're scaring me."

"I don't want to scare you, but until this is over, we have to be careful. I don't want any repetition of what happened last month."

"How can two men see all the way around this property?"

"Technology, sweetheart. This is the twenty-first century."

Fury interviewed the four nanny candidates and narrowed the choice down to two. Although he protested, she attempted to force Gray's participation in the final decision. "Do we need to have a background check run on the woman we choose?" Fury asked as they discussed the final two candidates.

Gray laughed. "Do you think that wasn't done on all the applicants? These ladies are eligible for National Security Clearance."

"Stupid me. Which one do you like better?"

"I'm not the one who is going to spend many hours a day with her. You make the final choice. I have no problem with either one."

"I don't know which one I like better."

"So, you want me to make the decision so you have someone to blame if it doesn't work out?"

"I do not," she said, annoyed that he was giving her a hard time.

"What is your criterion?"

"I want someone who knows more about taking care of babies than I do but doesn't act like she does—or try to tell me what to do. She needs to care about him like a mother or grandmother but understand that I am his mom."

"And you think there's someone like that?"

"There has to be."

He put his hands up as if to surrender. "I'm not having anything to do with your final decision. It's all up to you."

Grinning, Gray stood up from his chair at the breakfast table and walked around to her. He leaned over, and, with one hand on her shoulder, kissed the top of her head. "I have to go. I know you'll make the right choice."

As he walked away, Fury said, "Sometimes, you really annoy me, Gray MacGregor."

"It's in my job description."

As he disappeared down the hallway, Ella came in to clear away the dishes.

"Ella, have you got a minute?"

"Certainly." She sat down in the chair Gray had left empty.

"Help me make the final choice of a nanny. I've narrowed it down to Leah Brice and Corinna Garcia."

"They both seem like good women."

"I know, but I can only hire one. You're going to spend time with her. Which do you see living here and holding Quin?"

Ella thought for a minute. "I believe Corinna would fit in best. She's a bit older, not looking to remarry, and her only child lives in Pittsburg. She goes to our church and seems to live a good life."

"Then Corinna it is. Thanks, you've been a big help."

Ella smiled, got up, and finished clearing the table.

I'm glad I included her.

Three weeks went by without any negative activity. Mike came to dinner at Forglen, and afterward, the three of them sat in the small TV room. Quin was with Corinna upstairs.

"Dad, it's been wonderful that nothing more has happened, and I want to believe that it's gone away, but I'm living under a cloud, waiting for that other shoe. Plus, I hate living with so much security and being suspicious of everyone."

"I know you are, lass. It's no way to enjoy your life. Unfortunately, the print they lifted off your car wasn't in the system."

"Does that suggest that we're dealing with an amateur?" Gray asked.

"More than likely."

"What next?"

"I think it's time we punched the sleeping bear—flush him out," Mike said. "It may be uncomfortable, like ripping off the tape, but allowing him to be in charge is going to erode away your nerves."

"Why do you guys all assume it's a male?" Fury asked.

"I don't know that we do. But the odds favor a man," Mike said.

"You haven't seen *Fatal Attraction*."

"That was a movie," Gray said. "What do you suggest, Mike?"

"I've been chatting with Shawn's boy. He thinks that Fury should go public with her plans for the book, whether she plans to publish it or not. It may have been the reason or the excuse, but her defiance of the demands should provoke action."

"Any suggestions as to how to make that happen? We can't very well take an ad in the *Constitution*."

"I know, Gray. I can invite Caroline Elliot over for lunch," Fury said. "I can tell her that she was so helpful when I was trying to get an interview with you that I would like to show my appreciation."

"Who's Caroline Elliot?"

"Do you know any of your employees? She's a reporter for the *Gazette* who wrote a piece on you several years ago, and she wrote that piece about our marriage that mentioned my book. I bet that she'll see a story in the renovation of Forglen, the baby, or even the book."

Both men liked the idea, and ten days later, on invitation, Caroline visited with Fury at Forglen.

"I can't believe what you've done with the house. It is hardly the same place that it was last Christmas," Caroline said, as Fury showed her into the living room.

"I hope we've brought a little more warmth to it and matched the décor with the times."

"You certainly have. It's amazing how much it has changed." She looked around as she took a seat. "Tell me, since you've become a wife and mother, are you still writing?"

That was easy.

"Absolutely. I have a new romance due to my publisher the middle of next year, and I'm finishing up the preliminary work on my book based on some of the history of Arabella."

"I can't wait to read that one."

Throughout the visit, Fury watched the reporter for any indication that she might be the person behind the harassment.

Caroline took the bait, and the "Lifestyle" section of the Sunday Gazette carried a major piece about Forglen's history, the MacGregors, and Fury's book in progress, including photos.

"Mission accomplished. Now, it's a wait and see," Gray said as he laid the newspaper down on the breakfast table. "You're pretty sneaky, you know. I think I'd rather have you as a friend than as an enemy."

"You know the cliché, 'keep your friends close and your enemies, closer.'"

"That's an excellent idea. Let's go upstairs and see how close we can get."

It took only five days for the article to have the desired effect. Law enforcement had been incorporated into the plan, and the private security detail was on high alert. A second team of security had been installed inside the house in anticipation of a reaction from the stalker.

"I don't think that Ella or Edward had anything to do with the threats, but we're not taking any chances," Mike said. Gray agreed.

The inside security was made up of two, off-duty female police officers from Atlanta, hired by Gray. They posed as old friends of Fury from college.

At a minute after one a.m., a figure appeared on the screen, coming from a camera at the back of the estate. The team immediately alerted the inside detail and the Arabella police that a suspicious individual was approaching the property with what appeared to be a backpack. They allowed him to compromise the property. As he reached the center of the backyard and started to drop his backpack, the backyard lit up like a football stadium, and both teams converged on the man.

"Gray, what is happening?"

"I think a fish has taken the bait. You stay here. I'm going down."

By the time Gray reached the yard, the man was handcuffed, and Arabella police backup was arriving on the scene.

"We got him, Mr. MacGregor. He's a punk kid, but looks like he intended to start a fire of some sort. He had newspapers, rope, a jar of gasoline, and matches in his pack," a member of the security team said.

"Good work, guys," Gray said. "Has he said anything?"

"Not yet, but we're going to let the uniforms take him in. The detectives will grill him. We need you and Ms. MacGregor to take a look and see if you recognize him, but it would be best if you don't say anything to the son of a bitch."

"I understand. I'll get Fury."

The entire household was huddled in the breakfast room. Ella and Edward knew immediately that the commotion had something to do with what had happened in July, but Corinna was clueless.

"What has happened, Ms. MacGregor?" Corinna asked.

Fury told her only as much as Ella and Edward knew because she did not feel like reciting chapter and verse.

"They want us to see if we recognize this thug, Fury. You want to change?" Gray said as he walked in the house.

"I'll bring clothes down for you," Ella said. "What would you like?"

Neither Gray, nor Fury recognized the young man. As soon as they looked him over, he was transported to the Arabella Police Station.

"We'll need you both to come down to the station in the morning," the Arabella detective said as the marked car pulled away.

Gray turned to the private detail. "Will you be wrapping up and leaving now?"

"I don't advise that, sir. We can't assume that he is your man or that he is working alone. Better keep us here until we have more information."

"You're right," Gray said, putting his arm around Fury's shoulders. The detective agreed.

The MacGregors were in the Arabella police station at nine a.m. the next morning.

"He hasn't broken, yet, but we think he will," Detective Barrett said. "He's lawyered up with a green public defender whose license was issued about a week ago. If the newbie has any sense, he'll convince his client to cooperate."

"Why should he?" Fury asked.

"With all the agencies working this case, he's facing charges in two counties and Federal Court. Atlanta is all over this. Normally, in this type of case, they would have stepped out of the picture, but they're hot to trot. Your dad must be well liked over there."

"My dad is liked wherever he goes," Fury said, smiling.

"Well, the kid's got a clean record, but we've got him tied up pretty tight. His prints match the ones lifted from your car, and he was caught in the act last night. However, he's not the mastermind behind this crime."

"If he's not, then we're back to where we started, aren't we?" Fury said with panic in her eyes.

"Not at all. Our team is digging into everything about him that could connect him to you. There's a common denominator there somewhere. He's not the brain behind the computer hacking. He didn't finish high school and doesn't own a computer. We've tossed his trailer."

"Aren't all kids computer experts these days?" Gray asked.

The detective smiled. "Most. My kids run circles around me with this social media crap—whoops, I'm sorry, Ms. MacGregor."

"I've heard worse. My dad was a cop, remember?"

"As a matter of fact, we're expecting your father here any minute. He said that he has not talked to you."

"I wanted to let him sleep last night, but I guess you've filled him in?" Fury said.

"I hate to interrupt," Gray said, "but if there's nothing more you need from us, I should get to my office."

"I think we've covered it for now."

As they stood up to leave, Fury turned to Barrett. "Detective, you might want to look into whether the suspect knows Caroline Elliot." Gray looked at her with a puzzled expression.

"The reporter? Why would you think he should check on her?"

"I think she has a crush on you, Gray. Last Christmas, when you introduced me at the party as your date, she became very cool toward me, and I got the same vibes when she came to Forglen last week."

"Fury, I don't think that she would take such drastic action on a superficial interest in me—even if she has one."

"You never know."

"You've taken that *Fatal Attraction* movie far too seriously."

"Have you got a better idea?"

The detective watched as they bantered back and forth.

Gray shook his head. "Well, if that's the case, maybe they should check out your old boyfriends. What was the name of the last one?"

"We'll look into Ms. Elliot," Barrett interjected. "If anything develops, we'll let you know right away."

On the way back to Forglen, Fury looked at Gray. "You know, I despise the power your great-grandfather had in this town, but I'm beginning to like yours."

"Does that mean I'm going to get a little more respect out of you?" he said, teasing her.

"You're lucky you're driving, or I would kick you where it would hurt the most."

CHAPTER FORTY

Gray did not stay at the office long. By three-thirty, he was at Forglen.

"I'm surprised you came home this early."

"Everything at the office is on track. Is Quin asleep?"

"He is, but if his schedule is consistent, he won't be much longer."

"When he wakes up, why don't we take his carriage out on the back terrace and enjoy the pleasant weather? I don't think the two of you are getting enough fresh air."

"Okay." *Something else is going on here.*

Quin woke ten minutes after Gray arrived. Corinna prepared his bottle while Fury changed his diaper.

"Sure you don't want to do this?" she asked Gray as she peeled away the adhesive on the disposable diaper.

"You do it so well that I wouldn't want to interfere."

"Yeah, right. Admit it, you're a wuss."

"We'll check that out after the lights are out tonight," he said with a mischievous look on his face.

She smiled, looking down at her changed figure. *It's nice to be a wife again.*

They had hardly sat down on the patio when Ella came to the door. "Gray, Detective Barrett wants to speak with you."

Fury's eyes grew large as Gray took the cordless phone.

After a few seconds, he said, "We're on our way."

Turning the phone off, he turned to Fury. "Call Corinna to take over with the baby. We're going to the station."

"What's happened?"

"Apparently the kid finally gave them the information they wanted, and they have someone in custody. That's all he said."

When they walked into the station, the officer on the desk recognized them, picked up his phone, and called Detective Barrett.

"Glad you're here, Mr. MacGregor. We've got quite a bit of news."

"You have the person behind all of this?" Gray asked.

"We do. There's still one more person involved, but we've got the key player."

"Man or a woman?" Fury asked.

"It's a woman."

"Caroline? Was I right?"

"No ma'am. Mr. MacGregor," he hesitated as if reluctant to continue, "I'm afraid that it's your aunt."

"What the fuck? Valerie?"

"It looks that way."

"Why in the hell—?"

"She doesn't want your wife to write a book."

"You mean—where is she?"

"In the interrogation room with her lawyer."

Gray didn't wait for the Detective to escort him. He stormed into the office, shoving the door open. "What in the hell were you thinking?"

"Gray—"

"Don't say anything, Ms MacGregor," a gray-haired man in a navy-blue suit said.

"You, shut-up, Pierson." Gray was livid and turned back to Valerie. "What were you thinking, old woman? You could have caused me to lose my son, maybe even my wife. Have you lost all of your faculties?"

"She can't write that book, Gray." Valerie's tone was defiant.

"Oh, she can write that book all right. She can write any book she damn well wants to write."

"But, it could ruin our name if she tells everything."

"Ruin the MacGregor name. That's all you care about?"

"Now, Gray. There are things you don't know. She has to be stopped."

"First of all, she does not have to be stopped, and second, I doubt that there's much I don't know, other than what I've just learned, which is: you're as bad as the jackass who called himself my father."

"Gray!"

"Don't even think about justifying yourself to me, Valerie."

"There's a lot you don't know."

"You think so? Then, why don't you tell me."

She looked away. "No. I can't. Some things just shouldn't be talked about."

"You do realize that you're sitting in a police station, don't you? I think we're past the point of 'some things shouldn't be talked about.'"

"Gray, there are other people here." She looked around the room while twisting a lace handkerchief that she held in her lap.

"Pretend there's not."

She leaned forward and motioned for him to move closer with her index finger. He took a deep breath, shook his head from side to side, and then leaned closer to her.

"Your grandfather, my father, had another child," she whispered. "There was a son . . . older than Jack and me."

He straightened. "That's not a revelation, Valerie. Fury knows; I know. To put a fine point on it, that child is her uncle."

Shock registered on her face.

"*You* didn't know who your father's paramour was, did you?" There was a sneer in his voice. "She was Fury's grandmother."

"That can't be."

"Oh, but it can, and it is. Your father and Bridget Dolan were lovers."

Valerie sat quiet for several seconds. No one spoke until Detective Barrett broke the silence.

"Mr. MacGregor, I think that we should go into my office. Let Ms. MacGregor speak with her attorney."

"You're not going to let them put me in jail, are you, Gray?"

He looked at her with fire spitting from his eyes. "Don't ask me that question right now. You wouldn't like the answer."

Fury had been standing next to Detective Barrett, directly behind

Gray. Her face was pale. Gray turned, put his arm around her, and said, "Lead the way, Detective. I've seen all of Ms. MacGregor that I ever care to see."

When all were settled in Barrett's office, he spoke. "Mr. MacGregor, we don't believe that the emails your wife received were sent by either your aunt or young Jameson. But, she knows who sent them because she financed the operation. We have an idea of who it is, but we would like her to tell us."

"She'll tell you. Give me two minutes *alone* with her."

"I know how you feel. However, on advice of counsel, Ms. MacGregor is not saying any more until we have the Mercy County prosecutor here to negotiate. I'm surprised she said as much as she did to you." Barrett opened a file on his desk. "Chadwick will want to speak with Mrs. MacGregor and you before her first appearance in court as to your position on her release pending trial."

"She can stay in jail." Gray stood as if to leave. Fury took his hand.

"Gray, we have to wait and talk with the prosecutor. I'm just as angry as you are with her, but she is an old woman. Do you really want to see her spend time in jail? Do you know what women in prison are like? She couldn't survive twenty minutes."

"She should have thought of that."

Fury looked at him and neither spoke for a moment.

"I need to walk. I won't be far." Taking Fury's hand, he led her out of the building.

Once on the sidewalk, Fury was first to speak. "I don't know what to say, Gray. She never crossed my mind as a suspect."

"Nor mine."

"She is your aunt."

He shook his head and moved his free index finger toward his lips in a gesture of be silent. "No more talk."

When they returned, Mercy County's one and only prosecutor, Leo Chadwick, was waiting in Barrett's office.

"Nice to meet you, Mr. MacGregor. Sorry about the circumstances."

Gray shook his hand and nodded.

"I believe that Detective Barrett has mentioned to you that Ms.

MacGregor will appear before the court shortly, and it will be my job to ask for her remand to custody or for an amount of bond to be set for her release. How do you and your wife feel about that?"

"Leave her in jail. Valerie abused every moral code I know and several legal ones. However, my wife may be more forgiving."

"Mr. Chadwick," Fury interjected, "I think being caught has been a wake-up call, and it's stopped any further threats. I see her as a broken woman now."

"Fury, I sat by your hospital bed and saw the fear of losing Quin in your eyes, while Valerie was busy writing checks to hoodlums with her diamond-encrusted fingers. She paid to make your life hell. I think she should stay locked up. Isn't your book about how a MacGregor never paid the price for his illicit actions? Well, this one will."

"Mr. Chadwick, if it's my call, then make her give up the name of the person who sent the emails and make her pay enough to rattle her comfort zone. Don't keep her incarcerated."

Gray said nothing.

Valerie was released on a one-hundred-thousand-dollar bond that afternoon. However, she had to wear an ankle bracelet. Chadwick had argued that with her money, she was a clear flight risk.

Fury wondered how the Mercy County Court would have handled Valerie if the victim were not on her social and financial level. Chadwick had discreetly recommended to Gray that his presence or absence in the courtroom might affect the outcome.

That evening, Mike came to Forglen for dinner. He had spent the day with the detectives on the case. As he entered the house, Gray said, "Mike, I'm grateful for your work on the case. I'm not sure the locals could have cracked it without the efforts your team put in."

"I'm glad it's over and sorry it took so long. They picked up the computer hacker an hour ago. He worked for you, Gray, at the Marble Company office in the IT department. Your aunt had heard that he was having serious financial problems because of a child on drugs. His position in the company also gave him knowledge of Fury's research in the basement."

"Are they certain that no one else was involved—feeding her information?"

"Not knowingly. She may have picked up a word here and there from everyone from your household staff to the office, but there's no evidence that they were in on the conspiracy."

"How did she get that boy, Paul Jameson, to trespass and do what he did?" Fury asked.

"He is the son of her handyman. He helped his dad out with odd jobs at her house and talked about trying to save enough to buy a car. I have to give it to the old lady, she was a sly one."

CHAPTER FORTY-ONE

July 28, 2009

"Have you ever wondered how *anyone* knows who the right person to marry is?" Fury said as she put a birthday cake decorated with shamrocks on a crystal pedestal.

"I believe that there are recipes for bad marriages, but I don't know of a reliable recipe for a good one. I was sure that you had made the biggest mistake of your life when you married Gray, but I was wrong. Here you are with two precious boys and expecting a third baby."

Fury stopped what she was doing and looked at her sister. "Thank you. I think we are both pretty lucky."

The sisters were in the Forglen kitchen preparing the food for Mike's sixty-fifth birthday party.

Cory finished spreading the potatoes on a huge casserole of shepherd's pie. "Do you still believe that our grandmother's spirit orchestrated your marriage?"

Fury smiled. "Of course. The night that Gray proposed, we were here, in the house where she fell in love with his grandfather. She had to have been sitting on my shoulder, whispering in my ear, 'Marry him, lass. He's Graeme's grandson—a real keeper.'"

Cory shook her head. "You're impossible."

"How else would you explain it? If I had not gone in quest of the historical truth, we would never have met. What gave me that idea? Why did I dream about an uncle I never knew? The psychic I went to said I was right."

"You don't believe in that, do you?"

"We all choose what we want to believe. I choose to believe that the spirits of our ancestors are with us, and I believe that Bridget and Jim are happy that J.G. MacGregor's gold was used to establish the neonatal units, named for them, at the Arabella and Redbridge hospitals."

"Poetic justice, right? Taking the scoundrel's secret money and using it to help others and to honor those he harmed," Cory said.

"Everything that went wrong in the MacGregor family is directly linked to what an evil man he was. His abuse of Bridget and his standing in the way of Graeme's love for her led Graeme to marry a woman he couldn't love, which led to Dorothy's suicide. Her premature death contributed to how Jack and Valerie turned out, which led to Gray spending a miserable childhood and becoming the cold and detached person he was when we met."

"And along came Fury O'Quinn, true to the avenging goddesses whose title she bears, and saved the day."

Fury threw a peanut at her sister.

Laughing, Cory said, "All kidding aside, the endowment that you guys created with that gold has made Don a happy camper. He says that having state-of-the-art equipment onsite at his hospital is a Godsend."

"Zaira came up with the idea right after she moved back here, and Gray ran with it."

Cory slid the casserole into the oven. "I really like her, and it's good that Dad has a companion. They ought to get married. I think that Mom would approve, but Dad keeps saying that they're just 'keeping company.'"

Fury smiled. "Translation: Sleeping together."

"FURY O'QUINN."

"Stop shouting, and, my name is Fury MacGregor."

"I know; I know. You can't possibly think that our father is having sex with Gray's mother—at their age?"

"They're old, not dead, Cory. And I think it's great if they are."

"I bet your husband wouldn't think it was so great—she's his mother."

"We haven't talked about it—probably not the best topic of conversation. He's liberal, but that might be one mental image over his line."

"Well, I don't believe it. I think that they're just good friends."

"With benefits."

"FURY."

"Shhh. The boys are asleep."

"Well, they're not going to hear us in this big house. Not to change the subject, but yes, let's change the subject."

"Deal. I want you to know that I really appreciate your helping with the food. Ella is a great cook, but Irish cuisine is not her strong suit, nor Gray's."

"And, we all know that Fury MacGregor is a culinary disaster."

"Oh, come on. I've gotten better. I can make scrambled eggs. Quin and Conor love it when I make them green eggs and ham."

Cory smiled. "My sister, the chef—green eggs."

"You're just jealous, because all of your eggs are yellow."

"I prefer them that way. Who's definitely coming tonight?"

"All of Dad's old friends from the pub, Shawn, Frank, a couple of other retired cops, and all the wives. You know them."

"I haven't seen Frank and Maeve since the thank-you party that you guys had for all the guys who helped catch Gray's aunt and her accomplices. That has been over two years."

"Well, anytime you want to catch up, you can find them all at the Atlanta pub on a Friday night. Thank goodness we had them on our team with the Valerie mess."

Cory nodded. "Does Gray have any contact with her?"

Fury shook her head. "You know Gray, when he dismisses someone from his life, as far as he is concerned—they no longer exist. He was not happy that she got off with probation. The only time he has mentioned her name since the trial was when he read the advance reader copy of *From the Quarry: a tale of two families*. His comment was, "Send Valerie a copy and charge it to me."

JUDITH ERWIN was born in Atlanta but has spent the majority of her life in Jacksonville, Florida. She holds a B.A. in communications from Jacksonville University and a law degree from the University of Florida. She practiced family law for over twenty years.